EDGE OF
OBLIVION

Published by Montlake Romance
P.O. Box 400818
Las Vegas, NV 89140

ISBN-13: 9781612184197
ISBN-10: 1612184197

J.T. GEISSINGER

EDGE OF OBLIVION

A NIGHT PROWLER NOVEL

Montlake Romance

To Jay, my husband, boyfriend, business partner, and best friend.
The best part of every day is opening my eyes
in the morning and seeing you there.

*What judgment pronounce you upon him who
    though honest in the flesh is a thief in spirit?
What penalty lay you upon him who slays in the
    flesh yet is himself slain in the spirit?
And how prosecute you him who in action is a
    deceiver and an oppressor,
Yet who also is aggrieved and outraged?
And how shall you punish those whose remorse is
    already greater than their misdeeds?*

—KHALIL GIBRAN

PROLOGUE

Once, we were gods.

Ages ago, idyllic, uncounted centuries before man or his sly, sprawling civilizations had even been dreamed, we ruled sovereign over all other creatures in the deepest, virgin heart of equatorial Africa. Divine and resplendent, reveling in the bounty and glory of our many Gifts, we took the name *Ikati*—Zulu for "cat warrior"—because it most closely described our stealthy perfection, our feline, sinuous grace, our cunning and lethal prowess.

We lived and loved and raised our children there, beside the pristine, glimmering waters of the Congo, beneath the nourishing sun and the endless blue sky and the lush, dappled shade of the baobab trees. We wore crowns of gold and garnet and tanzanite; we walked naked among nature and one another and knew no shame. We honored our dead and hunted our food and slept in the fat, crooked arms of acacias and marulas; we passed the stories of our illustrious history to the next generation. We celebrated our Mother Earth and her great magic, and all was well. All was perfect.

But Time is a merciless thief, even for creatures so blessed as we, and slowly things began to change.

Invaders came. Clumsy, ugly, two-legged beasts with spears to stab hearts and arrows to pierce flesh and fire to burn homes. They stole through our forests and poached in our grasslands; they poisoned our rivers and captured our children, our old and weak. We fought our enemies back; we had no choice. Year after year we fought, decades of struggle, war, blood, death. Battles were won, only to begin anew with the next generation. There were so many of our enemy, and so few of us. In time, our numbers dwindled. In time, our enemies gained the advantage.

So, like all creatures must, we adapted to survive.

We learned the human ways. We spoke the human tongue. We wore human clothing and raised human crops and built homes of mud and grass, then wood, then brick, as they did. We learned to hide our true nature. And in this way, we began once more to thrive.

In secrecy. In silence. With seething hatred in our hearts.

Then one day came a different sort of man, a man with no spear or sword, a man with open arms and a gentle voice who claimed to be our friend. He offered a truce and the return of what was already rightfully ours, the rivers and the mountains and the verdant, untouched forests. *Trust me*, the man said, and, tired of so much war and bloodshed, we did.

For a long, long while, the arrangement suited us both and we prospered. Our children grew up together. Our clans lived side by side. Because we were so beautiful and Gifted, unfixed as they were in a single aspect of flesh and bone but mutable, pliable, evanescent, the two-legged invaders began to worship us as the gods we truly were. Offerings were made, statues of gold and ebony and oiled stone were carved, temples were built—the Sphinx, most famously—all in our name. We even mated with our former enemies, bearing half-Blood children, offspring that might one day be as Gifted and blessed as the pure-Blooded were.

Or might not.

A Queen arose from one of these unions. Cleopatra, she was called, meaning "the glory of her father," because he was *Ikati*, one of our own Blood. More beautiful and cunning and sensual than us all, she ruled empires and seduced hearts and convinced a human man to turn against his king. And with that, she sealed all our fates.

The coup failed. The Queen and her lover died. And the *Ikati* were hunted once again. We were hated. We were driven out of our homeland, nearly extinct.

The few that remained remembered how they had survived before the human pestilence came, before clever deceptions blinded their eyes and stole their glory, and made a pact to return to the old ways of pretending and lying, of keeping to themselves. They fled their beloved Africa and found other places in the world to call their own, small, wooded places, cloaked in silence, far away from prying eyes.

Untold eons have passed, and still we live in secrecy and silence, bound together by honor and betrayal and a tradition of ironclad rules to protect us from the greatest threat of all: forgetting.

Our kingdom of peace and perfection was stolen from us by *you*, covetous, ambitious, treacherous Man. And though we have learned to live alongside you, though we have learned to survive, though we may smile and nod as we pass you in the street, we are always, *always* ready to eat out your hearts.

Beware.

Certification of Assembly Resolution No. 218.4.9
Dated this 12th day of July, 20—
Concerning the legal disposition of Morgan Marlena Montgomery,
*   senior Assembly member, Sommerley colony, Hampshire, UK,*
*   accused of high treason, criminal accessory, et al.*

RESOLUTION AUTHORIZING EXECUTION

WHEREAS, the above-named Assembly member has been accused of and pleaded *guilty* to the following:

1. High treason
2. Criminal accessory
3. Assault with intent
4. Hate crimes
5. Mayhem
6. Terrorism

WHEREAS, the punishment for each of these crimes individually or *in plurali* according to the Law and common practice is death,

WHEREAS, we, the undersigned Assembly members, in a unanimous vote do find the defendant guilty of all charges,

THEREFORE, be it resolved the accused shall be executed. Punishment will be carried out immediately upon recording of this document.

IN WITNESS WHEREOF, I have ascribed my name and affixed the seal of this Assembly on 12/7/20—

Edward. Viscount Weymouth

KEEPER OF THE BLOODLINES

ONE

Nathaniel quickly descended the narrow, twisting wood stairs to the underground holding cells, a large flashlight gripped in one hand, an electric cattle prod in the other.

It was cold and dank, the pitch black unbroken except for the narrow wedge of his flashlight's yellow beam. The stairs had been built long ago—nearly two dozen generations of the Alpha's ancestors had inhabited the manor since—and they creaked in loud protest underfoot. His steps disturbed a choking cloud of dust and small, unseen creatures that went scurrying away to disappear into cracks in the rough stone walls, slick with moss and moisture. A cobweb drifted by, ghostly pale strands that lifted to brush his face. Somewhere far off—below?—he heard the muffled sound of flowing water.

He almost lost his footing on an uneven step, then regained his balance and, scowling, nervously pushed an errant lock of brown hair from his eyes. He didn't want this errand, was loath to do it, if truth be told, but he'd only today been voted in to fill the empty Assembly seat and was not in a position to say no. He'd just have to get it over with as quickly as possible and put the whole nasty business out of his mind once it was done.

He hated executions. The blood. The screams. The cold, unsmiling faces gathered to watch it all. A necessary evil, but he wished they'd been able to make an exception for *her*.

Not that he'd question. Not that he'd ever dare.

At the bottom of the steps he paused, grimacing. It smelled down here, like rust and rot and something sour and profoundly unpleasant, something he didn't want to take too much time trying to identify. His flashlight illuminated a long, primitive room with a dirt floor, a rough-hewn ceiling above, a row of windowless wooden doors lining either side, heavily locked.

His heart began to pound. The criminals and outlaws and deserters of the clan had always been kept here, deep in the bowels of the earth, so far below the manor their screams could not be heard. Shivering, he imagined the dying whispers of those screams still echoed off the walls.

He hurried to the third door on the right, paused beside it with one ear trained for any sound within. But all was silent. With a quick glance back to the stairs, he transferred the flashlight to his mouth, held it between his teeth as he fumbled at his belt for the ring of rusted, old-fashioned keys, frowning at each in the semidark until he found the correct one. He fit it into the lock, turned his wrist, and cringed at the harsh screech of metal against metal as it gave.

He had a fleeting thought that this might not have been such a good idea, coming down here alone. It was a test, he knew, and he wanted to prove himself worthy, but this place made his skin crawl with prickling dread, and he had no idea what was about to greet him on the other side. She might even be dead, for all they knew.

Or worse: angry.

The door swung slowly open with a long, eerie groan of rusty hinges. He tensed, awaiting any movement or noise, but there was nothing. He took the flashlight in hand and, with the cattle prod held out like a crucifix warding off evil spirits, eased into the cell.

The corpse of a rat lay disemboweled near a pile of rotten straw against the stone wall, its mouth frozen open, fur stiff with dried blood. There was a bucket of brackish water, an untouched plate of food on the floor near the door, a dirty wool blanket atop an empty pallet of hay. The air was grave-still and so cold he saw his exhalation in a cloud of frosted white. Did he have the right cell?

He set the tip of the cattle prod against the back of the door and gave a little push. The door swung farther open, and suddenly there came a sound that stood all the tiny hairs on the back of his neck straight on end.

A low, rumbling growl, from a back corner of the cell, a corner so black he couldn't fathom it. Rich and spine-chilling, with an unmistakable tone of warning, it was a sound he'd recognize anywhere. Then out of the blackness, a glow appeared, two almond-shaped points of hot, burning green.

A pair of eyes, beautiful and predatory, fixed on him.

He had the right cell after all.

"Miss Morgan," he whispered, holding his ground though he really, *really* wanted to turn and run. He cleared his throat, stood a little straighter. "Miss Morgan," he said again, his voice a bit stronger this time, though still threaded with hesitation, "it's time."

The growl deepened, electrifying and primal. The eyes did not blink.

Nathaniel felt his own predatory animal blink wide awake inside him, hackles raised, claws unsheathed. He took a deep breath to calm it. That wouldn't resolve anything, and he'd probably end up dead. She was the stronger of the two, the more experienced, by far the more lethal. He kept a hard grip on the cattle prod and, with his thumb, flicked on a tiny switch. The flashlight he kept angled toward the floor. It draped the walls and ceiling in gold and umber shadows.

"I'm sorry," he added, keeping his tone even with a surprisingly difficult exertion of will. "You know this is not my doing. You know this is the Law."

A hitch in that deep, snarling rumble, a telling note of something like agreement. It made him breathe easier, just the tiniest bit. Leaving the door open, he inched back over the uneven dirt floor, slowly, making no sudden movements, giving her more room. The cattle prod, however, he hadn't lowered. He didn't need to glance away from those glowing emerald eyes to know how hard his hand shook.

"I'm just going to wait here, Miss Morgan, right out here where you can see me, and you come out whenever you're ready." *Please, please don't make me come in there and get you. I only just got engaged last month, I'm only twenty-one*—"Whenever you're ready, I'll just be waiting right here."

He snapped his jaw shut so he wouldn't say anything stupid and continued slowly backing up until he was a safer distance away near the stairs. After a moment, the growling subsided to a disgruntled chirrup, then a final, huffing snort.

He waited by the stairs for what felt like a thousand years, nerves screaming, ears aching for the slightest hint of movement, sincerely hoping Leander and the rest of the Assembly had thought better of their decision to send him down alone and were on their way to assist. Then all of a sudden the frigid, dark underground prison hummed with a pleasant snap of electricity that sent a wash of honeyed warmth over his skin in wave after perfumed wave.

God, she was powerful. Feeling her Shift was like standing a few feet away from a lightning strike, just as electrifying, just as lethal. And she smelled of something warm and luscious, like maple syrup or brown sugar, only darker, finer, completely unlike his fiancée, who was scented of lilac and rosewater, girlishly sweet—

"Nathaniel," a voice purred, feminine and smooth, as dark and delicious as her scent. It sent a rash of goose bumps crawling over his skin. He saw movement beyond the open cell door. A figure glided forward through shadows without noise, maneuvering with unstudied grace and sleek elegance. A hand on the doorframe, then a face that seemed to manifest from thin air, arched brows and huge almond eyes and lovely full lips curved into a small smile that might have been sadness or disdain. She stepped forward past the door and into his puddle of weak yellow light, and Nathaniel could not stop the gasp that parted his lips.

She was naked. Incredibly, *perfectly*, naked.

His mind wiped blank. The cattle prod lowered to his side. Random words formed in his mind then vanished, swallowed by pleasure and astonishment: *lovely; full; curve; satin; slender; sweet; soft; want; yes, want—*

"Nathaniel," she said again, amused at his slack-jawed admiration. "The Williams boy. I remember you." Her gaze flickered over him, uncomfortably keen, then she smiled. "You're all grown up."

His tongue would not work. He could not form a coherent thought.

"I'm unfortunately without clothes," Morgan continued, turning her wrist in a slow, graceful motion to indicate her spectacular nudity. He tried to sputter out a reply, but she went on, ignoring him. "Would you be a dear and find me something nice to wear to my execution?"

The great hall of Sommerley Manor was noisy, crowded, and hot. The tall, lead-paned windows that lined the west wall were thrown open in their casements, letting in the heather-scented glory of an English country afternoon. A desultory breeze ruffled the ivory silk curtains but did nothing to cool the sea of bodies pressed shoulder to shoulder in the grand, gilded room.

Though the entire tribe had wanted to attend the proceedings, only so many would fit, so the Assembly had held a lottery. Feeling immensely pleased with themselves for both the turnout and the demonstration of faux democracy that so gratified the crowd, the group of fifteen men now sat pompous and preening on an elevated dais at the front of the room behind a long oak table draped in somber gray linen, nodding to the crowd and murmuring smug congratulations to one another.

Erected in the center of the crowded, cavernous room was a tall, evil-looking device atop a scaffold. A clever assembly of blood-darkened wood and shining metal and sharp, angled blades, the machine had been rolled in on a wheeled platform from its storage place in a well-avoided shed near the back of the property, once the gamekeeper's storage shack. Now it housed a collection of macabre items such as this, racks and crushers and saws and garrotes, used not infrequently. Beside the machine stood a hooded executioner, hulking and silent.

Though well entrenched in the twenty-first century, the soul of the tribe had not changed in millennia. Neither had its Law, nor the punishment for those who broke it.

And colluding with the enemy exacted the direst punishment of all.

Beside the dais on their own platform were two elaborately carved mahogany chairs, cushioned and large. In one sat a man, handsome and leonine, wolf-eyed and silent, black-haired like the rest of his kin. His posture was relaxed except for the tanned forefinger of his right hand, which kept a steady beat against the polished arm of his throne, belying his inner turmoil. The throne beside him, toward which he sent a swift, occasional glance, sat empty.

His wife had refused to attend.

They'd been close, everyone knew, the new Queen and the traitor the excited crowd awaited. And the Queen had taken the betrayal particularly hard.

It was common knowledge also that the Queen had thus far refused to intervene or even offer an opinion on what was to be done in the name of justice. This was taken as a clear sign of her approval of the Assembly's resolution, though it was well within her rights and authority to do exactly as she wished, even as far as granting a full pardon. She alone stood outside the Law that so tightly bound the rest of her kind; she alone was sovereign, even above her husband, the Alpha, strongest male of all the colony. Unlike the rest, if she wished it she could leave, or stay, or dance a naked jig atop the lighted ball that dropped on New Year's Eve in Times Square, so many thousands of miles away. She'd come from the outside world and was free to rejoin it yet had elected to stay with her clan of secretive, Gifted people and her handsome, distracted husband, who now waited to watch an execution he approved of but did not wish to witness.

Because she'd chosen to stay, her people adored her. And because she had chosen not to intervene in their business, the Assembly had—grudgingly—begun to offer her their respect.

With a slow, majestic pageantry that swiftly silenced the gathered crowd, the ivory-and-gold-leaf double doors at the far end of the Great Hall swept open, and everyone turned, breathless, to look.

Until she actually saw what awaited her, Morgan had thought herself prepared for this moment. She had stupidly hoped it would be swift and relatively painless: the guillotine, beheading by sword, a firing squad perhaps. Something she could endure with dignity that would cause more pain to her psyche than to her body. Something poetic or tragic or morbidly elegant.

How mistaken she had been. How naive.

This would not be over quickly. They were out for more than just her blood—they wanted to humiliate her, make her an example. They wanted spectacle. They wanted *theatre*.

The horrible machine, the rabid, hissing crowd, her heart clenched to a fist in her chest. The air so choked with malice and bloodlust she could barely breathe without feeling suffocated. A shouted accusation from the back of the room: "Traitor!" and the crowd began to jeer, taking it up in chorus, stamping their feet.

She prayed she wouldn't break too soon and give them the satisfaction of hearing her beg for mercy. She hadn't been broken yet, in all the weeks of isolation and deprivation and brutality suffered in the holding cell.

But this, oh, this...

She swallowed, hands trembling, fought the clawing animal fear rising to a scream in her throat, and silently repeated four words that encompassed everything she believed in, everything she had so desperately wanted, her lifelong dream turned to prophecy and curse.

Live free or die.

One or the other. She had chosen long ago.

She wasn't born to hide. She wasn't born to live like a domesticated animal, tame and docile, chained to a stake in the yard. She had never really fit in. Even as a child all she'd wanted was *more*, though she didn't know exactly more of what.

Live free or die. So be it.

With Nathaniel trailing a few hesitant feet behind her, still clutching his cattle prod, she advanced through the parting crowd with her head held high, her shaking hands hidden in the folds of her dress, her gaze fixed forward on the dais and its group of watchful, waiting men.

"Incredible," Leander heard one of the Assembly members spit under his breath. He didn't turn to look who it was; his gaze was trained too keenly on Morgan.

She was thinner, he thought; definitely thinner and paler, though it hadn't reduced her beauty or her sensual, magnetic appeal. He watched heads swivel and mouths drop in her wake, men, women, and children alike. Though all his kind were beautiful to the point of being meaningless, she outshone them all.

Somehow—as always—she'd found something glamorous and dramatic to wear, though she'd been sent to her cell almost four weeks ago in nothing more than bloodied rags. Now she wore simple, serious funeral black but made it look like the most elaborate couture: a long, sleeveless silk gown, one-shouldered, drifting over her lithe curves like enchanted gossamer; silver high-heeled sandals; thick mahogany hair swept back from her face in a stylish, casual chignon. Even unadorned, with no paint or ornament, even outcast and reviled and walking toward her imminent, grisly death, she was truly magnificent.

In spite of himself, he smiled. In this moment, she reminded him of his wife.

Proud. Regal. A born fighter.

He'd never really *looked* at her before, not like this, like a stranger seen for the very first time. They'd grown up together, after all, and he'd had nothing but admiration for her fire and intelligence, for her drive to succeed where no tribeswoman before her had. She was the first woman to serve on any Assembly in any of the Colonies, the first to jump into any fray, the first to seriously rebel against her role as a wife and, in time, valued breeder. She might have even intimidated him if he hadn't been the Alpha and therefore immune to that sort of thing.

But you are *Alpha,* the animal inside him hissed, angry, rising up to sting his skin. *And she almost killed your sister. She almost killed your wife. She betrayed you all.*

His smile faded. He relaxed back into the plush comfort of his enormous carved chair, inhaled a deep breath, and waited for it to begin.

"Morgan Marlena Montgomery," Viscount Weymouth intoned over the cacophony, staring down his aquiline nose through his spectacles. He took particular pleasure in his role in the proceedings because it was *he* whom she'd plotted to kill, after all, regardless of her failure to do so. "Daughter of Malcolm and Elizabeth, former sworn member of this Assembly, do you understand the charges brought against you?"

Morgan stood demurely before the dais, hands folded at her waist, head bowed. The jeering crowd fell suddenly into tense silence, and even the breeze creeping through the open windows seemed to still. Slowly, she raised her head and leveled the viscount with her gaze, calm and direct. Slanted sunbeams caught in her hair and haloed her head in glimmering auburn and bronze, a faerie crown of light, and she looked for a moment like a Michelangelo Madonna, pure and sweet, and nothing at all like the treacherous viper he knew her to be.

"I do," she answered, her voice soft but clear. "And I accept the will of the Assembly."

The viscount sniffed, displeased. She did not seem appropriately afraid. Well, no matter. She'd be afraid very soon, he assured himself. Very soon. He'd have her stripped and shorn and trussed like a turkey; he'd give her to the crowd to soften her up before fixing her to the Furiant, his personal favorite of the tribe's torture devices, so named in honor of the bohemian dance of spinning and flailing bodies and limbs.

Soon, he promised himself again, nearly salivating with anticipation. *I'll see you naked and begging soon, my duplicitous dove.* He snapped the thick sheaf of papers in his hands and moistened his lips, lowering his gaze once more.

"Then by unanimous resolution of this Body," he read, his sonorous voice carrying to the far reaches of the silent room, "we do hereby sentence you to—"

"Wait."

The voice came from behind him, clear and commanding, the American accent evident even with that single word. He turned, startled, and the room turned with him, all gazes now focused on the woman who'd appeared so suddenly beside the empty throne. She was lovely and pale, the palest creature in the room, golden-haired and delicate in a gown of ivory satin that nearly matched her skin. She stood there like a shimmering opal among a sea of black pearls.

He glimpsed her solemn face, registered the stubborn lift of her chin, and his heart sank.

"Majesty," he murmured, executing a low, practiced bow. The men on either side of him rose and bowed in turn, and so did everyone in the crowd, in utter silence. Like static electricity sparking in invisible bursts over all their heads, the sense of anticipation in the air ratcheted higher.

Her husband rose and took her hand, and with a quizzical arch of one dark brow he bent and pressed his lips to her fingers. When he straightened, she sent him a penetrating, sidelong look and let her hand rest in his as she turned to face the room.

"I have an idea," the Queen declared.

Beneath the starched white collar of his shirt, Viscount Weymouth began to sweat.

TWO

Morgan was having trouble remembering how to breathe.

"And that way," the Queen continued, calmly addressing the stupefied Assembly, "we can kill two birds with one stone. So to speak."

In the wake of this statement—utter silence.

They'd reconvened in the East Library, a smaller yet no less grand room than the formal hall they'd just left. It was peppered with priceless antiques and ticking clocks and plush Turkish rugs and a huge crystal chandelier that threw fractured prisms of light over the polished mahogany table and the silent, stiff group of nineteen seated around it.

Sixteen Assembly members, one Alpha, one Queen, and her.

The traitor.

To whom the Queen had just offered a lifeline, slim though it was.

Morgan kept herself calm as best she could by focusing on the view of the hills through the windows, rolling drifts of loamy earth carpeted in emerald fields and nodding wildflowers and miles of forest so dense only a faint memory of sun reached the silent forest floor from the canopy far above. Pale green rays filtered through but never fully penetrated the cool gloom.

The river Avon cut through the dark center of it, miles of snaking turns and crystal clear water that was bejeweled above by darting turquoise dragonflies and perfumed pine needles and gossamer tufts of drifting goldenrod, below by the mirror flash of rainbow trout. On a clear day like this she knew she'd be able to see straight down to the sandy bottom, to the waving tendrils of moss anchored to beds of smooth, dark stones, to the tiny, darting hatchlings and froglets. She'd spent hours exploring the New Forest as a child, many hours and days and months of her life. The memory dissolved like a bitter pill on her tongue; in all likelihood, she would never explore it again.

"With all due respect, my lady," said the viscount to the Queen past stiff lips, "I fail to see how your *plan* can be realistically executed."

From the corner of her eye, Morgan saw Leander's head turn in the viscount's direction. She didn't have to see his face to feel the particular heat of his answering stare: warning and blatantly hostile. Envying the lone hawk that circled far above in the stark cerulean sky beyond the windows, she fisted her trembling hands in her lap and practiced breathing.

In. Out. In…out.

The viscount began again in a more conciliatory tone.

"There's absolutely nothing to guarantee this female," he gestured toward Morgan with a curl of his lip, "who's proven herself a danger to the tribe by the worst possible act of treason, will do as you say. She'll simply vanish, never to be seen again. Or worse, she *will* find them. And reveal *everything*."

Morgan chanced a glance at him from beneath her lashes.

From his position seated straight-backed and dour near the head of the table, he shook his head. Two bright blotches of red stained his cheeks, a fine sheen of perspiration covered his brow, his hands curled around the arms of his chair so hard his fingers had turned white. She almost felt sorry for him.

Almost.

"No, she won't." Jenna turned her head and gazed across the room at her with luminous eyes of yellow-green, cool and assessing. "Will you, Morgan?"

Wordless, trying not to shake or blink or otherwise reveal the snarling terror monster in her gut, Morgan shook her head no.

Jenna turned back to the viscount and granted him a satisfied smile.

No one said anything for one long, frozen moment. Then a voice chimed up from the middle of the table, stronger than she would have given him credit for.

"I think it's a good plan."

Nathaniel, newly christened member of the Assembly, looked nervously around with a flop of dark hair falling over one eye. Morgan leaned against the overstuffed back of her rose chintz chair and exhaled a long, silent breath through her nose. *Quiet*, she willed, staring hard at him. *Please be quiet, or it's off with your head, you fool!*

He was sweet and young, and she didn't want to see him do anything stupid and get hurt, especially on her account. For not the first time, she wished her Gift of Suggestion could be used across empty space and was not limited to touch.

"Agreed," said Leander, to the obvious shock of everyone at the table except the Queen, who sat beside him, relaxed and elegant with one finely arched brow slightly raised, as if to say to the rest of them, *Go ahead, I dare you.*

"But, but—" the viscount sputtered, livid. He jerked out of his chair. "It's impossible! There is no guarantee—"

Another man stood, Grayson Sutherland, stocky and well-regarded. "The risk is too great, lord. Even you must see—"

"Yes, yes," someone else was saying loudly, "the risks *far* outweigh any advantage we could hope to obtain—"

"—she wouldn't just return—"

"—it's outrageous to think—"

"—she cannot be trusted!—"

"—the danger to us—"

"—think of the *consequences*—"

They were all on their feet now, arguing and shouting over one another, all except the Queen and her Alpha, who remained apart and silent, and Morgan, alone at the end of the table, shivering in her chair. Though it was warm enough in the room, she was cold, ice-cold, a freeze that went bone-deep. *Grave*-deep. She wondered if she'd ever feel warm again.

Leander stood abruptly from his chair, a lithe unfolding of limbs that was at once elegant and unquestionably menacing. "Silence," he commanded through clenched teeth, and, just as abruptly, there was.

White-lipped and petrified, Morgan smiled. If she had ever questioned the Earl of Sommerley's authority or his complete control and power over the tribe, his ability to send a group of sixteen savage, bloodthirsty males sinking back into their seats in silent, pale-knuckled fury with just a single word proved it beyond doubt. He was Alpha for good reason.

He stared around the table, and one by one every man in the Assembly glanced away.

"I will speak with my wife," he went on in that low, steely tone, "*alone.*"

The men shared sour glances; grumbles of assent were heard. They climbed one by one to their feet, and chairs were scraped back over the marble floor with grating screeches that set Morgan's pulse skittering and her teeth on edge. Someone came up beside her, gently touched her bare arm. She glanced up to find Nathaniel gazing down at her, smiling hesitantly, that lock of hair falling over one eye, stubbornly refusing to stay in place.

"Miss Morgan, I'll just take you back down to your—"

"*No touching!*" hissed Viscount Weymouth, coming up behind him. He wrenched Nathaniel's hand free of her arm, and Nathaniel blanched and stepped back, wide-eyed. "Do you want her to strike you senseless, boy? Make you her puppet with no more than *this*?"

He held up one finger as if it were a loaded gun.

Nathaniel took another quick step back. Morgan knew it was useless to argue, to tell him that of course she wasn't going to do any such thing, so she kept her mouth shut and rose from the chair unsteadily, still not understanding what had brought this all on.

Her confusion was overwhelming and well-founded. Jenna had almost died because of her. Why would she try and save Morgan's life?

But she wouldn't soon find out, because the snarling viscount had gone back to the table and snatched up the cattle prod Nathaniel had left behind. He stalked back across the room toward her, holding it straight out and threatening the way a lion tamer wields a whip.

She knew he'd turned it on even before he jammed it against her shoulder, but the jolt of electricity that stabbed through her like a molten spear and sent the room exploding into pops of red and white and then sliding, slipping black was more than confirmation.

At least she had time to grab his wrist before she blacked out.

It was going to rain.

Jenna felt it in her bones, though the sky through the tall windows of the East Library was still that perfect, unclouded blue. There was a dull ache in her chest that foretold the coming storm, just as in the past a fluttering ping in her stomach had indicated an imminent earthquake, a bitter taste on the back of her tongue had predicted snow, and that rare pain behind her right eye—experienced only once, when as a child she'd lived on one of the smaller Hawaiian islands— foreshadowed a volcanic eruption. Hurricanes brought on migraines, pounding and howling like the storm itself.

You will feel the very heartbeat of the earth, someone wise had once told her not so long ago, and he was right. Being *Ikati* meant being alive and attuned to the symphony of nature as no other creature on Earth was.

Behind her, back and forth across the marble floor and hand-woven Turkish rugs, that wise someone paced, silent as only a nocturnal predator can be.

"You didn't tell me," came his gentle accusation, low and faintly amused.

She didn't turn from the window. "I didn't know until this morning," she replied truthfully.

She'd been dreading this day for weeks. Over and over, she had turned it in her mind, working on it in the same stubborn, steadfast way a termite chews through wood. What was she going to do? Because she had to do something, obviously. She wasn't going to just sit by and let Morgan die. But what?

What?

It was a problem that defied solution. Pardon was out of the question. Execution was out of the question. Indefinite imprisonment was out of the question, because she knew that would be worse than death for someone like Morgan, so fierce and proud.

But her betrayal had cut Jenna to the bone, both literally and figuratively. And Leander's sister, Daria, was still in grave condition, most likely to be maimed for life.

There was the undeniable fact, however, that Jenna, though angry and betrayed and quite wounded herself, understood exactly why she'd done it. Which left her right back where she had started, pondering what was to be Morgan's punishment.

It hadn't come upon her until she'd caught herself staring blankly at one of the gilt-framed oils in the Gallery of Alphas. She'd gone nearly every day to stare at it, drawn by a combination of curiosity, nostalgia, and the faint, nagging feeling of something obvious that was being missed. It was a portrait done with care and precision, the image of a handsome, unsmiling man with a sharp jaw and a wide forehead, done in severe umbers and charcoal, lit from above. His blistering green eyes stared down from the canvas, just as feral and canny as her own.

Because they were. The portrait was of her father.

He'd been an outlaw to the tribe, too, and paid the ultimate price.

"She reminds me of my father, in a way," Jenna mused aloud, watching a skein of swallows rise from the tree line beyond the windows. They scattered in quicksilver flashes of gray and black, melting into the sky.

"Really?" Leander's murmured response was wry, not a question at all. The pacing stopped for a moment, then started up anew.

She turned to face him in a rustle of taffeta and satin, reminding herself to change out of this ridiculous dress as soon as possible. The Assembly inevitably required formal dress for these occasions, though she hated it. Even her wild Leander was dressed formally in a beautifully cut suit of navy so deep it was almost black, gleaming Italian loafers, cuff links, and a starched shirt and silk tie. Only his hair remained untamed, a glossy jet tangle that brushed his shoulders, always appearing windblown even just after it had been combed.

Naked. He looked far better naked. Though she supposed he needed to wear *something*, clothes only served to mask his true glory.

The formal-dress problem would soon be remedied, she told herself firmly. She was fully healed now from all her wounds, and it was time to step up to the plate and begin revising the old rules.

The first item of business was Morgan.

"They're both rebels—"

"With *very* different motives," he interrupted, still wry, still pacing with his hands clasped behind his back. He shot her a measured, heated glance from beneath sooty lashes.

Her mouth quirked. "One for love, one for freedom. Both noble ideals—"

"Noble?" He came to an abrupt halt and gazed at her from across the room. His expression bordered on severe. "Jenna."

He said her name in that particular way he did when he thought she was being unreasonable, chiding yet stroking, tender yet reproachful, and she was abruptly angry. She pushed away from the window, crossed her arms over her chest, and went to stand in front of the massive, unlit hearth. She kicked at the foot of the scrolled iron screen that shielded it and was rewarded with a black smudge of ash across the toe of her ivory satin slipper.

"You couldn't understand, Leander. You've had your freedom your entire life. She's been locked up, locked away, denied the most basic rights—"

"For her safety. For *our* safety," he reminded her.

When she didn't answer, he came up behind her and stood with the broad expanse of his chest pressed against her back. His hands lifted to gently encircle her shoulders. He brushed aside the gold mass of her long hair and pressed a soft kiss to the bare nape of her neck. She scowled down at the ashen, chunky remnants of some long-dead fire and refused to turn around and wind her arms up around his neck, though she wanted to with a desire so strong it still took her by surprise.

Always, always this need for him. For his body and his heart and his proximity, even when she was irritated with him, even when he was driving her mad with his cold, calculated logic. She simply could not imagine being without him, for one second of one day. Just the thought of it caused her physical pain.

Love, she had learned, was its own kind of prison. With chains and locks invisible but just as real and unyielding as those of steel.

"You know what's out there," he murmured. His lips brushed her skin with a gentleness that left gooseflesh in their wake. "You know better than most."

She closed her eyes and inhaled, letting him draw her nearer, letting his scent of spice and smoke and virile man envelop her. His lips slid down her neck; the soft press of his teeth against her jugular made her shiver in delight. But she was still angry with him. Definitely.

"Everyone deserves a second chance," she said, leaning into him. She let her head drop back and rest against his shoulder. He turned his lips to her cheek.

"Hmmm," he murmured, unconvinced. He wound his arms around her in a gentle, possessive embrace and nuzzled his face into her neck. She had to press the smile from her lips. He sensed the shift in her mood and pressed his advantage. "Compromise," he whispered near her ear, "can be a beautiful thing."

Her eyes blinked open. Instantly on guard, she stiffened. "Compromise?"

He breathed a low laugh down her neck that sent warmth surging through her entire body. It softened her, made her think of pillows and sheets and their very fine bed, of him ardent and warm and naked beside her.

Inside her.

Angry, she reminded herself. *Angry.*

"I know this is important to you," he said in that soft bedroom voice, stroking his palms up and down her arms, slowly rocking her back and forth in his strong embrace. "And I know once you have your mind made up, well…" He lowered his lips to her neck again, opened his mouth over the column of her throat, heat and softness and a gentle suck that fluttered her eyelids. "…I might as well try and stop the north wind."

"Exactly," she said, scowling now at the carved figurines that decorated the long mantel, row after row of obsidian and porcelain and glass panthers in miniature, crouching, leaping, lazing in the limbs of a tree.

His muffled laughter shook them both. He turned her in a practiced, fluid motion, his hands gently coercing her hips, his palms flattening against the small of her back, drawing her in again. In spite of herself, her arms reached up and twined around his shoulders. He bent his head and pressed his lips to her temple, her cheek, one corner of her mouth.

"But perhaps, great Queen, you might allow me one or two conditions of my own," he murmured, spreading his hand around the back of her neck. He tilted her head up and rained feathered kisses over her eyelids, her brow.

She made a wordless noise of protest and kept her eyes closed, frowning, feeling the heat and muscle of him burn her straight through their clothes. "Stop trying to bribe me."

"Never bribing," he breathed, skimming his lips over hers, lightly, oh so lightly, just enough to make her pulse jump and have her rising on her toes to better meet them. Her lips parted and she felt the fleet, electric shock of his tongue against hers. His arm tightened around her so she felt his heartbeat drumming against her chest, staccato and strong, to match her own. "Only asking."

With one hand still cradling her head and the other wound hard around her body, he covered her mouth with his and kissed her deeply, making her forget all about the difference between a bribe and a simple question, making her sorry there was a manor full of restless, feral-eyed *Ikati* waiting for their decision, making her regret the terrible inconvenience of their fine and formal clothes.

She pulled away first, breathless and flushed, and gazed up at him from beneath her lashes. "One or two," she said, still stubborn, alight in the dark, glowing burn of his eyes. "But we agree she can try?"

A figure tottered by outside the sun-hazed windows, glassy-eyed and slack-jawed, stumbling blindly over the manicured lawn, headed toward the dark line of trees in the distance where the forest began. Without looking she knew it was Viscount Weymouth, wandering aimlessly in his mustard waistcoat and old-fashioned cravat, completely naked below the waist.

Leander smiled down at her, wolfish, and the flush spread over her cheeks and down her neck. "She can try," he relented, tilting his head to hers again. "And when she wakes up from that shock Weymouth gave her, maybe you can get her to Suggest to him that he put back on his pants."

"He's lucky. If I had her Gift and he'd shocked me with that thing, he'd be naked *and* lying in a pool of his own blood." Jenna sighed, leaning into Leander, pressing her lips to his again. "Shall we retire to the bedroom, my love?" she murmured, fingering the knot of his silk tie. "I find myself in need of...a change of clothes."

THREE

The assassin stood gazing out the same tall expanse of Tudor windows in the East Library that Jenna had looked out the day before, watching the mass of black thunderclouds that hulked overhead, ominous and opaque. Rain sheeted down in a silver, sideways slant in the wind and smeared the view of the fields and misted forest beyond to plots of muted gray and brown and green. A flash of lightning forked through the clouds, brilliant white, and illuminated the hills and trees in spare, pagan lines before dissolving again to smoke and shadow. A low rumble of thunder shivered the glass.

The storm had broken just as he'd disembarked from the Earl of Sommerley's private plane at Heathrow this morning and showed no signs of letting up. It reminded him of the monsoons that drenched his own colony in Brazil every summer. But this squall, vigorous and lusty as it was, seemed somehow less primal. More predictable. More...restrained.

Everything in this sophisticated, sprawling English colony was so restrained. The architecture, the people, the land—even the weather. Only their Law was the same, he mused. He'd seen the evidence of that in the medieval-looking device still standing in the great hall. It exuded an animal hunger all its own, just as the machines kept by his tribe did.

"I don't follow," he said to the windows. "If you know where they are, why not send a garrison? Why not send a full force to wipe them out?"

"We don't know *exactly* where they are. And until we do, we can't mount a direct assault. We can't risk the exposure or the manpower. Most of our forces are readying the tribe for the move to Manaus. And since they know about all the colonies except yours, moving the tribe to safety is our first priority. Once everyone is settled we can focus on strategy, but in the meantime we can't just strike out blindly. We need more information."

Leander's tone was just tight enough to reveal his irritation. Xander had known the earl for decades and knew how he hated questions, hated explanations. Which meant that in addition to needing information, Leander needed *him.*

"More information." Xander turned from the window and looked at Leander with one eyebrow cocked.

Kill first, ask questions later—that was his own motto, and it had served him well. But this man who reclined so casually against the back of his elaborate chair in his elaborate drawing room within his even more elaborate manor house couldn't live by the simple creed of an assassin. He was Alpha, which meant careful decisions, careful questions, careful plans.

Politics. He loathed it. Thank God the role of Alpha of Manaus had gone to his half brother.

"Yes," said Leander, gazing at him now with unveiled irritation in his sharp green eyes. He shifted in the chair, restless, and something in his expression suggested he had his own, unspoken problems with this plan. "Exact location, exact numbers. How they live. What, exactly, they know about *us*."

Xander studied him, wondering what he was missing. "If you're looking for that kind of information, you don't need an assassin. You need an infiltrator. A mole."

"As it happens, we need both."

Apparently no longer content to sit, Leander rose from his chair and moved to an elegant sideboard of polished cherry that displayed a variety of cut crystal bottles filled with amber and gold and clear liquids, set out on a silver tray. Xander watched in mild surprise as his host poured a generous measure of scotch into a glass, threw back his head, and quaffed it in one swallow.

According to the long case clock in the corner, it was barely past noon. The vague feeling of something being off solidified into surety.

"Both?" he prompted when Leander didn't continue.

There was silence in the room for several moments, unbroken except for the thrum of rainfall against the windows and the ticking of the clock. Then Leander spoke, low, to the empty glass in his hand.

"Have you ever been in love, Alexander?"

The assassin, trained from childhood to act and not to feel, was caught completely off guard. Against his will the fleeting image of a pair of chocolate-brown eyes, liquid dark and smiling, flared in his memory. He blinked and the image vanished, leaving behind a ghost of dull pain that throbbed and mewled in his chest before he ruthlessly smothered it.

"No," he answered flatly.

"Neither had I, until recently," he went on, still low, still to his empty glass. Xander knew he spoke of his new wife. The Diamond Queen, they called her; just as beautiful, just as rare. She was famous in all four *Ikati* colonies, as famous for her Gifts and charm as she was for her past and her parentage.

The only freeborn *Ikati*, daughter of an outlaw Alpha and his fated, forbidden love.

A human, of all things. The enemy.

"It's more powerful than I ever would have guessed," Leander mused, almost to himself. "Elemental. Transformative. And painful." He gave a soft, humorless laugh. "Like fire."

"Like death," Xander rejoined, still in that flat, emotionless tone.

This conversation was headed down a very dark path, a dangerous path, one he didn't care to follow. Love *was* an element, he knew too well, as cruel and violent as hurricanes or tornadoes or floods. Even speaking about it invited disaster.

Another rumble of thunder rattled the windows, and Leander seemed to snap out of his reverie. He set the empty glass down on a beaded coaster and turned abruptly, his face wiped clean of emotion.

"We want you to accompany a member of our colony to Rome to hunt the Expurgari."

Xander's eyebrows shot up. "They're in Rome?"

"I know," Leander said. "I always imagined the Expurgari lived in the worst places in the world, the desolate or diseased places. Somewhere like Calcutta or Death Valley."

"Or Chernobyl," Xander added, very dry.

"But perhaps they never left Rome. It all started with a Roman emperor, after all. One of his descendants might be their leader now."

"But why me?" Xander persisted. "I'm not a bodyguard, as you well know. In fact, I'm quite the opposite. If your tribesman needs muscle, there are far better choices than I—"

"No," Leander interrupted, gazing askance at Xander. He inhaled a slow breath that lifted his shoulders, then walked across the room and sank back into the plush comfort of his ornate, high-backed chair. He trained his gaze on the storm outside the windows. "It's not a bodyguard we're after. Your particular skill set is exactly what's required. For our *tribesman*."

There was something ironic in the way he pronounced the last word, something mocking. Xander waited, knowing he'd get the answers he was looking for if he waited long enough. His patience was legendary, almost as much as his precision and efficiency, his total lack of emotion.

"Once in Rome," Leander said quietly, still gazing out the window, "you will stay two weeks, not one day more. And if in that time period the exact location of the Expurgari headquarters is not determined by the person you will accompany, if the detailed information we seek is not gathered, you will do what you do best." He turned his head and his gaze flicked over Xander once in keen, cold assessment. "You will kill her."

"*Her?*" Xander echoed, shocked, though his expression remained stoic as ever.

But before he could say more, there was a sharp knock on the library door. When it opened to Leander's curt "Come," Xander was shocked once again, this time into silence.

FOUR

"That's the best I can do," Jenna said, her voice strained, and released Morgan's fingers. She fell back into the riot of scarlet and pink peonies that decorated her overstuffed silk chair and rested a pale, shaking hand over her eyes.

Morgan sank back into the spine-numbing chill of her own metal chair set across from Jenna's and tried very hard not to vomit. She still fought against that sideways, lurching pull, that disorienting loss of gravity, those vivid images that had popped and flared and drunkenly reeled from the first moments Jenna had grasped her hand.

The Queen's Gift of Sight was extraordinary, as powerful and elegant as the woman herself. She could read a person's thoughts with a touch, see future plans and past remembrances, glean information, and find the truth behind lies.

She could also replay that information back to someone else in a kind of silent, maniacal movie, just as she now had. But Morgan had never thought being inside someone else's mind—someone else's memories—would be quite so terrifying. Or quite so nauseating.

She'd seen everything. Everything they'd done to the Queen, everything she'd suffered at the enemies' hands, and it literally made Morgan sick.

A guard stepped forward, black-clad and muscular, one of the dozen or so that stood watching with hawklike intensity near their facing chairs in the solarium. It was a soaring, glass-ceilinged chamber of enormous potted palms and frescoed walls and silk sofas, surrounded on all four sides by arched windows, slick with rain. The room housed an extraordinary variety of exotic birds in hanging gilt cages, beating clipped wings impotently against the bars. Morgan thought it a perfect allegory for her entire life. Their chirps and whistles made an eerie symphony with the relentless drumming of the rain on the glass panes overhead.

"Majesty," the guard murmured, throwing a dark glance in Morgan's direction. He stepped near and hesitated a few respectful feet away. "Are you unwell?"

"Fine," Jenna said, cross, waving him away. "I'm perfectly fine. It wasn't her," she added, knowing they suspected Morgan of some nefarious Suggestion, akin to the little scenario with the viscount yesterday. The Queen pinched the bridge of her nose between two fingers and muttered, "Always this *hovering*. It's enough to drive you mad."

"Yes," Morgan said, very softly. "It is."

The guard retreated to his place with the other men, and Jenna opened her eyes and leveled her with a look so clear and compassionate it made her want to shrink away in shame, so undeserving was she of the kindness there. But she couldn't shrink away; all she could do was close her eyes to avoid it.

"I'm so sorry," Morgan whispered. Her face grew hot; tears threatened behind her closed eyes. "I'm so sorry for what they did to you—that I'm responsible—for *that.*"

With a rustle of fabric, Jenna leaned forward in her chair. A gentle hand touched Morgan's knee. "I know you are. I know you didn't mean...I know that wasn't what you wanted." Almost as an afterthought she added, "I can See it, you know."

Morgan opened her eyes, looked into the pale, somber oval of Jenna's face, and endured a moment of self-loathing so gut-ripping it felt like she'd swallowed a grenade. "Why are you doing this for me? Why not just let them kill me?"

She didn't think it possible, but Jenna's face went a shade paler. She removed her hand from Morgan's knee and leaned slowly back, settling into her chair with the barest of melancholy sighs. It was a sound with a lifetime of pathos behind it. Her gaze drifted over Morgan for a silent moment before she began, low and halting, to speak.

"I made a promise to you once. Not that long ago. Do you remember?"

Yes, she wanted to say. *I remember. Of course I remember. My freedom for my silence.* But she didn't say that. There were others here—men, guards, unquestioning loyalists— who would never understand how the seed of friendship can take root and flourish in the dark soil of a shared secret. "But that was before..." she began in protest, then trailed off, unwilling to even speak it aloud.

Jenna's lips quirked, and for some bizarre reason, Morgan thought she might be hiding a smile.

"My father used to tell me, 'A promise made is a promise kept.' He never went back on his word and neither will I. All I'm offering is a chance, Morgan. A chance for us to gain the upper hand and for you to make things right. If it pans out, you'll be pardoned. You can come back to Sommerley or move to one of the other colonies and start a new life for yourself. Realistically, it's not much of a chance—Rome is a very large city. I didn't see anything specific from the Expurgari who tortured me"—she said it, *tortured*, unflinchingly, and Morgan's face again—"that would lead us to their headquarters there. No address, no outstanding landmarks, not even a general idea of neighborhood. Only that hideous room full of..."

Heads, the Queen didn't say. Heads preserved in formaldehyde, row after row of them in glass jars lining an entire wall in a large, windowless room of dark stone and antique furnishings and colorful, crested flags hung near the ceiling. Heads of their kin, murdered *Ikati*, a few from only months back and desiccated, shrunken others from God only knows how many long centuries ago.

It was the enemies' trophy room. And Morgan's targeted, nearly impossible-to-find destination.

Jenna cleared her throat and lowered her gaze to her hands resting on her lap. "You only have two weeks. Half a month to find a needle in a haystack isn't really that much of a chance, but it's all I can do. It's a...compromise. Find them and all's well that ends well. If, however, you don't find them in time..." She trailed off just as Morgan had done moments before, not needing to articulate the obvious.

If she didn't find them in time, she would die.

Jenna must have seen how she blanched, because she leaned forward suddenly, grasped both of Morgan's hands between her own, and spoke in a low, urgent voice. "Fate will have its way with all of us, Morgan. I can't predict how this will end because that is out of my hands, but I *can* give you a chance for redemption. *Everyone* deserves at least that. The rest is up to you. Find the Expurgari and let the tribe get their vengeance somewhere else."

Mute, Morgan gazed at her while the hovering guards began to mutter and rustle and move forward, alarmed at this new contact. Two of them swooped in and pulled Morgan roughly back by the shoulders, dragging her chair back several feet.

Jenna shot to her feet. "That's not necessary," she hissed as one of the guards wrenched Morgan's hands behind her back and twisted a pair of biting cold handcuffs around her wrists. She clenched her teeth against the sudden pain and—worse—humiliation of being bound. The guards hauled her to her feet, shoving aside the chair with a kick.

"Lord McLaughlin's orders, Your Highness," the larger one answered, surly, breathing his malty breath down Morgan's neck. "No contact except for the transfer—"

"Release her this instant or *I'll have your head,*" Jenna shot back, bristling, and the guard stiffened in what should have been terror but was more probably outrage. She could quite literally have his head, quite easily, but no one in this patriarchal society as yet was used to a woman wielding that much power. Especially since Jenna hadn't flexed those particular muscles since becoming Queen. Morgan knew it would only take one bloody instance to have them all cowed and toeing the line, but she didn't want to be the cause of any more bloodshed.

"It's all right," she said to Jenna between her clenched teeth. "You've done enough. Please, you've done enough."

She flicked her gaze to the smaller guard, the worried-looking one with soft eyes and a turned-down mouth. "We're done. I'm ready."

He nodded and curled a gloved hand around her upper arm, careful to lean as far away as possible while still holding on to her.

"Morgan." Jenna stepped forward with an outstretched hand, but the two guards had already begun to lead her away, tripping backward in the same heels and gossamer gown from the day before, rumpled now because she'd slept in it. The other guards came up to surround her in a booted knot as they made their way toward the door with their prisoner.

"I'll be back," Morgan said over their shoulders, her voice not quite even, not quite strong. She watched the lone figure of Jenna recede among the clustered palms and rioting birdcages, pale hair and skin stark as snow against the gray, rainy day. "I'll make it right. I *promise*," she added, just as they reached the door.

"Good luck," Jenna called. But in the heavy, doleful undertone of her soft voice, Morgan heard the farewell and knew what *good luck* really meant.

It meant *good-bye*.

The guard with the malty breath—Matthew was his name— was the one who knocked on the carved oak door of the East Library. Somehow he fancied himself in charge, though Morgan and all the other guards knew full well he was unranked and the least Gifted of the group. His only advantage was a clumsy kind of strength, which he used judiciously to drag her through the crypt-quiet shadowed halls of the manor, yanking her along by her elbow when she slowed or stumbled on a bump in a thick-pile rug.

She'd known Matthew all her life, of course, just as she'd known everyone in the tribe since the day she was born. She'd been there the long-ago day his mother had dropped his newborn sister—tiny, puling, and deformed—into the yawning black mouth of the Drowning Well, then turned and walked away without even shedding a tear. Waist high and frightened among the somber, gathered adults, Morgan had clutched her father's hand and felt terrified and proud there was nothing wrong with her, no deformity or weakness that would compel the tribe to shun her, compel her own mother to make a trip to this unholy place or risk death for all her other children and herself.

But her mother was dead by then. And Morgan had no weakness.

Well, no weakness they could see.

She recalled another memory of Matthew, leering at her with two sloe-eyed friends from the leafy shadows of a twelve-hundred-year-old yew on the eve of the Equinox Festival one winter when the snow was ankle high. She'd been fifteen then, at the brink of her first Shift, only just beginning to notice she was different from the other girls of the tribe, uninterested in boys and marriage and whispered, giggling talk of what happened after the Matchmaker and the Keeper paired you off in a proper Blood match and you were allowed to be alone together.

Wandering aimlessly off on her own as she almost always did, she found herself far away from the bonfire and the dancing in the town square and amid the dark cathedral of trees and crystalline silence of the woods. They came up on her silently as she was inspecting the bristled perfection of a pinecone hanging from a snow-dusted bough and knocked her to the ground with a shove from behind. She didn't have a chance to run or even get on her feet before they were on her, grabbing at her clothes, laughing and growling and egging one another on like the young savages they were.

She had a weapon, though. A sharp, double-edged letter opener, stolen from her father's desk.

She was different but she wasn't stupid. She'd noticed how they watched her.

After that they left her alone, Matthew and his two friends, one of whom had to wear an eye patch for the rest of his life to hide the gaping hole in his skull.

She stood now behind him, surrounded by the phalanx of guards, staring at the back of his head and wishing she had the unheard-of but very convenient-seeming Gift of Enemy Skull Exploding.

"Come," barked Leander from behind the closed door. Matthew pushed it open. Not satisfied to merely enter the room with her trailing behind, he turned, grasped her by the arm, dragged her over the threshold, then released her abruptly, as if he'd been burned by touching her.

So of course she fell. Of course she did.

Caught on one of the heels of her shoes, the hem of her dress tangled beneath her feet. The delicate fabric gave way with a soft ripping noise, and she pitched forward, unable to throw her arms out for balance because they were cuffed tight behind her back. She fell to her knees on the cold marble floor with a bone-crunching jolt that startled a pained gasp from her lips, but just before she fell flat on her face, something stopped her.

A pair of hands. Strong and warm at her shoulders.

She was caught and steadied, pushed gently back to her knees, where she rocked, finding her balance. Then she lifted her head and looked up—

—into a pair of eyes, brilliant amber rimmed in kohl, that stared out from a sun-darkened face of such cold, savage beauty it sent a thrill of pure fear humming along every nerve. Adrenaline lashed through her body, primitive and chemical, and abruptly awoke the animal inside that bristled and hissed and screamed *danger!* at the top of its lungs.

He was huge—tall and thickly muscled, far larger than any of her lithe, sinewy kin—and had shoulders so wide she crouched in a pool of thrown shadows at his feet. His black hair, tipped on his wide forehead to a widow's peak, was cropped close to his head. His clothes were black as well, simple and form-fitting, made for ease of movement. On his back was a pair of crossed swords, sheathed in leather scabbards. On his belt and boots were more weapons, gleaming wicked in the light.

But all this paled in comparison to the more imminent threat of his eerie, amber eyes.

They fixed on hers, unblinking, unfeeling, and she realized with another jolt that this man staring back at her in absolute stillness with that beautiful face and those scorching, firelit eyes wasn't anything she'd ever seen before. He was alive, his *body* was alive, but behind that mask of perfection, there wasn't a shred of humanity or mercy or kindness or feeling. There was nothing. He was dead.

Soul dead.

Next to the Furiant, he was the most terrifying thing she'd ever seen.

"Xander," said a voice from her right. Leander's, she supposed, aware on a molecular level of her thundering heart, her frozen muscles, the stranger's gaze, which had dropped to the pulse beating wildly in the hollow of her neck. His nostrils flared with an inhalation, and for one wild, horrified moment, she thought he might lean down and tear out her throat with his teeth.

But he didn't. He only lifted that piercing gaze back to hers and, in a motion of fluid, predatory grace, drew her to her feet. He released her and stepped back, never blinking, his attention never wavering, those piercing dead eyes never leaving her face.

"Xander," Leander said again. "This is Morgan. Your flight for Rome leaves at one o'clock."

FIVE

Morgan was fairly sure the assassin was plotting the details of her death at that very moment, though he wasn't paying her the slightest bit of attention and hadn't spoken a single word to her the entire flight.

She chanced another glance at him from beneath her lashes. He sat still as death in a seat opposite hers at the front of the luxurious cabin, just as he'd been for the last two and a half hours, large hands spread over his muscled thighs, head tilted back against the seat, eyes closed. His chest rose and fell in a calm, steady rhythm, but she knew he wasn't sleeping; his forefinger tapped a silent beat against his leg, and every once in a while a muscle in his sharp jaw would flex. She had the impression he was barely restraining himself from leaping from his seat.

Plotting her death. Definitely.

When Leander had spoken his name she'd known instantly who he was. What he *did*. Infamous throughout all four colonies of *Ikati*, Alexander Luna was called The Shadow or The Hammer or, in his native Portuguese, *Ira de Deus*, The Wrath of God. He was a killer, a very good one, sent on special assignments all over the world by the Alphas to track deserters or eliminate threats.

Or accompany convicted felons on needle-in-haystack hunting trips.

Killer or not, he was a beauty. All muscle and sinew and spare, hardened grace, he moved like nothing she'd ever seen, effortless fluidity and instinctual, unstudied prowess. He had a potent, menacing kind of charisma about him, the kind that drew the eye and held it, the kind that captivated the attention to contemplate the disparity of those sensual lips with that merciless expression, that soft, satin skin made for touching with the cold, burning threat of those dead amber eyes. He was carnal and elegant and forbidding, so forbidding even the air seemed to hold its breath as he passed through it.

A jolt of turbulence rattled the cabin, interrupting her study of him. Morgan gasped and stiffened in her seat.

As plush and comfortable as the buttercream leather seats of Leander's private plane were, she'd soon rip hers to shreds if the turbulence kept up. She *hated* flying. She was a creature of the earth, born to slink through tall grasses and climb the sap-perfumed trunks of trees and laze sleepily in sunlit glens until her tongue was lolling and her fur was hot. Flying was for lesser creatures, for prey—the birds.

Another jolt—this one strong enough to dislodge her duffel bag from the overhead compartment and send it tumbling to the floor—and a sudden drop in altitude that sent her stomach into her throat. She clutched the armrests and closed her eyes, swallowing hard, willing herself not to throw up.

And when she opened her eyes again the assassin was sitting right beside her, staring into her face.

"What—" she blurted, startled, but before she could get it out, he reached over and grasped her wrist. He pressed his thumb and forefinger into the tendon from either side, not hard but not gently either, and the urge to vomit vanished.

"Oh," she said, and then, "How?" because she couldn't think of anything else.

"The inner gate."

His voice was deep and soft, the accent indefinable. Between that, his sudden, molten proximity, and the cold fire of his unblinking tiger's eyes, Morgan was abruptly speechless, and spinning. *The turbulence,* she thought. *I'm dizzy from the turbulence.* She made a little, wordless questioning sound and tried unsuccessfully to look away.

"It's an acupressure point," he added, by way of explanation. He still hadn't blinked, and she wondered if that came from years of staring down gun sights at fleeing prey. Her wrist was still grasped in his large, warm hand.

"You're white," he said when she didn't reply, and now she wondered if he only spoke in two- to four-word sentences. Perhaps he wasn't too bright.

"I'm fine," she snapped and pulled her wrist from his grip.

Really, what the hell? she wanted to shout at him. *You don't want me to throw up but you're perfectly okay with putting a gun to my head and blowing my brains out?*

She assumed it would be a gun. He looked like the type who would own a lot of guns.

"We'll be landing soon," he said, and she found herself counting.

Four. Four words. She was overcome by the sudden, incongruous urge to laugh.

In two weeks, if she hadn't completed her impossible task of finding the never-before-located headquarters of an elusive, cunning enemy in a six-hundred-square-mile city of almost three million people, she was going to be killed by a beautiful idiot. She leaned her head back against the seat and sighed. Her mother must be rolling over in her grave.

"You probably shouldn't touch me." She stared up at the curved ceiling and its rows of softly glowing recessed lights. "Or didn't they tell you that?"

"Suggestion doesn't work on me."

Morgan turned to look at him. He really was stupid. Or maybe just stupidly cocky. She resisted the urge to reach out, touch the side of his stupidly beautiful face, and whisper, *Quack like a duck.*

"It works on everyone," she said drily, emphasizing the last word. "No matter their intelligence level."

One of his eyebrows lifted, but that was all. He seemed to be waiting for her to continue.

"I can make you do anything I want," she said, enunciating every word, trying to be clear so this blunt instrument sitting next to her would understand. "It's my Gift. All I have to do is touch you, Suggest something I want you to do, and you'll do it."

His lips curved into a smile that was both wicked and challenging. And not stupid at all.

"Then by all means," he drawled. He held out his hand in invitation. *"Touch* me."

Her heart screeched to a stop inside her chest. Then her mind took off, wild and careening, shooting a million miles out into space in the expanse of one second to the next.

She could make him forget.

She could make him forget and make him unconscious and then do the same for the pilot—well, maybe after they landed—and escape into the never-ending maze of Rome's storied, sun-washed streets and never be seen again. It was only the three of them, it would be so easy, Leander hadn't even sent any other guards. She could travel to Paris and Prague and even Iceland if she wanted, she could find her own way in the world and leave Sommerley and the Law and the *Ikati* all behind, forever.

She could be free.

Before he could change his mind, she seized his outstretched hand.

Warmth and a charge of electricity, a tingle up her arm. "Forget me," she whispered, vehement, staring into the depths of his kohl-rimmed amber eyes. "Forget me and sleep."

Then, quite inconveniently, nothing happened.

Never, never, never, it's never happened before. Since infancy I've had this Gift, and no one is impervious, no one can resist. I trained for years to be careful not to touch, not to hug, not to think any random thoughts that would hurt one of the tribe—

"*Meu caro,*" the assassin murmured. He gazed into her eyes, still with that sly, wicked smile, his hand grasped in hers. "My dear. How could one ever forget a woman like you?"

It hit her like a wrecking ball, swift and solid and just as devastating: immune. He was immune. And *toying* with her.

"Son of a bitch!" she hissed and snatched her hand away.

That earned her a laugh, dark and dangerous. "Son of an *Alpha*," he corrected, reaching behind him to grasp something clipped to his belt. He pulled it out in a move so fast all she registered was the glint of shining silver, the musical *chink* of metal sliding against metal, solid and sleek.

Then his hands were around her throat.

She screamed and pushed back, but she was held in place by the lap belt, her feet struggling to find purchase against the slick, low-nap rug. He was suddenly on top of her, muscle and heat and a low, growled curse, his leg over hers, his arms around her shoulders, his fingers tightening on her neck, cutting off her air. She swung out blindly and connected with his jaw, found a handful of his shining jet hair and yanked as hard as she could. Another curse and then he was off her, standing a few feet away, breathing hard and staring at her with glittering, wary eyes.

She tore off the lap belt and leapt to her feet, lissome and lightning fast, and stood facing him in the middle of the aisle, her feet spread apart, legs flexed, hands balled to fists. Shaking and furious, she realized with a shock that her neck was throbbing and sore where he'd wrapped his hands around it.

He'd *hurt* her.

The urge to Shift came over her in a blinding white spark, violent and primal. Reason and caution and calm were stripped away, replaced by the instinctual and over-powering urge to claw her way out of her human skin and fly roaring through the air to land on top of him and slash out his eyes, tear off his arms, eat out his heart.

"You are going to die," she snarled and stepped forward.

The heated charge came, then the flare that sparked and caught like gunpowder, then the scent of smoke and honey, the swift and terrible flash of pain as her muscles and tendons and bones began to transfigure into her other self, her *real* self. She inhaled, savoring the pain, savoring the thought of his blood on her tongue.

And then...nothing.

She faltered. The pain in her throat increased, pressure and an odd, electric hum that sent agony flaring down her spine and held her just at the brink of the turn. She lifted her hands to the pain, searching for the source, for the circle of fire that ringed her neck.

Her fingers touched cool metal. There was something around her throat.

"No," she whispered. Her heart became a sudden, frozen weight inside her chest.

"I'm afraid so," the assassin answered without regret. He took a step back down the aisle, watching her carefully, his face blank, barren of all emotion. "Your Gift of Suggestion can't harm me, but I'm afraid fangs and claws are another situation entirely."

She was horrified. Horrified. She might as well be dead. "You *collared* me!"

He didn't answer. He didn't need to; the evidence was right there, cold and tight against the throbbing pulse in her throat. He just kept backing away toward the front of the plane, toward the closed door that led out of the main cabin into the dining room and media room beyond.

"I can't live like this! I can't go two weeks without Shifting!" she shouted, digging her fingers into the skin around the collar, searching for a way to get it off. But even as she did it, she knew there wasn't a way. The locks, once fitted together, fused closed. It could only be removed by a welder's torch in a dicey process that often left hideous scars. It was the *Ikati*'s most effective means of punishing minor offenders, and one of their most feared. Living with the collar meant never being able to Shift. It meant staying in human form, for as long as was deemed necessary to foster a more cooperative attitude.

"Find the Expurgari sooner, and it won't be two weeks," the assassin suggested, cold as ice. He reached the door and opened it, paused for a moment to gaze at her. She stared back at him in impotent, white-faced fury, her mouth open in horror. "Or perhaps in the meantime," he said with an evil glint in his eye, "I'll *forget* why I put it on in the first place." He turned and disappeared through the door, closing it with a definitive thud behind him.

Morgan sank to her knees in the middle of the aisle, her fingers still clutched around the cold links encircling her throat. "Son of a bitch!" she shrieked.

From behind the closed door, there might have been laughter.

SIX

Rome. Spectacular city of living history, of emperors and poets and lovers, of red-tiled roofs hugging a kink in the dark river that winds serpentine through it, of saints and artists and ancient monuments erected in exaltation of long-dead gods.

From the air it looked like a magical fairy-tale city, Morgan thought, gazing out the airplane window to the sprawling maze below. Painted in warm washes of terra cotta and cinnamon and ochre, surrounded by verdant, hilly countryside dotted with crumbling ruins, it glittered rare and beautiful like a topaz against a backdrop of emeralds. The streets were snarled and writhing and interlocked like a drawer full of snakes, forested with bell towers and palazzos and cathedral domes that gleamed gold in the afternoon sun. She felt a thrill of real excitement that she'd soon be walking those streets, which was followed by the sour, jarring realization that *he* would be walking right beside her.

Her fingers stole up again to trace the rigid metal rings of the collar. He better not be in the room with her when it came off, because slicing his face to ribbons with her claws had moved to the very top of her priority list.

The plane shuddered as the landing gear was engaged, and she leaned back into the plush confines of her seat.

First things first, she thought bitterly, watching the city rise up to meet them. *Beautiful bastard. I'll find them first, and then I'll take care of you.*

"There's only one bed," Morgan declared bitingly and turned to gaze at him in frozen, green-eyed hostility.

"Observant," Xander replied drily and brushed past her into the plush opulence of the Nijinsky suite. The door swung shut on silent hinges behind him.

The Hotel de Russie was not the most famous hotel in Rome—that honor went to the Hassler, hands down—but it was the best. He'd stayed here on many occasions and appreciated its lush, terraced gardens, its central location between the Spanish Steps and the Piazza del Popolo, its uniquely Roman air of sexy, sophisticated gentility. It was immaculate and beautiful, decorated in classic Italian luxury: silk-paneled walls; gilt-framed oils; copious use of creamy marble and glistening mirrors and the kind of outrageously expensive, decadent bedding found only in five-star hotels or the very finest brothels.

But even the best brothels didn't offer a pillow menu. It was here he'd first found he had strong feelings on the matter of duck feathers for his pillows versus goose.

He set the small bag with his clothes and the locked leather case that housed his collection of knives—the small collection, for traveling—on the large glass-topped desk in the main room, then walked across the expanse of vanilla carpet to the curtained windows. He pushed aside the ivory silk with one hand and gazed down at the piazza six floors below, at the Egyptian obelisk of Pharaoh Rameses at its center. Relocated to Rome by Caesar Augustus from its original home in Heliopolis—City of the Sun, oldest of the old Egyptian settlements—it was carved in hieroglyphs and towered over one hundred feet tall, a stark reminder of the blended, bloody history of the two empires.

The Romans had held public executions in the square below for centuries, right up until the last one in 1826. The thought struck him, not for the first time, that the *Ikati* really weren't all that different from the humans they so despised. More Gifted, perhaps, but just as violent.

Perhaps even more so.

"I'm not *sleeping* with you," Morgan spat from behind him.

Against his will, he summoned the vivid, heart-stopping image of the two of them naked, entangled in the sheets on that very large and decadent bed, Morgan arching and moaning his name beneath him.

"Don't be stupid," Xander said through clenched teeth, banishing the lucid illusion. "And don't flatter yourself. This is only for convenience. I'm not letting you out of my sight." He turned from the window and leveled her with a lethal stare that drained the blood from her cheeks.

But—*God.* Even with her blood-drained cheeks and travel-rumpled clothes and the hostility that pulsed off her in waves, her loveliness was astonishing and otherworldly, the kind he'd seen only once before in a painting of an angel by Caravaggio. The kind that made every male in the airport and hotel stop and gape as she passed by.

The unforgettable kind. The *dangerous* kind.

Even now as he glared murder and mayhem at her, a flash of heat tightened his groin at the ghost of that wanton fantasy of the two of them together on the bed, the same blistering heat that had enveloped him the first time he'd glimpsed her at Sommerley. Tall and lithe and slender as a sapling, with the eloquent eyes of a silent-movie star, she'd walked in the room and all the air had gone out. Then she'd tripped and he'd reacted on pure instinct to catch her and had taken in a lungful of her scent, warm skin and woman and exotic, dark muskiness, a perfume unlike anything he'd experienced before, fine and feminine and powerfully provocative.

Traitor, he reminded himself. *Traitor and liar and mark.*

"Well then," she said, still frozen and fierce. "I hope you enjoy the floor."

They stared at one another, deadlocked in silent animosity, until there came a tap on the door. An accented male voice called out, "Porter. I have your bags, sir."

Morgan sent him one last baleful glare, then moved with stiff grace toward the wheat-and-cream striped sofa in the sitting room. She dropped her handbag unceremoniously on the floor and perched on the sofa's overstuffed arm with her arms folded across her chest. One leg, slender and bare, clad in a strappy, high-heeled shoe that seemed useful only for accentuating the delicate bones of her ankle, swung back and forth in agitation.

He gritted his teeth again. Why in God's name did she have to be wearing a *skirt?*

He went to the door, let the bellman in, and indicated where the man should set the bags. There was an inordinately large amount of them—all Morgan's—and he had to make several trips back and forth from his bell cart in the hallway. The man kept throwing heated glances at the sofa, where Morgan perched while she watched him like a cat when it hears the can opener, all eyes and appetite.

Xander went to get his billfold from the duffel bag on the desk. When he turned back, the porter stood slack-jawed and silent in front of Morgan, stupidly gaping. She brushed her hair back from her face, a gesture that seemed somehow unnatural, as if her hands had just been doing something else, and smiled at him.

"Porter," Xander snapped. Watching men fall to pieces all over his mark was going to get old, fast.

Blinking, the man turned. Xander held out a fistful of euros and jerked his head toward the door.

"Yes, sir," the porter murmured and walked over to him—more correctly stumbled over—his face gone a curious and very unnatural shade of green. Xander frowned.

And was able to leap out of the way just as the porter opened his mouth and sent a jet of hot, yellow vomit spraying onto the vanilla carpet in the exact spot he'd just been standing.

Disgusted, he barked a string of curses. The man went to his knees, coughing and spitting, blathering apologies in Italian. From the sofa behind him came a laugh, low and pleased, and he looked up to find Morgan smiling at him, sweet as saccharine and just as fake.

"Oh my," she said, still casually swinging her foot with its finely turned ankle back and forth. "I wonder if it was something in the water. Too bad you weren't able to assist him with a dose of your wonderful *acupressure*. It looks like his 'inner gate' could use a little oiling."

He felt the tiniest twinge of admiration that she would risk something so bold purely out of spite, right before it was swallowed by a wave of blistering anger so strong he had to curl his hands into fists to control the itch to curl them around her neck.

"Try something like that again," he said, his voice very low in his throat, "and you'll find yourself missing a pair of hands."

She flushed red, and he was gratified to see it. The porter struggled to stand. He found his footing and backed away toward the door, wiping his mouth on the sleeve of his beige linen uniform, still stammering apologies and assurances that someone would be up directly to attend to the mess. He reached the door and disappeared through it at a run.

Morgan bent and retrieved her handbag from the floor, then rose, all without the slightest bit of haste or discomposure. She retrieved one of her smaller suitcases from the row against the wall, then walked in easy, graceful strides to the door of the master suite. Inside the door she paused and turned, her hand on the doorframe, a smile on her face, the picture of untroubled elegance.

Only her eyes gave her away. The heat in her emerald gaze scorched the air between them like a lit fuse.

"And if you ever threaten me again, errand boy," she said quietly, swinging the door shut, "you'll find yourself missing your *di—*"

The door slammed closed before he heard the final word, but he didn't have to. He knew exactly what it was.

When the woman from housekeeping arrived twenty
minutes later to clean the carpet, Xander was still standing
in the middle of the living room, staring hard at the closed
bedroom door.

SEVEN

It was two hours before she was sufficiently calmed to leave the master suite, and by then Xander was gone.

The shower helped. It was a mosaic-tiled, glass-enclosed expanse of luxury with silky lavender shampoo and French-milled grape seed oil soaps and three sets of jets set at various heights, the better to massage a body with hot, pulsing water from all angles. Seething, she spent what felt like forever under the sprays before she began to relax. When she emerged—puckered—there were Egyptian cotton towels, plush and pristine white, there were ivory cashmere robes hung from a gleaming silver dowel, there was a marble fireplace and what appeared to be a real Picasso hung above the dressing table. There was even a window with a view to the faraway, sunset-emblazoned hills.

What there was *not* was a gun. Which she very much would have liked to find hidden in one of the vanity drawers.

Bastard. Cold, arrogant bastard. If it weren't for her promise to Jenna, she would put a bullet in his head and burn this place to the ground.

But she had work to do and couldn't afford to spend any more time envisioning putting a gun against his temple or pushing him off the balcony or Suggesting to one of the hotel staff they poison his food. The sooner she found what she'd come for, the better.

And then to hell with him.

She dried her hair and dressed, then went out to the living room, expecting to find him skinning kittens or swallowing live goldfish, but there was only a pair of black kidskin gloves—women's gloves, supple and delicate—laid out beside a handwritten note on the glass-topped desk in the living room.

Dinner. Eight o'clock. Downstairs. Don't be late.

A pair of gloves and seven words, all harmless in themselves. Yet nothing in as long as she could remember struck such a raw chord of bitter resentment deep in her heart. The collar, now *this*. Did he really expect her to humor him and wear the gloves, voluntarily giving up the final Gift at her disposal? Leaving her defenseless, completely at the mercy of fate?

No. Her hands would remain bare, and God help him if he tried to force them on. As for dinner…she'd rather have dinner with the devil than with him.

She ignored the gloves, balled up the note, tossed it to the floor, and went down to the lobby, where she hailed a taxi and disappeared into the purple-blue haze of the warm Roman dusk.

From his position behind the spreading branches of a potted raffia palm in the lobby bar, Xander watched her go and won a bet with himself. Then he took the next cab and instructed the driver to follow her.

Morgan had no idea where she was going until she saw, ethereal and enormous and uplit in a vivid wash of gold, the jagged stone outline of the Colosseum. It was the hugest thing she'd ever seen, an ellipsis of pale yellow blocks of travertine and tufa the length of a football field with a three-story façade of superimposed arcades, arched hollows where enormous statues of gods and emperors had once stood. The dark hollows stared out over the city like rows of empty eyes.

"There!" she said to the driver, excited, pointing through the open window.

He glanced at her in the rearview mirror. He was graying and paunchy and utterly nondescript, but his eyes were like dark chocolate, liquid and sweet, and she saw the echo of the younger man he'd once been.

"*Dove?*" he said around his cigarette, pulling the two syllables out in a languid, sensual tenor that also belied his age. And made her appreciate his ambition.

"The Colosseum," she said, hopeful. Surely that translated to any language?

"*È chiuso.*" He made a gesture with his hand that sent pale gray whorls of smoke rising in ghostly circles from the cigarette now held between his fingers. "*Tour fermano a cinque.*"

She recognized only one word of this languidly delivered answer, which was *chiuso*—closed. "It's okay." She gave him

the international sign for approval: a thumbs-up. "Please—
per favore—take me to the Colosseum."

He shrugged and kept on through the snarl of evening
traffic, several times barely avoiding hitting one of the dozens of scooters that whizzed by the taxi at lightning speed.
They turned onto Via dei Fori Imperiali, and Morgan
watched it grow closer and closer, a hulking giant erected
right in the heart of the city nearly two thousand years ago.
The cab slowed to a stop at the curb. This garnered a chorus
of irate honking and shouts of *"Spostati!"* from the line of
cars behind them.

"Grazie," she said, the only other Italian word she knew
besides *please.* She leaned over the front seat, touched her
hand to the driver's shoulder, and met his eyes in the rearview mirror. *"Grazie,"* she said again, softer. He nodded,
slowly, and she left him with a smile and the impression he'd
been paid for the ride. And handsomely tipped.

Though denied access by locked iron gates, three times
the height of a man, that closed off every arched entrance,
throngs of people still strolled around the grassy perimeter
of the Colosseum, talking, laughing, smoking, taking pic-
tures in front of it. She felt like a tourist herself, awed and
amazed, craning her neck to gaze up in wonder. She'd only
ever been allowed out of Sommerley once, on a trip with
Leander to Los Angeles, and that city was so elementally different from this one that trying to compare them would be
like comparing water to fire.

But Rome. Oh, Rome.

Even the air was different here, warm and soft and filled
with life, ripe with birdsong and honking horns, nearby
laughter and far-off singing, heady with the scent of fresh-
baked bread and sun-warmed stone. A stocky, bespectacled

man with a mouth like a dried prune approached and said something to her in Japanese, gesturing to his camera and his tiny, smiling wife standing a few feet away beside a low fence.

"Of course. Yes!" she said, without realizing she'd never held a camera in her life and had no idea how to operate one. Her confusion became quickly apparent, and the man, in broken English, gently showed her how to focus the lens and which button to push.

When it was done they were beaming and bowing and shaking her hand, and Morgan experienced a feeling so unfamiliar and strange it took her a moment to identify. Like optimism but stronger, a buoyant confidence and goodwill and sweet anticipation all rolled into one.

Hope. She felt hope.

The Japanese couple thanked her one last time and moved away, leaving her standing stunned and alone, awash in sentimentality for this new bud of feeling she'd glimpsed, which she knew without question wouldn't live long.

And neither will you, a small voice whispered in her ear, *if you don't get going.*

She stared up at the golden stone bulk of the Colosseum.

One look inside, she decided, just a tiny bit of sight-seeing since she'd most likely never have the opportunity again, and then she'd figure out where to begin her search.

Starting off at a casual stroll, Morgan made her way across the greenbelt of grass and around the cobblestone-paved perimeter, wondering at how open it was, how accessible even with the iron gates. She could walk right up and *touch* it. And she did, running her fingers over cracks and bumps and warm, roughened stone, over a small, faded patch of blue-and-black graffiti on the inner curve of a graceful Ionic column, missed by whoever was tasked with removing it. She moved on, noting with no small satisfaction that she was alone and unwatched—practically *free*— in a foreign country, something that even two months ago would have been unthinkable, a total impossibility.

She couldn't help the wicked smile that curved her lips, wondering what *he* had done when he'd discovered her gone. She hoped it involved a stroke.

Around a turn where the outer façade abruptly gave way to what was left of the shorter, inner amphitheater walls, she paused to look around. Few tourists were near this section, only a group of teenagers sitting cross-legged perhaps fifty yards away in a semicircle under the boughs of a gnarled fir tree, smoking something sweet and acrid that didn't smell like tobacco. One of them snorted and punched another in the shoulder, and they all fell into fits of giggling.

She doubted very much if they'd notice what she was about to do.

The strappy heels she kicked off into a corner, though she hated the thought of leaving her favorite pair of Chanel sandals out in the open like sitting ducks. Then with one final, furtive glance around, she wrapped her hands around the cold iron bars of the gate, looked up, and began to climb.

Caught between fury, disbelief, and that same odd, fleeting admiration he'd felt at the hotel when she'd—almost—made a porter regurgitate his lunch on him, Xander watched the lithe, confident figure of Morgan scale the outer façade of the Colosseum like a spider advancing up a wall.

There were hundreds of people within shouting distance, hundreds more speeding by through evening traffic on the boulevard just beyond. She was totally exposed. Only one of them would have to look up to see the pair of long, bare legs, the dark hair like a brushstroke down her back, the white blouse stark as daylight against the night.

What was she thinking? *Was* she thinking? If any of the lingering tourists snapped a photo of her—worse, a *video*, nightmare of nightmares—they'd *both* lose their heads.

He'd seen *Ikati* executed for far less egregious offenses than this.

Secrecy. Silence. Allegiance to the tribe. That was all there was, for all of them, since the beginning of time, all that kept them safe against exposure, against discovery.

Evidently Morgan was done with all three.

For the third time since he'd made her acquaintance less than eight hours ago, Xander was spun on a wheel of emotion, from anger to amusement to surprise and beyond, all of it fighting for dominance at once. He hadn't felt this—*much*—in nearly twenty years, since he was sixteen, deep in the throes of an agony so profound he'd never been able to speak of it again.

He darted out from beneath the gloom of the row of shaped cypress where he'd been standing, ran with long, silent strides to a stretch of wall where no tourists lingered, and pressed his body full against it. He exhaled, took a step back, and melted into the warm, scratchy stone.

"Wow."

There was simply no other word to describe it.

Morgan stood in her bare feet at the very top of the uppermost arcade, looking down on what was once the sandy floor of the Colosseum. The floor had long ago been removed except for a re-creation of it at one end. The structures beneath were now exposed, a two-level network of tunnels and crumbling subterranean chambers, winding and shadowed in the starlight.

A warm, light wind buffeted her body, swirled her hair into her eyes. Wanting to feel the rocky earth and tufts of green grass beneath her feet, she decided to go down and explore it. Just as she made a move to jump down to the next level of worn stone seats below, there came a voice, low and hostile.

"What the hell do you think you're doing?"

She froze. For a single, horrifying instant, she pictured herself in prison—human prison this time—locked away for trespassing on a national treasure. But then she turned and it was Xander, not one of the local *polizia*, renowned for their ferocity.

Morgan didn't know which was worse.

"What do you think I'm doing, genius?" she said coldly, squaring her shoulders. "What I came here to do: search for the Expurgari."

"Really?" he replied, just as cold. He appraised her with a slightly curled lip. "Because what you're doing seems closer to sightseeing than searching."

"You can read minds?" she snapped, folding her arms across her chest.

That curled lip of his drew back even farther, and she desperately wanted to slap the smirk right off his face.

"Doesn't take a genius to figure it out," he said, his voice dripping with sarcasm. "You're practically hyperventilating with excitement."

He put a slight emphasis on the word *genius*, and the urge to slap him grew exponentially stronger. Smug bastard. And she was *not* hyperventilating.

"And by the way," he continued before she could reply, "let's get something straight. You need to ask—nicely, which I know will present a challenge for you—for permission to leave the hotel. And if I grant that permission, it's only on the condition that I'm coming with you. I need to know exactly where you are at all times, so in the future you're not to go anywhere without asking me first. Understood?"

Morgan had heard the term *blood boiling* on many occasions, but she suddenly, completely grasped its true meaning. Fire flowed through her veins, scorching hot.

"I'm not going to ask your permission for anything, ever," she enunciated slowly. "But I'll *inform* you that I'm going to go down there," she pointed to the shadowed floor of the amphitheater, "to take a look around."

Xander took a single step forward out of the shadows. His amber eyes burned like embers in the hard, dark angles of his face. Dressed entirely in black, he looked as if he'd been caught in an unexpected dust storm: a fine coat of pale yellow dust clung to his clothes and skin, even dulled the shine of his gleaming jet hair. She hated to admit it, but even dirty and angry, he was the most gorgeous man she had ever seen.

In a tone filled with dark threat, he said, "I wouldn't do that if I were you."

"Well, obviously you're *not* me. And going down there is exactly what I'm going to do."

"No," he replied, emphatic. "You're not."

Morgan pushed her windblown hair from her eyes and glared at him. "I'm not asking permission!"

"And I'm not making a suggestion. You're not going anywhere but down those stairs"—he jerked his head, indicating the wide stone steps that led to the lower levels and the street—"and back to the hotel. With me. *Now.*"

His hands were empty and flexed open. He stood with his legs apart, knees slightly bent, weight on the balls of his feet. Fighting stance. She recognized it from years of fencing lessons she'd been forced to take by her father. His archaic ideas of femininity were probably surpassed only by those of this dust-encrusted Spartan glaring daggers at her.

"I didn't realize Leander sent you along so you could irritate me to death."

He smiled—grim, without a trace of humor or warmth—and answered in the most menacing tone she'd ever heard, delivered soft as silk. "Whatever works."

Oh, oh, and *oh.* The flush of blood that crept up her neck to spread throbbing over her ears was hot, painfully so. She felt shamed and unsteady, unduly exposed, and knew without question he had aimed for exactly that.

Don't let him see it! Don't let him win!

"You're lucky you collared me." Her voice was steady, her face was composed, but everything inside was a riot of lashing emotion. The need to Shift ate through her blood like acid, but she was crippled by the damn collar. That'd *he'd* put on. She cocked her head and let her gaze travel over him. Measuring. "But I'll bet..."

"What?" he prompted. His fingers flexed.

She smiled sweetly at him. "I'll bet I'm still faster than you."

A heartbeat before he recognized the challenge, then his expression changed, a microscopic shift from flat contempt to something more heated, closer to curiosity, or anticipation. "Don't even think—"

Before he could finish his sentence, Morgan turned, took two long, running steps, and launched herself off the Colosseum's highest wall and out into empty space.

EIGHT

When she was fifteen years old, Morgan Shifted for the first time.

Tremors of it had been surfacing for years. A flash of illusory pain in her bones, an unexpected sharpening of smell and hearing. All the *Ikati* had heightened senses from birth, but suddenly she was able to smell a bird on the wing from miles off and know if it was hawk or starling, suddenly she was able to see every dewdrop on every blade of grass on the lawn outside from the window of her second-story bedroom. She heard the fir trees humming with sap, she tasted rain days ahead, she felt the earth turn beneath her feet. All of nature came into brilliant, perfect focus, and she was at the very center of it all, a locus of awareness.

Then, on the morning of her fifteenth birthday, she finally Shifted to panther and discovered that in addition to strength and agility and sharpened senses, she could run so *very* fast.

She knew that even with the collar she'd still have that lightning speed. And there was no chance in hell Mr. Rules and Regulations would Shift to pursue her, because the Law expressly forbade them from Shifting in front of humans.

He'd have to follow her on foot.

She sailed through the warm evening air, suspended for a breathless moment—heart pounding, arms spread wide, hair snapping in a long, dark flag behind her—and landed on a patch of grass just feet from a stone bench where two lovers were locked in a passionate embrace. They broke apart with gasps and began to exclaim in startled Italian, but she ignored them and concentrated instead on regaining her equilibrium. The ground was hard and the jolt hurt like hell, but she knew no bones would be broken. A fifteen-story free fall really wasn't all that bad; she'd once fallen twice as far from the top of an ancient, towering fir in the New Forest at Sommerley and barely been bruised.

Breathing heavily, still crouched on the ground, she looked over her shoulder and craned her neck to where she'd just been to see if he'd followed.

But he hadn't. He stared down, a small figure in black awash in gold lights, alone at the top of the Colosseum, watching her with those canny amber eyes. Feeling strong and alive and *free*, she blew him a kiss, then took off at a run.

NINE

From the uppermost arcade wall, Xander watched as Morgan, in a truly astonishing display of impudence, lifted her hand to her face, puckered her red, generous lips, and blew him a kiss.

In spite of himself, he huffed a short, disbelieving laugh. He was *Ira de Deus*. Famed, feared assassin. Bringer of death.

No one—*no one*—had ever treated him with such disrespect.

His regard for her grew in exact proportion to his outrage. He'd never met anyone who'd dared take such liberties as this. She was cocky and defiant, definitely reckless, and seemed to care not a damn about his reputation or the very real and imminent possibility he would be the one to end her life.

She was…fearless. He'd never met anyone like her.

For a brief, deranged moment as he watched her rise from her crouch on the grass and sprint off barefoot across the boulevard, traffic screeching to a halt in both directions as she passed, he was held fixed by surprise and admiration and simply watched her run. She bounded graceful and fleet like a Thomson's gazelle through the snarl of cars and taxis and Vespas, even clearing the hood of a red Fiat that didn't stop in time in one graceful, long-legged leap.

His hand lifted automatically to the Ba Gua Zhang crescent moon knives sheathed in a slim leather scabbard at the small of his back, hidden inside his belt. Gifted to him by his capoeira master when he was just a boy, they were fifteenth-century throwing knives, folding and perfectly weighted, in pristine condition though frequently used.

He hesitated, then dropped his hand. Had it been anyone else, there would have been a blade protruding between those swiftly retreating shoulders by now. Deserters were a dire threat to the tribe, and he'd caught—or killed—every one he'd been sent to look for.

But it isn't anyone else. The thought rose, errant, to needle him. *It's her.*

Without bothering to examine exactly what that meant, he lifted his gaze to the sky and saw the twinkling stars, the fat, perfect pearl of the rising moon. Then he closed his eyes and let it rise to a burning peak within him, the writhing bright power of the Shift, ever there just beneath his skin.

Then, without noise or warning, he dissolved into mist.

It was the same every time, effortless as breathing, a mere focus of the will. As if an eyelid had been peeled back to reveal everything around him in vivid color from all angles, he perceived above and below exactly as he perceived forward and back. There was no impediment to his sight, though he lacked eyes through which to focus or even, for that matter, a head. He existed as a part of the very air itself, weightless, and moved through it by applied thought—*up, down, fast, slow.*

The one inconvenience was his clothes. Anything he wore or held in his hands simply dropped to the ground as his body dissolved into mist. He'd never been able to take things with him as Vapor, but he had another utterly unique and powerful Gift at his disposal for that.

He'd come back for his clothes and knives later. Right now he had a runaway to catch.

In a sinuous, pale gray plume of mist, he rose into the air and caught the heated updraft of wind from the boulevard below. He used it to lift him, riding it until he was far above the Colosseum, far enough that anyone looking up would see what appeared to be a small cloud, if oddly swift. Beneath him Rome was laid out in glittering splendor, bedecked in shimmers of copper and gold. The streets were pulsing arteries filled with traffic, snaking away in all directions in streamers of red and white. Above him was the night sky, sapphire dark, dusted with stars.

And there, standing fixed on the sidewalk as pedestrians parted around her like flowing water around a rock, stood Morgan.

Even from this distance he saw her shock, her blank disbelief. She'd gone pale, almost as white as her blouse. She'd felt his Shift; that much was obvious. Had he lips he would have laughed out loud.

Yes, I can Shift to more than just panther, meu caro. *I have my mother to thank for that.*

———
77

He pushed through the atmosphere, up and forward, flying, easy as air, knowing without a doubt that at this exact moment she was cursing his name and recalculating plans. No matter. She could run, she could hide, but she wasn't getting away.

Ever.

He kept well above as she turned and began to push her way through the throngs of chattering tourists and strolling lovers and elderly women in head scarves and sensible shoes heading out to evening mass. He felt curious and unhurried, the luxuries of self-confidence, and tried to keep out of easy sight as he tailed her, camouflaging himself with varying degrees of success around belfries and chimneys, in the foliage of trees. She kept looking up and behind as she ran but never stopped or even slowed her pace.

She went north, keeping to well-traveled and well-lit streets, darting in and out of churches and trattorias and coffee shops, entering in the front and exiting the back or some other side door, trying to shake him. It was amusing, and he found himself hoping it wouldn't soon end.

He was having something like—fun.

Then she ran down a flight of steps into an underground entrance to the Metro and he began to worry.

He flashed down the steps behind her, startling a bunch of chortling pigeons on the rail into shrieking flight. He followed the sight of her bobbing dark head—easily identifiable from behind with that fall of shining dark hair that gleamed like sunlight on water, so different from all the others crowding around—into one of the sleek silver cars just as its doors were closing. He flattened himself against the ceiling, spread as thin as he could go around the fluorescent tubes that illuminated the car.

It was packed. Morgan was nowhere in sight.

"Terribly foggy in here," remarked a white-haired man in Italian, squinting up at the ceiling from his plastic seat below.

"It's your eyes," replied his dour wife, waving a dismissive hand at him. "How many times do I have to tell you to get new glasses?" She fumbled around in a lumpy knit handbag, came up with an eyeglass case, and handed it to her husband without another word. Xander took the opportunity to slink away, molecule by molecule, over cold metal and hard gobs of dried gum, toward the rear sliding door.

Morgan wasn't in the next car. Or the next.

He didn't begin to really panic until the third stop, after he'd gone through every car on the line and hadn't found her. Oddly, he found no scent of her anywhere except near the door where she'd entered. As he floated unseen overhead, listening to a pair of pimply teenagers argue the pros and cons of rap versus metal, it hit him.

Morgan had gotten on and off at the same stop.

As he waited for what seemed an eternity, spread thin as smoke against the graffitied tile wall on the Metro platform for the next car that would take him back to the Barberini Fontana di Trevi, Xander began to reevaluate the situation.

Morgan had always wanted a tattoo.

Nothing big, nothing that could be seen by the casual observer, and nothing silly. She wanted it to mean something, something special and soulful and not an idle decoration like a butterfly or a heart.

Not that she'd ever seen a butterfly or heart tattoo. Not in person. Those kinds of whimsies were not allowed in a place like Sommerley, where every duty was to the tribe. Your life and your soul and even your *flesh* belonged to them and them alone. A tattoo, to most of her kith and kin, would be an abomination. Something profane, something to mar their sacred birthright: beauty.

Something forbidden.

Which was precisely why she felt the need to get one.

"Buonasera," purred the young man behind the glass counter, sizing her up with eager eyes. He was tall and stooped with greasy skin, hair that badly needed washing, and breath like he'd been on a three-day bender, which she could smell from where she stood. She smiled at him, pretending not to notice.

"Buonasera."

The shop was small and lit by flickering fluorescent lights in vivid blue and yellow and purple that lent a night circus atmosphere, surreal and dreamy. Several leather chairs lined one wall; hundreds of sample tattoos lined the others. Aside from the man behind the counter, she was the only one in the shop.

All in all, it was perfect.

He moved out from behind the glass counter and came to stand near—too near. His gaze never lifted from the level of her chest. He said something else in Italian that she didn't understand, a question.

"Tattoo?" She pointed to her right hip. "Here?"

He let his gaze rove down from her chest to her hip. *"Sì,"* he answered, not altogether steady, and moistened his lips. More unintelligible Italian followed, but she didn't miss the undercurrent of suggestion or the way he looked at her bare legs.

She turned, went to the front door of the small shop, locked the door, and drew the shade. When she turned back to him he was staring at her with an amusing combination of terror and anticipation, wringing his hands together.

She walked toward him slowly, still with the smile. "Yes, this is your lucky night. Unfortunately for you, my unwashed friend," she added, reaching out to touch his arm, "you're not going to remember any of it."

After the tattoo—which made her happy in the way small children are happy on Christmas morning—she strolled up Il Corso, the main thoroughfare back to the hotel. She was tired and hungry and sore from her earlier jump and from where the needle had pierced her skin. Who knew a *hip* could be so sensitive? All she wanted now was something to eat, a bath, and bed.

The gelato shop was charming, small like all the other shops on the Corso and still filled with people though the hour was late. She selected pistachio—large—and ate it with a small wooden spoon while she wandered, thoughtful, up the boulevard.

What was Xander doing right now?

She had no doubt of his fury. In his place, she'd feel the same. But she didn't feel sorry for him. She thought he very much needed a bucket of water to douse the fire that was his ego. So sure of himself, so confident. So domineering. So *irritating.*

Though a tiny part of her was glad for the distraction. It kept her from thinking too much about the ticking clock of her assignment.

Perhaps she'd gone too far, though. If he truly thought he'd lost her, he'd be on the phone with Sommerley in a heartbeat, calling in reinforcements. She had no doubt she could escape him again, but a city full of *Ikati*, all intent on finding her, was another situation entirely. The thought gave her the chills.

She pressed on to the hotel at a quicker pace, tossing her empty gelato container in a sidewalk trash can as she went.

Nothing. He found nothing of her, not even a trace of her scent. Not at the Barberini Fontana di Trevi station, not at the baroque masterpiece fountain of Triton plashing in the plaza above, not along the elegant and bustling Via Veneto, not in the shopping districts or the labyrinth of tiny streets built in the Middle Ages of the Piazza Navona.

She was gone. Vanished.

And she didn't even have the Gift of Vapor to explain it, though she was collared and wouldn't have been able to turn anyway. He flew high over the city, district after district passing by below in blurs of painted color, his fury with himself increasing with each passing second.

A known criminal. A threat to the tribe. A pawn of the enemy. How could he have let her escape?

When the light showed faintly green along the eastern horizon, he finally gave up. He flew back to the Colosseum and resumed his human shape, retrieved his clothes and crescent knives, dressed, then took a taxi back to the Hotel de Russie, all the while trying to figure exactly what he would say to Leander and the Sommerley Assembly.

So sorry, but I've lost the one person who could destroy us all. Oops?

Somehow he didn't think that would be sufficient.

At the hotel he brushed past the bowing doorman and took the elevator to the top floor. Once outside the door to the Nijinsky suite, he didn't even bother with the key. He just Passed through it, clothes and all, and came to an abrupt stop inside the marble foyer.

A softly breathing bump was burrowed into the king-size bed.

Someone was *sleeping in the bed.*

Just as the thought flashed over him and he reached for his knives, he smelled her, warm sugar and woman, and froze in disbelief.

She came back.

She came *back.*

It kept repeating in his head like a broken record, anchoring him to the floor with the sheer impossibility of it. Then another, even more confounding thought: Why?

Freedom was hers. She'd—inconceivably—outwitted him, she had the resources to orchestrate her escape to any far corner of the earth, but she came back. The relief that surged through him was cool and prickling, as palpable as rain. It was followed by a gripping desire to know exactly what made this dangerous, maddening, lovely woman tick.

Without making a sound, without turning on any lights, Xander crossed the elegantly furnished living room and went into the master suite to stand beside the bed. He stared down at her sleeping face for several minutes, just watching her. Her hands were folded beneath her cheek as if in prayer; her lashes made a silken black curve over her cheeks. Her hair spilled dark chocolate and mink over the pillows; those full lips, ever red even without lipstick, were soft and slightly parted. She looked beautiful and innocent and totally at peace.

He would be well within his rights to kill her now and not wait the two weeks.

No, he thought immediately. *No.* That body, that face, those plush ruby lips...no.

Then he cursed his own stupidity and wondered what the hell was wrong with him. She was a deserter! She was a traitor! She was...*beautiful. Mysterious. Strong.*

He closed his eyes, stretched his neck back, and hissed a long, quiet breath through clenched teeth. Then he retreated to the safety of a leather armchair, set diagonally across from the bed in a corner of the room, removed his knives from their sheaths at the small of his back, and settled back with one gripped in each hand, to wait.

TEN

When Morgan opened her eyes in the morning, Xander was standing at the edge of the bed, staring down at her with searing, molten eyes. Clutched in his hands was a pair of wicked-looking knives.

She sat up so abruptly the goose-down pillows slid off the bed. Even as she looked around wildly for something to stab him with—the pen on the night table, yes!—he was backing away, lowering his hands to his sides.

"I'm sorry," he said. "I didn't mean to scare you."

He seemed to mean it because he retreated as far as the bedroom door before he put his hands behind his back and sheathed the knives at his waist. Then he stood there looking at her silently with his hands loose at his sides.

"Excellent plan," she said, heart thundering, "because standing over a sleeping person while holding knives is very *non*scary."

No response. The way he looked at her, searching and burningly intent, brought the blood to her cheeks. She pulled the sheets up to her chin and stared defiantly back.

"You came back." His voice was different than yesterday. Just as grave, but softer somehow.

"I never left," she answered, cross. "I just…I just…"

He cocked his head in a sharp, birdlike movement that brought to mind a raptor she'd once seen hunting a white rabbit in the New Forest. It hadn't ended well.

She stood, pulled the sheet from the mattress, and wrapped it around her body. She wore a camisole and panties and nothing else and suddenly felt very exposed. "I'm starving. I think breakfast is in order before we get started."

He frowned at her as if she were speaking in a foreign language and let his searing gaze drift over the sheet, puckered to folds in her fist. "Started," he repeated, his voice gone husky.

The blood in her cheeks flamed hotter. He looked starving, too, but perhaps not in quite the same way she was. The thought unnerved her. "With our little mission here."

He blinked. His gaze traveled back to her face.

"Finding the Expurgari," she articulated when he still didn't speak.

One of his eyebrows lifted and, surprisingly, so did one corner of his mouth. "Oh. That. I thought you might have meant get started with *gloating*."

Her lips quirked. "I think I had my fill of that last night, while I was…" *getting my tattoo*, she almost said, but thought better of it. Her free hand drifted down to trace the sore flesh on her hip, and his eyes followed the movement, avid. "Sightseeing," she finished.

They stared silently at one another. Outside in the pink flush of dawn, church bells began to toll, beautiful and melancholy. Sunlight streamed pale gold and glittering through the slit in the silk curtains to pool on the carpet between them, so bright it almost hurt her eyes.

"Are you going to run away again?" His voice was oddly courteous. It made her suspicious. Perhaps he was having a laugh at her expense.

"Only if you leave any more rude notes," she shot back, then swept around the end of the bed, headed for the bathroom. She paused at the door and looked back at him over her shoulder.

"No," he said, quite serious. "I won't."

"Well, good then." She still wasn't sure if he was mocking her. But the way he looked at her was not mocking at all. His expression was at once grave and faintly confused, ineffably curious. And...hungry.

A surge of heat passed between them, bright as danger. It made her take a step back, beyond the bathroom door. The marble was a cold shock beneath her feet.

"Ah, do you mind if I...?" She gestured to the shower, being careful not to allow her hand to shake.

"Of course," he said, inclining his head. He stepped back, too, into the living room. "I'll be waiting for you."

That, she thought, firmly closing the bathroom door, *is exactly what I'm worried about.*

Morgan was under much better control by the time breakfast was served.

The café was quaint and sunny, situated directly across from the Keats-Shelley Memorial House at the base of the Spanish Steps. It boasted an excellent view of the terraced garden staircase with its fuchsia riot of ruffled azalea beds, the imposing Renaissance bulk of the Trinità dei Monti church perched at the top, and the tourists that flocked past on the Piazza di Spagna like so many chattering, exotic birds. It was Xander's choice; he had guided her to it with one hand held lightly under her elbow the entire four-block walk from their hotel.

They sat now in silence in the shade of a white umbrella, looking at everything but one another.

The aproned *cameriere* came with their demitasse cups of espresso and departed with a bow.

"So. What is your plan?" Xander took a sip from the tiny porcelain cup. In his big hand it looked like a child's thing, small and easily breakable.

"I rather hoped you had one."

Morgan shifted in her chair, settling better against its cushioned back, and lifted her own cup to her lips. She swallowed and tasted heaven: a tiny dose of coffee so fine and strong and sweet it was nearly dessert, topped with a creamy fluff of foam. "God, that's good," she said. She finished it in one long draught and sighed in pleasure.

Beside her, Xander smiled. "You don't have espresso in England?"

"Tea," she said. "Very fine tea, but nothing at all like this. This is—" She struggled for a moment until he supplied the perfect word.

"Decadent."

He turned his head to look at her, and the sunlight behind his head caught in his dark hair and haloed it with blue flame. It struck her again how beautiful he was, how savagely graceful, at once mythic and menacing. There was something oddly doomed about him, too, an air of weary sorrow like the memory of too much sin.

Like a fallen angel, she thought, and had to glance away.

"It's better than what we have in Brazil also."

She glanced back at him, watching as he drained his cup and set it down, every movement elegant and spare. He looked up at her, rested his elbow on the arm of his chair, then rubbed one finger across his full lips in a slow and thoughtful gesture that also managed to look profoundly erotic.

"Our espresso is grown at lower altitudes, in nonvolcanic soils. Italian blends are more refined."

"Why does the altitude make a difference?"

"Like wine grapes, only coffee beans grown at high altitudes in rocky, inhospitable soil produce the best fruit."

She lifted an eyebrow.

"It's the struggle that refines them," he explained, "the challenge. Give them too much water, sunshine, and fertile soil and they grow fat and tasteless, like a Concord grape, appetizing only when saturated with sugar and made into jelly. Or they wither and die of boredom. Like people. The best ones are survivors. Stripped of chaff, refined by struggle and hardship, they're rendered complex and potent by their very endurance and ability to thrive in spite of deprivation."

Poetic, she thought. *My assassin is poetic.*

"So," Morgan said, gazing at him askance from beneath her lashes, "which are you, then? A fat jelly grape?"

He smiled, wry. "No." His gaze flicked over her, once, hotly assessing. "And neither, I suspect, are you."

The food arrived. Plates loaded with prosciutto and honeydew and *cornetto*, biscotti and boiled eggs with heirloom tomatoes, toasted bread and more of the wonderful espresso. Morgan dug in, trying to avoid the burning stare Xander aimed in her direction.

"I thought perhaps the most crowded areas first," she offered around a bite of buttered toast once the waiter had retreated. "The touristy areas. Ancient Rome, the Palatine Hill, places like that."

"More sightseeing," he said, with a tone that indicated his disapproval of this plan.

She swallowed her bite of toast and sent him a frosty look. "It's just a numbers game. Jenna didn't See their direct location, so I have to start somewhere. We can eliminate the bigger, more obvious tourist traps first, then move to the outer areas if we don't find anything. But I have a feeling we will."

"You think they're hiding in plain sight?"

"Why not?" She shrugged. "We do."

There followed a long, uncomfortable silence. She ate, trying to ignore him while he sat still as stone in his chair, examining her with a gaze so heavy it was *touch*. Heat across her cheekbones, fight-or-flight adrenaline coursing through her veins. But she was not—*not*—going to look at him.

At last he spoke, and she instantly wished he hadn't.

"Why did you do it?"

Concentrating on the contents of her plate, she speared a ripe piece of melon on the tines of her fork, folded a paper-thin strip of prosciutto over it, and lifted it to her mouth. It melted on her tongue, savory and sweet.

"I thought I told you. I wasn't running away. I just wanted to look around a bit before we got started."

"That wasn't what I meant. Which you know."

His voice was quiet, barely audible over two elderly gentlemen at the next table arguing vigorously over a game of chess. In spite of herself she glanced at him, expecting to find derision or contempt. But there was only curiosity, that and something deeper, something indefinable that glittered dark in the golden depths of his eyes. The air between them crackled.

Apprehensive and uncomfortable, she dropped her gaze to her plate. "What difference does it make? What's done is done." She savagely speared another cube of melon, then dropped her fork to her plate with a clatter and sat back against her chair, her appetite vanished.

"As a matter of fact, it makes a great deal of difference."

"To *who*?" she replied, unhappy. Her sentence was ironclad, her fate was sealed. Whys no longer made any difference to anyone.

"In the end, everything matters" was his cryptic response. "The big triumphs and failures are what we most remember, but all the little mindless moments, all the forgotten details of your life matter, too. It all matters, because it all adds up to who you really are."

Surprised, she glanced up at him. That look of curiosity was still there, intense and unflagging, and she was held in it, suspended like a fossil pinned in liquid amber. All at once her apprehension and unhappiness disappeared and she felt only that odd bud of hope again, the one that had first taken root last night. It burned through her heart like a spear of fire.

"Who I really am," she repeated, uncertain. Was this a test?

He nodded, the smallest motion of his head.

"I'm nothing. I'm no one. I'm…" she cleared her throat, wretched, "…a traitor."

"Are you?" he murmured, with an almost imperceptible accent on the first word.

His eyes were hypnotic, sunlight and shadow, searching and searing and washed with ancient sorrow that darkened their pure luminosity but allowed her a glimpse into a well of torment so deep, so unfathomable, it was frightening. For a moment as he watched her, his mask of perfect indifference slipped and she glimpsed beneath it something that she recognized all too well.

Pain. Just like her, this beautiful, unrepentant killer was in pain.

In the space of one moment to the next, something vital changed.

"Haven't you ever wanted a different sort of life?" She blurted it, unthinking. It came out small and pleading. Raw.

"A different sort of life," he echoed, hollow.

"That's all I ever dreamed of, since I was a little girl," she rushed on. "Something more. Something…else. *Anything* else." She gestured to the people strolling past, the whistling waiters, the arguing chess players, a pair of nuns in black habits walking arm in arm up the steps toward the church. "What they have, but I never will."

He sat in absolute stillness, watching her with unblinking eyes, his face rigid. "Freedom."

"Yes," she said, surprised he had guessed. "Liberty and independence and, *especially*, the choice over who we can love." His face turned ashen when she said those words, but she pressed on, ignoring it. " 'One should die proudly when it is no longer possible to *live* proudly.' Do you know who said that?"

He didn't hesitate. "Nietzsche."

She laughed, surprised again. "An existentialist assassin! Yes, Nietzsche. And he was right. Death is always preferable to a life in chains. If nothing else, at *least* we should be allowed that." Her hands shook. She pulled them into her lap, clasped them hard together. "But we're not. We're allowed nothing. And for me, for a woman..."

Her voice faded. There was silence between them for a moment before she resumed, low, to her hands. "I thought becoming an Assembly member would change that. I thought being more Gifted than most of the other men in our colony would change it. I thought if I worked hard and tried my best to be like them...to fit in...I thought things could be...different."

He hadn't moved or, it seemed, taken a breath. She looked up at him, searching.

"But I was wrong."

"The new Queen—" he began, but she shook her head and cut him off.

"I didn't know. It was before. And now..." She bit her lip, fighting the sudden, horrifying onslaught of tears. "Now it's too late."

"They promised you freedom. The Expurgari promised you freedom." He said it softly, not as an accusation but as if he understood.

Morgan knew in her heart she was a coward. She was bold and smart and self-sufficient, she was many things her mother would have been proud of, had she lived to see it, but she was a coward because she couldn't stand it. The isolation, the oppression, the secrecy, and the silence, the crushing weight of the legacy of her Bloodlines and her Gifts.

Everyone else in the tribe could stand it. They had for millennia. But not she.

She would rather die.

"When I first Shifted at fifteen," she said, struggling to maintain her composure, "I was taken before the Keeper and the Matchmaker so they could determine who would be a proper Blood match for me. Because I had Suggestion, I was more valuable to them." She looked up at Xander. "As a breeder." She took a breath and went on. "They wanted to breed me into the Alpha's line, but I knew what that meant—the least possible amount of freedom conceivable. So I threatened to kill myself. You can't imagine the uproar it caused." Her hand drifted upward to linger at the metal rings around her neck. "They threatened the collar, but I wouldn't budge. They relented, in part I think because my father was too valuable to them—"

"Why?" Xander interrupted, intense.

She lifted her gaze to his. "Money. He handled the tribe's investments. He knew everything, where it all was, how much we were worth. Everything. Day and night, counting, counting, counting. Ledgers and holdings and bank accounts. That's all there was for him." She turned her head and looked out at the bustling piazza, at a Gypsy child with huge dark eyes and dirty clothes, begging for money at the base of the Spanish Steps. "Especially after my mother died."

"He loved her?"

Startled, she looked back at him. He watched her with laserlike intensity, unblinking.

"Yes. They...it was Matched, but they did love one another."

"So you were a child of love."

She stared at him, blank. *Love?*

EDGE OF OBLIVION

"You were conceived in love," he insisted.

"I...yes. I guess so, if you put it that way. I suppose I was."

He nodded, as if this pleased him, and she flushed red, embarrassed at the turn in the conversation and completely confused. Why the hell was she talking about love with the man tasked with ending her life if she failed her mission?

"Were *you*?" she shot back, defensive.

His face changed. A flicker of unnamed emotion, here then gone. "My mother suffered the fate you were lucky enough to avoid."

She blinked, understanding. "The Alpha."

He nodded. A muscle twitched in his jaw.

"She's Gifted."

"She *was*," he corrected, flat, and now, realizing what he meant, she was sorry she'd asked.

"Oh. I'm—I'm sorry. What happened?"

He held her gaze for another moment, still intent, then inhaled and leaned back in his chair. He looked away and ran a hand over his cropped hair and held it there for a moment, an unstudied gesture, masculine and unconscious and somehow intimate. His voice came very low.

"He was not a gentle man."

It chilled her. She could only imagine the atrocities behind those simple, succinct words. Even Leander, Alpha of Sommerley, with all his sophistication and elegance and finery, even he was a killer beneath all of that. All the Alphas of their kind were born and bred for one thing, and one thing only: domination.

"No," she said quietly after a moment. "They never are."

He didn't respond, and she sat staring at his profile, outlined stark against the morning sun, brutally handsome and hard. She'd met the Alpha of his colony once before, a man named Alejandro…

"You're the son of an Alpha," she said, curious. Leander would never allow anything to come between him and his birthright. "Why aren't you Alpha of the Manaus colony now?"

That twitch in his jaw again, but that was all. He glanced back at her, his eyes searing gold. "Fate chose my path. And I followed it."

She frowned at him, waiting for more, but he only turned his head and directed his gaze to the passing tourists, bobbing by in a sea of color and noise.

"You are the strangest assassin I've ever met," she declared, undecided again if he was mocking her or just being evasive. This entire conversation made her head spin.

"You're acquainted with many assassins?" he said drily, to the view of the palazzo.

She speared another ripe piece of melon, lifted it to her lips, and ate it. "Not any who've read Nietzsche and talk about love and fate all in the same breath," she muttered.

He chuckled softly. "I've had an unusual education."

She snorted. "I'll just bet you—"

He went rigid in his chair and whipped his head around so fast it was a black blur in her peripheral vision. He hissed, low, through his teeth, and a deep, warning growl rumbled through his chest. All the tiny hairs on her arms stood on end.

"What is it?" she said, stiffening.

The air around them seemed to warp and shimmer, and she felt his anger and adrenaline pulse over her skin in heated, dangerous waves. The arguing men at the next table fell silent, and she wondered if they felt the sudden atmospheric change, but she didn't dare look over.

"Open your nose," he growled, scanning the palazzo. His lips peeled back to reveal a set of perfect, gleaming white teeth. His hand went to his waist.

She glanced around. The café, the passing crowd, the bright, sunlit morning—she saw nothing out of the ordinary.

"Your *nose*," he hissed and shot to his feet. His chair skidded back and toppled over with a clatter to the cobblestones.

There was a twitter from a table of young women as they noticed Xander for the first time; a few soft gasps rose from another. Conversation all around them ceased except for a few startled murmurs. And she could understand why. At his full height, on full alert, the assassin exuded a current of feral, crackling electricity, virile and potent, that rocked her back in her chair and left her breathless. Even the humans must have been able to sense it, but if not, there was still the fact of the taut, leashed lines of his body, those massive shoulders and arms, the face of a destroying angel, perfectly beautiful and perfectly cold. She stared up at him, startled, as an exquisite rush of heat flooded through her veins.

"Xander, there's nothing," she said, horrified by her body's response. What the hell was the matter with her? "Will you *please* sit down, you're making a scene—"

But then she sensed it. Hot and heavy and peculiar, a wave of power unlike anything she'd ever felt. Enveloping. Burning. Surrounding. It felt at once intimate and alien, probing, and she knew without doubt it was meant for her. On instinct she inhaled and caught the scent of lightning and smoke, a lingering sting like gunpowder on the back of her tongue. Sweat and musk and succulence, masculine and heady.

"Alpha," she breathed, tasting the truth with every nerve in her body. "My God, it's an *Alpha*."

And not one of their own—no one from any of the four *Ikati* colonies felt like this. Though it was undoubtedly one of their kind, a male of their kind, he smelled different. He tasted different. His aura was scented dark, so dark, like mulled wine and spice and violence, like secrets and whispers and tunnels beneath the earth. Intoxicating and frightening, it held her frozen in her chair, hypnotized.

"*Find him*," Xander commanded, his eyes raking the passing crowd.

Without hesitating, Morgan closed her eyes and concentrated.

The crowd vanished. Everything fell silent. There was only warm air, the chair firm beneath her, and the glass edge of the table, cool under her wrist. She cast out her awareness in swift, concentric rings, enveloping everything around her. Warm humans and solid buildings and the corded sinew of trees, canvas umbrellas and all manner of dull, inanimate objects and the sweet, fleet wind brush of starlings flitting through the air. Cars passed by a few blocks over, a plane flew by overhead, hard and fast and metallic.

And then—oh, and then—

She collided with him and gasped.

He was power and darkness and black, grasping need, a frightening, gravitational pull, strong and elemental. She felt as if she'd entered the atmosphere of a massive black hole and was in danger of being sucked in and swallowed.

"By the steps," she panted, pulling back from the contact with an effort that caused her an almost physical pain. "At the top of the Spanish Steps—he's there!"

She opened her eyes, turned her head, and through the sea of people and color and movement, found him.

He stood fixed and silent on the uppermost terrace of the sweeping white staircase, leaning on the balustrade with his hands gripped so hard over the curved edge his knuckles were white. He was tall and large—not as muscular as Xander, but just as substantial—with black hair just beginning to gray at the temples. Dressed in elegant, spotless white, he stood out in the riot of color around him, and the power of his shining, bright presence made everything else fade to gray like a brilliant ray of sun against the clouds.

His face was severe yet appealing, blessed with the hard grace and undeniable beauty shared by all *Ikati*, a beauty that made heads swivel for another look as he stood staring back at her with eyes so sharp and strange she shuddered.

They were black. Coal black. Flat and endless. She had the impression of being sucked into that gravitational pull again, of falling. Of drowning.

Then Xander moved and set her free. He took off at a run, brutally shoving his way across the piazza, leaving a swath of cursing tourists in his wake. He sailed over the enormous plashing fountain in its center in one flying leap and landed on the other side—a feat no human would ever be able to achieve, evidenced by the astonished gasps of everyone that saw it—and kept running in a beeline toward the wide, sweeping staircase and the man standing near the top.

The man in white didn't move as he watched Xander approach. He held perfectly still, his gaze trained on him, wearing an expression of mild irritation but not fear or surprise, almost as if he expected exactly this scenario.

His gaze went again to Morgan. She sat perfectly still under the cold weight of it, rigid as stone, finding it difficult to breathe.

There came a voice inside her head, and then breathing became impossible.

You will be mine. Beautiful stranger, blood of my blood, you will be mine.

Just as Xander reached the first level of steps, the man in white turned and vanished into the crowd.

ELEVEN

Xander saw him turn and vanish, and he ran even faster.

In a flat-out sprint, he took the steps three at a time, pumping his arms and legs hard, shoving past people or colliding into them, knocking them over—but he didn't stop or even slow.

An Alpha. In Rome.

Impossible.

In all the four colonies of *Ikati*—England, Brazil, Quebec, and Nepal—there was no one unaccounted for. Travel was severely restricted, Bloodlines were carefully kept; everyone knew everyone and always had. There weren't even any stray half-Bloods anymore, not since the new Queen had been found. And the few deserters they'd had over the past decades were all caught and returned, or killed, most to his own credit. The fact that a male of his age and potency had gone undetected and unnoticed was impossible.

But somehow it had happened.

He reached the top level of the terraced staircase and skidded to a stop, scanning the crowd, inhaling deep. He caught the unmistakable scent of *Ikati* to the west, a glimmer of power fading fast down a narrow, tree-lined side street. He took off after it.

He was dimly aware of people scurrying out of his way, of the cobbled pavement flying by beneath his feet, of his own heart pounding in his chest, of his lungs, which burned like fire. The only thing he focused on was running, as fast as he could, and the single thought his nerves and blood and bones kept screaming inside his skull.

Enemy! Enemy! Enemy!

Because of course the man in white was their enemy. A feral Alpha—with the possible exception of the Expurgari there was nothing more dangerous to the tribe than that, a fact proven time and time again over the centuries. Alpha males of the four known colonies were highly aggressive and violent toward other Alphas. They fought for dominance, almost always to the death.

If he knew of the other colonies, he would make a move to usurp their Alphas. It was in his blood, in the structure of his DNA. And total domination was the only acceptable outcome; also in his DNA. Which meant death for one Alpha or the other.

Which meant war.

Xander had smelled the Alpha's desire first—aimed at Morgan, animal pheromones thick and pungent—and the shock of fury it gave him sent a flood of murderous aggression through his veins. He could only imagine what he wanted from her, wanted to do to her, an unmated female, in her lush, exquisite prime—

He cursed and ran faster.

Around a bend in the road, and he saw a flash of white disappearing into an alley. He lunged forward, anticipation seething in his blood. He bared his teeth in victory. The man in white would be trapped—

Xander rounded the corner of the alley and ground to a sudden halt.

There, at the end of the long alley, stood the man in white.

Holding a gun.

Smiling.

There was a loud report, a crack of noise that ricocheted off the tall brick buildings on either side. A bright flash of light and the smell of smoke, and Xander just had time enough to concentrate before the bullet hit him.

It was a perfect aim. Four inches below the collarbone on the left side of his chest.

His heart.

The bullet went in the front and out the back, piercing a perfect, round hole in the fabric of his shirt. It left behind the scent of scorched linen. He staggered back with the force of it and lifted his hand to his chest.

"Shit," he muttered, frowning.

He really liked this shirt. He looked back up at the man in white, who had lowered the gun to his side and was staring at him in stunned incomprehension.

"Surprise," he said and offered the stranger a smile of his own. Then he reached for his knives.

Morgan had to shuck off her heels so she could run—the second beautiful pair deserted in less than fourteen hours, these a snakeskin, red-soled Louboutin—and had just reached the top of the Spanish Steps when she heard the shot.

She froze. Her blood chilled to ice. Everyone around her froze as well, exclaiming in various languages, and gazed at one another, wide-eyed. There were shouts in Italian that mentioned the word *polizia*, and she didn't want to stick around for that. She turned and sprinted down a side street with Xander's scent flaming hot in her nose.

She rounded the corner of the alley just in time to see him hurl a throwing star at the man in white. Just before impact, his target dissolved into a fine spray of mist, and the throwing star caught the collar of the now empty white shirt and embedded it into the brick wall behind him with a *thunk*. It hung from the throwing star's spikes like laundry hung out to dry. The mist that had been the man in white coalesced and rose quickly in surging gray plumes.

The force of his Shift made her gasp. He was incredibly powerful, just as powerful as the throb of energy that had so shocked her when Xander had Shifted at the Colosseum the night before.

It was always like that with an Alpha. Power and passion and heat. Past her shock, she wondered again why Xander wasn't the Alpha of Manaus—he was far stronger than Alejandro, the one who ruled now.

Moving fast, the gray plume of mist disappeared above the roofline, pants and shoes and underthings left behind in a heap on the dirty cement. Xander ran to the pile of clothes, crouched down, and quickly combed over them. He pocketed something, then noticed her standing there, staring.

He stood and stared back. His eyes were fierce, firelit gold, unmistakably dangerous and wild. She felt the surge of bloodlust crackling through his body and took a step back, her hand at her throat.

"Get back to the hotel." He was breathing heavily but his voice was perfectly controlled, perfectly cold. "Wait for me there. Don't let anyone in but me, no matter what happens. *Entendido?*"

She nodded, backing away, her hand still at her throat. If she'd had any illusion of the truth of what he was, if she'd harbored any secret hope because of their strange conversation at breakfast, it was quickly stripped away and burned by the sheer pulsing force of the rage and hatred that burned in his eyes, bright as comets.

Killer, she thought. He was a killer. Of that, there was no doubt.

Then he turned away, walked to the very end of the alley where the brick walls met behind a pair of reeking Dumpsters, and simply melted into the building, leaving behind not a single trace he was ever there.

He didn't want to leave his knives behind, so Xander simply used Passage instead of Vapor, a convenient Gift he'd more than once been grateful for.

This way he could simply Pass through solid material— or it through him, like the bullet—keeping his clothes and anything he carried with him. Anything that wasn't too heavy, that is. He'd once tried to Pass a three-hundred-pound deserter from his colony through the steel bars of the country jail he'd found him in, piss drunk, and had made the unfortunate and gruesome discovery that there were weight restrictions to this particular Gift. The man had made it halfway through before things really got ugly. Xander had had to abandon the body, but he burned the jail to the ground so there was no evidence of the deserter's unusual demise.

In another life he'd have been a cat burglar. He'd more than once dreamed of the riches he could accrue, all with no more effort than it took to concentrate.

The building he'd entered through the back had once been a multilevel private home, converted now into a modest hotel. Once through the walls, he found himself in a laundry room, steamy and strewn with mountains of unwashed sheets, pillowcases, and towels. He oriented himself for a moment, finding the muffled energy of the Alpha far above him, moving fast over the roof. Then he started to jog, dodging washing machines and ironing boards and two old Italian women folding towels who shrieked as he went past.

He went through the kitchen, the dining room, and the small, deserted front lobby—not bothering with finding doors, just Passing through the walls as he went—and ran out into the street. His prey was there, high above, a streak of pale gray moving swiftly and silently through the sky.

Though it was all he could do to keep the animal under his skin from clawing its way out, Xander forced himself to fall back to a safer distance. A plan formed in his mind. He could always Shift to Vapor if necessary, but not only did he not want to play that particular hand just yet, he wanted the man in white to think he'd lost him in the tangled maze of Rome's streets, and—hopefully—lead Xander to his lair. If he thought he was still being followed, the chances of that happening were exactly zero.

Xander ran to a tall stone pine, umbrella-shaped and ubiquitous around the city, and scaled the trunk quickly, forgetting in his haste to even look around for watching eyes of pedestrians below. He reached the top and steadied himself between two massive branches and looked out, his view obstructed by nothing but a small branch with clusters of dangling needles he brushed aside.

Over the landscape of rooftops and treetops and church spires there rose one massive, iconic structure, a cruciform basilica topped by the tallest dome in the world. It dominated the skyline, glittering enormous and diamond white in the morning sun.

Xander watched in arrested curiosity as the small gray cloud of mist made its way above the city, angled down toward the dome, and disappeared into the cupola that topped it.

"*Meu deus*," he breathed, frozen in horrified shock.

This was even worse than he thought.

TWELVE

Morgan awoke in warm darkness to the sound of Xander's voice somewhere nearby, pitched low and tense. He paused intermittently between sentences as if he were listening.

"Yes, I'm sure. I know. I did, but he'd vanished. I'll try again in a few hours. I've been at it all night. Yes, she—no. *No.* Leander, that's *not*—"

He exhaled in a long, aggravated hiss, then fell silent.

She sat up from the couch, blinking in the dark living room. She sensed it was still a while before dawn; the birds hadn't even started singing outside the windows in the trees yet, and the city still held that slumbering quiet of very early morning. She stretched, wincing at the crick in her neck, and rose from the couch, pushing the ivory cashmere throw aside.

It had been one of the longest nights of her life.

Pacing hadn't helped. Worrying hadn't helped. Four shots of very fine whiskey hadn't helped. Only sleep had provided an escape from the state of anxiety she'd been in since she returned to the hotel after finding Xander in the alley, and that had been a temporary solution. Now that she was awake, the anxiety came flooding back full force.

What happened? Did he catch the Alpha? Did he discover anything? Were there more stray *Ikati* wandering the streets of Rome? Why was he gone the entire night? How could he walk through *walls*?

Was he hurt?

His voice had come from the master bedroom, and she looked toward its closed door, wondering if she should knock or just wait for him to come out. The sound of running water decided for her. Xander was taking a shower.

With a heavy sigh, she rubbed her eyes and went to forage for something to eat in the kitchen. She had only breakfast yesterday, and now her stomach was tied in hungry, disquieted knots.

In addition to the sprawling living room, master suite, sitting area, and a twenty-five-hundred-square-foot balcony that overlooked the rooftops of Rome, the Nijinsky suite boasted a full kitchen, a bar, and a separate dining room for ten. She looked around the marble-and-chrome kitchen and thought she could quite happily live here for the rest of her life. Except when she opened the refrigerator door there was nothing but cold air to greet her.

She pursed her lips, debating. Wait for Xander to finish his shower, knock on the bedroom door, and get down to dealing with reality—or order room service?

She thought about reality—her mission, the quickly dwindling days to its end, what would happen if she failed—and decided to order room service. Reality sucked.

She found the menu on the desk in the living room and ordered what amounted to a meal large enough for five people. It arrived in less than fifteen minutes, and she let the black-suited man who arrived with it set it all up on the long polished wood table on the terrace, beside a trellis covered in scarlet bougainvillea.

When he was finished and bowed out the door, she stared down at the white linen napkins and silver domed dishes and the glasses of fresh-squeezed orange juice, stalling. It was still dark, and the air held a cool, dewy tinge, but there was a faint hint of lavender along the eastern horizon and she knew the sun would be up soon.

Another day. Her third day in Rome. Only eleven left, and then her fate would be decided.

She caught her lower lip between her teeth. *And this assassin you just ordered breakfast for,* she thought in a fit of agitation, *will be the one to decide it. You moron!*

"Oh, for God's sake, I still have to eat," she muttered, and stalked off in the direction of the master suite.

When she knocked on the door, there was no answer. There wasn't an answer to her call, either, so she pushed open the door and peeked around it.

"Xander," she said into the steamy room. "I've ordered breakfast."

No response. She imagined him silently bleeding out on the tile in the shower, and her heart did a strange little flip-flop inside her chest.

"Xander," she said, louder, moving past the door and into the center of the room "Are you all right? Where are—"

But she stopped abruptly because she caught sight of him standing with his back to her, head bowed, hands flat on the marble sink in front of the large, misted mirror. He was naked from the waist up. His bronzed skin dripped with water, his hair made a dark, damp cap against his head. A white towel was wrapped around his hips, and she was afforded a spectacular view of his quite perfect physique, the musculature and proportion even a bodybuilder would envy.

But his back. Oh God, his back.

She'd never seen scars like that. Long welts raised in white, crisscrossed in dense patterns all across his shoulders, upper back, spine. Imagining exactly what had caused them stole the breath from her lungs and made her legs go weak.

He slowly raised his head and met her gaze in the mirror. He wore that dead expression again, the absence of all feeling that had so frightened her the first time she'd glimpsed his face. He straightened—slowly, as if it pained him—and then she noticed his chest, reflected in a clouded outline in the mirror.

If she thought his back a painful sight, his chest was a maddening riddle. On both sides of his sternum at the level of his heart there were fields of straight lines. Black hatch marks on the right side in groups of four lines with a diagonal fifth, red hatch marks on the left, over his heart. There were dozens of them, more than that, row after row of stark, unembellished marks. They were the strangest tattoos she could imagine having.

"It's a count," he said very low to the mirror. She started.

A terrible idea began to form in her mind, one that she felt like icy fingers invading her brain. She pushed it back, horrified.

He turned and faced her, without hurry, without expression, his arms hanging loose at his sides. He made no attempt to cover himself, no attempt to hide from her open-mouthed alarm, as if he were inviting her disgust. As if he wanted it.

"Red for *Ikati*, black for others," he said tonelessly.

And then she knew.

"Kills," she whispered, understanding beyond the impulse to bury it. Her gaze skipped over his muscled chest, trying not to add, trying not to imagine all the lives reduced to short, blunt hatch marks on an assassin's chest.

She lifted her gaze to his face. "Why?" she said in a small voice.

His hands curled to fists. "Why what?"

"Why do you keep track?"

The question startled him. He blinked and it was there again, that depth of urgent pathos, welling to the surface. A flash and it was gone, vanished behind the expression of emptiness she'd come to recognize as his mask, a very good, very practiced one, one that hid his genuine feelings well.

Almost.

He answered without inflection, his eyes as empty as his voice.

"So I always remember exactly what I am and what I have to answer for. So I can never fool myself into thinking I'm anything but a monster."

She breathed in sharply. A monster. That's what they'd called her, too.

Her heart began to ache, but not just for the carnage she witnessed carved into his bare flesh, and not for the red line she knew was waiting for her, the final one that would finish off an uncompleted group of four just above his left nipple.

Her heart ached for him. For the terrible toll all that death must have taken on his soul.

Haven't you ever wanted a different sort of life? she'd asked him just yesterday, thinking only of herself. She wondered now how many times he must have wished for that very thing.

"I ordered some food," she said, clearing her throat of the frog in it. "I thought you might be hungry."

He stared back at her as if this were the last thing on Earth he had been expecting. She knew exactly how he felt.

"I'll just...wait for you to get dressed."

She turned and walked slowly from the room, leaving him staring silently after her.

In a dream, he dressed.

Underwear, pants, shirt, shoes. Knives in his boots and belt, hair combed carelessly with his fingers. Teeth brushed, watch strapped to his left wrist, his heart like a splintered piece of wood inside his chest.

That was new. He wasn't thinking about it.

I thought you might be hungry, she'd said in response to his unrepentant admission of sin, and that was all it took. The blood on his hands had soaked so deep, into every pore and atom; the things he had done were so awful they could never be atoned for. He was beyond salvation, so far beyond the pale he was almost a cliché of evil. And yet she hadn't condemned him. She had just looked at him with those huge green eyes, looked *into* him, almost as if she...

Not! Thinking! About it!

He found her sitting at the table on the sweeping terrace, gazing out into the lifting pink radiance of dawn. He simply watched her for a moment through the sliding glass door. Her hair was mussed and spilled dark over her shoulders, around the cashmere throw she'd wrapped around them to ward off the chill of the morning. Her skirt was wrinkled; she must have slept in it. He wondered if she'd waited for him. How long might she have waited before she'd fallen asleep in her clothes? The metal collar around her neck took on a rosy gleam in the light, and he felt a ping of discontent at the sight of it against the fine skin of her throat, delicate as a foal's.

Twice. She'd had the opportunity to flee now, twice, and hadn't taken either one.

He inhaled, marshaling his fragmented emotions with effort, pushing down the thought that rose unbidden inside him like a lure that bobbed up, unwelcome, from dark water.

You can trust her.

No. Trust was for children and fools. He was neither.

Her head turned and she looked at him through the slider. She sent him a fleeting, quizzical glance then directed her attention to the many silver domed platters on the table. She lifted one, sniffing its contents.

Bacon. He smelled it through the glass, and his stomach growled.

He stepped out onto the terrace and took a seat opposite her. Neither of them spoke for several minutes while they filled their plates and ate. Birds began to chirp in the trees beyond the plant-filled patio, hesitant little sleepy peeps at first that grew into full-throated songs of welcome as the sun rose over the horizon.

"You didn't catch him," she said, stating the obvious.

He tore apart a croissant with his fingers. "No. I know where he went, though. I'm going out again."

"That must be handy for an assassin." She glanced up at him. "The walking-through-walls bit. I've never seen that before. And you have Vapor, too. You're very Gifted."

He didn't reply. Church bells throughout the city began to toll.

"I like that," Morgan said quietly between bites of scrambled egg. Xander froze with his fork halfway to his mouth.

"The bells," she said, looking down at her plate. "We don't have church bells in Sommerley."

"Oh." His heart eased out of his throat. *Fool.*

When he was able to breathe again, he sensed something different. She was so somber. Her finely arched brows were drawn together, her generous mouth turned down.

"Are you all right?" he said, low, not quite looking at her.

She blinked up at him, startled. "Me?" She let out a small, brittle laugh. "I'm...yes! Of course I'm fine! I'm just...so very..."

Then she carefully put down her fork, dropped her face into her hands, and fell silent.

"Morgan," he said, harsher than he intended.

She put up a hand. "Just give me a minute." Then she put the hand back over her lowered face.

The impatience that lashed through him was almost unbearable. He held himself immobile, staring at her gleaming dark hair, the fine sweep of her collarbones exposed at the open neckline of her blouse, her long, tapered fingers that were just slightly trembling on her face.

He said her name again, softer. She inhaled, then let her breath out in a sharp exhalation that sounded like she had come to some kind of decision. She lifted her head and looked straight at him, and her gaze was steady and clear.

"I have to know how you're going to do it."

He frowned. Do *what?*

"It's just the not knowing. I think if I know, I can…it will be easier for me."

The food he had eaten turned to a sour lump in his stomach.

"Please tell me," she whispered. The look she gave him then, pleading and vulnerable, shattered the dull hunk of wood in his chest to pieces.

Glowering, he shoved his chair back from the table and strode across the patio, stopping only when it ended in a balustrade of pink marble lined with baskets of flowers. He had a wild thought to jump off. Somehow that seemed much preferable to answering her question.

How are you going to kill me? was what she was asking.

How, indeed?

He heard her walk up behind him, slowly, her step soft over the stone. He didn't turn to look at her when she stopped just inches beside him. He felt her gaze like fire on his face.

"I'm not going to run away from you," she said, very quietly. "You have my word, if that means anything at all."

There seemed to be a steel band tightening in degrees around his chest with every breath. He crossed his arms over it and stood still as a rock, glaring daggers at a potted red geranium.

"And I want you to know that I'm sorry."

That got to him. He looked at her, shocked. "You're *sorry.* For what?"

She smiled, and he thought he had never seen anything so sad in his entire life.

"For us. I'm sorry for both of us. For the way things are. For the people we could have been, in another life. And

I don't blame you." She shook her head. "I know it's just your…"

She faltered, dropped her gaze from his, and turned to the view of the city, dusky rose and amber in the morning light. "I know it's just your job."

He was staggered. If this was a ploy to disarm him, it could not have been better planned or targeted more perfectly.

I know it's just your job. She was granting him absolution for having to kill her. She was *forgiving* him.

"We're going to find them," he said roughly, only half believing it.

"Maybe," she agreed softly. "But if we don't, I have to know how you're going to do it. I have to know. I can't go on like this, imagining every possible thing you could…" She made a vague gesture with one hand, and it was so helpless and resigned and utterly sweet he wanted to scream in impotent rage.

But he didn't. All he did was lift his hand, reach out to her, and place two fingers very lightly on the nape of her neck between the C1 and C2 vertebrae.

Her skin was warm and so very soft. Her hair was cool and heavy and silken on the back of his hand, as if he had plunged wrist-deep into water. She closed her eyes and bowed her head, and he couldn't remove his hand no matter how many times he told himself to.

"A knife?" she whispered.

Wordless, he nodded.

"Will it hurt?"

"No," he said, his voice suddenly hoarse.

She took a breath and seemed to gather herself. She lifted her head, and he allowed his hand to fall. The sudden loss of the heat of her skin was a cold shock against his fingers.

"Well then."

She looked at him without fear or reproach, her eyes vivid and shining, almost relieved. She exhaled. She smiled. The change in her was immediate and profound, as if invisible shackles had been released and dropped to her feet. "Let's finish breakfast, shall we?"

And she turned and walked back to the table, leaving him, once again, stunned and silent.

THIRTEEN

"The *Vatican?*" Morgan turned to Xander in shock.

He gave the cab driver instructions in Italian, then gave a curt nod, ignoring with great effort the view afforded him as Morgan's skirt rode up over her knees and a pair of long, tanned legs emerged in all their toned glory.

Christ, he thought, gritting his teeth. *This is a goddamn disaster.* He sat back against the hard taxi seat and stared out the window.

They'd finished breakfast quickly, and she'd showered and changed at the hotel. He wanted to get an early start, picking up where he'd left off yesterday, and she'd insisted on joining him. Two heads are better than one, she'd said, only with her scent in his nose and the sight of that body displayed so spectacularly in a simple black skirt, a fitted red blouse, and those sky-high heels she favored, only one of his heads was working. And it wasn't the one on top of his neck.

He really needed to get some sleep.

"But—but—how can that be?" she was saying, leaning forward.

By chance, Xander glanced in the rearview mirror and saw the taxi driver gaping in slack-jawed admiration at the reflection of her cleavage, peeking out in all its creamy, rounded perfection from the undone top button of her red blouse. He bared his teeth, and the man blanched and snapped his eyes forward.

"Aren't the Expurgari associated with the church? Why would one of us go anywhere near the Vatican? Does he not *know?*" Morgan leaned even closer, so close he could smell exactly where she'd dabbed perfume at the hollow of her throat. To his great horror, his mouth began to water.

"Sit *back*," he snapped, glaring at her, "and stop asking so many damn questions!"

She stared back at him, cool, with her eyebrows raised in twin dark quirks, not one iota impressed with his display of anger.

Wonderful. She wasn't even scared of him. He'd told her exactly how he was going to kill her, and even that had failed to frighten her. If anything, it made her *happy*.

Of all the deserters and criminals and threats to the tribe he'd tracked in his lifetime, he had to get stuck in Rome for two weeks sharing a hotel room with a headstrong, sexy, intelligent, fearless woman who also happened to be so beautiful it stopped men dead in their tracks in the street.

Shit.

She eased back into the seat, crossed her legs, and calmly said, "Well. I suppose if you're not interested in my input, I probably shouldn't tell you that our new friend is a telepath."

The cab bounced along the road. American rock music played on the taxi's tinny radio. Sunshine streamed through the windows, lighting her hair to a blaze of shining, coppery brown. And his blood ceased to circulate throughout his veins.

Telepaths were unheard of in the tribe. Of all their Gifts—Vapor and Suggestion and Foresight and Passage and many, many others—he'd never encountered a telepath. Even their new Queen's Gift of Sight was limited to touch. His mind raced with the possibilities.

"And you know this because…?"

Inexplicably, she flushed red. She dropped her lashes and began to inspect her flawless manicure with great interest.

"Morgan," he said, an imperative. She looked up at him from beneath her lashes.

"Tell me what he said."

But he could guess. From the flush on her cheeks to the way she squirmed under his penetrating stare, he could guess.

"He didn't threaten you—"

"No," she said, too loud, then cleared her throat and looked away. Her voice dropped. "No, he did not threaten me."

His voice came flat and accusing. "He knows you're unmated."

Her flush deepened, spreading down her neck. She nodded, once, and he wanted to break something.

It was the scent that gave it away. Unmated females exuded a different scent—wilder, more primal—than their mated counterparts. The bonding scent was subtle but distinctive and softened the sultry siren's perfume of an unmated female *Ikati*.

An *Ikati* like Morgan.

He'd trained for years to become immune to it, in the same way he'd trained to become immune to pain or fear or Gifts like Suggestion. *A soldier can't afford distractions*, his capoeira master had told him as a very young man, over and over, even as he was becoming ensnared by the most dangerous distraction of them all, one that no one thought to train him to resist because no one thought it was possible.

"This is too dangerous for you. You're going back to the hotel," he said through clenched teeth, but she sat up ramrod straight and caught his arm just as he was about to lean onto the sliding plastic window that separated the front seat from the back and bark instructions to the driver. Her fingers clenched so hard into his bicep he thought he felt a bruise form.

"This is my *life* we're talking about," she snapped, eyes blazing a hot, brilliant green. "*I'm* the one who's supposed to be tracking the Expurgari, *I'm* the one with everything to lose, so I'll be damned if I'm going to let you boss me around and decide what's best for me just because you're bigger and carry a bunch of knives!"

He felt the cab driver's worried glance in the mirror, but he didn't turn away from Morgan's livid, pale face. "This is not a game, Morgan," he said harshly. "Do you know what a feral Alpha will do if he catches you? Do you have *any idea* what he will do?"

"Yes," she said icily. "And that's far preferable to what *you* are going to do to me."

Her words hit him like a fist in the gut. The cab slid to a stop—he didn't turn to look where—and she released his arm and gave him a one-two punch before opening the door and stepping out into the street.

"And at least I'll get to have sex before I die." She muttered it, then slammed the door behind her, turned, and walked away.

If a grenade had gone off in his lap, it would not have had near the explosive effect those words caused on his body.

Everything went into instant overdrive. His heart rate, respiration, hormones, everything spun wildly out of control, including his thoughts, which were saturated with the most carnal, vivid images of Morgan's naked body, wrapped around his own.

He hunched over, clenched his hands into his hair, and sat there with his eyes squeezed shut, breathing in great gulping breaths of air, until the taxi driver cleared his throat.

"*Mi scusi, signore. Stiamo andando in?*"

"No." He took a few more ragged breaths. "I'm going."

He pulled some money from his back pocket and threw an uncounted wad of euros through the little plastic window. "Keep it," he said in Italian as the driver protested it was too much.

Money. Who cared about money? Leander would wire him as much as he needed for as long as he needed it. No, money was not the most pressing problem at hand. And neither, if truth be told, was Morgan.

The problem was him.

This woman—this *mark*—had somehow managed to splinter his control every time he got near her. Everything about her got under his skin, from her eyes to her scent to that smoky, come-hither voice, that fire and passion, that fragile, appealing *lostness* that leaked from her in unguarded moments when she thought no one was looking. And the things she said, the impossible, crazy things! Things that lingered in the back of his mind on replay for hours, one on top of another, a layer cake of confusion and fantasy and horrible temptation and worst of all—

Understanding.

Somehow, impossibly, he knew she understood that he didn't want to kill her but he would because he had to. Because that's who he was. That's all he was and all he had been, for so long he couldn't remember anything before. And her acceptance of that was the worst thing he could imagine.

Haven't you ever wanted another sort of life?

He stood on the street corner as the cab slid away into traffic, watching her walk away, watching the heads turn in her wake, hearing the chorus of whistles that followed those swaying hips, and for a brief, terrible moment, recalled another woman who had spoken those exact words to him, so many years ago.

A woman who'd died because of him.

And if they didn't find the Expurgari, Morgan would have to die, too.

FOURTEEN

Son. Of. A. *Bitch!*

She was almost blind with rage. If she'd had a machine gun in her hands, she might have mowed down everyone in sight, all these cheerful Italians and chattering tourists and those stupid nuns. There seemed to be a thousand nuns to every church in this city. Honestly, it was starting to freak her out.

"This is too dangerous for you," she mimicked under her breath as she stalked down the busy sidewalk, not bothering to get out of anyone's way. "Ha!"

Too dangerous. Oh, I'm sorry, you're right! I've never been in any kind of *danger* before. I've never been convicted of treason and locked up for weeks and faced my imminent, gruesome death. I've never fought off a pack of wild panther boys or kicked ass over all those other savages who wanted my spot on the Assembly or shared a hotel room with a *killer!*

She raked a hand through her long hair and cursed out loud, garnering a disapproving stare from another of those multifarious nuns who stood outside a little sidewalk café, sipping espresso.

"Stuff it, sister," she said, and walked on.

Where the hell was she, anyway? She paused for a moment to look around and get her bearings.

They'd gone only a few blocks from the hotel in the taxi, and she didn't have a map or speak Italian. She had money so she could hail another cab, but when she put a hand to her forehead to shade her eyes from the sun she saw, unmistakable and huge, the dome of St. Peter's Basilica less than a mile away on the other side of the sluggish, winding Tiber.

She decided to walk.

It was a beautiful day, bright and sunny, and every bird in the city seemed to be singing sweet little melodies from the pockets of trees that were everywhere. She crossed the river over an arched stone bridge, mossed and dark with age, and made her way along the tree-lined boulevard, dodging pedestrians and leaping out of the way of insane Vespa drivers who all seemed to share the same death wish.

She passed fountains and ruins and one ancient, weathered fortress that turned out to be the emperor Hadrian's mausoleum, topped by a massive, sword-wielding bronze angel. The city was a feast of art and architecture, all casually laid about in plain view for everyone's enjoyment. She loved the vitality of it, the open green spaces and the ancient buildings and the sense of magic that permeated everything, even the air.

And Italian men, she thought, eyeing one spectacular specimen lounging idly against a tree, *are pretty magical, too.* They dressed well. They moved well. They were tall and dark and elegant, much like her own kind. Even the slouchy, paunchy, balding ones had a certain *je ne sais quoi.*

The lounging dark-haired boy lifted his head, caught her looking, and whistled, low and husky. His eyes burned. She looked away, kept walking, and tried not to think of other burning eyes, kohl-rimmed, amber, and endless.

Xander watched as Morgan bypassed the noisy line of hundreds of people waiting to enter the Vatican, sashayed to the uniformed officer operating the metal detector at the entrance, and touched his arm.

The guard, smiling a glazed, faraway smile, led her away by the hand into a private side entrance. Xander rolled his eyes and snorted.

She was shameless.

But he wasn't about to stand in line himself, especially with that metal detector and the knives concealed in his boots and belt, so he strolled around until he found a relatively unpopulated area—no easy feat—and backed himself against a soaring granite wall. He closed his eyes and concentrated, sending his awareness out, looking for the warmth and motion that would indicate the presence of people on the other side. There was nothing. He took a breath and pushed back.

The stone was cool and very old, much harder than brick or marble and harder to Pass through. The drier, dustier volcanic tufa of the Colosseum had left a residue on his clothes and skin, but granite left nothing but a slight alkaline taste in his mouth. He concentrated on moving forward through the dense mass of it, his legs and arms and chest pressurized as if he were underwater. It was harder to breathe in this type of rock, too, and he didn't attempt it.

When he came out on the other side he was in a small service corridor that was featureless and brightly lit. He inhaled, relieved to be free of the granite, and followed the corridor around to a set of double steel doors. He paused with his ears open beside them, listening, tasting the air.

People. Statues. Glass cases and bronze figurines and... mummies?

He opened the door and stepped into the room, making a swift inspection. It was an Egyptian collection of some sort, with sarcophagi and funerary urns and statues of various pharaohs and animal gods. He smiled at a beautiful basalt sculpture of the cat goddess Bastet in a lighted case and put two fingers to his forehead in salute. Then he moved silently through the chamber, ignoring the speculative glances of the tour group he passed on the way out.

He had Morgan's scent again. Exotic dark muskiness and heated woman, unmistakable and utterly unique, overlaid by that floral perfume she'd applied this morning. Lilies, he thought, shouldering through the crowd. Lilies and lovely hot readiness.

Snap out of it, soldier!

He ground his teeth together and kept on through the adjoining rooms, finally clearing the Egyptian wing and moving through the picture galleries and the tapestries and the ceramics, the statuary and mosaics and oils, all the masterpieces he'd seen in the dark as he'd prowled through the same halls last night in search of any trace of the man in white.

He followed her scent into the Sistine Chapel, which was very small, no bigger than the living room of their suite at the hotel, thick with tourists and uniformed officers who shushed the crowd at regular intervals and prevented photographs. He took a moment to look up and admire the work of one of their more famous kin, Michelangelo, and chuckled to himself. No one but the *Ikati* would ever know.

Down several narrow flights of stairs with crawling claustrophobia at the hot, pressing crowd, through a short gap in the buildings, and he was into the soaring majesty of St. Peter's Basilica.

It was hushed and vast and eerie as a graveyard, dense with flickering candles and incense and whispers that echoed off the vaulted ceiling far overhead. Hazy sunshine spilled down like spotlights on the elaborate inlaid marble floor from the sixteen windows in the enormous dome above the altar, but here in the portico all was dim and silent.

He caught sight of a red blouse far ahead in the nave, a wave of dark hair spilling down a woman's back, and quickened his pace. He threaded through a group of whispering tourists, went around a massive column, and she was abruptly there, flushed and panting, leaning stiff against the column with one hand at her throat and the other held out to stop him from coming any closer.

"Get away," she whispered, hoarse. Her eyes were half-lidded, the pupils dilated so wide they nearly swallowed all the surrounding green, leaving only odd, flat black.

He froze, knowing instantly something was wrong. He cast out his awareness, opened his nose and his ears, but found nothing unusual. He stepped closer, and she let out a soft, keening moan that raised every hair on his body.

"*No closer,*" she insisted, oddly weak and breathless. Beneath her flawless café-au-lait complexion she was very pale. A sheen of sweat had formed on her brow.

"What is it?" he said, low, watching her eyelids flutter, the pulse beating wildly in her throat. His danger sense grew to gnaw against his skin.

"He's here." As she said the words, her brows furrowed and she gasped, a little startled intake through parted lips. "Somewhere—nearby—"

She choked off with another gasp. When Xander stepped closer she shuddered and moaned, arching against the column as if she were in pain.

"That's it. We're getting you out of here." He made a move toward her, and she shook her head, vehement, hissing like a snake.

"No! Please! I'm trying to get him out! I have to get him *out!*"

He looked around again, wildly, searching and scanning, but detected nothing of that dark, violent scent and feel of the Alpha he'd detected yesterday. That greed.

"What the hell is he doing to you?"

She inhaled, long and shuddering, and looked up at him from beneath dark lashes, a concentrated look, full of heat and need and longing. "Everything," she whispered. Her cheeks went a deep, flaming red.

With a cold shock of recognition that felt like ice water down his neck, Xander understood.

His capoeira master had once told him that the best way to win a war was to break the enemy's resistance without ever fighting. There were better ways than direct attacks, ways to outthink and outmaneuver and outplan that were superior to engaging in a bloody, costly battle.

And a Gift like that of Telepathy—where you could insert yourself right into your enemy's mind—might even make resistance impossible.

It might even make your enemy feel something so unthinkable as *desire*.

"What can I do?" he said, helpless, wanting to pick her up and carry her away to somewhere safer but not wanting to do anything to make matters worse. "I don't feel him anywhere, Morgan. I can't sense him—"

She gasped and arched hard against the column. With her eyes closed and her head back, she bit her lip and made a low sound deep in her throat. His heart stopped. Then she put her hands into her hair and stretched back like a cat, thrusting her chest out so he saw with perfect clarity the outline of her full breasts, her nipples straining taut against the red silk.

He stopped breathing. Instantly, he got hard.

"Do something!" she pleaded, hoarse.

He told himself in the next moment that he was only helping her, that this was the best, most effective way to distract her and break the mind link, but even as he was telling himself these things he didn't really believe it. He knew himself far too well.

In two quick steps he closed the distance between them, wrapped his arms hard around her body, put his mouth over hers, and kissed her.

And, unexpectedly, with heat and fervor and a passion that unlocked something deep within him he'd put away long ago, she kissed him back.

Time spun away, sound faded out, everything ground to a standstill. Her hands were in his hair and his were on her soft curves, her jaw, the dip of her waist. She arched into him, soft and lush, and he thought he'd never felt anything so fine as her and this and the sweet warmth of her mouth, of her tongue on his, gliding and sensual and wantonly demanding.

More, her body said, straining against him. *More*, her soft mouth said, hungry. *More!* that little mewling noise in her throat demanded when he pressed his pelvis to hers and she felt the full length of his arousal, throbbing hot.

And he wanted to give her more. In that moment he wanted to give her anything and everything—whatever she asked for, whatever would quench this aching burn in his chest and the roaring in his ears and the poison eating through his blood, poison he'd had his first taste of the moment they'd met.

He wanted to be inside her. He wanted to hear her moan his name. He wanted—

Suddenly she broke away.

She stood there staring at him, blank, panting, her arms still tight around his neck. Then, with a horrified cry, she skipped back and slapped him hard across the face.

"Son of a bitch!" she cried, distraught.

He worked his jaw where she'd hit him and tried very hard to concentrate on the fact that she no longer seemed to be happy about the kiss. Inside him, his desire for her *pounded*.

"You do realize that's not my name," he said drily.

"What the hell do you—how could you—what the hell were you *thinking*?"

That last bit was shrieked, and the cathedral's vaulted marble ceiling conducted it, splintering it into an echoing symphony that shattered the silence in the vast halls all around them. Startled exclamations and muttered reprovals came from various angles, but he ignored them.

In spite of the uncomfortable strain against the front of his pants and the horrifying realization that perhaps it wasn't *him* she'd been thinking of when they shared that passionate kiss, Xander kept his voice carefully neutral and businesslike when he answered.

"You asked me to help—"

"I didn't mean like *that!*"

"And because I couldn't sense him anywhere nearby, that was the most expedient way to break the link. Otherwise I would have gone after him." He cleared his throat. "Obviously."

She was shaking and flushed and clearly free of whatever spell she'd been under. With her rigid bearing and glittering eyes and flustered distraction, she was utterly lovely. She was also *pissed.*

Right now he was very glad for that collar.

"You're trying to tell me you knew that would work?" she asked, dubious. She crossed her arms over her chest and narrowed her eyes at him.

He crossed his arms as well, rose to his full height, and coldly gazed down his nose at her. "Of course. Why *else* would I kiss you?"

Her nostrils flared. She tossed her hair back over one shoulder with a shake of her head. "I see," she said, regaining a little of her fractured poise. "Am I that repulsive to you?"

He paused, regarding her with a look he knew was mercilessly forbidding, willing himself to do the right thing and be done with all this foolishness. But he couldn't bring himself to say it. He couldn't make himself say *yes.*

She took his silence as an affirmation anyway and went even redder. "The feeling is mutual, Ace."

He sent her a grim smile and sidestepped that. "Let's get back to business, shall we? Do you feel him now?"

She swallowed hard and looked around. "No," she said, low. "It's broken."

"And when you first felt"—he floundered for an appropriate word—"when you first felt the connection, where were you?"

She jerked her chin to a nearby chapel, decorated with mosaics and statues, featuring a prominent wood, stone, and marble altar that housed the lighted, ghoulish remains of a dead pope in a crystal casket.

"I want you to come with me over there, and if you feel anything—anything at all—we're going to leave and I'm going to come back alone. Understood?"

She didn't answer. She wasn't looking at him, and he wondered if she ever would again.

"Morgan," he said more softly, trying a different tactic. "Are we agreed?"

After a moment, she jerked her head up and down: yes. Progress. Good.

He opened his palm to the chapel. She went before him, hesitating only when she drew near the altar.

It was topped with eight taper candles in bronze holders, just in front of a massive mosaic depicting the martyrdom of St. Sebastian. There were pink marble columns and corbels with carved cherubs and gold leaf slathered on every available surface.

"Anything?" he murmured, close behind her.

She held very still with her head cocked, as if listening. She looked left and then right, frowning a little, her chin lifted. Her gaze traveled up the soaring marble columns to the vaulted ceiling far above, and she paused, considering.

Then she dropped her lashes and looked at the floor beneath her feet.

"It's...odd," she finally said. "There's a faint echo of something. Almost like déjà vu. But I can't put my finger on where it might be coming from. It's like he's everywhere. And nowhere."

Xander was disappointed, primarily because he'd found only the same thing in his search the night before. It made him a little harsher than he should have been. He was really looking forward to getting his hands on this bastard.

"Well, that's helpful. Maybe it's *God* you feel."

Her lips flattened. She turned to look him full in the face. "You," she said, "are an unmitigated *ass*."

He stared back at her, wrestling with the urge to kiss her again. Those damn *lips*—

"And you're not trying hard enough," he said, his voice tight. "If he's close you should be able to find him, like you did yesterday. Just concentrate."

"If it were that easy, I'd have found him already!" she said, exasperated. "Maybe it's this building." She wrinkled her nose at the lighted casket. "There's too much weird juju in here."

He had to admit the dead guy was giving off a really funky odor beneath all that careful casket sealant. And there was something else he couldn't place, something unnerving, a whiff of ancient earth and dead air and cold, unlit corridors. It reminded him of a crypt. It also very inconveniently interfered with his own ability to sense his surroundings as fully as he normally did. Everything was oddly muted.

It had been the same last night. He'd waited for the sun to go down before attempting to infiltrate the cupola where the man in white had disappeared. The scent of

Alpha was on the stone outside and the glass panes, even lingered like an afterthought in the air above the altar, but then it evanesced and disappeared altogether. But there was something, some indefinable energy, in the very walls of the cathedral itself, vibrating from the foundations...

It made no sense. None of this made any sense.

The only reason he could fathom why an *Ikati* would go anywhere near what many considered the holiest church in Christendom was total ignorance. Since the half-Blood Queen Cleopatra had incited the rage of Caesar Augustus in AD 30, the *Ikati* had been hunted and persecuted, had long ago retreated into silence and small, well-fortified colonies to survive. The situation worsened in the thirteenth century when Pope Gregory IX instituted the Inquisition. Along with heretics, cats were declared diabolical. That set the stage for massive, church-approved executions. Cats were witches' familiars, associated with the devil, dirty animals not to be trusted.

Too bad for humans. Because by the time the Black Plague hit a century later, there were barely any cats left to eat all those disease-carrying, flea-infested rats. Half of Europe's population was wiped out in just a few years.

"Maybe we should go back to the Spanish Steps and try again there." Morgan looked hopefully toward the massive doors behind them that led outside into fresh air and sunlight.

She didn't look completely recovered from whatever spell the Alpha had put her under; she was still a little too flushed. And if he was still lurking around somewhere, Xander definitely didn't want to give him another chance to get inside her skull.

"All right. We'll come back tomorrow." He made a move to take her arm, and she sent him a look of such frozen hostility it held his hand in place.

"I'm not an invalid," she said.

He pressed his lips together to keep from smiling. "Clearly."

"And you already know I'm not going to run away."

"So you've said," he replied, curt.

"Then why do you keep taking my arm whenever we're walking?"

Because I like to touch you.

"Habit." It was the first thing out of his mouth but not what he'd been thinking and obviously not what she was expecting, either, if her expression was any indication.

"So you're a *gentleman* killer," she said with soft scorn. "Did they teach you that at Assassin Academy? How to Make Nice with Your Prey One O One?"

He closed his eyes for just longer than a blink and found the memory of another soft, feminine arm he'd once loved to touch ready to torture him with fresh pain. Being around Morgan was peeling back the scabs on some old, nasty wounds, and he didn't know what to do about it.

"My mistake. It won't happen again."

His voice was shorn of all emotion, but something dark moved within him, something angry and violent that needed an outlet. He felt the urge to fight, to beat something bloody, so keenly she sensed it and took a quick step back, blinking. He stared at her, cold as stone, then turned his back and walked away, out into the blinding bright sunshine of St. Peter's Square.

And there, ringed around the base of the soaring granite obelisk in its center, stood six huge *Ikati* males, feral as wolves, staring right at him.

FIFTEEN

Adrenaline blasted like dynamite through his veins. Xander spun around, took four long running strides back inside the cathedral, grabbed Morgan's arm, and yanked her hard against him.

"*Run!*" he hissed into her ear. He shoved her in front of him.

She yelped in surprise and slipped in her heels over the slick marble, but it didn't matter because he was right behind her, shoving her forward, holding her up when she stumbled.

"Xander! What's going on! What are you—"

He didn't listen to a word she said, didn't listen to the startled gasps of the people he shoved by, didn't slow or look back to see if they were being followed. He knew his best—his only—chance of getting Morgan to safety was to move fast.

Faster than *them.*

The two of them skidded around an enormous marble column, her heels clattering against the floor. She lost one then the other as he towed her mercilessly toward the great, golden papal altar where morning service was being held in the shadow of the colossal *Baldacchino,* a ninety-five-foot-tall bronze monument carved by Bernini.

He felt the *Ikati* males enter the front of the cathedral one by one, dark bursts of energy that stung his skin like needles.

Morgan felt it too because she gasped and stiffened, turning to look over her shoulder.

"No!" he shouted, pulling her forward. His shout splintered to a thousand *nos* that collided and crashed together overhead in the vast sunlit dome like the broken chiming of bells. The red-robed bishop conducting mass didn't miss a beat—he looked about a hundred years old and was probably deaf—but several dozen worshippers turned in their chairs and craned their necks to get a look at the disturbance.

They flew by the worshippers, ran into the massive, semicircular, white-and-gold transept, skidded around red velvet ropes on stanchions erected to keep the public out of this off-limits area, and headed directly for the altar and its mosaic of the martyrdom of St. Processus.

"Hold your breath!" Xander shouted, towing Morgan behind him like a tug. Up and over the marble steps, across the altar, right to the wall with the colorful mosaic—

Morgan balked, panicking. "Where are you going? There's no way out!"

But of course there was. "Just hold your breath!" he shouted again and tightened his grip on her hand. He hit the wall first and her shocked scream cut off into silence.

Cold, hard stone. Heavy, crushing weight. Hazy darkness and utter quiet and the feel of her hand in his, heat and softness and life among all the dead rock Passing through his pores.

And then they were through it.

They emerged onto a strip of grass along the busy street behind the cathedral, and Morgan fell to her knees, gasping and coughing. The sudden sunlight was blinding.

A double-decker tourist bus rumbled past. Xander, without giving her a chance to recover or start cursing at him, hauled Morgan to her feet. He had to put his hands under her armpits to get her moving forward because her legs seemed incapable of carrying her weight.

"Get on that bus and get back to the hotel," he growled, shoving her into the street, stopping oncoming traffic with one vicious look. He picked up speed and she ran along with him, breathing hard, finding her balance. The tour bus was only yards ahead. "Lock yourself in. If I'm not back by sundown, call Leander and tell him there's a feral colony here, not just the one male we saw yesterday. And then get the hell out of here. But wait until sundown, you understand?"

"A *colony*?" she sputtered, panting. They reached the bus and ran alongside it for a few paces. Then she grabbed a bar at the back where a set of stairs rose to the second deck and hopped on. She turned and stared at him with huge, frightened eyes. Her hair swirled all around her face in the wind.

His nostrils flared. There was something darker in the scent that hit his nose, something even warmer and more spiced than her usual, natural perfume. His pulse, already pounding, responded to it as if he'd been injected with adrenaline. Every muscle in his body tightened, and he felt a sudden surge of aggression that was not related to the males they'd left behind.

Sweet Jesus, he knew that scent. He knew what his body was telling him.

And he had to get the hell away from her. *Right. Now.*

He stopped running abruptly. He stood in the middle of the street with cars honking and people shouting at him and watched the bus drive away. Morgan clung to the brass rail as it bounced along, watching him with those huge green eyes, face flushed, legs long and bare beneath her slim black skirt.

"Wait until sundown!" he shouted. She nodded. The bus rounded a corner and disappeared.

"*Abiit cum femina,*" said Aurelio, staring hard at the colorful mosaic the two interlopers had just disappeared through. Though she was gone, he still had her scent in his nose, lingering sweet on the back of his tongue, and it was like nothing he'd ever tasted. Rich. Sensual. Arousing. His entire body ached with need.

A full-Blood female. New, ripe, and beautiful. No wonder Dominus wanted her.

"*Proin invenisti eam,*" answered Celian. *We'll find her.* Though they could each speak several languages, when they were together, the brothers spoke only Latin. Still in Latin, he added, "You and Lucien go after her. I'll take Constantine, Lix, and D for the male. Rendezvous at the sunken church at sundown, with or without. *Constat?*"

Everyone nodded in agreement. Celian was second-in-command, Dominus's right hand, and in his absence Celian's word was law.

"Be careful with that male," Aurelio muttered, shooting Celian a dark look. "He's trained."

"And full-Blooded," added Lix. He stood off to one side, examining the mosaic the two had disappeared through for clues. He raked a hand through his too-long black hair. "You ever hear of something like this?"

"Dominus will know what it means," said Celian. Dominus always knew what everything meant. Which was why he was *Rex*.

King.

"Let's get going."

The brothers turned away from the mosaic of St. Processus and made their way back through the vast, echoing basilica to the main entrance, ignoring the gawking stares and whispers that traveled in their wake. Leading the group, Celian knew how menacing they must look. Not one of them was less than six five, and all were thickly muscled from years of fight training, boxing and swordplay and martial arts. Their chosen attire didn't help, either: black leather, a lot of it, topped by long black trench coats that disguised an array of weaponry. He had a random thought that the male they had just chased would have fit right in with them.

A human woman gaped at him as he passed by, and he winked at her, lascivious. She shrank back against a marble column, pale, her hand to her throat. He smelled the sour tang of her fear sharp in his nose.

That's right, deliciae. *I will eat you for lunch.*

The *Bellatorum* reached the main entrance of the church, then split up and went in opposite directions without another word.

Xander felt their approach like waves of stinging needles on his skin. Except there were fewer of them...four, he thought, concentrating on the energy they emitted. Only four now. Which meant they'd sent two after Morgan.

Shit. He was going to have to work fast.

He stepped out from the line of tourists waiting to enter the Vatican and looked right at the four males in black who stood silently on the steps of the basilica, looking around, testing the air with their noses. He was all the way across the vast, cobbled plaza, but they found him right away. Four dark heads swiveled in his direction; eight flat black eyes zeroed in on him with cold, calculated precision. No one moved.

Then Xander flipped them the bird and all hell broke loose.

Instead of running after him—as he anticipated, as any *Ikati* trained to secrecy and silence, the tribe's two cornerstones of existence, would have done—the largest male in the middle simply reached beneath his coat, pulled out what looked to be a Glock semiautomatic, and started firing.

The crowd split apart like stampeding wildebeests, screaming and shoving, pounding the pavement. Hundreds of bodies pushed in every direction, panicking, as more shots rang out over the courtyard. Perfectly still and silent, Xander stood in the middle of the chaos while a hurricane went on all around him.

Damn, they were bold. He'd never have attempted something like this.

The first bullet pierced his thigh. The second hit him in the left bicep. By the time the third bullet ripped through his chest, he was smiling.

The shooter lowered his gun. His companions on either side stared at him, hard, without fear but definitely surprised. Then just because he really wanted to piss them off, Xander lifted his hand to his mouth and faked a yawn.

The shooter's lips curled back over his teeth. He took two steps forward just as a dozen members of the Swiss Guard appeared on the steps of the basilica. They looked truly ridiculous in their Renaissance uniforms of blue, yellow, and red stripes, puffy collars and black berets. But the assault rifles they carried didn't look so ridiculous.

"Lay down your weapon!"

The shooter, whom Xander began to think of simply as Big, sent the guard who'd shouted at him in Italian an irritated look. Then he said something to his three companions, and all nodded their heads.

As the Swiss Guard began to slowly approach the men in black, they simply disappeared into mist. All four, all at once. Their clothes and weapons fell to the cobblestones in large, lumpy heaps.

Xander went cold.

Not only could they Shift to Vapor—which only the most Gifted of his kind could—they had absolutely no problem doing it in full view of humans. Hundreds of them. Which meant *they didn't care* if humanity knew of their existence.

Which meant they were now the worst threat to the tribe. Even more of a threat than the Expurgari.

He watched as they surged above the clamoring crowd, moving fast. The Swiss Guard had frozen in place, craning their necks to look up. Three of them made the sign of the cross over their chests, five more took a few paces back, eyes bugging wide. The rest were apparently too stunned to move.

The four clouds of Vapor went west, opposite where he'd sent Morgan. He watched, torn, until they disappeared past a far grove of fig trees. Then he turned and started to run, the sight of Morgan's flushed face receding on the bus vivid in his mind.

SIXTEEN

Morgan's hands shook so badly she could barely fit the plastic door key into the electronic reader. She finally did it, and the little red LED light changed to green. The door clicked open.

She fell into the hotel suite and slammed the door behind her, turned the deadbolt and turned the flip lock, then collapsed against the door, gasping for air.

She had run all the way from the tour bus's last stop near the Termini station to the hotel, a span of several miles, hoping her scent trail was diffused throughout the city as the tour bus wound through it, hoping the fact that she hadn't left St. Peter's on foot would help disguise her.

Hoping that Xander knew what the hell he was doing.

Her first urge was to pick up the phone and call Sommerley. Leander would know what to do. Leander might even come and get her! Her heart leapt at the thought of returning home, then fell as she realized there would be no mercy for her if she failed to find the Expurgari. And so far she had failed. Finding a stray colony of *Ikati* would hardly appease the Assembly. She'd still be made to pay with her life. And probably accused of working with the feral males all along.

She shuddered and passed a hand over her eyes. *God,* were those males feral. If she'd thought her own kin untamed beneath their thin veneer of civilization, those six males she'd sensed at the church were absolute savages. They exuded that same rabid, violent need she'd felt from the man in white, but where he was crystal cold, a silent void of darkness, they were all pulsing heat and fever, hot carnage wrapped in black leathers. She knew what they were.

Soldiers. Barbarian soldiers to an ice King.

She pushed away from the door and staggered a bit, feeling hot. Too hot. Her face was still so flushed. And she was sweating. It must be the run. She normally ran only so far in animal form.

She went to the kitchen, put her wrists under the cold tap, splashed her heated face with water. She stood there a moment, trying to clear her head. Through the living room windows, the sun streamed in bright, directly overhead.

Noon. That left...six hours until nightfall. She needed a stiff drink.

Just as she turned away from the sink, the first tremor of heat hit her.

She froze midstep. Listening hard, stretching her senses, she stood there, breathless, still. Only her heart seemed to be working, and it hammered away in her chest like a jackhammer.

Something was near. Some*one*.

Her hand flew to the collar around her neck. She couldn't Shift. She couldn't protect herself if they came for her.

Another tremor, more substantial this time, accompanied by the faint, masculine scent of spice and gunpowder. Warning heat pulsed over her skin.

She shot to the heavy wood block of knives on the marble countertop, grabbed one, and whipped it to her side, gauging the best spot to make a stand. She didn't want to be stuck with her back against the wall in the kitchen. She *definitely* didn't want to try hiding in the bedroom, and the living room offered no hiding places at all. Not that they couldn't find her by scent alone. This was impossible! Where was Xander?

Stricken by paralyzing indecision, she was able to move only when she thought she heard a footfall in the hallway outside the front door.

She crept slowly from the kitchen with the knife clutched in her sweating hand and glanced around. Everything in the living room looked normal. The open door into the master suite offered a partial view of the room, but nothing looked amiss. The scent of spice and virile man faded, leaving only the bitter, metallic taste of fear on her tongue. The footsteps outside the door had ceased.

Do you know what he'll do to you if he catches you?

God, she'd been so flippant when she'd answered Xander's question. And now...there were six of them. Plus the leader. Which meant there were *seven* feral males looking for her. Maybe more.

She swallowed around the raw panic clawing at her throat.

With real regret, she remembered the tattoo she'd gotten only a few days ago, remembered too how freedom was so precious to her she'd risked her life on more than one occasion to obtain it. She decided right then and there that if she were captured she'd kill herself. No *way* was she going to let herself become some kind of sex slave.

That decided, she felt a little better.

She moved silently through the living room and eyed the front door. Unease made its way through her body like a thousand army ants marching up and down her nerve endings.

A sound from the terrace. She whirled around, lifted the knife, and gasped.

On the other side of the glass stood one of the huge *Ikati* males from the basilica. His hands hung loose at his sides, his legs were planted shoulder-width apart, his eyes burned glittering, soulless black. He was enormous, big boned and heavily muscled, without a spare ounce of flesh on his entire body. She saw that quite clearly because he was completely nude.

And aroused.

Terror gave her wings.

She whirled around and leapt for the front door as the horrible, ear-splitting crash of shattering glass filled the room. She didn't have to look to know he'd smashed right through the slider. With her heart in her throat and a strangled scream on her lips, she flew through the living room, through the marbled foyer, and in her haste crashed straight into the door. She stepped back and flung it open only to be met with fresh horror.

Another one. Hulking and black-eyed in the doorway. Naked.

Survival instinct took over. Her arm jerked up and slashed out hard with the knife. The male in the doorway feinted right, avoiding her thrust, and grabbed her wrist just as the knife whizzed by his head. She yanked back, growling through her teeth, and met the resistance of stone.

He said something in a language she didn't recognize and bared his teeth at her, eyes blazing. Instinct told her he was commanding her to back down. To submit.

"Fuck you!" she screamed, struggling against his grip.

His eyebrows shot up. Then he backhanded her so hard fireworks detonated behind her eyes and all the bones in her neck popped. Tasting her own blood in her mouth, she slid to the floor, where she remained, stunned, her wrist still caught in his grip, her body dangling from his huge hand. In her stupor, she noticed both males had large tattoos on their left shoulders, a stylized black eye that looked like an Egyptian hieroglyph.

The one who'd hit her pried the knife from her fingers, then moved into the foyer and closed the door with a kick of his foot. He set the knife on the console table and silently stared down at her. The other male stood in the living room with piles of ruined glass around his feet, watching them. He said something in that strange language. It sounded amused and also seemed to anger the one with his hand around her wrist.

He jerked her to her feet so hard it felt like her shoulder would pop out of the socket. He loomed over her, exuding menace and raw power, and she shrank back to the length of both their arms. He allowed her to hover there, tethered, pulling hard against his grip, and wouldn't let her go farther. The marble was cold and slick beneath her bare feet.

"I am Lucien," he said in perfect English.

She kept her eyes focused on his face, knowing what would meet her gaze if she allowed it to travel down farther. Black dots floated in her peripheral vision. She licked blood from her lower lip. "Charmed," she said, staring him in the eye. "I'll call you Lucy for short."

He blinked. The one at the patio door snorted, then walked nearer. She glanced at him, wondering through her fog of pain how the two were so easy with their nudity. They'd obviously followed her as Vapor and materialized without all that black they'd worn back at the cathedral, which had revealed the general fact of their massive physiques but kept hidden the details. All the muscled, masculine, golden-skinned details. Involuntarily, her gaze drifted down.

She blanched. The *size*—

There came a low laugh and she snapped her gaze up to his face.

Dear God, he was smiling at her.

"Do you see something you like, female?" His voice was husky, amused.

The black dots in her vision subsided just enough to see him glower at her cold response. "I see something I'd like to *chop off.*"

Lucien growled deep in his chest and tightened his fingers around her wrist so hard she thought the bones might snap. It hurt like hell, but she bit her lip to keep back the moan of pain. The other male just stood there looking at her with his head cocked.

"You are fierce for a female," he murmured. His gaze flickered over her, taking in her bare legs, the short skirt, the blouse she now wished was much baggier. He slowly licked his lips, a gesture that might have been seductive on another man as well-formed and virile but on him was utterly chilling. A bloom of heat washed through the air. It was followed by the dark, spiced scent of desire.

"Aurelio," Lucien said, sharp, then something else in that language of theirs. His lips flattened, and the bloom of heat cooled a few degrees.

"She isn't claimed yet," Aurelio said, hard.

"Brother! That's treason!" Lucien hissed, glaring at him.

"Only if the King finds out." He stepped closer, glaring at Lucien with something like murderous rage. Neither one seemed to notice they'd switched to English. Aurelio glanced back at Morgan, and something in his eyes made her flinch. His voice dropped several octaves. "I want a taste before we relinquish her." His nostrils flared. "She smells so *good.*"

"We don't have time for the daily mutiny, Aurelio," Lucien snarled. "She belongs to the King. Back off or I'll make you wish you hadn't gotten out of bed this morning!"

Aurelio curled his hands to fists and growled at Lucien, Lucien bared his teeth at Aurelio, and Morgan took the opportunity to reach out with her free hand and touch the hand Lucien still had wrapped tight around her wrist.

"You're going to let me go and kill Aurelio now," she said very clearly.

That flicker of amusement appeared again on Aurelio's face as he shifted his attention to her and gave her the once-over with those black eyes. "Beautiful and fierce, but perhaps a bit demented, eh, Lucien?"

But Lucien didn't answer. He blinked once, then released his grip on Morgan's wrist. Aurelio didn't have time to react before his brother slammed his fist into his face.

Morgan jumped out of the way as Lucien followed the wild swing by slamming his huge, naked body into his brother's, toppling them both to the marble with a flat thud. They struggled madly, Aurelio cursing and shouting, Lucien eerily silent except for several hoarse grunts as he tried to get his hands around his bigger brother's neck while being punched and wrestled. She sagged to her knees against the wood console, terrified, trying to work up the nerve to make a run for it. All she saw was flailing huge limbs and acres of bare, toned flesh and the occasional flash of a heavy, swinging male member. She had the insane urge to laugh.

At that exact moment, Xander crashed through the door.

SEVENTEEN

When he caught sight of Morgan cowering and bloody against the console, staring up at him with huge, terrified eyes and a bruise blooming garish blue and purple across her cheek, Xander experienced a flood of rage so overwhelming he literally lost his mind.

With a roar so fierce it pulled the two fighting males up short and fractured the oval mirror above the console into a web of splintered glass, he bared his teeth, unsheathed his knives, and lunged at them.

He hit the bigger one first. His charge was so powerful it knocked them both off their feet. They flew through the air and landed on top of the glass coffee table in the living room, which shattered into a million pieces with a hideous crash. The male beneath him grunted in pain but wrapped his arms around Xander's back with such force he thought his spine might be crushed. They rolled over the broken glass together and slammed against the sofa, which was shoved back several feet by the impact.

He heard Morgan screaming something but was too focused on the fight to make it out. His arms were trapped in the male's vise grip; his weight pinned him to the floor. He was wedged against the sofa, but none of that mattered. In a swift, practiced move, he thrust up with his dagger and sank it deep into his opponent's side. The male arched back, howling, and gave Xander perfect, unobstructed access to his throat.

Xander took the opportunity and slashed his other dagger straight across his carotid artery.

Blood sprayed out in a huge red arc, splattering his face, his chest, the floor. The male rolled to his back, clutching his throat and writhing, and Xander freed himself from beneath him and leapt to his feet, ready to fight the other one. He whirled around to find him standing only a few feet away, shaking in rage, his black eyes wild.

"He was *mine*," he hissed, curling his hands to fists.

Xander frowned. It almost sounded as if he was mad at him for killing the other one first. He didn't have time to figure it out because the male lunged at him like a madman, snarling and swinging. Xander waited in a crouch for him to get near enough; then, in a blindingly fast move practiced hundreds of times, he stepped swiftly aside, used the other's forward momentum against him, and shoved the male so hard from behind he stumbled right into the half of the glass terrace slider that hadn't already been destroyed.

The huge male hit it face-first. It shattered like a bomb.

Arms flailing, he went flying through a field of razor-sharp, glinting glass and landed on his chest with an ugly *smack* against the pink marbled terrace. He lay there stunned while shards of glass drifted down all around him, catching the light like diamond flakes. With adrenaline roaring through his veins Xander leapt across the room, landed in a crouch beside the male, withdrew a dagger from his boot, and sank it deep between the bones of the male's neck, severing his spinal cord.

He jerked then exhaled in a sputter. On the marble beneath his body, blood began to pool.

Breathing hard, Xander noticed a sharp pain in his abdomen, blooming with heat. He stood and looked down at himself and was amazed to find a widening circle of blood seeping through the front of his shirt.

"Xander."

Morgan's voice jerked him back to reality. He turned. She stood in the suite's foyer, shaking, leaning against the wood console for support. Her beautiful face was nearly white.

"Are you hurt?" He fought a sudden wave of dizziness. Instinct made him reach around to his back, where he discovered a thick, jagged piece of glass sticking out at an angle from his shirt. He touched it and it sent a wave of pain shooting through his body. A hot rush of liquid spilled over his skin and pooled around the waist of his pants.

The table. He'd hit the coffee table, he'd rolled in the broken glass—

"Are you hurt?" he said again, harsher this time, taking a step over the blood-splattered ivory carpet toward Morgan.

"No." Her gaze flickered down to his waist. He put a hand over his abdomen and felt his own blood seep hot and thick between his fingers. A tiny sliver of glass pricked the tip of his finger.

Christ. It went all the way through. He'd seen enough knife wounds to know that a perforated bowel was not going to be pretty. And he was bleeding like a stuck pig, which meant there was a distinct possibility one of the abdominal arteries had been compromised. If he had any chance of survival, he needed help.

Fast.

"Listen to me very carefully, Morgan," he said, his tongue strangely numb. "I want you to get my cell phone from the leather case on the desk and call the first number on the speed dial. No one will speak when it's answered, but tell them you're with me, and I'm hurt. When they ask for it, the password is Esperanza."

He felt both hot and cold, and sweat had bloomed over his chest. He took another step toward her and almost stumbled. She jerked forward with both hands out and crossed the room.

"Say you understand. Say it, Morgan."

"You're bleeding." Her voice cracked. "Here, sit on the couch. Let me take a look."

She guided him to the couch, and without protest, he let her. With pain now radiating out from the wound in throbbing hot spikes, he held perfectly still as she quickly unbuttoned his shirt and smoothed it over his shoulders, then pulled it off his body. She knelt next to him and touched his side, probing, her fingers featherlight on his bare skin. Her movements were careful, almost reverent, and he realized she was taking care to avoid hurting him.

She didn't want to hurt him.

That thought gave him as much pain as the blade of glass embedded in his body. He closed his eyes, concentrated on his breathing, and let the deep, warm scent of her skin wash over him.

Not bad. This wasn't a bad way to die. Here, with her, with her scent in his nose and her fingers soft on his skin. Of the thousand ways he'd imagined his death, one as pleasant as this had never been included.

"It's clean, but I won't lie—it's bad," she said. "I'm not going to remove it because that will only make it worse." He smiled, wondering how she knew that. "Do you think you can lie on your side?"

He opened his eyes and looked at her, and when she looked up into his face he saw not fear or panic but something cool and detached that looked worryingly close to calculation. It froze his heart to stone in his chest. And that's when he realized she wasn't going to call anyone for help. She was going to let him bleed out here on the wheat-and-ivory striped silk sofa, and then take her freedom once and for all.

And really, could he blame her?

The room tilted. He didn't have much time.

"I want you to know I understand," he murmured. His gaze roved over her face, memorizing the perfect planes and angles, the plush lips, the dark arch of her brows. She pulled back, blinking, and he caught her hand. "I know this is something you need to do, and I understand. And…I don't blame you."

She frowned at him. "You don't blame me for what, exactly?"

"For letting me die."

As her eyes widened, he lifted his hand to her cheek and traced a finger down the curve of her cheekbone.

Satin. Perfect.

He smiled at her. Then he slumped down onto the sofa's plush cushions and passed out.

The wave of emotion that hit Morgan was so overwhelming she had to take a moment to breathe against it because she was afraid she'd pass out like Xander just had.

Anger. Shame. Sadness. Regret. Outrage. Disappointment. All of it flooded her at once.

He'd saved her life. And then he'd insulted her. *Again.*

He thought she was a liar—that much was abundantly clear. She'd already given him her word she wouldn't run away, but obviously that held no water. He also thought she was low enough to leave him there to bleed out on the couch after he'd risked his own life to save hers. And the way he'd looked at her at the church after he'd kissed her to break the link with the man in white—that had hurt more than she liked to admit.

Because she'd liked that kiss. She'd been lost in it. With his lips on hers, she'd felt something she hadn't felt in years: connection. Real and warm and illuminating, like someone had turned the lights on in a room kept always dark.

But he'd only been doing his job. The disgusted look on his face after she'd broken away was clear evidence of that.

All of this was only his job, she reminded herself, gazing around the wrecked room. If she died on his watch, he'd be held responsible. It was nothing more than that, and that was as it should be, but she couldn't seem to get her heart on board. It ached, it throbbed, and she didn't want to know why. She really didn't.

Still shaking, she rose to her feet and found the cell phone in Xander's bag, right where he'd said it would be. It was hard to dial the number because her hands were trembling and slippery with Xander's blood, but she did it. She lifted the phone to her ear and listened.

It was picked up on the second ring but not answered, just as he'd said. Only silence greeted her on the other end. She didn't even hear anyone breathing.

Her voice came low and tremulous. "Xander told me to call this number. He's hurt, and he told me to call—"

"We have your coordinates," came the clipped response. It was a male voice, brusque and gravelly, with no discernible accent. "What is the password?"

"Esperanza," she whispered.

Silence again. Then: "Do not move from your current location."

"Please hurry—"

The line went dead.

She dropped the phone on the desk and went back to Xander. He looked so massive and male on that dainty sofa, so overpowering and at the same time oddly peaceful with his closed eyes, his deep, heavy breathing. Like a napping bull.

A beautiful, half-naked, bloody, napping bull, with a chest full of hatch marks.

She picked up the shirt she'd removed from him and pressed it softly against the oozing wound on his abdomen. He jerked, moaning.

"Shhhh," she murmured. "I need to keep pressure on it. To help stop the bleeding. I'm sorry. I'm sorry if it hurts. And I'm going to stay right here with you. I won't leave you."

He muttered something that sounded like the password she'd just whispered into the phone, then sank back into unconsciousness.

EIGHTEEN

"They're not coming."

It was Celian who finally said aloud what everyone had been thinking for the past thirty minutes, and true to his nature, his voice was stone-cold. He was the largest of the group at almost six foot eight and 280 pounds of solid muscle, and about as cuddly as a shark. He was dressed, as they all were, in one of the many sets of spare clothes kept tucked away in nooks and crannies all over Rome for occasions such as this, when escape as Vapor was necessary and their leathers and weapons were abandoned. This latest cache had been retrieved from the bell tower of an abandoned fourth-century church.

"Let's wait another five minutes," said Constantine, flicking a glance at Celian's hard face. They all knew what failure meant and that the brunt of the punishment would fall to the first-in-command. And for failing to return with either one of their intended targets, the consequences would be very bad.

Lix growled an agreement, and Demetrius—known to the *Bellatorum* simply as D—remained characteristically silent. Ironically named after a Greek orator who died in the first century BC, D often went days at a time without speaking a word. In addition to his menacing silence, his head was shaved, he sported several eyebrow piercings and sinister neck tattoos, and he was prone to outbursts of unprovoked violence. Though all the *Bellatorum*—the warriors—were feared by their people, he was downright dreaded.

Celian glanced up at the deep blue bowl of sky visible in small slices through the windows ringed around the upper few feet of the stone ceiling. Above the ancient subterranean church whose rooftop rose just a few feet above street level, stars were beginning to wink to life. "No sense putting it off," he said, practical as ever. "The longer we wait, the worse it will be when he finally hears it."

He pushed off the crumbling Doric column he'd been leaning on, walked across the worn stone floor, and disappeared through a hidden door behind the altar. Lix, Constantine, and D shared a look, then followed.

The corridor they entered was barely more than shoulder-wide and so low in some places they had to duck their heads. It was chilly and damp and near black, but they had lived here for so many years they were accustomed to the temperature and didn't need lights to guide the way. They walked in silence for more than ten minutes, descending farther into the earth as they followed the main corridor and its worn, winding stairs. Other corridors yawned open and snaked away into darkness as they passed. None of them glanced up to admire the age-worn frescoes of gods and vineyards and cherubs at play on the rough ceiling above; none paid heed to the empty hollows where centuries ago bodies had been wrapped in linen and lain to rest. Except for the scuffs of their boots on the dusty tufa, it was quiet as a crypt. And just as cheerful.

"Over forty catacombs beneath Rome, and we have to get stuck in the one that smells like feet," muttered Lix, bringing up the rear.

"It's the biggest one, Felix," said Constantine, knowing Lix would hate hearing his given name and hoping to divert another one of his legendary diatribes about the smell of the catacombs where the *Bellatorum* and the soldier class of *Legiones* lived and trained. The *Optimates*, the *Electi*, and the *Servorum*—the aristocracy, the chosen females of the King's harem, and the servant castes—lived in nearby catacombs that were accessed by a series of connected tunnels they'd dug themselves. All the catacombs had been deserted for centuries, and many were still undiscovered by the outside world. "And thank Horus for it, because I'm going to have to go somewhere far away to get away from your constant complaining. You're like an old woman."

"Watch yourself, beauty queen," shot back Lix, taking the bait. "Or I'll torch that shoe collection you've got. What are you up to now, about ten thousand pair? And are all those hair products really necessary? You could start your own salon."

Constantine snorted and tossed his head, sending glossy jet hair spilling over his shoulder. He was, by all accounts, the most beautiful male of the kingdom. Some said he was even more beautiful than the *principessa* Eliana herself.

Females swooned over him, and he took great advantage of it, but he had unswerving loyalty to his brothers and was always the first to put himself in harm's way for one of them. Which was lucky for him, or else jealousy would have most likely made everyone hate his guts.

"At least I bathe," said Constantine, taking a loud and pointed sniff in Lix's direction.

"And you smell like a damn rose garden! Is that *perfume*?"

"Put a sock in it, ladies," growled Celian over his shoulder. "Unless one of you wants to be the one to explain our situation to the King."

That silenced them. No one ever wanted to be the bearer of bad news to Dominus. There was only a fifty-fifty chance your tongue would stay attached.

A few more minutes of walking through the silent underground labyrinth, and finally they arrived.

The corridor opened abruptly into a vast, soaring space decorated like the keep of a Gothic castle. There were no windows in this place, but there were Egyptian statues and ancestral portraits and beeswax candles in iron braziers dripping wax to the stone floor. There was chunky wood furniture and Persian rugs and a long table with carved high-back chairs that seated thirty. Red velvet sofas lined one wall; shining suits of armor flanked a massive glass case of antique weaponry.

In the center of the room sat an elaborate throne of dark wood with clawed feet and crimson cushions. Its back curved up to a high, sharp point, atop which perched a grinning human skull, cocked askew on a spike.

Upon the throne sat a man. He was large yet lithe and dressed in snowy white, as always, which contrasted with the burnished honey-bronze shade of his skin. From his neck hung a golden talisman on a chain: the Eye of Horus, symbol of the ancient Egyptian god of war and vengeance. Dominus believed himself the reincarnation of Horus, and all the warriors had the symbol branded on their left shoulders when they were indoctrinated into the *Bellatorum.*

"Gentlemen," said the King. His deep voice carried easily over the distance between them. "How fare you?"

"Well, sire." Celian bowed his head. The others, lining up beside him, followed suit and remained silent.

"Well?" Dominus repeated in a questioning tone. In turn, the warriors each felt the sharp, fleeting sting of the King's gaze upon them. "Indeed?"

Celian lifted his head and met his master's gaze. "We four are well, sire," he equivocated, "but as for Aurelio and Lucien, I cannot say. They did not return to the rendezvous point as agreed."

All the candles in the chamber sputtered in a sudden cold breeze. Celian felt his brothers beside him tense and concentrated on keeping his own body relaxed, his breathing regular. The King thrived on fear and sensed it like a snake senses a mouse. If he hadn't seen otherwise for himself, he'd have thought the King's tongue was forked.

"The rendezvous point," the King drawled, sardonic, lounging against the back of his throne with one leg crossed casually over the other. "Which means you split up."

"The male escaped through the wall of the Vatican, sire—"

"Through the wall?" Dominus said, sharp. He sat forward, eyes glassy and hard like obsidian. "You mean he evanesced, as we do?"

Celian took a measured breath, calculating. How to describe it? "I mean he moved through it. He…melted. Into it. He's impervious to bullets, too."

The King's black eyes did not blink. But they burned. By God, did they burn.

"Yes. I found that out myself. Very interesting. And inconvenient." He paused for a moment, contemplative, then very softly said, "And the female?"

Celian was dreading that. The King had made no bones about his desire for that female.

"He took her with him through the wall."

The King's nostrils flared, but that was all. He still hadn't blinked.

"We reengaged the male outside, but the female was gone. Aurelio and Lucien went after her, and we tried to lead the male in the opposite direction, but he didn't follow. We circled back but lost his scent. And Aurelio and Lucien didn't return at the agreed time."

Celian knew it wasn't his imagination that had the temperature in the room dropping by several degrees. Next to him, Lix shifted his weight from one foot to another.

"Unfortunate," the King said, with an edge like a blade. "So very unfortunate. Especially since I made my instructions perfectly clear."

A chilled breeze stirred around their shoulders as the first spike of pain throbbed through their skulls. Only Celian remained still against it, having been subjected to the King's excruciating Gifts many times before. Their lord and master didn't actually read other people's minds so much as *inhabit* them, and when he wished, his anger inhabited them as well.

In this case, the King's anger felt like a fanged viper slithering around inside his head, spitting poison into his brain.

The others began, subtly, to fidget. D rolled his shoulders; one of them cracked. Lix shifted his weight again, and Constantine flexed his hands open and closed.

"*Facilis*," Celian murmured. Easy, boys. Take it easy.

A cat, one of hundreds that ran wild throughout the catacombs, appeared from behind the throne, where it had been sleeping on the stone floor. Pure black and sleek, it was a perfect miniature for their kind in their true animal form. Except for its eyes, which glowed vivid yellow in the candlelit room. The *Bellatorum*—born in darkness, raised in darkness, trained to fight and kill in darkness—had black eyes, to a one. The cat rubbed its face against a leg of the throne, then jumped in one graceful leap onto the King's crossed legs.

He began to stroke it behind the ears. It purred and settled into his lap.

"We will wait until midnight to see if Aurelio and Lucien return with what is mine," said the King softly. "And if they do not"—he turned his burning black eyes to Celian and his lips curved to a smile—"I shall require compensation."

Celian's skin crawled. He knew what compensation the King required. One thing and one thing only bought atonement from the King's displeasure: pain.

Pain would be his tithe for failure.

"Yes, sire," he said, his voice very low.

A growl rumbled through Constantine's chest, and the King smiled even wider. "Ever the protector, Constantine. And yet how you displease me with this show of concern for your brother. Your fealty lies with me first, does it not?"

Constantine raised his head and met the King's cold, cold eyes. "Yes, my lord."

"Good. Because it will be you who will dispense Celian's punishment if your other brothers do not return with the female."

Celian felt Constantine stiffen and wanted to reach out and cuff him upside the head. Defiance could get him killed. He wasn't worth it.

"As you desire, my lord," said Constantine, slowly, anger darkening his face.

The King settled back into his throne, thoughtful, stroking the cat. He looked them over, one by one, calculating. "Consider yourselves fortunate, gentlemen. I am in good humor, as three males of age survived the Transition this week alone. We have several more *Liberi* who will soon be tested, and we have the promise of a new full-Blood female at our fingertips. Things are looking up, would you not agree?"

The warriors answered as one, their voices echoing in the stone chamber. "Yes, sire!"

Dominus chuckled. "And I am closer than ever to perfecting the antiserum. Yes, things are most definitely looking up."

None of them knew exactly what he was talking about, but no one commented or questioned. Questions were never allowed.

Dominus sighed and waved them away with a flick of his wrist. "Prepare yourselves, then. I will join you in the *fovea* at midnight."

The brothers bowed and backed away toward the exit but stopped when they heard the King's voice.

"And Constantine?"

He turned. "Yes, sire?"

"Make it the barbed cat-o'-nine-tails." His lips curved into a smile, cold and red. He glanced at Celian. "I want to see blood."

NINETEEN

Three hours after Morgan made the call on Xander's phone, she heard a sharp knock on the door of the hotel suite.

By then she had little hope the assassin would survive. His pulse fluttered fast as a hummingbird's, then stalled out for seconds at a time, his skin was gray, and his breathing was weak. And the blood. So much of his blood had leaked from his wound she thought there couldn't be anything left for his heart to pump through his veins.

She'd crouched on the floor in front of him for as long as she could, with his blood-soaked shirt pressed to the wound, until her legs had cramped and she'd repositioned herself on the sofa beside him, ignoring the blood that seeped through her skirt and blouse from the sofa cushions, between her fingers from the gash on his stomach. She hadn't moved since. Her mind refused to consider the implications of his death and instead kept up an endless loop of images of Xander since they'd met. His burning tiger's eyes rimmed in a thicket of black lashes, his wicked smile, the way he moved like a silent, deadly hunter, those scars all over his back. His tender, blood-lost expression when he'd said he didn't blame her for letting him die.

That kiss.

That was the one that refused to fade, no matter how much she tried to push it aside.

So when the knock finally came, she was relieved. For about five seconds, until she opened the door.

There in the hallway stood three males. Two were obviously *Ikati*, big and glowering and exuding the kind of menace and power only a male of her kind did. One had dark hair to his shoulders and stormy, oddly colorless eyes; the other had hair trimmed short like Xander's and eyes the exact shade of new grass. Both had guns drawn, pointed right at her face.

They flanked a third male, smaller, older, bespectacled—

—And human.

She didn't have time to wonder about that because she was summarily shoved aside as they pushed past her into the room.

The human fell to his knees in front of the couch, dug a stethoscope from the black leather bag he'd carried in, and listened to Xander's heart. He did a cursory physical exam with nimble fingers that were both gentle and sure: pulse rate, wound inspection, pupil dilation, lifting first one lid then the other to shine a pen-size flashlight into his eyes. The two *Ikati* performed a swift, silent sweep of the rooms and the terrace, looking behind doors, checking locks and exits.

When satisfied no threats lurked inside, the green-eyed *Ikati* holstered the gun in the front of his waistband and went to stand over the doctor while he worked. He watched silently while the other male did a quick check of the two bodies that had lain on the floor for the past few hours. Gray and stiff, they were beginning to emit the faint, distinct odor of decay.

"And?" said the green-eyed *Ikati*. His voice was deep and gravelly.

The human adjusted his glasses and made a small, dissatisfied noise. Cottony tufts of white hair wreathed his head like a crown of miniature clouds. "He's lost too much blood, Mateo. I've got to do surgery to get this piece of glass out and stop the bleeding, but we can't move him to the safe house like this. He'll die before we get him there."

Mateo ran a hand over his head and cursed. The other *Ikati* male finished his inspection of the bodies and stood, surveying the room with those smoky mirror eyes. "I told you we should have brought a donor."

"We didn't have *time*, Tomás," Mateo responded, sharp. "And where the hell would we have found one, anyway?"

"Excuse me," Morgan said. Everyone ignored her.

"Let's get him up on the table," the human said, gesturing to the glossy mahogany dining table. "I can work better up there. And I'll need towels and blankets, and something for him to bite down on if we're going to do the surgery here. A wooden spoon is good."

"Um, gentlemen?" Morgan tried again. And failed again. The two *Ikati* took hold of Xander's shoulders and legs while the human rushed over with his medical bag and began clearing the silk flower arrangements from the center of the table.

"Easy, watch his head!" the human man chastised as Mateo and Tomás laid him out on the table. Xander jerked and groaned when he was set down, but his lids remained closed. "Roll him on his side, like this," the man said, working over him. "Gently, please. Gently."

"Guys—"

"*Meu deus*, he's lost a lot of blood," Tomás muttered. He stood at the head of the table, looking down at Xander's pale face, his blue lips.

"He's strong," Mateo said, by Xander's feet. His face was as almost as pale as Xander's, his jaw clenched tight. "He's made it through much worse."

Morgan cleared her throat. "May I just have a word—"

"He won't last long without a transfusion," murmured the doctor, peering at Xander's bare lower back. "You'll have to find someone local, and quick because he's fading—"

"You let him die, and we'll have your head, Bartleby," snapped Tomás, bristling.

"Not helpful," said Mateo, noting how the man blanched under the assault of Tomás's anger. He addressed the doctor directly. "There *is* no one local. There's no colony in Italy, and obviously it can't be either of us since his body will reject blood from another male. You'll just have to find a way to make it work without—"

"*Hello!*" shouted Morgan.

Three heads swiveled in her direction.

"I can give him blood," she said, calmer now that she had their attention. "I can be the donor."

Frozen, Bartleby glanced first at Mateo, then Tomás, both of whom had turned to stare at her with the flat, killer gaze of jihadists. No one moved.

"You are the mark," said Mateo. Dispassionate, his gaze traveled over her body.

"I am the Morgan, actually," she answered tartly.

"*Mark* means *target*," Tomás cut in with a curl of his full upper lip. "Hit. Job. Pigeon. Victim—"

"How enlightening," Morgan interrupted, folding her arms over her chest. She glared at him so hard she thought her eyes might cross from the effort. "Thank you for the vocabulary lesson. Now are you going to let me be the donor or let your boy bleed to death on that lovely Cassina table?"

There followed a long, crackling silence.

Morgan was at the very end of her reserves of patience, a well that was shallow under the best of circumstances. She was exhausted. Her body ached, her bones ached, even her *teeth* ached, and her blood was boiling like someone had lit a fire beneath her feet. If she had anything to compare it to, she'd have thought she was coming down with the flu. So the fact that there were two *more* strange, hostile males staring at her as if she were lunch didn't freak her out as much as it should have.

"He can only take blood from an *Ikati* female," she said, exasperated at their continued silence, their narrow-eyed hostility. "And if he doesn't get it soon, he's going to die. Right?" she added, glancing at the human. With a quick, birdlike dip of his white head, he nodded. She nodded back, already knowing the answer before she asked. *Ikati* had no blood types, no blood-borne diseases, and human blood was useless to them, as weak as water. Only a female could give a male blood and vice versa.

"So I'm offering," she said in conclusion.

Still no response. Mateo and Tomás stared at her while somewhere outside a dog began to bark.

Morgan exhaled and dropped her arms to her side. The exhaustion sank down to stain her bones, and it felt suddenly as if her skin were too tight. "Fine," she said, bitter. "It's on you, then. When the Assembly asks what happened, it's on you."

She turned and was about to walk to the phone on the glass-topped desk in the living room to call Leander when Mateo's gravel-rough voice stopped her.

"Why would you do that?"

In her stiff, blood-encrusted clothes, Morgan turned back and looked at him. He gazed back at her, all muscle and bulk and green-eyed menace, the light shining raven blue off his hair.

"If I'm not mistaken, his assignment is to kill you, if you fail in your task. Why would you give him your blood?" he persisted.

Good question. Unfortunately, she didn't have a good answer. At least, not one that made any kind of sense. She stood there for almost a minute, thinking.

"He just saved my life," she finally answered, gesturing to the two bodies sprawled in gory proof on the terrace, the living room floor. "I owe him the chance, at least. He deserves that much from me. And...because I want him to live." She blew out a long, exhausted breath, realizing how insane she sounded for even saying it, realizing too it was God's honest truth. "Even if it means..." *that he's ultimately going to have to kill me,* she thought. *And that I am a self-destructive moron with a death wish.* But she didn't say that. Instead she lamely ended with, "...you know."

A nerve behind her eye throbbed, sending a spike of pain through her skull. She pressed her fingers against it, thinking this was going to be the mother of all migraines.

And how was that possible, since she'd never had one before? Only humans suffered headaches. Humans and *Ikati* females who were about to—

"You honor us," Mateo said, husky.

Blinking, she dropped her hand from her face and looked at him. He was gazing back at her with something like...awe.

"What?" She glanced at Tomás, whose expression had changed from one of total suspicion only seconds before to one that looked alarmingly close to gratitude.

"What you do to any one of us, you do to *every* one," Tomás replied, cryptic, his mirror eyes gone curiously round.

Morgan looked back and forth between the two *Ikati* males and the frozen, dumfounded human doctor. "Uh..."

"It's their code," the doctor said with a swift glance to his companions. He pushed his glasses up farther on his nose. "The assassin's code. *Cross one, cross us all. Kill one, kill us all. Love one...*" He cleared his throat. "*Love us all.*"

"More assassins," Morgan said, a little more feebly than she would have liked. She closed her eyes. "How many of you are there, exactly?"

"Four," said Mateo and Tomás together.

Could have been worse. At least it wasn't four hundred. She glanced down at Xander, back up to them. "Where's the other one?"

It was Mateo who answered this time. "Waiting downstairs with the car."

"The car?"

His rough voice was tinged with something like amusement. "You didn't think we were going to *fly* out of here, did you?"

A girl can only hope. "Okay. Let's get this over with," she sighed.

"Hop to, Doc," Mateo said to Bartleby.

The doctor leapt into a blur of action. He snatched up his black bag and removed a large, wicked-looking syringe and a length of plastic tubing with pointed silver cannulas at each end. He threaded the tubing through the syringe, readied a small glass bottle that smelled like alcohol, a stack of white bandages, and cotton swabs, and set all of it on the table beside Xander's still form. He snapped on a pair of thin latex gloves.

"On the table, if you please." He motioned with an open hand to the long dining table. Morgan sat on the edge with as much dignity as she could muster in her bloodstained clothes with her bare legs dangling over the side like a child's. She crossed then uncrossed her legs, noting with no small trepidation that neither Mateo nor Tomás was looking at anything but her.

She felt like an ant under a very large—very *male*—microscope.

"You should lie down," said Bartleby gently. He made to lift a hand to her shoulder, but a low snarl from Tomás quickly divested him of that idea. His hand dropped to his side. His face went pink. "Would you *please* lie down?"

"Is it really necessary?"

"You might find yourself a bit light-headed," he said, glancing between Mateo and Tomás. When he spoke again his voice was apologetic. "And it's going to sting."

She looked down at Xander, beautiful and unconscious and on the verge of death, and wondered if it would sting as much as a knife thrust between the vertebrae of her neck. The thought made the blood drain from her face. She lay down beside him in one quick motion. The doctor rolled up the sleeve of her blouse and swabbed her arm with alcohol.

"How long will it take?"

"Not long." He carefully swabbed Xander's arm, then repositioned it, palm up, trying to balance it on his hip. It didn't work. "Hold it like this, if you would," he said to Mateo. The assassin complied, silently, looming so large over the table he blocked out the orb of light from the lamp on the ceiling above.

She closed her eyes, breathed in through her nose, and tried not to think about the colossal stupidity of what she was doing.

There was a prick of pain at her arm, the bite of cold steel sliding into her vein, a pull as the syringe was depressed and her blood was pumped out of her body. Then nothing.

She spoke into the hush without opening her eyes. "Is it working?"

"Perfectly," Bartleby murmured. "Just a moment more and it will hit his vein—"

Xander gave a jolt as if he'd been electrocuted.

Her lids flew open. Beside her, his large body had jack-knifed into a straining, muscled bow that both Mateo and Tomás were doing their best to subdue by wrestling him back down to the table.

"What's wrong?" she cried, panicking. She sat up abruptly and was dizzy. "What happened?"

"It's fine, it's completely normal," Bartleby soothed, reaching out to check the needle in her arm and the connection with Xander's. He sent her an odd, sideways look. "It's just your blood hitting his system. Please remain as still as you can. He'll acclimate to it in a moment."

And, as she watched in startled fascination, he did.

The muscles of his arm relaxed first. Then his jaw unclenched, his back, his legs. With a low moan that reverberated all the way through her body, Xander slumped back against the cool, polished wood and gave a long, shuddering sigh. Heat radiated out from him in pulsing waves as if he were engulfed in invisible flame.

Mateo and Tomás relaxed as well and blew out hard, relieved breaths. They gave each other one of the looks the doctor had just sent her, and she was abruptly embarrassed.

She'd overreacted. They thought she was a hysterical female.

"I've never actually seen it done," Morgan admitted a little sheepishly. She was the only girl in a brood of five, and though her two sets of twin brothers were younger, they were—accorded by their gender—given far more leniency and privileges than she. Even though she was smarter, stronger, faster, as a girl she'd been almost sequestered because of her sex. Until her mother had died, and then she'd run wild...

She glanced up at them. "I didn't think it would be quite so...dramatic."

"It usually isn't," said Bartleby. A tiny frown rucked his brows. He shot a quick, furtive glance at Mateo. "It's nothing abnormal, but that kind of reaction usually only happens with—"

"Check six, Doc," said Tomás, hard. "Unless you want to end up looking like a bag of smashed asshole, this evolution does not require your input."

Bartleby went white, swallowed, and sat abruptly down in one of the cushioned dining room chairs.

"*Unsat*," Mateo growled back at Tomás. "We need him, so you're going to ease up on that shit. And keep your soup cooler clean in front of the *ultimecia*. We clear?"

Tomás stared at him long and hard as if he were contemplating the merits of strangulation versus a hard kick to the chest. Unblinking, Mateo stared right back. After a jaw-grinding moment, Tomás took a breath, stepped back, and said, "Clear as a fucking bell, brother."

Morgan looked back and forth between them, wondering what Bartleby had been about to say, why Tomas didn't want him to say it, and what the hell an *ultimecia* was. But she was too tired to do anything about it. And hot. The room suddenly felt like an oven. She lifted her hand to her forehead and was surprised to find it covered in sweat.

"Do you have anything in that bag for a headache, Doctor?" She rubbed her left eye. "I'm feeling a little…"

"Weak?" he supplied from his chair, peering at her from behind his round glasses with an oddly intense look. "Achy? Feverish?"

She nodded, frowning. How could he know that?

He stood and rummaged through the bag, came up with a digital thermometer. "May I take your temperature?"

The nod again, and he came to stand beside her. He brushed aside her hair, inserted the thermometer into her ear. In five seconds there came a beep. He withdrew the little plastic item and gazed down at it. His face went even whiter. "Oh, dear," he said.

Panic began to churn her stomach to knots. "What? Am I sick?"

"No, no, nothing like that. You're perfectly healthy," he mumbled, distracted. He turned back to his black bag and deposited the thermometer within, then measured Xander's pulse at his wrist and quickly took his blood pressure with a Velcro cuff around his bicep.

"What is it, then?" she pressed.

He glanced pointedly at Mateo and Tomás, then back at her, trying, it seemed, to communicate something crucial. "It's just a little..." he coughed, "...female things, you know...I have something for it." His face flamed bright, crimson red.

Morgan narrowed her eyes. *Female* things?

"Let's get this show on the road, Doc," interrupted Mateo, glancing at his watch. He pulled a phone from a pocket in his cargo pants and dialed a number. "We're coming down in five," he said to whomever it was that answered on the other end. "Keep frosty." He snapped it shut and shoved it back into his pants, then addressed Bartleby. "Good to go?"

"Yes, yes," he said, fluttering over Xander. "He's had enough of the transfusion. He's strong enough to move." His gaze flickered again to Morgan, then he turned away and finished packing his things.

Mateo held a hand out. "Are you ready?"

Morgan took a breath and gazed back at him. "Ready as I'll ever be." And she took his hand in hers.

TWENTY

Xander woke up laid out flat on his back in a quiet room with his tongue glued to the roof of his mouth and pain throbbing sharp in his abdomen.

He kept still from old habit, his eyes closed, measuring his surroundings with his senses. Anyone looking at him would have thought him still asleep, but he was on instant alert, primed and ready to fight though he was supine, that pain in his side was substantial, and he could tell by the light-headedness that he'd lost a lot of blood.

No one was in the room with him. He cast out his awareness farther, through the walls, through empty rooms, until he came up against a cold lead wall where his exploration abruptly stopped. Good. This was good. Lead meant a safe house, which meant they'd come for him.

Which meant Morgan hadn't left him to die after all.

The thought of her sent a lance of pain through his chest. His eyes blinked open and he lifted his head, looking around. A narrow bed, some plain furniture, a bathroom accessed through a door ajar, surgical instruments and bandages on a rolling silver table nearby. There were no windows, but he sensed it was close to sunrise. How long had he been out?

With an effort that sent pain radiating in wicked lashes up his spine and all the way down to his toes, Xander pushed the sheet aside and sat up.

He was naked, clad in only a large white bandage wrapped tightly around his waist. It was stained rust with blood in erratic circles on the right side. He inhaled, testing the limits of his tolerance, and found he could take a full breath without effort. His ribs weren't compromised, and since he could move his arms and legs, his spine wasn't compromised either. That was a relief, because the last thing he remembered before passing out was a terrible deadness in his legs.

He stood carefully, balancing his weight over his bent knees. His back protested with a sharp, stabbing ache, but it was tolerable, less than when he had first sat up. He was alive, if not perfectly well. But no matter the injury, he'd heal quickly. If he wasn't dead, he'd be fine within days.

He crossed the room, found the black pants and shirt that had been left folded on a chair, and pulled them on carefully with gritted teeth. His weapons were laid out in a neat row on the top of the plain dresser, and he smiled as he donned those as well, strapping the knives around his waist and ankles. He pulled on a pair of new black boots, size fifteen, government issue, and laced up the ties.

Then he walked out the door and went to find her.

The safe house—one of dozens the Syndicate kept in every major city across the globe—was a refurbished villa in the hilly and moderately affluent Aventine section of Rome. It boasted 360-degree views of the city and over ten thousand square feet of living space, the vast majority of it underground. From the street, it was a modest turn-of-the-century affair of brick and mortar surrounded by a tall iron fence, with gardens and trees and a bearded, chubby lawn gnome by the front gate whose pointed red hat had long ago faded to pink, and a security system to rival that of Fort Knox.

The bedrooms and lounging area were on the bottom floor, the kitchen, dining area, and media rooms on the second floor, the gym and training center on the first floor belowground. Aboveground it was simply a house. A beautifully decorated, unoccupied house, because no one ever ate or slept or lived there. Aboveground was all for show. Once you descended beyond the reinforced lead door to the "basement," you entered another world.

He walked past six unoccupied bedrooms and found himself alone. A staircase twisted up to the main room, which was a large, open space decorated in dark charcoals and brown and beige without a hint of feminine softness. Beyond it were the dining room and kitchen—modern and masculine as the rest of the belowground areas—and as soon as he reached the top step of the stairs, he heard Mateo's gravel-rough voice drifting in from that direction.

"I can't take it much longer, T."

There came an agitated grunt, then the sound of boots pacing back and forth over tile. "*You* can't! I feel like I'm gonna crawl right out of my fucking skin."

"If he doesn't wake up soon, we'll have to leave Bartleby here with him and come back when it passes."

Xander froze, listening.

"How much longer we got?"

"Three days minus sixteen hours," muttered Mateo. "And counting."

Groans. "Jesus Christ."

He waited, but they didn't say more. Curiosity got the better of him, and he made his way silently to the kitchen, where he stood there in the doorway, unnoticed, looking them over.

His boys. His brothers, in heart if not in Blood.

They were assassins like him—collectively referred to as the Syndicate by the rest of their kind—and like him they were disgraced sons of powerful males who'd been handed over as children to the brutal tutelage of the capoeira master Karyo, a human the Manaus colony kept on retainer because he was both a perfect killing machine and perfectly tight-lipped about his "unique" students and their kin, who paid so handsomely for his silence. It was either study under Karyo or be tossed into the Drowning Well; bringing shame to one's family name was not well tolerated by his kind, and at least the Academy offered a chance to save face.

It offered their *fathers* a chance to save face. The young boys who would become the hardened killers of the Syndicate never gave a shit about things like that.

Mateo was the son of a duke, of the *Grandes do Imperio*— Great Ones of the Empire. At six years old he'd called his pompous father a *cachorro puto*—dog fucker—in front of the entire Manaus Assembly. He now leaned against the counter by the sink, muscled arms crossed over his chest, chewing his lower lip.

Tomás, eldest son of the colony's Matchmaker, had burned his family's home to the ground when he was eight in a fit of rage after his father had spanked his bare ass in the middle of Sunday church services when he wouldn't stop squirming in the pew. He sat at the big square wood table with one knee jumping up and down beneath it, his head bent over, hands clasped over the back of his neck.

Julian, a giant skull-crusher of a male with shaggy dark hair who always drove the getaway car no matter the job, had stolen apples from a neighbor's tree. He sat hunched over a bowl of pasta at the table, mechanically shoveling it into his mouth with a blank-eyed stare as if he didn't even know he was eating.

And he, Xander, had simply been born to the wrong woman.

They had trained together in Brazil since boyhood in the fine arts of murder and mayhem, until his three adopted brothers had gone into the American military as spies of sorts and he had gone slowly insane.

They were the only three souls in the world he trusted with his life. They knew all his secrets and he knew all theirs, and if anything was finer than that, he hadn't seen it.

"Boys," he said.

Uncharacteristically, all three of them jumped. They gaped at him as if he were Lazarus, risen from the dead.

His brows arched. "What's doing, gentlemen?"

And then they were on him like a pack of enormous, rough-and-tumble puppies, hugging him, slapping him on the back, making him see double in pain with arms squeezed around his middle.

"You look like shit," Tomás said when it was over. He stepped back to peer at him with a critical eye. "You shouldn't be up yet."

"How's the gash, man? Thought we lost you there for a minute, bro. You were pretty chopped up," said Julian, his big hand wrapped around Xander's shoulder.

Mateo merely looked him up and down and shook his head. "You're one tough fuck, you know that?"

"And you're just as ugly as I remember," Xander answered, grinning. "But I guess a jarhead isn't supposed to be pretty, right?"

"Navy SEAL, asshole," growled Julian from beside him. "Jarhead's a marine. And we have better hair."

"Yeah, well, you're all cannon fodder as far as the military is concerned. But we know better what you *really* are, don't we?" He winked, and the big male grinned at him, nodding, and slapped his shoulder.

"He's a shitty driver is what he is," Tomás said in an affectionate tone, looking sideways at Julian. "We would have gotten to you sooner at the hotel, but Driving Miss Daisy here took his sweet time leaving Monte Carlo."

Julian scowled at him. "I made a seven-hour trip in under three, jerkoff. Top that!"

Tomás shrugged. "Would have been quicker if that bus of bikini models hadn't been unloading in front of the Fairmont." He smiled, the lines around his mirror eyes crinkling. "Thought you were going to have whiplash. Or a heart attack."

"You drove here from Monaco?" Xander said, surprised. "What were you doing there?"

The three of them knew how to fly—and hijack—anything from a single-engine Cessna to a military fighter aircraft, so he'd assumed they'd come by plane. Fortunately they had been close enough to get to him quickly. If they'd been in Quebec or Manaus, his chances of survival might have been exactly zero.

Tomás and Mateo shared a dour look. "Ali Baba sent us to do recon on some big-shot casino owner named Stark," Mateo said. "Seems he's into this guy Stark for some serious cash and is looking for a way out of it. And if Stark has a little *accident*, so to speak, Ali Baba won't have to pay at all."

Xander's jaw tightened. "He's gambling again," he said, and the three other assassins nodded.

Ali Baba was their nickname for Xander's half brother, Alejandro, who ruled as Alpha of the Manaus colony. A preening, undisciplined, shifty-eyed male with an ego the size of a small country, Alejandro was also incredibly lucky. Hence the nickname. Though he had a knack for winning big at casinos—and occasionally losing big, which it seemed he had been recently—that wasn't what had earned him the sarcastic moniker first coined by Tomás years ago. The Syndicate called him Ali Baba because he'd been crowned Alpha only by a lucky turn of fate that propelled him to a position of power he hadn't earned and didn't deserve. He wasn't as Gifted as Xander, or half as strong or smart.

But he *was* the firstborn son of their father's new wife. The new wife who hated Xander with an elemental ferocity and was ultimately responsible for having him shipped off to the Academy. The new wife who'd taken Xander's mother's place when she died. More correctly, when she was killed.

By his father.

Ancient history, that. But some scars never fade. Like the scars on his back where his father had whipped him whenever he was disobedient and then poured salt over the flayed skin just to hear him scream. So the mention of his half brother's name brought his blood to a boil.

"The gambling will have to stop when the rest of the Alphas convene on Manaus," Xander said, dark, thinking of the move all the colonies were preparing to make. Since it had been discovered the Expurgari knew the locations of all the colonies except Manaus, preparations had been in the works to combine all four colonies into one mega-colony. Logistics were proving to be a nightmare, but once Alejandro was surrounded by three other snarling Alphas, he wouldn't stand a chance of getting away with his usual idiocy.

And hopefully he'd do something to piss one of them off and there would be a bloody—deadly—fight.

"Maybe," said Julian. "But our friend Mr. Stark still might not wake up in the morning."

"Speaking of morning, how long have I been out?" Xander asked, curious how long it had taken him to heal this time. He wasn't fully operational, of course, but a human wouldn't have survived the hit he'd taken, forget about being up and around.

Silence, sudden tension, and furtive looks passed back and forth. Mateo said, "Sixteen hours. Exactly."

Xander's nervous system went on instant high alert. They'd been talking when he came in the room, *three days minus sixteen hours,* Mateo had said…did that have to do with Morgan—had she been hurt? Where was she? Something in his chest went cold.

His voice lowered an octave, he said, "What's wrong?"

"How's your sniffer, X?" said Mateo, watching him from hooded green eyes.

Xander was confused. And he *hated* to be confused. "What are you talking about?"

Mateo glanced at Tomás, who said with a lifted eyebrow, "*Inhale,* man."

When he did, Morgan's scent hit him like a wrecking ball. Fire and fever and a dark, searing need, laced with her normal perfume of exotic spices and warm skin and lush woman, all of it overlaid with the distinct, exquisite aroma of a female, aroused.

The Fever. She was deep in her Fever. And there was absolutely nothing more irresistible to an *Ikati* male than that.

He staggered back, wide-eyed. An erection sprang to rock-solid life in his pants.

"Yeah," Tomás said sarcastically, by way of explanation. "So there's that."

He swallowed, his throat like a desert. "Where is she?" he croaked.

"Bartleby's with her," said Mateo with a glance upward. "In the gym—"

"The *gym*?" He was aghast at the thought of her sprawled over athletic mats, writhing in unfulfilled need. "Why in God's name isn't she in one of the bedrooms, comfortable—"

"One of the bedrooms next to *you*?" Julian interrupted with a pointed look at the front of his trousers. "You think you'd have slept the last sixteen hours through that?"

Sweet Jesus, that's what they'd been talking about when he came in. He couldn't believe they'd stood it for as long as they had; a female in her Fever emitted an irresistible siren call to a male, a call that on a purely biological level was almost impossible to ignore. The Fever in females of young-bearing age happened once a year and lasted for three days, and mated or not, it was a dangerous time for the female and any nearby males, as well.

Competition festered. Fights broke out. Animal impulses reigned supreme.

In his colony any female in Fever was kept on full lock-down until it passed. And now—

"Bartleby's been giving her drugs to keep her calm," said Mateo. "And we've been doing a little self-medicating with our friend Mr. Daniels over there," he added, glancing at a bottle of Tennessee whiskey on the counter. "And now that you're up, we can clear out until—"

"I'm not leaving," Xander said emphatically. "I'm not leaving her here alone."

Silently they assessed him. "She'll be with Bartleby, X," said Tomás.

He met the male's cool, tintless gaze. "I'm not leaving her."

"We'll be back in a few days," said Mateo, trying to be reasonable. "She's out of danger. You took down both those deserters who broke into the hotel room, and no one but us knows we're here. She'll be perfectly safe here with Bartleby for a few days—"

Xander turned to him, his gaze flinty. "You're not listening to me. I. Am. *Not*. Leaving."

Mateo stared back at him. "Because…?"

"Because she's my responsibility."

Mateo cocked his head. His eyes narrowed. "That sounds strangely familiar, Alexander."

A rush of vicious fury, blinding white, and before he knew what he was doing, his fist connected with Mateo's jaw.

Tomás and Julian jumped between them as Mateo snarled and moved to retaliate, his own muscled arm cocked back to strike, all of them shouting at once. It took a few minutes before they could be separated. Julian dragged Xander back into one corner of the kitchen, Tomás pushed Mateo, cursing, into the other. They stood staring at one another on opposite sides of the room, breathing hard, straining against the arms that held them.

"You did it again, didn't you?" Mateo panted, flushed and angry, held tight in Tomás's arms.

Xander bristled. "One more word and so help me God—"

"You *bonded* with her, you fucking idiot!" Mateo shouted. "You bonded with your mark! Are you crazy?"

"Don't be ridiculous!" Xander snarled, straining against Julian's grip. "I'm just doing my job!"

"Oh, yeah? Tell that to the arm that just took a swing at me! Tell that to your *blood*!"

Xander froze. "What did you say?" he whispered, staring hard at Mateo. All the light in the room was suddenly bright, so horribly bright—

"Get off me," Mateo spat, and broke free of Tomás. He circled around the kitchen, throwing off heat and flexing his muscled arms, staring black murder at everyone and everything. Finally he turned and looked at Xander, and when he spoke his voice sounded like he'd been swallowing rocks. "Doc did a transfusion, direct from her to you. Yes," he said when Xander went stone stiff. "Her blood. In you. That's how you made it through." He turned away, sat down heavily in the kitchen chair Julian had occupied, and stared down at the plate of cooling rigatoni.

"She did that? She did that for me?" Xander barely had the breath to speak. His body went completely lax. Julian released him but kept a wary hand on his shoulder.

Mateo glanced up at him. After a moment of weighted silence, he exhaled a heavy breath through his nose. "Yeah. Maybe you're not the only one who's bonded."

"I'm not bonded," he said, hoarse.

A bonded male was aggressively territorial, insanely jealous, and utterly devoted to his female. He would kill for her, he would die for her, he worshipped the very ground she walked on.

He didn't feel any of that. He felt...not like that. He didn't. He *couldn't.*

"Oh, man," said Mateo, glaring. "Shut the fuck up. Who do you think you're talking to here?"

Xander stared at him, his mind an utter blank. "I don't even know her."

"Apparently you know enough. When her blood hit your system you jacked like you were riding the lightning."

If he'd felt any shred of humor at the moment, he might have laughed at Mateo and his amusing colloquialisms. "Riding the lightning" meant being electrocuted. In the electric chair. Which is how it looked when an *Ikati* received blood from their mate.

From their mate.

For all *Ikati*, love was much more than a state of mind. It went deeper than emotion, deeper than wishes or vows made in a chapel or a lifetime of shared values and goals. It changed something within, on a physiological level. It left a mark, a fingerprint, a *soul*print that was never erased. Though some of their kind were Matched for propagating the race in hopes of imparting Gifts to their offspring and some of them were mated in love, as true lovers and soul mates and friends, *all* of them were mated for life. "Until death do us part" wasn't just five words spoken on a Sunday. It was an ironclad pronouncement by fate. Among their kind, there was no divorce, no affairs, nothing at all that came between mates. Ever.

Except death.

No! his mind screamed. *It can't be! It cannot be!*

Mateo stood and jerked his chin at Julian and Tomás. "Either which way, we're out of here for the next sixty hours or so. There's enough food and meds to last until we get back. Bartleby will stay to take care of you both." He strode to the staircase that led upstairs and took the steps two at a time. "And you're welcome for rescuing your sorry ass," he muttered just before his boots disappeared from sight.

The three of them stood in uncomfortable silence until Tomás finally spoke.

"He'll get over it. He's just worried about you. And he's probably just jealous. That girl of yours is one serious piece of—"

Cut off by Xander's deep, warning growl, Tomás threw up his hands. "Point taken! I'm not saying another word."

Julian spoke. "You won't be able to stay here without... you know. That's a physical impossibility."

"I can control myself," he said, stiff.

Julian glanced down at the bulge straining in Xander's pants. "Sure you can."

"X," said Tomás, very quietly. Their eyes met, and Xander saw something he'd never seen there before: pity. "Don't make this another Esperanza, man. You couldn't save her, and you can't save this one either. Don't be a fucking tragedy."

Xander walked up to Tomás, pressed his chest against the other male's, and stood looking at him, eye to eye, nose to nose, vibrating rage. When he spoke, his voice was low, controlled, and cold as ice.

"Back off, Tomás. You're stepping into a minefield. And we all know what happens to fools who take strolls in minefields."

They stood like that, eyeball to eyeball, unblinking, until Julian intervened. "Jesus fucking Christ," he spat, shoving them apart. "What the hell is wrong with you! We're on the same team, you idiots!"

"Tell that to your friend Romeo," Tomás snarled, then turned his back and headed for the stairs. He went up, but stopped halfway. He turned and fixed Xander with a hard look. "Take the next three days to get your head straight, bro. Fuck her, don't fuck her, I really don't give a shit. But if you don't finish her when you're supposed to, you *know* what happens. The Assembly will come to us. Then we'll have to take her out, and *you* too, you dumb fuck. Otherwise we're all dead meat. So don't put us in that position. We've been through too much together to get killed for a skirt."

Then he stalked up the stairs, leaving Xander alone with a pensive Julian.

"Sorry, X," he said, sounding as if he truly were. "But he's right. You know he's right." He clapped a hand on Xander's shoulder in farewell, then, like his two brothers before him, made his way to the stairs.

"There's a feral colony somewhere in the vicinity of the Vatican," Xander said to Julian's retreating back. The big male spun around to face him, eyes wide. Xander went on, his voice dull, his heart clenched to a fist in his chest. "Those two males you saw in the hotel room weren't deserters. They're feral; they don't belong to any of the known colonies. They were with four others when I first saw them. And there's another, an older male who I think is their leader. So if there's that many males, there's females. There's a colony nearby."

"How?" Julian said, shocked.

Xander looked at the white tile floor, shook his head, took a deep breath, and blew it out. "I don't know. But they want Morgan." He looked up into Julian's wide eyes, and his voice took on a darkly menacing tone. "And I'm not going to let them have her."

"Oh, man," said Julian, shaking his head. "This situation has gone totally FUBAR."

Xander allowed himself a small, mirthless smile. FUBAR was one of the many slang terms that peppered the speech of the three members of the Syndicate who'd trained in the American military. The abbreviation stood for *fucked up beyond all recognition.*

"Just remember," Xander said without a hint of sarcasm, knowing from experience he was right about this, "things can always get worse." Then he crossed the kitchen, clapped his hand on Julian's shoulder, and took the stairs three at a time, heading for the gym.

TWENTY-ONE

D was dreaming.

A part of his mind—the part that was always lucid, whether he was asleep, awake, or stone-cold drunk—recognized this fact and began to record the details of the dream so he could access them when he woke. Many of his dreams meant nothing; many more held fractured clues that he had to fit together like puzzle pieces over a few days or weeks in order to see the full picture of the future his dreams painted for him.

But some dreams, like the one he was enmeshed in now, arrived fully formed and presented him with an image of the future as vivid as a van Gogh.

He'd had the Gift of Foresight since birth, long before he was able to Shift to Vapor or panther, long before he realized what the dreams actually were. And though it was an incredibly powerful Gift—one he'd been careful to downplay just as he minimized his intelligence and maximized his ruthlessness because he believed that being underestimated and misunderstood put him at a distinct advantage with friend and foe alike—he hated it with every fiber of his being.

Because knowing exactly how and when everyone you loved was going to die was not a walk in the park.

Someone was dying in this dream, too, but not someone D loved. It was the strange male with the flaming orange tiger eyes Celian had fired on at the Vatican, the one who had so impressed the *Bellatorum* with his display of fearlessness and bravado, the one who had taunted them with lewd gestures and feigned boredom and a mocking smile.

The one who could walk through walls. Whose body filtered bullets like a fan filtered air.

In the dream a knife protruded from the male's back, sunk hilt-deep between his shoulder blades. There was a great deal of blood, spurting from the wound and splattering over the black stone floor, running in tiny crimson rivulets over the fist clenched around the blade of the knife, the fist that twisted the blade and sent the male crashing to his knees with a bellow.

It was Dominus who had plunged the knife into the male's back. Dominus who twisted it. Dominus who stood grinning over the male as he collapsed sideways onto the floor and lay there, silent and still, leaking out his life in swiftly widening circles that pooled beneath him and glinted red in the candlelight.

The beautiful full-Blood female was there, too, chained naked to the *fovea* wall behind them where Celian had been whipped near to death at midnight when Lucien and Aurelio had failed to show up. Thrashing against the steel cuffs that held her wrists overhead, she screamed something he couldn't make out, screamed with such force and anguish it sent a concussion like a detonated bomb through the room and buffeted Dominus forward several feet, knocking him off balance.

None of this surprised D's dream self. Dominus always won. He always had. And clearly the male would have to die if the female was to be taken. Whoever he was, he was dangerous, and powerful, and wouldn't give her up without a fight. She was obviously powerful, too; all you had to do was be near her to feel the unique, humming current exuded by the most pure-Blooded of their kind.

What surprised D was when a coldly smiling Constantine appeared behind Dominus, pointed a gun at his head, and pulled the trigger.

"D! D! *Demetrius!* Wake up!"

Lix's voice pierced the dream like a dagger punched through skin. He sat up abruptly in bed and looked wildly around, weighing the darkness, feeling his heart like a hammer in his chest. Everything was exactly as he'd left it when he'd fallen asleep—how long ago?—the six metal cots, the wood lockers lined at their feet, the bare walls, the spartan, undecorated space.

The catacombs where the *Bellatorum* lived and slept and trained were designed and decorated much like a military barracks, with sleeping quarters, dining quarters, armories, and meeting rooms, with training areas that included a gym, fighting arena, and shooting range. Because they were the elite of the King's guard, they had more freedom and privileges than the half-Blood soldier class of *Legiones* who lived in the nearby chambers, but were given nothing in the way of luxuries that would make them soft.

So the blanket D had squeezed between his fists was scratchy and thin.

"What time is it?' he said to Lix, his voice a harsh scrape in the quiet. He ran a hand over his head, breathing in deep to counteract the sudden dizziness—dreams like the one he'd just had took a while to recover from.

Crouched on his heels next to D's low cot, Lix said, "Haven't looked at the clock recently, but the *Servorum* are coming in. Must be close to dawn."

Unlike the *Bellatorum*, who came and went as they pleased, the servant class was allowed out only at night. But at least they were allowed out: the chosen females of the King's harem, the *Electi*, and the neutered males who guarded them, the *Castratus*, weren't allowed to leave the splendor of their sprawling catacombs at all. Neither were any of the hundreds of offspring that lived with the *Electi*, offspring of various ages and strengths of Blood.

Only full-Blooded members of the *Bellatorum*, the *Optimates*, and the King's close relatives—with the exception of the *principessa* Eliana—were allowed to come and go at will.

D stood and yanked on the clothes he'd left folded atop the footlocker at the end of the bed. He laced up his boots and got his gear strapped on: Glock nine millimeter on his right hip, kukhri—tip dipped in poison—on his left, push daggers in each of his boots, other knives tucked into pockets in his pants. He looked at the two empty beds that belonged to Lucien and Aurelio, and his mouth tightened.

He had a terrible suspicion they wouldn't ever sleep there again.

"Where's Constantine?"

Lix stood and crossed his arms over his chest, and D felt the other male's anger like a burning weight in his own chest. "With Celian," Lix answered, dark.

They exchanged glances. Celian was laid out facedown on a cot in the infirmary, bloodying towel after towel that was pressed to his mangled back. The cat-o'-nine-tails was infamous for its brutality—he'd be out of commission and in a lot of pain while the chunks of scored flesh grew together.

D said, "How is he?"

Lix shrugged. "Lost a lot of blood, but he'll be fine in a few days, you know that. Celian's a badass—"

"I meant Constantine," D snapped, shrugging on his long overcoat.

Lix inhaled deep, then passed a hand over his face. He dropped both hands to his waist and exhaled. "He's not talking."

Which meant he was taking it hard, as he always did, as Dominus, of course, knew.

The King knew everyone's weakness, and Constantine's weakness was his brothers. He was more loyal to them than to their cruel King, and when they hurt, he hurt. Especially when *he* was the cause of that hurt. Like tonight, when he'd been forced to whip Celian into unconsciousness while the King watched, amused. Dominus had been measuring Constantine's loyalty to him with gruesome tests like these for years, and D had wondered how long it would be before Constantine finally snapped.

D cursed under his breath, remembering the dream, the particular look on Constantine's face as he pulled the trigger: hatred and deep satisfaction. Evidently he would snap, and soon.

"Had a dream," he said to Lix, who sent him a wry smile in return.

"I know. That's why I'm here."

D looked up at Lix, his brows drawn together in question, but Lix only shrugged again, the motion not exactly nonchalant. "Dominus," he said simply.

D realized with a cold chill over his skin that the King had sensed him dreaming, as he did when the dreams were particularly vivid. And now he wanted a full report.

"Shit," D muttered, eyeing the arched corridor at the end of the room that led out to a mess hall and connecting tunnels beyond. Those tunnels, winding and dark, led directly to the King's chambers.

"Just tell him the truth, D," Lix said quietly. "Just tell him what he needs to know."

He doesn't need *to know everything,* D thought, ever the rebel, but aloud he said only, "*Recte.*"

Right.

The antiserum that would allow half-Bloods to survive the Transition was almost perfect.

Dominus had been working on it for the past three decades, had in fact started the first experiments before he had earned his degree in cell and gene therapy as a young man. It had confounded him then more so than now, since he had almost solved the maddening riddle of exactly which component of human DNA warped the superior genetic characteristics of *Ikati* DNA. Because it so clearly did: over several thousand years of his race's recorded history, only a tiny percentage of mixed-Blood *Ikati* were ever known to survive their first Shift at twenty-five.

The first and most famous was a female named Cleopatra. Ruthless and cunning, that one, almost as fine a strategist as he. And his spies informed him another female had recently done the same, and even been named Queen of that massive colony in the ancient woods of southern England he'd had his eye on for so long.

He'd never take a half-Blood Queen for himself. Though he'd kept human women—captured and held prisoner, tourists mostly, the choicest ones—as part of his harem since his beloved Sabina died so long ago, that was pure pragmatism: humans bred like rabbits. A single female could produce a child—or two or three—every nine months for decades during the entirety of her breeding years. Full-Blood *Ikati* females were only fertile once per year and rarely got pregnant. It was the reason his kind had all survived on the edge of oblivion for centuries. Humans were simply outbreeding them.

Not for long, though. He was going to turn their fertility against them.

Three of the six *Liberi* injected with the latest version of the antiserum had survived their Transitions this past week alone. Close. So close. Only a few more trials, and he was sure he'd perfect the compound, and then he'd inject the hundreds upon hundreds of his half-Blood bastards and put the final stage of his plan into place—

"Sire."

Dominus looked up from his perusal of the latest DNA sequence and variance report from his privately funded, state-of-the-art lab in Milan to find D and Lix standing at the arched entrance to his library. Like windows, doors were absent in all the catacombs.

Except the heavily guarded doors that led to the outside world, of course.

"*Salve, Bellatores,*" he said, laying aside the report on his desk. He leaned back into the comfort of a large leather chair and gazed at them while they stood in silence at the doorway, waiting for his command. They wouldn't enter unless invited, and he had half a mind to let them stand there and sweat, but he knew they were both on edge from the incident with Celian. He liked to occasionally push them to the far edge of their constraints: anger kept a warrior razor sharp. "Better to be feared than loved," his own father had told him, wisely.

He'd felt neither for the old man and had killed him as soon as he was old enough to lead, but still, it was good advice.

Motioning them forward with his hand, he said, "Come in. Sit with me."

The two huge warriors sat in the two chairs opposite his desk—dwarfing the furniture and looking profoundly uncomfortable—and Dominus had to press the smile from his lips. He looked first at Lix, long-haired and unshaven, then at D, tattooed, bald, and emitting his usual aura of violence, dark as a lightning storm and just as dangerous.

Tell me, Bellator, he thought. With a clenched jaw, the warrior began to speak.

"The full-Blood male we encountered at the Vatican," he said, moving only his lips. His entire body, big as it was, had fallen still as stone. He hated when Dominus was inside his head, which, of course, the King found highly amusing.

He made a noise of interest and gestured for D to continue.

"He was here, in the *fovea*." He licked his lips. "With the female."

The King's eyebrows shot up. He leaned forward, put his elbows on the desk. "Go on."

"She was naked," he said tonelessly, "chained to the wall."

At that, blood began to pound through the King's veins. Naked. Chained. Two more beautiful words could not be found in any language. He'd think more on that later on, when he was alone. Perhaps when he was with one of his human concubines; they were so much easier to scare than their *Ikati* counterparts, and he loved them to be scared when he took them. He loved them to scream. "And the male?"

Here D inhaled and dropped his gaze to the edge of the King's desk. "You stabbed him in the back. You killed him."

"So I win," he said, very soft. D glanced up at him, stone-faced. His voice came very low.

"You always win, sire."

Dominus sat back in his chair, pleased beyond measure. That male he'd encountered had powers he'd never heard of and smelled of death and carnage and the kind of hardened soullessness he'd only ever found in himself, all of which had given him considerable worry.

But this made everything so much easier. The warrior's dreams were never wrong, and like the one that had alerted him to the arrival of the two strangers, this one had been so strong he'd felt the echoes of it from half a mile away. He watched as Lix shifted in his chair, still uncomfortable, and abruptly decided the two of them deserved a little reward.

"It's three days until the next *Purgare*," he said, thinking of the ritual burial ceremony that took place at midnight under every full moon for all the *Liberi* who hadn't survived their treacherous first Transitions over the previous month. Their mothers, the *Bellatorum*, and the rest of the upper classes gathered to scatter the ashes into a secret spot of the river Tiber along with flowers and murmured farewells, and he'd come to hate each and every *Purgare* as a personal affront to his pride.

But not for long. This next could be the last.

"Take the next few days off," the King continued, gratified when the two warriors looked at him, shocked. "Go out, get drunk, Shift in the Villa Borghese if you like. Silas will give you money." He motioned to his most trusted servant, who glided forward silently from the shadows of the room and bowed in their direction. "Enjoy yourselves."

"Thank you, sire," said Lix, sounding more than a little confused, and he tried not to smile again. The King wasn't known for leniency or charity, but he dearly loved to keep them guessing.

"Take Constantine as well," he added, in a rare swell of benevolence. The male had taken his task of punishing Celian exceptionally hard and might not leave his bedside until he healed. A small gesture of generosity would go a long way toward mending his raw emotions. After all, a king needed his warriors loyal. And as the very intelligent human Niccolo Machiavelli once said, "Severities should be dealt out all at once...but benefits ought to be handed out drop by drop, so that they may be relished the more."

"Father," said a female voice from the door. The two warriors leapt to their feet and stood at attention, eyes fixed on some far-off point behind the King's head.

Dominus rose from his chair. "Eliana," he said, his voice warm.

She walked toward him over the hand-knotted Persian rug with the poise and grace of a runway model and paused beside him, offering her cheek.

He leaned down and kissed her, thinking she was too thin. Her cheekbones stood out in the perfect oval of her face, which made her dark eyes look even larger than normal. He brushed a lock of her choppy black hair from her forehead and wished she'd grow it longer. He didn't like this modern look on her.

As beautiful as her mother had once been, his only daughter was twice that and had his intelligence and drive to boot. Trained in martial arts—unnecessary, but it kept her occupied—an expert in computer science, and fluent in several languages, she was worth a hundred of someone like her older brother, Caesar. The boy was cowardly and unGifted and had he not been his son Dominus would have given him over to the *Castratus*. But Eliana was his pride and joy. Unfortunately she chafed just as her mother had at the life of sheltered privilege she'd been forced to lead.

But Dominus would never risk allowing her the leniency to roam free in the world. She was the only thing he truly loved, the only precious spark of light in his life of war and darkness, and he protected her from the dangers of the outside world just as he protected her from the ugly truth of what he was and all the things he'd done to get that way.

But someday, if his plan worked, she could live free as a bird. As could they all.

Forever.

She turned to the warriors. "*Bonum mane, Bellatores*," she murmured, gazing at D. Lix gave a murmured hello, but D remained silent. His gaze flickered to hers, and he inclined his head, then glanced away. That muscle in his jaw flexed again.

Dominus smiled. He'd noticed it before, the hunger that wafted from the tattooed warrior like perfume whenever his only daughter was near, and he welcomed it. Eliana would never find him attractive; of that he was sure. She had suitors aplenty and was quite literally out of his class. And Demetrius—rebellious, insubordinate, combative Demetrius—had more than once been induced to follow some order he found egregious simply because he'd had Eliana utter it for him.

Oh, how he loved to prey upon weakness. Just thinking about it warmed the frozen cockles of his heart.

"I heard a rumor a strange full-Blood male was spotted near the Vatican," Eliana said, turning back to him with a little furrow between her dark brows. "An Alpha. Are you in any danger?"

He smiled down at her. Out of necessity, he'd told her—everyone, actually, he'd told everyone long ago—that they were being hunted by others of their kind, that they'd be massacred if found by these savage interlopers.

That his own father had been killed by one of them.

"That's nothing for you to worry about, love," he said with a meaningful glance at D. The big male met his gaze straight on.

Isn't that right, my friend?

Slowly, D nodded his head yes, and the King's smile grew wider. "That's nothing for you to worry about," he repeated, and sent the warriors on their way.

TWENTY-TWO

When Xander opened the door to the gym and stuck his head inside, the perfume that hit his nose was so lusciously overpowering he sagged against the jamb, momentarily stunned.

"Who's there?" came Bartleby's aggravated voice from behind a folding screen erected in one corner of the darkened room.

Morgan's scent, a voluptuous bloom of heated woman and exotic dark loveliness, drew him forward, had him salivating like one of Pavlov's trained dogs. Following it was a compulsion, a decision made in some deep, animal part of his brain that overrode all logic and restraint. He pushed off the doorjamb and let the door swing shut behind him.

It was hot in the room, a tropical heat, the air humid and perfumed. Along with the lack of light it reminded him of a night he'd spent once in Bali, but there hadn't been this amazing, sensual force pulling him forward then. There hadn't been this *need.*

Because it was need. As basic as the need to eat or breathe or Shift, the urge to mate with the source of all that lovely, deep, feminine scent was a lashing demand in every cell of his body.

He took several steps into the room but froze when he heard a low moan.

Morgan's moan.

"Go away," hissed Bartleby from behind the screen, "you'll make it worse!"

Just going to move her to a bedroom, Xander thought, one ragged part of his brain still functioning. *Just going to get her off the floor, get her comfortable...*

He staggered across the polished bamboo floor of the gym one step at a time, trying not to breathe too deeply because it sent the animal inside him into a frenzy of snarling hunger. Morgan moaned again, and the doctor cursed. Xander rounded the side of the folding screen and froze, looking down with his lips parted and his heart a sudden throbbing clench in his chest.

She was lying on her back on a futon unfolded on the floor, arms and legs akimbo, a sheet bunched up around her waist as if she'd been thrashing in it. She was clothed, but not by much: a simple camisole gone see-through with sweat, a glimpse of plain, girlish white panties beneath the wrinkled sheet. Her hair was a tangled dark mess over the pillow beneath her head, her eyes were closed, her skin shone with the Fever and a fine sheen of perspiration. Strands of hair curled mermaid damp across her brow, clung to her neck, and he itched to push them from her skin with his fingers.

Looking at her, every atom in his body, every nerve, screamed, *I want! I need! Mine!*

"I told you, it'll make it worse if you're—"

Bartleby, crouching over Morgan with a syringe in his hand, turned while he spoke. When he saw Xander standing there, he broke off in surprise and came to his feet. "You're up! How are you feeling?"

Xander's mouth felt like baked stone. He didn't take his gaze from Morgan when he answered. "At this exact moment?" he said, his voice shaking. "Like King Kong on Viagra."

"It's the hormones she's emitting," Bartleby said, sending a worried glance toward Morgan. As if she knew he was looking at her, she let out a whimper. Her head rolled back and forth on the pillow, and she arched on the futon, radiating heat. Bartleby glanced back at Xander, whose mouth had begun to water. "You can't be in here. You know that," he said, moving between Xander and Morgan so he blocked the view.

A low, warning growl rumbled through Xander's chest. He couldn't help it.

"Alexander," said the doctor, careful to keep his voice mild, "I'm only trying to make this easier for her. She is in a lot of discomfort—pain, actually—and though I've just given her a shot of morphine, she'll still be able to feel you here and it will make the pain worse. You need to leave. For her."

He didn't move. His brain sent the command, but his feet refused. His entire body was in mutiny. Desire pounded through him in wave over dark, powerful wave, and he stood there fighting it, fighting the almost overpowering urge to rip off that sheet and those innocent white panties and take her right here, on the gymnasium floor.

"Why would Leander send me with a female about to go into her Fever?" he wondered aloud. His voice cracked over every other word. "Why would anyone be so stupid?"

Bartleby sighed and set the syringe down on a low table that was filled with towels and water bottles and various medical supplies, then turned back to Xander. "He didn't know. She said it's her first Fever."

Xander started. He'd never heard of a female going into Fever for the first time later than puberty. "What? That's impossible! She's—how old is she?"

"Twenty-six," came the reply. "And, yes, it's almost unheard of to happen this late. But not impossible." His tone shaded with sarcasm. "Clearly." He put a gentle hand on Xander's bicep and gave a small push. It was like trying to move a building.

"I just want to move her somewhere more comfortable," Xander said, licking his lips. "I can't stand seeing her on the floor. Just to one of the bedrooms, downstairs." He glanced at the doctor. "Will it hurt her if I move her?"

Bartleby shook his head. His eyes were worried. "But it might hurt you." A flush spread across his cheeks.

"The wound is healing," Xander said. "It hurts, but you know I heal fast. And she probably only weighs a buck ten, a buck twenty at the most—"

"It's not your wound I'm worried about, old friend," said the doctor, then sent a pointed glance at the front of Xander's trousers, at the bulge straining there. Bartleby coughed into his hand and glanced away.

Xander dismissed that. He was under control. If he had stood here with the scent of her readiness pummeling him for the past few minutes and had done nothing to satisfy the screaming need it unleashed in him, he could control himself.

He was relatively sure of that.

He brushed past Bartleby and knelt beside the futon. He leaned over Morgan. His gaze traveled over her flushed face, her tangled hair, her chest...

He squeezed his eyes shut, banishing the sight of hard pink nipples straining taut through the sheer, clinging fabric of the camisole, of her breasts, so full and round.

"Morgan," he whispered, opening his eyes. She made a little sound in her throat and her brow furrowed, but her eyes didn't open. "I'm going to move you to a more comfortable place, to a bed. All right?"

She didn't answer. He smelled the drug the doctor had given her, smelled the chemical harshness of it in her blood beneath the amazing, opulent scent of the Fever, and knew it wouldn't last long. Her body was burning through it even as he knelt there.

He gathered the sheet around her, carefully slid his arms beneath her body, and pulled her against him, cradling her to his chest. He lifted her and stood up. Her head fell against his shoulder, she breathed a little, discontented sigh. Her skin was hot, so hot—

The fingers of one of her hands curled around the front of his shirt. Eyes closed, she burrowed against him, inhaling, breathing his own scent into her nose. Then she made another sound in her throat, but this one was purely erotic.

A shudder wracked him. He had to get her to that bed, and fast, and then he had to get the hell away from her.

Without another word to the doctor, he crossed the darkened gym, kicked open the doors, and headed toward the stairs.

Morgan was on fire.

Everything burned, everything hurt, her skin and her muscles and her bones. Even her thoughts—chaotic and disjointed as they were—scorched a painfully blazing path through her brain, pounding one word over and over.

Mate. Mate. *Mate.*

She'd never felt anything like this incinerating, elemental urgency before but supposed she shouldn't have been so surprised; her own mother had her first Fever late, though not as late as this. Once Morgan passed puberty without a sign of it appearing, then twenty, then twenty-five, everyone just assumed she was an anomaly. That possibly her powerful Gift of Suggestion came with a darker side. Infertility.

But no. She was fertile. Now she felt it to the very marrow of her bones.

And there was a male holding her. An *Ikati* male, not the human doctor that had tended to her since the first signs of the Fever hit. She smelled the difference between them, the power, the strength of this male carrying her in his arms. She smelled his lust, dark and deep.

Her lids were so heavy from the drug she couldn't open her eyes, but she *could* inhale, and she took that heavenly scent of lust into her lungs. This close, it was thick and sweet like candy, delicious. It sent a spike of heat straight down between her legs.

She made a little noise of longing in her throat. The male began to walk faster.

There came the sound of heavy doors being kicked open, then light behind her closed lids that hurt enough to make her turn, wincing, and bury her face in the hard chest she was cradled against. Movement and breathing, her body swaying with his steps, the motion rhythmic and calming except for the pressure of her breasts against his body, the aching awareness of him and his beautiful scent like something she wanted to eat.

Yes, taste him, her mind urged, churning. *Taste all of him! He is what you need!*

She arched her back, slid a hand up around his neck, and opened her mouth over the column of his throat.

Salt and musk and masculinity, heat and rightness, the throb of his pulse beneath her lips. He stumbled and cursed, yanked his head away, but she wanted more, she wanted to run her tongue over all his smooth, lovely skin, and then she wanted to bite him and straddle him and take him deep inside—

"Touch me," she whispered, arching into him again. His arms tightened around her. He made a low, rough growl deep in his chest.

They kept moving.

Faster now, down a set of stairs, another, the male breathing hard and nearly stumbling several times as he hurried along. Her nose was in his hair, her lips were on his skin, her teeth nipped at his earlobe, his shoulder, the soft spot between his collarbone and neck. It sent shivers through his body, delicious ripples of hard muscle that drove her own need even higher. She heard the sound of another door being kicked open, then there was cool darkness and she was abruptly deposited onto a bed.

"Morgan," a voice said, hoarse, and then she knew. His voice sent a wash of pleasure through her body, pure and sweet, like sunlit honey.

He would help her, help ease the pain. Though he despised her, it was his *job* to keep her alive and well. At least for a while.

"Xander." She writhed against the mattress, reaching out blindly. "Please, Xander."

A sheet was pulled over her body; her wrists were caught and pinned. She fought against it; she didn't want the sheet on top of her. She wanted *him* on top of her.

"Morgan," he said again, and this time he really sounded as if he were in pain.

She managed to open her eyes, and he swam into view, hovering above her with his lips pulled back in a grimace and a fine sheen of sweat glistening on his brow. His eyes stared down at her, searing, molten amber rimmed in black lashes.

He wants you! the animal inside her hissed, writhing to be set free. *Take him!*

He'd pinned her wrists against the pillow above her head, and she knew she couldn't get them free. He was far too strong for that. So she didn't bother to try.

In a single, swift motion, she arched off the mattress, stretched out her neck, and put her mouth on his.

He moaned against her lips but didn't pull away. He didn't move nearer either. He just allowed her to kiss him, to suck at his lips and slide her tongue into his mouth, all the while holding her wrists down so hard against the pillow his arms began to shake.

"I want you," she whispered through frenzied kisses. "I need you."

"It's just the Fever," he groaned, his brow furrowed, his eyes half-lidded, watching her. "It's the hormones. And the drugs. You don't know what you're saying."

"*I need you,*" she insisted, teasing her tongue in and out of his mouth. He turned his head away, panting, and she took the opportunity to put her lips against his throat again, to press her teeth into his throbbing jugular.

The snarl that ripped from between his clenched teeth was like nothing she'd ever heard and sent a thrill of exhilaration zinging along every nerve.

He surged against her, throwing the length of his hard body on top of her as that snarl kept coming, fierce and animalistic. He kissed her like an animal, too, all teeth and greed and rough intent, an Alpha taking what he wanted without restraint or apology, his hands all over her body, squeezing her breasts and bottom, tangled in her hair.

She moaned and stretched full against him, lost, no longer herself but someone else, someone consumed in flame and flesh and pleasure, in the pounding pulse of two heartbeats, in the roar of desire like the swell of the ocean cresting over her, tumbling, crashing—

And then with a horrified cry, Xander broke away.

She was left breathless, spinning, every nerve like an open wound scraped raw.

"Jesus," he whispered, backing away toward the door. "I'm sorry, Morgan, I'm so sorry…"

"Please, Xander, don't go, it's all right," she said, struggling to sit up. The room spun. She shook her head to clear it, but the drugs—the goddamn drugs—

"I'm so sorry," he choked again, then fled through the door and slammed it shut behind him.

Morgan sagged back against the mattress, pain in her skull like needles driven through her eyes, in her body as if she'd been set to burn on a funeral pyre.

"But it hurts…" she whimpered to the empty room.

Then she passed out.

TWENTY-THREE

If he were human, D would have had trouble hearing Lix over the thumping bass of the techno music that screamed from the overhead speakers in the VIP section of their favorite bar and nightclub, Alien. But unfortunately D heard him clear as day.

"That's bullshit," said Lix, and knocked back another shot of Patrón.

It was his fifth. He was just getting started.

Watching Constantine disappear around a darkened corner on the far side of the room with a human female wearing a dress so short it was almost a belt, D sighed and ran a hand over his shaved head. "I'm telling you, Lix, there's something weird going on with Dominus and that

Servus, Silas. I just don't know what it is yet." He shook his head, frowning. "Something's just not right."

He'd dreamed of it in bits and pieces, clues that hinted at nefarious plots and well-kept secrets, tantalizing but ever out of reach. Unlike the dream he'd had this morning that had arrived in full—though he'd edited it in the retelling, a practice he knew would get him killed if discovered—and the one that showed him the full-Blood female and her orange-eyed Alpha had arrived in Rome, he'd been getting morsels of something else over the past few months. Years, even, maybe. It was hard to tell.

"Talk like that can get you killed, D. You better not mention that around any of the *Legiones*; they're just dying to take us down a notch. They're only soldiers because they weren't Gifted enough to make *Bellatorum*, but they're not stupid. One of them will turn you in just to earn a day off."

"Imagine what they'd do if they found out I was following him," D said in a wry voice.

Lix gaped at him. "You wouldn't. You couldn't be that stupid. He'll catch you!"

D had been spying on the King and Silas for several months now, trying to gain any kind of information that would satisfy the nagging feeling they were up to no good, but one glance at Lix's horrified expression told D he shouldn't have said anything. Not that he was going to stop.

Though he should have been used to it by now, he hated feeling like a chess piece, a dumb cog in the King's machine. He planned to keep searching until he found some answers.

But to his brother he only said, "You're right. I'm not that stupid. Bad joke."

Better to have Lix ignorant, anyway. It was safer for him that way.

Lix relaxed back against the white leather booth and motioned to the hovering waitress for a refill of his tequila. "Jesus. Don't scare me like that, asshole."

The waitress darted over from where she'd been standing at the bar, staring, and leaned over Lix. A fall of bottle-red hair spilled over her shoulders; her large breasts almost erupted from her low-cut top.

"*Si, signore?*" she breathed, fluttering her lashes.

D rolled his eyes. Another human female throwing herself at a warrior's feet.

The *Bellatorum* were larger and different and far more dangerous than their human male counterparts, exuding a primal power that parted crowds wherever they went, and they didn't care who noticed. Dominus himself didn't care. The King required only that they keep the location of their lair a secret, but as far as Shifting or standing out in a crowd...

"Humans are so stupid they can't see what is right under their noses," the King was fond of saying, "and even if the rare one does, all the rest will call him crazy."

D grudgingly admitted he was right. Though those werewolf rumors had persisted for centuries, mistaken as they were. It was common knowledge they originated from some drunk Greek of antiquity who had seen an *Ikati* Shift; as if a *dog* would be able to change its shape.

He'd long ago tired of the attention. Yet the other *Bellatorum* hadn't, so he found himself spending another night in this underworld playground, paroled from purgatory, watching the circus unfold.

Lix gave the human waitress a dangerous smile. His eyes lingering on her décolletage, he licked his lips. "*Alium,*" he said, low.

Her brows furrowed in confusion. Lix had forgotten he was speaking Latin, not Italian. He wasn't thinking with the right head.

"Bring him water," D said to the waitress in Italian and waved her away.

"*Gratias, matrem*," Lix said sarcastically, then shouted after her swiveling derriere to bring him another tequila as he'd originally asked. He turned back to D, his expression sour. "Who shit in your cereal?"

He didn't bother answering. Tense, he leaned back against the booth and stretched his arms out. His gaze darted over the sweating, gyrating crowd on the dance floor below.

"Ah," said Lix, drawing D's gaze back to his face. The long-haired male was nodding. "I get it. You saw Eliana today. You're always in a piss-poor mood after you see the *principessa*."

D sent him a baleful glare but didn't respond.

"She likes you, you know," Lix said, smiling.

Now D spoke, and his voice was like flint. "Shut up, brother."

Unperturbed by the hostility that pulsed from D like another beat of the music, Lix shrugged. "I'm just stating the obvious. You should make a move on that before one of those sissies of the *Optimates* mates her and she's out of commission forever."

"Speaking of talk that can get you killed," said D pointedly, glaring at Lix.

Though the *Bellatorum* could have any female they liked and were highly sought after as breeding partners for unmated females, females of the *Supremus*—the King's direct relatives—were strictly off-limits, on pain of death.

And his only daughter...D shuddered to think of the punishment that would follow if it were discovered he'd bedded her. Or even kissed her, for that matter.

Lix made a face at him and stretched his legs out under the table between them. "Maybe Aurelio was right after all. You ever think of that? Maybe it *is* better to ask forgiveness than permission."

D's expression soured. "Forgiveness? Like the forgiveness Dominus granted Celian? Because that kind of forgiveness I can do without."

It was Lix's turn to scowl. He sent a glance over his shoulder to the corner Constantine had disappeared around. His voice low, he said, "I thought he was going to make Constantine kill him."

D shook his head, ran a hand down the back of his neck, and squeezed the tense muscles there. "Constantine would kill himself before he'd do any lasting damage to one of us, which the King knows. So making him whip Celian is all just part of his..."

Sickness, he didn't say. Cruelty. Insanity.

"...thing. And Celian heals faster than anyone. He'll be up and around in a few days."

But in the meantime, Constantine would punish and anesthetize himself in any way possible, including getting drunk, getting into fights, and having rough, anonymous sex with human females. As he did every time the King played one of his sick games on him.

For the thousandth time D wondered what the hell it was all for, anyway.

Lix sat forward in the booth, crossed his arms over his knees, and said, "You think Lucien and Aurelio are coming back?"

D met Lix's intense gaze. The music pounded, lights strobed, bodies swayed and writhed.

"No."

Lix didn't even blink. "Me neither. So what do we do about it?"

D watched as Constantine reappeared around the dark corner of the nightclub, disheveled and grim, looking as if he'd just attended his own funeral. The human female stumbled after him, weaving shakily through the crowd. She headed to the bar and collapsed onto a barstool, trying in vain to adjust her demolished clothing. "We don't do anything," D said with a slight emphasis on the first word.

"Because?" Lix said, surprised.

Constantine moved closer. Though he was so beautiful Michelangelo could have modeled the *David* after him, a feeling of darkness moved with him, the subtle chill of death. The crowd parted to let him pass, shoving one another in their hurry to get out of his way.

"Because this situation is going to take care of itself."

Lix's face clouded, then cleared. "Your dream—that's right. Dominus killed that male in your dream." He sat back. "Not that it makes me feel any better. I'd like to get my hands on that bastard myself." His gaze searched D's face. "Did you see anything else? Anything before—or after?"

D shook his head and avoided Lix's gaze. He just couldn't chance the King's finding out about his treason during one of his regular trips through Lix's brain.

He'd learned how to hide things. He'd learned how to tuck things away into small, unseen places in his mind, places the King never bothered to go. There he kept his fantasies of Eliana, the visions of her soft body and soft eyes and soft mouth, there he kept his suspicions of her father, there he kept the snippets of dreams he edited, those dreams that hinted at terrible things to come.

There he kept his fear.

It was the fear that kept him awake nights, bathed in sweat, his body rigid and his mind a churning inferno. He didn't know exactly what was coming, but he knew *something* was, something vast and dark and cold that felt like oblivion. And now that the two full-Blood Shifters had arrived just as his dreams foretold, he felt an unseen clock ticking down to zero hour.

But to what? *What?*

"I need a drink," said Constantine, who had arrived to stand dead-faced and hulking beside their table.

D was about to open his mouth to speak but froze, the breath stolen from his lungs. Constantine and Lix froze as well; then all three turned in unison to look down at the dance floor below as the crowd parted to let three enormous, muscled males pass.

Ikati. Strangers.

Enemies.

The three strangers looked up at them just as Constantine said, "On second thought, a fight will do just fine."

"A *bar?*" complained Julian from behind the wheel of the Maserati he'd stolen in Monaco. He, Tomás, and Mateo were randomly driving through the dark, rainy streets of Rome, making a game of seeing how close he could come to pedestrians without actually hitting any of them.

He was fairly sure that nun on the Via Veneto would survive.

"It's a nightclub, not just a bar," grumbled Mateo, staring out the window at the buildings flashing by. He still wasn't over the incident with Xander, though it had been a good twelve hours prior. Those seven words were more than double what he'd spoken all day.

"And a good one at that," added Tomás from the backseat. "I heard Angelina Jolie was there just last week."

"Please," sneered Julian, steering the car around a corner so fast the two right-side wheels lifted a few inches from the ground. He narrowly missed crashing into an elderly couple crossing the street. "She's too busy making movies to hang out in bars."

The car fishtailed as Julian overcorrected. Mateo and Tomás were thrown against the windows. "Do they even have food in a bar?" Julian continued, unperturbed by the curses that were being hurled at him. "Answer me this: What is there in a bar that I'd be interested in? Do I dance? No. Do I drink? Well, okay, yes, but I'm not paying twenty bucks for a shot of watered-down whiskey. Do I like loud music? No. The only thing I'm going to find in a bar is—"

He stopped speaking abruptly, but it wasn't the Vespa he'd just clipped with the right front fender, sending its helmeted driver into a tailspin that launched him over the handlebars and off onto the grassy strip beside the road.

He stopped before he could say *women*.

The only thing to be found in a bar was human women. Lots of them. Like the one Xander had loved so long ago. The mere mention of which had caused the entire day to turn into a steaming pile of shit.

"He's got a hero complex," muttered Mateo to the window, knowing exactly why Julian had shut up so quickly. "Always looking to save the damsel in distress."

But in reality, she hadn't been in distress until she'd fallen in love with Xander.

It was a tragic tale, a cautionary tale, one still whispered about in their colony in Brazil, though of course never to Xander's face. Esperanza had been the bright, captivating daughter of Karyo, their capoeira master, whom Xander had gone to live with at six years old when his father remarried and his dead wife's offspring was banished from his new wife's sight.

The five of them practically grew up together, there in that joyless compound and its morbid array of weaponry. No one ever knew what happened to Karyo's wife or if he'd even had one; no one cared. The *Ikati* cared only that their human pet kept his mouth shut and kept churning out trained killers like the ocean churns out waves. And so he did. Karyo was a brilliant teacher. His students were brilliantly Gifted. Everyone was brilliantly pleased.

Everyone except Xander and Esperanza, who, as the years progressed, in between his grueling training and her schooling and subsequent betrothal to an older man she'd never met, had somehow found the time to fall in love.

It was said later that it had been inevitable. Take a damaged, wrong-headed boy like Alexander Luna—warped beyond repair by his father's savage beatings, beatings that were soon transferred to his wife when he saw how quickly Xander toed the line when his mother's pain was used as a deterrent—and put him in the path of temptation, give him a taste of forbidden fruit, as it were…what did anyone expect?

For years, Xander and Esperanza kept their secret well hidden. As of course they should. Had the relationship been discovered sooner, the *Ikati* would have moved to terminate it.

Permanently.

But as it will, fate had its own cruel way of dealing with things.

Karyo discovered them. The details of how and where, the other members of the Syndicate never knew. The only sure thing was the fact of Esperanza's lovely, broken body discovered one misty morning lying in a pool of her own blood on the cobblestones in front of the training center.

Her neck was broken. She'd been thrown from the roof.

Julian, Mateo, and Tomás had all been there when Xander found her, when he confronted Karyo, who stood by watching, his face like a slab of stone.

"You killed her!" Xander screamed at the wiry old man.

"Better that than see her defiled by an animal," Karyo coldly responded.

And then, at sixteen, Xander committed murder for the first time.

Afterward he was inconsolable. The *Ikati* didn't much care that he'd killed Karyo. Humans, after all, were expendable. His own father, however, cared about the gossip it brought and came to the compound to give Xander a ruthless beating.

Then Xander committed his second murder.

After his father's death—judged by the Assembly a justifiable homicide for reasons of self-defense—his half brother, Alejandro, had been installed as the new Alpha of Manaus, and Xander had forsaken any shred of mercy, had slaughtered any tender feeling within himself that would ever allow him to feel pain, love, or happiness.

He died.

He walked, he talked, he became the best assassin the tribe had ever seen. But he was nothing more than a corpse. A zombie.

"FUBAR," Julian muttered under his breath, then blew out a long, hard breath. "All right, show me the way to this joint. I suppose I could use a watered-down drink." He banked hard left, turning down a one-way street, scaring pedestrians into squealing, scattered flight. "But don't expect me to like it. And you're paying, Tomás."

The first of the screams erupted from somewhere above them.

Even before the screams Mateo sensed it, and Julian and Tomás weren't far behind. As they made their way across the dance floor, watching humans skitter away like frightened puppies before them, the stinging hot recognition that there were three other *Ikati* males somewhere in this club hit all three of them like a heavyweight punch.

They looked up in the direction of the screams at the exact moment three huge, black animals reared up on their hind legs and set broad paws on the metal railing of the second-floor balcony. Yellow eyes, unblinking; long tails, snaking back and forth; fangs exposed, white and sharp. One of them roared a challenge.

"Aw, shit," said Julian. "I knew this was a bad idea."

The music thumped, the lights flashed, and it didn't seem as if anyone on the dance floor noticed what was happening up above until the bodies started dropping.

Suddenly there was a stampede. People couldn't get away fast enough. Screaming and shoving, they formed a

thronging mob that began to flow down the stairs. Some
didn't bother with the stairs and leapt clear over the rail-
ings, flailing, to land atop unsuspecting revelers below. It was
chaos.

"We can't Shift!" hollered Mateo over the music when
he smelled Tomás's intention as a gunpowder sting in the
back of his throat. "If the Assembly finds out we Shifted in
public—"

Tomás sank to a crouch, baring his teeth. "Special situation. And rules are made to be broken."

"No, Tomás!" Mateo shouted, gripping Tomás's fore-
arm. "No!"

Too late. Above the screams, the music, and the pounding of footsteps, a sickening crackle was heard as bone and
tendon transformed, then the loud rip of fabric as it was
shredded to pieces. On his other side, Julian Shifted as well,
the most enormous of any *Ikati* he'd ever seen—his huge,
wedge-shaped head with its tapering nose and long, silver
whiskers was above shoulder high to his own. He made a
grizzly bear look like a Chihuahua. Clothing lay in tatters
around his feet.

The three *Ikati* balancing on their forepaws on the railing above took it as an invitation. They pushed off with powerful hind legs and sailed over the second-story railing to
land in a noiseless, menacing crouch only a few yards away
on the dance floor that was now cleared of anything but the
six of them.

In unison, the five panthers crouched, sprang, crashed
into one another head-on in midair. They went tumbling
over the floor, clawing and biting, their snarling loud and
vicious enough to drown the music.

Then to his great horror, Mateo spotted a human female in the far corner of the club crouched beneath a cocktail table, holding something out in her trembling hand. His first thought was that it was a gun. He focused, then almost wished it was.

A small metal object, a glowing blue screen.

A phone.

A camera.

The entire thing was being filmed.

TWENTY-FOUR

"Why do you suppose it is," said Bartleby to Xander as they sat on the back lawn of the safe house in two folding chairs, "that you have kept me in your employ all these years?"

Xander sighed, feeling a lecture coming on. He stared up at the glimmering Milky Way peeking through rifts in the rolling, velvet dark clouds above. The cool tang of moisture in the air and the tingle of electricity that lifted the little hairs on his arms told him it was going to rain, and soon. He said, "Because of your charm and good looks, obviously."

But that wasn't it. The truth of Xander's loyalty to the doctor lay somewhere far darker.

Bartleby had been Karyo's personal physician. In desperation—his mind unable to grasp that Esperanza was gone, really *gone*—Xander had called him on that terrible day so long ago, had watched through his tears as the doctor examined her, met Xander's gaze, shook his head in wordless confirmation of the horrible truth.

He'd been kind that day, the only kind older male Xander had ever known, human or otherwise. Since then the Syndicate had kept Bartleby as their own physician. He was trusted and respected and had saved their lives on more than one occasion.

Because he knew the doctor so well, Xander didn't even have to look over to feel the sour look his old friend shot him.

"Wrong. Because I'm the only person who's ever honest with you," the doctor declared.

That definitely sounded like a pending lecture. Xander watched the neighbor's beagle stare at him through a small hole in the back fence, fifty yards away. The dog was growling and trembling, and Xander had half a mind to get up from his chair and really give the dumb beast something to tremble about. "Don't want to hear it, Doc."

"I know you don't want to hear it, Alexander, but the truth might do you a bit of good."

Bartleby stood from the chair, stretched his arms overhead, rolled his neck back and forth. Then he turned and stared down at Xander, his balding head crowned by a corona of stars.

"But first, a question."

Xander braced himself.

"Are you in love with Morgan?"

He drained the last of the bottle of very fine scotch he'd been drinking for the last hour as they sat looking at the gathering storm and swallowed around the searing lump in his throat. "You've been watching too many soap operas."

"Well," Bartleby persisted after a moment when Xander said nothing more, "*are* you?"

"You're a pushy bastard, you know that?" Xander grumbled and climbed to his feet. He tossed the empty scotch bottle at the back fence and was gratified to hear the beagle go yelping off into the night when it shattered against the wood.

"And you're avoiding the question." The doctor peered up at him through his spectacles and adjusted his bow tie. "Not that I blame you, mind you, but I think if you get some clarity on this issue it will make things easier for everyone involved."

"Clarity," he repeated disdainfully, drawing the three syllables out. "Now I *know* you've been watching too many soap operas."

"My point is," continued Bartleby, undeterred by Xander's sarcasm, "that you can't decide what you're going to do until you are clear on what exactly it is you feel for this female of yours."

"Mark," Xander corrected, hard. "Job. Pigeon."

"Mmmhmmm," said the doctor.

"And there is no decision regarding what I'm going to *do*. I'm going to…"

What? He was going to what?

Bartleby raised his eyebrows, waiting. Xander made a cutting motion across his throat with a hand.

"Please," scoffed the doctor. "You're not going to hurt a hair on her head."

"I don't even want to hear your theory on why that might be."

"Because you're in love with her! Even your Blood knows you're in love with her! Why don't you just admit it!"

Xander sighed and massaged his temples. "You're fired."

"Again?"

It was a running joke between them. Xander had fired Bartleby at least three dozen times over the last twenty years. It never stuck. The old man had grown on him like a barnacle.

In what he hoped would be the final period in the sentence of this unwanted conversation, Xander turned and made his way back toward the house. A breeze rustled through the trees along the fence, a rumble of thunder rattled the windows. Just as he lifted his hand to open the back door, Bartleby said, "She asked me not to give her any more drugs."

Xander spun around, shocked. "What? I thought you said it helped her. I thought you said she was in pain—"

"She is. And will be for the next two days." He tipped his head back and looked at Xander through his bifocals. "But she said she didn't want you to have any more excuses."

Xander's chest tightened. His lungs refused to expand or contract. His voice came low and wary. "Excuses for what?"

The doctor smiled. "For not finishing what you started earlier."

Dear, sweet lord in heaven. He stood there, staggered, while Bartleby gazed at him, serene as Buddha, moonlight shining soft off his spectacles. A low rumble of thunder broke the silence, and somewhere off in the distance, a dog began to howl.

"Go on, then." The doctor waved him away and sat back down in his chair. He stretched his legs out over the grass and tipped his head up to the sky just in time to watch the moon slip behind a thundercloud. "Go find clarity, my friend, and maybe with it you'll find some peace of mind. After all these years, you deserve it."

For not finishing what you started.

It repeated in Xander's head like a broken record as he slowly made his way through the dark house, down two sets of stairs, to the bedroom level where he'd woken up early this morning. He paused at the landing, staring down the long corridor to the door at the end where he'd left Morgan—fled her—his heart pounding so hard he'd thought it might break through his ribs and explode, killing him.

She was delirious. She was joking. She was just trying to get a rise out of him so she could torment him later about his stupidity.

Right?

Her scent teased the air, wound up inside his nose, luring, tugging him forward. The energy of her Fever throbbed in exquisite, crackling pulses over his skin. Knowing exactly what waited for him behind that door, he wondered if this was God's way of punishing him for everything bad he'd done in his life. It definitely felt like punishment.

A little moan from behind her closed door, and again he thought he would die. Desire flamed in him, hot as the sun, consuming. A noise like tremendous static roared in his ears.

His feet moved him down the hall.

He placed his open palms on the closed door and stood there with his arms braced against it for seconds, minutes, what seemed like hours, fighting against every raging instinct in his body.

You will not do this. You will maintain control. There's no going back from something like this, there's no good that can come of it—

The low moan came again, and his will began to fracture. He put his hand on the knob and slowly turned it.

The scent that slipped from the open door was so heady and overwhelming he was rocked back on his heels as it hit him in wave after wave of perfumed beauty. Ferocious, the animal inside him hissed and writhed to be free.

Xander pushed the door open farther. When he saw what was inside he froze.

The room was in shambles. Broken things lay scattered across the floor: a lamp, a yellow vase, a flat-screen television that had hung above the narrow credenza. A framed oil had been shredded to pieces, tossed to a corner. The bedsheets were in disarray, the satin comforter lay in a rumpled pile at the foot of the bed...the bed itself was empty. Frantic, his gaze darted over the darkened room. Morgan wasn't on the floor, in the chair, anywhere he could see—

From the adjoining bathroom there came the sound of running water, followed very quickly thereafter by a loud crash.

He bolted across the room, threw open the bathroom door, and came to a skidding halt beside the sink. She was crouched on the tiled floor of the shower—naked, shivering, knees drawn up to her chin—as water poured all over her, poured all over the shards of frosted glass that lay scattered around her.

The shower door was demolished. Ragged bits of glass stuck out from the metal frame like shark's teeth. A few of them fell tinkling to the tile.

"Morgan!" He frantically searched for blood, for signs she'd been hurt. "What happened? Did you fall? Are you—"

She glanced up at him through dark lashes, and her agonized look punched an aching hole into the very center of his chest.

"It h-hurts less if I b-break something," she said, teeth chattering.

The relief that washed over him was so strong he had to close his eyes for a moment to manage it. "You did this on purpose."

He opened his eyes to find her nodding into her knees, her dark hair fanned over her shoulders and back, dripping wet. "S-stupid d-*door*."

Steam curled up in feathered wisps from her shoulders, and as he reached in to turn off the faucet he was shocked to realize the water pouring over her was ice-cold. The steam came from her *skin*.

She was burning up.

"You need the morphine," he growled, reaching for one of the towels that hung on a rod beside the sink. He knelt beside her and carefully draped it over her shoulders.

She pushed it away. "Water," she said, her voice cracking. "I need cold water."

Reaching an arm up to the faucet, she made a move to stand but staggered. Before she could fall Xander had her in his arms, had her—shivering, wet, and burning—pressed against his chest. He kept his eyes on the ruined door as he maneuvered them past it, avoiding jagged glass and the view of her naked breasts, both inches away. He snatched the other towel from the rack and awkwardly tried to pull it over her while she squirmed in his arms.

God, the fragrance of her—the *heat*—

"Stop fighting me," he said through clenched teeth.

"*You* stop fighting *me!*"

"Jesus, woman. You'll be the death of me!"

He carried her, writhing, to the bed, where he gently laid her down atop the sheets. The towels were still covering her—mostly covering her—but he quickly shook out the comforter and laid it over her wet body. She kicked it off.

"Too *hot*," she moaned, writhing.

He stood there above her with his hands laced behind his neck—as if that could keep them from reaching for her—while she tossed and thrashed and begged him to put her back in the shower to cool her off.

It wasn't cold water she needed. Xander knew what she needed. It was the same thing every female in her Fever needed in order to ease the pain.

A male. She needed to mate.

She refused the drugs…

…for not finishing what you started…

Don't do it, Alexander. Don't do it. You'll hate yourself afterward—she'll hate you afterward. You know it's stupid, it's dangerous, it's—

She looked up at him—her eyes incandescent, bright as stars—and spoke his name. He'd never seen such raw need, such hunger. It made his legs go numb.

Slowly, feeling like he was outside himself, he knelt beside the bed. He reached for her arm, and it didn't surprise him at all that his hand shook. His fingers brushed her skin—hot, so hot—and she shuddered, made a little animal mewl in the back of her throat.

It's just the Fever, she's not in her right mind—

"I didn't take the drugs," she panted. "I didn't want them."

"I know," he whispered, fighting against every impulse in his body to hold her, kiss her, love her—

She rolled to her side and the towels fell away, exposing her breasts and belly, her lovely rounded hips. He squeezed his eyes shut. Her hand, hot and shaking, touched the side of her face.

Very throaty, Morgan said, "You know what I want. And I know you want it, too. That's why you're here, isn't it?"

Xander moaned, low, a tortured sound. She inched nearer. Her hand slid down to his chest, her fingers curled around the front of his shirt. She tugged at it.

"I can't—can't take advantage of you when you're like this," he said, his voice hoarse, his nose filled with her heady scent as she pulled him closer, closer—

"I know," she murmured, coaxing, "you're the gentleman assassin. You'd kill me before you'd take advantage of me. But I…" Her hands cradled his face. Her soft lips touched his cheek, his chin, his mouth, and his will began to crack. "…I can take advantage of *you*. We can hate each other later, Xander, but for one night, just for tonight, let's be the best of friends."

She slid her tongue between his lips, and then he shattered.

He crushed her to him. She was velvet and fire and soft curves, shaking in his arms, pulling his head down hard with both hands wrapped around his neck and her body arched against him. He couldn't breathe, he couldn't move, he couldn't even think. All he could do was *feel*, so he let the fury in his heart and body take over.

As another boom of thunder shook the windows in the house above, Xander pushed her back against the mattress, stared down, panting, at her. She stared back with that same hungry look, expectant now, her lips parted, cherry red against her white teeth. Her hair spread dark and curling wet over the pillow; her hands reached up to touch the hem of his shirt, to tug it free from the waist of his pants.

He tore it off. He couldn't get everything off fast enough. She helped him, shaking, both of them shaking and panting and kissing all the while, touching and exploring while his clothes fell to the floor. He rolled on top of her, and she ran her hands over his back, stroking the scars there with something like reverence.

"My beautiful assassin," she said against his mouth, her voice so tender it hurt.

"No," he said, hoarse, his palm cupped around her face. "Tonight I'm not an assassin. Tonight it's only Alexander and Morgan. Tonight it's only me and you." He kissed her, hard and delicious, and her legs lifted to wrap around his waist.

She writhed against him, ready, but he wasn't ready. He wanted to taste and explore and take his sweet time, because he knew this was only a one-time pass; tomorrow it would be over. Tomorrow she would be back to hating him as she had from the beginning.

But tonight...

He tangled his hands in her hair, pulled her head back to expose her throat. He kissed from the soft spot below her ear all the way to her collarbone, skipping over the cold links of the damned collar, wanting to rip it from her neck, free her from it. He stroked his tongue over the hollow in her throat, over the pulse that pounded there, her skin hot silk against his lips. She made a little noise of impatience and rocked her hips against his, the heat and wetness of her sex pressed against his erection, but he ignored her demands, focused instead on the beautiful curve of her breast in his palm, the weight of it, the satin texture and color, caramel tipped in raspberry.

He took her nipple into his mouth, sucking with his lips, lapping with his tongue. She gasped and arched against him, slid her hands into his hair. He bit down gently and she moaned his name.

It made his heart pound even faster. He wanted to hear her do it again.

He drew his tongue between her breasts, cupping them together in his palms, teasing her nipples with his thumbs. He slid his hands to her slender waist, over her soft belly, down her curved hips, letting his gaze follow his hands, learning her secrets, learning all those hidden places he'd fantasized about since the day they met.

The first of the rain began, drumming on the roof three stories above, just as he spotted a small, dark mark on her right hip: a tattoo. A fresh tattoo, he could tell from the ink. He moved to it, kissing his way down her body, then paused when he was close enough to discern it in the dim room.

In perfect, cursive letters, it read: *Live free or die.*

His breath left his lungs in a rush. For a moment he felt sick; he felt light-headed. Reeling with guilt and sudden self-loathing, he closed his eyes and pressed his forehead against her soft stomach.

And of course she knew. Beautiful Morgan, mysterious Morgan, rash, defiant, intuitive Morgan—she felt his pain and understood.

"Xander. Xander. *Xander,*" she murmured, as if to say, *Stop that, stay with me, look at me.* She stroked her hands over his hair, and he lifted his head to stare up into her eyes. Vivid and searching, they were full of some emotion that made his heart ache. Softly she said, "We both know how to live broken. But the past is just that. Past. And the future is out of our hands. Neither one has a place here with us now. Let it all go and be with me."

She slid down the bed when he stayed frozen with guilt and cupped his face in her hands. She said his name again, whispered it against his mouth, kissed him so gently he was gripped by a sudden, terrible urge to possess her, all of her, not just her body but her heart and her soul and every thought she might ever think and every emotion she might ever feel, all of it just so he could keep her here with him like this—soft and vulnerable and, yes, *loving*—forever.

Drawn into the rightness of her lips, Xander kissed her back. Warm and soft and tentative, it opened a door inside him that had been locked for years.

"Love me," she whispered into his ear, and the door blew wide open.

He was lost now; he knew it. Somewhere in the darkest corner of his heart he'd known it all along. So he no longer bothered to hold anything back.

He let himself fall.

He reared up on his knees and stared down at her, let his hands drift over her body, his gaze following every stroke and kneading pinch. She arched to meet his touch. She gave a little, soft sigh, and her eyes closed.

He stroked his hands down her parted thighs, bent to test the tender flesh there with his teeth, with his tongue. She moaned and her hands were in his hair again, trembling. He licked his way down to where he really wanted to put his mouth, taking his time, teasing her because he loved the little moans and the rocking motion her hips made. He stopped just inches away from the most sensitive, secret part of her, a low growl rising in the back of his throat.

Ambrosia. Sugar and spices and hothouse flowers...she smelled like heaven.

He spread her open with his thumbs and blew a breath over her wet lips, just to make her say his name again, which she did. He dipped his head and tasted her, and they both moaned at the same time.

Delicious. Perfect. Sweet and succulent and mine, mine, MINE—

Heavy-handed instinct pounded through him. The beast in him took over.

He slid a finger inside her, abrupt, invasive. He sucked at her greedily, grazing her swollen nub with his teeth, licking her all over. He didn't know if he was being gentle enough. He didn't know how long he could hold himself back; she was moaning and rocking and gasping his name, her nails dug into his shoulders. With his free hand he cupped her breast, pinched the hard nipple, watched the effect it had on her, and reveled in it.

"Come for me," he growled, and slid another finger inside her.

She cried out, her thighs trembling against his shoulders, her body taut as a bowstring beneath him. She froze for a moment and even seemed to stop breathing. Then it began, a little throbbing clench against the fingers he'd thrust inside her, and she shuddered.

"Xander, God, Xander," she gasped, writhing.

With an animal snarl, he drew himself up her body and plunged himself deep inside her.

She cried out again, so did he. Fire and satin and tight wetness, she was like nothing he'd ever felt, and her orgasm was still coming, gripping the length of him buried inside her, a delicious friction that threatened to send him over the edge too soon—too soon—

Panting, he bent and kissed her lips. "I'm too close—I have to slow—stop—"

"No!" she groaned. "Don't stop! We'll do it again—and again—just don't stop yet—"

"Morgan—"

"Xander." She wrapped her legs around his waist, her arms around his shoulders. She looked up into his eyes and took him deep with a feminine, fluid motion of her pelvis. *"Don't stop."*

She kissed him and rocked beneath him and with her hips coaxed his body to where it wanted to go. He began to thrust, a primal motion disconnected from his will, which wanted him to slow, to be gentle—

Morgan moaned her approval beneath him. His hips took over and he thrust harder.

He heard thunder, he heard rain, he heard the metal headboard smacking against the wall, sending repetitive, hollow clanging through the room. He braced a hand against it, gripped Morgan's hip in his other hand, and lifted her up so only her shoulders were on the bed. So deep, so deep, he didn't think he could go any deeper—

"I'm going to come again," she breathed. She gripped his arms, meeting every thrust of his hips with one of her own, staring up at him with those searching eyes that carved a hole into his heart. "Come with me. Come with me, Xander."

Breathing hard, sweat blooming over his entire body, he let go of the headboard and clasped her hips hard in both hands. He plunged into her again and again, wilder and harder, with every thrust losing himself to her and the storm and the magic they made together, here in the succoring dark.

"*Amada mio*," he hissed through clenched teeth, teetering on the edge as a wave of heat surged up his spine. Every muscle in his body flexed. "*Eu me comprometo a você.*"

She stiffened and cried out, her head tipped back into the pillows. His eyes slid closed and he heard a roar, only dimly aware it had come from him. Pleasure, searing white, rocketed through him and he jerked, emptying himself inside her, surging again and again as his orgasm tore his breath and every coherent thought away. For a blinding moment there was nothing but the two of them, joined as one. It spun on and on, dreamlike, and then—

He collapsed on top of her. Shaking. Panting. Wordless. He buried his face into her neck.

Her arms came around his shoulders. She cradled him, murmured soft things into his hair that he could not comprehend, so great were his agony and his bliss. He drifted on a current of gratitude so pure it was almost sweet.

She had let a monster into the most precious part of her, had reminded him of what it was to feel passion and pleasure and tenderness, had given him a glimpse of things he didn't deserve.

Happiness.

Hope.

He wanted to tell her that, wanted to say, *You have shown me the way back from hell.* But there was a terrible pressure in his chest and a stinging in his eyes and a tightness in his throat that threatened to choke him if he opened his mouth.

"It's all right," she murmured, knowing him already too well. "We're safe from the world now, for a little while.

We can have this. It doesn't have to change anything. We can have our night and go back to who we were tomorrow. Just for tonight, we can have that different life we always wanted."

He stayed silent, while inside he wept.

TWENTY-FIVE

Eliana watched in horror as a wet and bloodied D staggered into the cool, candlelit opulence of her father's private library.

"Demetrius!" She leapt from her chair, scattering the newspaper she'd been reading in a flurry across the floor.

He was bare-chested and panting, his face was bruised, gashes on his neck oozed blood in dark rivulets that coated his tattooed chest in a sheen of red. On his left bicep just below the Eye of Horus a deep, ragged wound exposed muscle and a sliver of bloodied white: bone.

"What happened?" demanded Dominus, rising from his desk.

"There were three new males—like the one we saw at the Vatican—three of them were at Alien—"

"Three more!" said Dominus, astonished.

"You were in a fight!" cried Eliana. She rushed to his side. "My God, your arm—"

"You never said anything about three other males," Dominus interjected, stepping around the desk, his tone menacing. "You told me you only dreamt of the female and the orange-eyed male—"

"Father! He's hurt!" Eliana protested, hearing the threat in his voice. How could he be so insensitive?

"Where are Constantine and Felix?" His gaze flickered over the warrior, assessing.

Wincing as he stood straighter, D said, "Here. In the infirmary. Lix got it pretty bad—"

"So what you are telling me," Dominus interrupted, "is that *all* my *Bellatorum* were bested by these interlopers?" A frigid breeze swept through the room. With a sneer, he said, "I'd no idea you were all so weak."

D stiffened and so did Eliana. Calling a warrior weak was the worst possible insult. Had it been anyone but the King, the offender would have been dead by now. She couldn't understand why he was treating D this way. What was *wrong* with him?

With a clenched jaw D replied, "They got it just as bad as we did." His voice turned scornful. "*Sire.*"

Their mutual enmity crackled in the air, raising the hair on her arms. As her father stepped forward with a snarl, Eliana made a split-second decision and stepped between the two bristling males.

"I'm sure the particulars of who injured whom can be sorted out later," she said quietly, gazing calmly at her father. For her own selfish reasons she didn't want to see done to D what had been done to Celian, and she knew his only chance was if she intervened. "The good news is the *Bellatorum* are alive, and the sooner they get to healing, the sooner they can go back out and take care of the problem. So perhaps since Demetrius was kind enough to come straight here to inform you of the problem, he might now be allowed to go to the infirmary and have his injuries tended?"

A beat of silence. Her father's wolf-eyed examination of her face.

For the millionth time, she was thankful he couldn't read her mind. The impenetrable veil that surrounded her thoughts was another of her Gifts, one she secretly referred to as The Blessing because she had far too many dangerous secrets, secrets that other members of her colony couldn't afford to keep.

Not the least of which was her forbidden fascination with D.

Finally Dominus smiled, then sent a flinty gaze to the bloodied warrior in the doorway. "Is there any imminent danger?"

D shook his head. "No. They don't know where we are. They couldn't follow us after the *polizia* arrived—"

"*Polizia?*" Eliana gasped. He might as well have said *butcher*. Over the past few years alone, six of her kin had been killed by the local police. It had been all over the newspapers; the outside world assumed some deranged exotic animal enthusiast was releasing captive panthers into the suburbs.

D nodded, his gaze averted from hers. "Shots were fired. We got out unscathed, but one of them may have been hit—"

"You're hardly unscathed!" she protested.

Dominus said, "Unscathed or not, you and the rest of the *Bellatorum* will find yourselves well enough to attend the *Purgare*, Demetrius. Do I make myself clear?"

D inhaled sharply and grimaced, a look she had seen on a hundred different faces when her father was displeased. No one ever spoke of it—no one dared—but Eliana had a dark suspicion that her father's mind reading wasn't his most potent Gift.

"Perfectly," said D between clenched teeth. He gave a stiff, pained bow.

"Eliana." Her father turned to her with a small smile, some unknown intent burning bright in his eyes. "Would you be so kind as to accompany Demetrius to the infirmary? He looks like he could use some assistance."

D blanched. "I'm completely capable of—"

"Of course," Eliana said, cutting off D's growled retort. She was anxious to make sure the warrior was all right, even more anxious to have a few moments alone with him, though of course he would practically ignore her, as usual.

With a clenched jaw, D bowed again, turned, and limped from the room. Her father drew her nearer, and they watched D's muscled legs take him, haltingly, down the shadowed corridor.

"And see if you can get any more information from him," her father murmured, eyes narrowed.

She sighed, suddenly mournful. "I don't know why you think I'd be able to. He can't stand me. Haven't you noticed? He can barely even *look* at me."

Her father looked pleased by that and also inexplicably amused. She understood the pleasure; it was, after all, forbidden for the two of them to be together. He was not of her caste and so there was no chance for them, and that's how it had always been, forever. She'd resigned herself to it. But the amusement? What could it mean?

Still smiling, her father said, "Yes. There's really nothing worse than wanting something and knowing you can never have it."

And everything inside of her ground to a halt.

D *wanted* her?

A million memories flashed through her mind, a million looks he'd sent her, hot and fleeting, his jaw as hard as the flat line of his mouth. The way he recoiled whenever she came near, the way he sometimes flushed. She'd always thought he despised her, she'd felt certain that jagged ache in her belly when he was near was only one-sided, but... could it be?

She stood breathless with the possibility. But what was she willing—if anything—to do about it?

"Don't look so surprised, my dear," said Dominus, drolly. "It's rather obvious to everyone but you." His face darkened. "But there's something else going on with him lately. I think he's hiding something." He glanced at her. His dark brows cast his eyes in shadow, but they glinted with a new cunning. "This requires a more delicate touch than I have patience for today. Go along and see if he'll tell you anything interesting, Ana. See if he'll tell you anything he won't tell me."

He gave her a gentle push when she stood frozen like a stalagmite to the floor.

"Yes, yes," she murmured, elated, trying very hard not to show it. "I'll...go...talk to him. Now."

Then she remembered how to move her feet and used them to walk slowly away, her step casual and slow because she felt the weight of her father's gaze on her back like two heavy, cold hands.

Lix and Constantine were already laid out on two cots in the infirmary when D limped in, muttering curses.

"*Quomodo ire?*" said Constantine, lifting his head from the pillow to watch D stumble toward another empty cot at the end of the long, brightly lit room. It was one of the only bright places in the catacombs, awash in harsh fluorescent lights run by generator. The *Bellatorum* were too few and too valuable to Dominus to be subjected to surgery by candlelight.

Celian lay on his stomach on a cot near the door, loudly snoring into his pillow.

"It went just wonderfully," spat D, and dropped to the bed. The metal frame squealed and nearly buckled under his full weight. *It went exactly as it always does,* he thought, furious. *The King was so understanding and supportive and thankful and even gave me a big hug at the end.* He stared up at the curved ceiling and did not look over when Eliana's soft step echoed through the room.

"*Principessa,*" said Constantine and Lix in unison, surprised.

"No, don't get up, *Bellatorum,*" she insisted, "please. Rest yourselves."

D closed his eyes, unwilling to watch them—injured— try to rise and bow to her, unwilling to watch her approach. Just having her scent in his nose and her lilting voice in his ears was torture enough. Pain throbbed through his body, and he knew it wasn't just because of his injuries.

Someone new entered the room. He cracked open an eye to see one of the *Servorum*—young, female—carrying a tray of bandages, salves, and metal instruments. She went to work on Lix first, as his leg was badly shredded, nearly bitten clean through by that huge male at the club. The *principessa* murmured something to her. He caught *good care* and *please*. Clenching his teeth, D closed his eyes again. He heard movement, low conversation, the sound of Lix's barked curses as his wounds were attended.

A hanging curtain was drawn around the bed with a swish of rings on a metal rod, and then Eliana was beside him. "I need to take a look at that arm," she said quietly.

His eyes snapped open. He stared up at her. Light flared like a nimbus around her head, obscuring her face. He tried to sit up, but she pushed him back down with a palm flat on the center of his chest, and the skin-on-skin contact was so unexpected it stunned him into submission.

"It's fine," he said, hoarse, pulse thudding in his ears.

"Puh."

He didn't know what that meant, so he kept his mouth shut and concentrated on not looking at her. He stared at the bare rock wall, brown and bumpy, but God, how he wanted to look at her. Pixielike and delicate with the elongated limbs and grace of a ballerina and that shock of choppy dark hair that on anyone else would have looked masculine but on her only served to more perfectly highlight the flawless symmetry of her features, those almond doe eyes—

No. He didn't need to look at her. He'd already memorized it all. He closed his eyes, and beneath his lids, she danced.

Her fingers on his skin, tentative, a flash of pain that stabbed through his gut and made him shudder as she probed the deep wound on his bicep. Her gentle sigh, a tingle as her breath, featherlight, brushed his bare chest. He heard a clatter as she pulled over a rolling metal tray of supplies from its position against the wall.

"I'd ask you if it hurts, but I already know what the answer will be."

She sounded dissatisfied. He wondered why, then screamed silently at himself to *stop* wondering why.

He breathed in. He breathed out. He breathed in again. She touched a pad soaked in alcohol to the edges of the wound on his arm and he flinched—even that minor contact, even when it brought pain—it was too much. It made him think of things he could never have. It made him *ache*.

He brushed her hand away. "Leave it," he said, hard. "Have the *Servus* do it. You shouldn't even be in here. This is no place for you."

There was a moment of silence, then she sighed. "Oh, Demetrius."

Startled by the quiet sorrow in her voice, he opened his eyes and found her staring at him, a furrow between her arched brows. She sat down on a stool beside the bed and dropped her gaze. Her lashes made a curving dark smudge against her cheeks.

"What have I done to so offend you?" she whispered.

He could not have been more astounded. "Offend me? *Offend* me?"

He repeated it twice because he couldn't think of a single coherent thing to say. She'd never done anything to offend him. On the contrary, she'd done everything to *entice* him, to enthrall him, to make him dream of her in night-sweat agony—

"I know I've done something because you are always so... so cold, but I don't know what it could have been because I only want to..." She glanced up, her gaze lingered on his lips, and his stomach clenched to a fist. "My father has asked me to attend you, and so I must, but…but if you wish it I can tell him…that you're fine, that you don't need my help—"

D couldn't help himself. He leaned over and grasped her wrist. "I do want you—I want you—your *help*," he corrected, stumbling over his words in his rush to get them out, "and you have done nothing to offend me. On my life, I swear it."

She sucked in a quick breath. Her eyes widened, her mouth made an "o" of surprise. The look on her face was pure revelation, amazement that turned quickly to something that had he not known better he would have thought was desire.

His body didn't know the difference, however. Heat saturated the air between them, rushed pounding to his groin.

He released her wrist as if her skin burned him, which it did. He lay back against the cool sheets and closed his eyes once more, thinking that of all the things her father could have done to torture him, this was by far the worst.

Forbidden fruit was always the most tempting.

The clock on the wall, ticking, the low drone of fresh air that was pumped through the catacombs, Lix and Constantine flirting unabashedly with the *Servus* at the other end of the room. Then Eliana's voice, low and tentative. "I…I'll need to clean the wound first, before I can suture it. It will hurt, but I'll try and be as gentle as I can. All right?"

He nodded, then because he didn't want her to think he was being cold, added, "Yes. Please. Thank you."

He hissed a breath through his teeth. What a disaster.

She worked on him a while in silence, wiping away blood and raindrops with soft towels, cleaning shallow scratches with pads dipped in alcohol, trailing her bare fingers over his skin. Pain and yearning lashed through him hot as the sun, and he wondered if she knew exactly what she was doing to him as she leaned over him, warming him with her scent and her nearness, addling him as if he'd had too much to drink.

He stiffened with a thought: Was this a trick? Was Dominus using her to—

"Here come the sutures," she murmured. "Please hold as still as you can."

The pain of the needle was nothing compared to the pain of lying half-naked next to her, thinking illicit thoughts, wondering if she was, even now, manipulating him. A little noise escaped his throat, and she froze, misunderstanding.

"I'm fine," he said, jaw tight. He nodded to emphasize it. "Solid as a rock. Go on."

She did. It was quiet between them for a moment, but not peaceful. He managed to keep his breathing even with an astonishingly difficult exertion of will.

He said, "When did you learn to do—this?"

She made a sound in her throat. Though sardonic, it was low and feminine and sent a rash of gooseflesh up his spine.

"Caesar used to pick a lot of fights when he was younger. He never won. But he didn't want Dominus to know, so I had to be the one to fix him up. I learned early on to make sutures so fine they'd never even leave a scar." Her voice took on a melancholy edge. "Learning new things has always helped me pass the time."

There was a beat as he processed that. His regard for her stood in exact opposition to his loathing for her brother, who, though highborn, was unGifted. And the kind of coward that had to pick on others to make himself feel bigger.

He wondered what it had been like for her, kept like a prized, exotic bird in a cage her entire life, cleaning up her brother's messes.

"You call your father Dominus?"

"Not to his face."

He cracked an eye open to gauge her expression. Her shell-pink lips were twisted in a little, secret smile. She caught him looking and her smile deepened. "No one calls him anything to his face, isn't that right?"

He let his silence be his answer.

She shrugged, a movement that seemed both casual and full of meaning. "I know. You can't talk to me. *No one* can talk to me. I don't blame you, I know what he's like."

"*Do* you?" he said harshly, before he could think. The minute it left his mouth he bit his lip, cursing himself. Her smile vanished.

"I...actually, no," she said, very softly, surprising him. "He's my father, of course I love him, but..." She trailed off, biting her lip. "But over the last few years he's seemed so... he seems..." She glanced up at him, questioning, and he found himself wondering again if this was some trick to get him to reveal himself.

"He is as he has always been to me," he said coolly.

Her expression soured. She cinched one of the sutures tight, and he sucked in a breath, surprised—it *hurt*.

"I'm going to tell you a little secret, Demetrius," she said through stiff lips, looking askance at him through her lashes as she continued to sew up his arm. "You can trust me. I can't make you believe that, of course, but—" She sat up a little straighter. "Wait, no, I can!" She sounded excited. "If I tell you something that no one else knows, something that would get me in trouble—*serious* trouble—if it's found out, will you trust me?"

He narrowed his eyes. "Whatever you're about to say—*don't.*"

She leaned in, so close she could have kissed him, so close he saw every detail of her poreless skin, the line of her dark lashes, the perfect Cupid's bow of her upper lip—

"I'm not a virgin," she whispered, staring deep into his eyes.

He suddenly felt as if he were conducting fire through his veins. Hearing that word on her lips—*virgin*—was like an alcoholic hearing the words *happy hour.* His mouth literally watered.

Then his rational mind kicked in: Was she toying with him?

"I'm not in the mood for games, little girl," he growled low in his throat.

At that, her brows lifted. "Little girl?" She smiled again, a woman's smile, knowing and mysterious. "I'm twenty-three, only eight years younger than you." Her voice dropped an octave. "And you're not looking at me like you think I'm a little girl, Demetrius."

Face flaming, he sat up abruptly, the last of his patience shredded. "What is this?" he hissed.

"This is me being honest with you," she said, unperturbed, surprising him again. This time because she wasn't afraid of him. *Everyone* was afraid of him. "I doubt you get much of that, so you might be unfamiliar with it, but, quite frankly, I think you could use a little more honesty in your life."

"You do realize just talking to me like this could *get me killed.*" Anger threaded through his voice, though he was careful to keep it low so the others didn't hear.

"And me?" She was defiant under his fierce gaze. Unblinking. "You don't think there's any danger for me?"

"You're the King's daughter," he snapped, livid now. "You'll be given a slap on the hand. I'll have mine cut *off*."

Inexplicably, her gaze dropped to his lips. "No, you won't."

He stared at her, waiting.

She met his gaze again and softly said, "I would never let him hurt you. Seeing you is the only thing I have to look forward to around here."

His heart dissolved to his toes.

"Stop this," he said through gritted teeth.

She went on calmly as though he hadn't spoken. "I was seventeen. It was one of the *Legiones*. Varro was his name. He was twenty. It was after the Christmas *Purgare*. He was killed a week later in a street fight; they said he was drinking—"

D suddenly realized what she was talking about. "Jesus!"

"—which made sense because he liked to drink. He was a troublemaker—"

He seized her wrists. "Stop!" he hissed close to her face.

"—and I was probably attracted to that because I've always had to be such a perfect little princess, so sheltered and doted over even though I wasn't born a boy, the eldest—"

He jerked from the bed and planted his boots on the ground, towering over her, shocked at what was coming out of her mouth, helpless to stop it. "Please—"

"—even though I killed my mother coming out when I was born—"

"Eliana!" he begged.

"—I was still put on a pedestal and given every privilege, but if it was ever known that I'd given away my virginity to someone outside my own caste I'd probably be floating down the Tiber on the next *Purgare* with all those other unfortunates who didn't make the Transition."

He couldn't breathe. He stared down at her, frozen.

"So now you know something about me." She was breathing a little too hard, her head tipped back, her eyes glittering dark. "Now you know a secret that could get *me* killed. And don't fool yourself, Demetrius. He would kill me. I'm his favorite, I'm his prize, but there is nothing more important to him than honor. Not even me. I may not know much about him, but *that* I know to the marrow of my bones."

With a fluid turn of her wrists, she released herself from his grasp, stood, and stepped back. She smoothed her hands down the front of her simple black dress, ran a shaking hand through her hair. Then she pulled her shoulders back and jerked a thumb at the cot. "Lie down. I'm not finished with that arm."

Dazed, speechless, he did as he was told. He felt as if he'd just been run over by a truck.

The sting of the needle again, the pull of thread. "So," she said, curtly, after a long silence. "Do we understand one another?"

He sensed diminutive life watching them from the carved rock ceiling far above, a spider crouched in shadow, spinning her web. He felt real surprise; no insects lived in the catacombs and no animals ever ventured near, save the feral cats. They all knew what lived in the perpetual darkness here, they all fled. Except for that sole, intrepid arachnid above, tenacious as the feline before him.

"You'd make a great general, you know that?" he finally said, grudgingly admiring.

"I'll take that as a yes."

His internal compass began to slowly adjust, magneti-
cally drawn to her as if the earth had rotated on its axis
and she was—suddenly, absolutely—true north. He was a
thinker, an analyzer, an *over*analyzer, as cold and calculated
as a computer, but the proximity of Eliana crashed his moth-
erboard and caused all his circuits to short.

Danger! a distant alarm screamed, flashing red. *Danger!*
Abort!

D cleared his throat. "I remember him."

Eliana's fingers, deft and warm, froze on his arm.

"Varro. He was strong. Brave. Reckless, but brave."

A shadow crossed her face. Sorrow? he wondered.
Regret? Did she miss him? The thought made him simmer
with jealousy and brought out his ruthless side. "I would've
thought you'd choose someone a little prettier, though," he
snapped. "He was no Constantine, that's for sure."

She glanced at his chest, his neck, the silver rings in his
eyebrow. Their gazes met again. Her answer came very low.
"Some girls don't want a boyfriend who's prettier than they
are. Some girls like tattoos. And piercings."

Heat passed between them again, bright as sunlight, just
as burning. There was a pull, a softening, and he felt himself slipping, felt the room tilt. His heart rate skyrocketed.
"Eliana—"

"What's it like?" she interrupted.

Thrown off balance—again—he frowned. "What's what
like?"

She dropped her gaze to his arm, watching intently as
an errant drop of rain still beaded on his skin began to track
slowly over his bicep. "Outside."

He drew a breath through his nose, calculating. She
could be manipulating him still. She could be testing him,

or using him—though she could have anyone she wanted to use, why him?—she could merely be making conversation.

But...no. Eliana didn't make small talk. And he sensed on a cellular level that he wasn't being manipulated; he had a sharp nose for that, having served her father for so many years.

She really wanted to know. And after he told her...she was going to ask him to take her outside. He knew it. He *knew* it.

He should get up right now, go back to his own bed, let his wounds heal by themselves and never, ever speak to her again. Yes, he should do that.

Instead, he opened his mouth and in a husky, halting voice said, "It's...everything."

Her breathing stilled. She met his gaze.

"It's terrible and harsh and cruel. It's beautiful and grand and dazzling. It's..." he faltered, searching, "...it's heaven and hell and your worst nightmare and your fondest dream, all rolled into one. And you never know what's going to come next because *anything* could, and that's what makes it so goddamn amazing. And so awful."

Their gazes held, the moment deepened. Her fingers kept a faint, lovely pressure on his arm. She said, "I want to see it."

"You can't."

"I want to."

"Your father—"

"What my father doesn't know," she said, dark eyes glittering, "won't hurt him."

His heart was suddenly like a wild thing in his chest, gnawing, twisting. She wasn't talking only about going outside. She was talking about him. About *them.*

"You don't mean that," he said, his voice low and husky.

"Don't I?" She didn't blink. He saw something in her face he'd never seen before: steel.

There was no mistaking that voice, that look. He was well acquainted with it, having lived in silent mutiny his entire life. But there was something else too, some ineffable quality, longing or loneliness that stirred the beast inside him to frenzy.

Was he wrong? Was he misinterpreting this entire thing? Was this just—wish fulfillment on his part?

He had to know. He had to. He had to make her say it.

"You can have any male in this colony, *principessa*. There are a thousand males who'd fight for the privilege, a thousand more who'd take a death sentence just to kiss your hand. You don't need me."

Her face softened. "I don't want them. I don't want them, Demetrius. I want you."

A war erupted inside his body. Withering heat, storm and fury, a lightning strike of desire against his fortress of good sense, blasting chunks of caution away.

They stared at one another a long, long while, silent, her fingers on his arm, his eyes searching her face, the sounds of other conversations unheard. He knew she smelled his pleasure and hunger, knew she felt his pulse throbbing beneath his skin, and knew without doubt that though it was stupid and dangerous and utterly forbidden, he was going to take this precious thing being offered to him because he wanted it with every atom of his being, and had for years.

Very low, he said, "When?"

Her eyes flared. "After the *Purgare*. He'll be distracted. He's always distracted then. I'll meet you at the sunken church."

That pull between them again, stronger. The need to kiss her was almost overwhelming. To manage it he said something—anything. "Wear black."

She broke into a smile, brilliant, heartbreaking. "Don't I always?"

Then she leaned over and kissed him on the lips—swift and soft as goose down, leaving him reeling—and went back to work on his arm.

TWENTY-SIX

When Morgan awoke sometime in the night—disoriented, thirsty, and sore—she was for a moment completely unfamiliar with her surroundings. The darkened room, the strange bed, the heavy leg flung over both of hers—

Memory came hurtling back, sharp as daggers.

She turned her head very carefully on the pillow, and there he was beside her, large and male and slumbering.

Xander. Her killer. Her lover.

She wasn't sure which was worse.

She didn't regret it, though, not really. Well, not yet. Because the Fever still burned like a swallowed sun within her, and even now her hormones were rising again like a tide. She let herself be carried with it, floating toward the inevitable, toward what they'd done over and over until finally they both had fallen into exhausted sleep and the pain she'd felt had—at last—subsided.

Now it was back. She needed him again. She'd worry about the consequences later.

She shifted beneath him, rolled to her side, pushed him to his back with a hand flat on his chest. He made a low sound in his throat and stretched—she felt it, the way his muscles lengthened and pulled taut and shivered, then relaxed—but didn't wake. She nuzzled her nose into his neck, and his arm wrapped around her shoulders, pulling her closer.

He mumbled something in his sleep that sounded like her name.

She trailed her fingers over the expanse of his chest, over the field of hatch marks, over the bare mark above his left nipple she assumed would soon be filled. She pushed the thought aside and let her fingers drift farther down, over the bandage still wrapped around his waist, over the hard, flat muscles of his lower belly, over the downy trail of hair that led from his belly button straight down to the curling soft patch of hair and the erection already hot and throbbing stiff against her hand.

"I told you that you'd be the death of me," he murmured into her hair. She couldn't help it: she giggled.

"All's fair in love and war," she quipped.

She felt him come wide awake. She looked up into his eyes, warm, endless amber, shadowed by those dark lashes.

"We're not at war," he said, very serious, and brushed a lock of hair from her forehead.

"Not until the sun's up," she reminded him, stroking her fingertips down his hard shaft. The skin there was so soft, the softest thing she'd ever felt, like silk poured over steel.

He shuddered, frowning, and pulled her closer. "Not ever," he whispered into her ear.

She found a rhythm with her hand, coaxing a response from him, coaxing his hips into that push and pull that she so loved, the masculinity of it, the raw power. He pressed a kiss to her temple, her cheek. She stroked him until his breathing was ragged and he kissed her on the mouth, hard and demanding.

He said something to her in that language of his—musical, magical Portuguese—and her hand slowed. Her fingers gently squeezed and released, exploring, teasing. He groaned, his face turned to her hair.

"What does that mean?"

"It means you're driving me *insane.*"

"No, what you just said." She ran her fingers over a throbbing vein on the underside of his shaft, around and around the full head atop, and he groaned again, louder. Her own breathing grew irregular; she loved him like this. Like putty in her hands. *Hard* putty.

He framed her face in his hands, kissed her again, deeply. "It means," he said, almost panting, "don't stop."

It had been far too long to simply mean "don't stop," but she didn't push it—she was distracted now by his hand on her breast, pinching her nipple, drifting down to stroke the soft wetness between her legs.

She gasped when his finger slid inside her, and she saw the flash of his teeth when he grinned.

"Two can play at this game, love."

It thrilled her, hearing that word on his lips. *Love.* She hid it by turning her face to his chest and nipping his nipple. He jerked and yelped, "Ow!"

She flicked her tongue out and licked where her teeth had just been, sucking and kissing, stroking with her tongue. He relaxed back against the mattress with a low moan, and she kept on, kissing her way down his chest, running her hands over his skin, rubbing her cheek against his belly, reticulated muscles hard against her face. He shuddered as she kissed him there, brushing her lips across the ridges of his abs, dipping her tongue into his belly button. He slid his hands into her hair, pushed it off her face so he could watch her.

She looked up at him, mischievous. As he watched, stiff and breathless, eyes wide, she trailed her tongue lower, lower, until she felt his heat and hardness against the column of her throat. Holding his gaze, she cupped him in her palm, licked her lips, and watched him tremble.

"Should I keep going?" she whispered, teasing, already knowing what his answer would be before he nodded emphatically *yes.*

She dipped her chin, flicked her tongue out, and slid it over and around that hard, velvet head. He gasped. Then she lowered her head and took him into her mouth, sucking and greedy and wanting to hear him moan.

He did, loudly. He arched from the mattress, his head kicked back into the pillow, his hands tightened in her hair, trembling, hot. He moaned her name and she loved the sound of it, loved the power she felt, the way he moved, instinctive and helpless in her hands, in her mouth, the taste of him and his heat and smoky scent—

He dragged her atop him and without preliminaries, with only a swift, hard motion of his hips, impaled her so deep their pelvic bones met.

Morgan heard him moan her name again, shuddering beneath her, but she was somewhere else, drunk with pleasure and heat and this new curling hunger that rose up inside her like a wave, like a demon, dark and devouring. She began to move atop him, rocking, making tiny circles with her pelvis, her head tipped back and her eyes closed, the air cool against her burning skin, the smell of rain and lightning in the air. His hands lifted to cup her breasts, he murmured something unintelligible. It sounded like a plea. She didn't stop; she couldn't. She was outside herself. She was floating.

He sat up and grasped her around the waist. She grabbed hold of his shoulders and took him even deeper inside, met his thrusts with her own, arched back against his knees, opening to him like a flower. Her hair spilled down his spread legs.

White fire and aching, friction and stroking, the sound of his beautiful voice muffled against her breasts as he kissed her there, urgent, warm lips on her nipples, drawing against her skin. The culmination was rushing at her, bright as a comet, and she was gasping, shaking, saying his name—

"Look at me," he said, hoarse, and cupped her face in his hands.

Morgan opened her eyes. He was gazing up at her, a look of something like anguish on his beautiful face. "Oh—God—I'm almost—I'm—"

"I want to see you. I want to watch you. Let me watch it happen." His voice was soft, so soft, almost as tender as his eyes, and it broke her apart.

Half moan, half sob, and she was over the edge, shuddering and shattering and staring down into his face, alarmed at the moisture swimming in her eyes, helpless to stop it.

"Yes, baby, yes," he whispered, reverent, as her body clenched around his.

He was so beautiful to her then, rapt and wide-eyed at the pleasure he was witnessing—the pleasure he was giving her—that it hurt—it *hurt*. It burned like acid in her throat.

She started to cry.

"Goddammit," she sobbed, burying her face in his shoulder.

He stilled, tightened his arms around her. "It's okay," he whispered, stroking her hair. "It's going to be okay."

"No, it's *not*," she said, sobbing harder. "It's *not* going to be okay! Don't say that! Don't lie to me!"

"Shhh."

He cradled her, he rocked her, he stroked his hands down her back and smoothed her hair. All she could do was hide her face and shake in his arms. He was still inside her, still throbbing hot, unrelieved, and though she wanted to run away and hide he was so warm and so strong and so... damn...wonderful.

God, he was wonderful.

"I *h-hate* you," she sobbed against his shoulder.

"I know," he murmured, stroking her. He pressed a kiss to her hair. "I know."

He let her calm down, let the crying slow, then stop. He eased her down onto the mattress and settled beside her, brushed her tears away with his knuckles, kissed her hot cheeks. He gazed deep into her eyes and softly said, "I hate you, too, beautiful girl. So much." He brushed his lips against hers, barely stroking, tender. "So much."

She bit her lip, turned away. She couldn't take it—the emotion was too crushing, too terrible, too *much*. His hand stroked her face, he turned her back to him with gentle fingers beneath her chin.

"Don't hide from me. You don't ever have to hide when you're with me."

That horrible tightness in her chest again, the welling in her eyes. He kissed the tear that slid over her cheek, caught another with his fingertip and brushed it away. She wanted to turn away again but didn't, and he saw it, and then there was moisture in his eyes, too.

"*Tu és o amor da minha vida,*" he murmured, his voice breaking. He kissed her with a desperation that took her breath away, a desperation that was matched only by her own. She clung to him, and he moved between her legs and pushed inside her.

"Say it again," she begged, not knowing what he'd said but *knowing*, feeling as if she would drown. "Say everything. Tell me everything, Xander, tell me now, before it's too late."

And he did. His lips on hers, his body moving inside hers, his heartbeat thudding strong and erratic against her chest, he let the words pour out. Soft and broken and in a language she did not understand, it poured out of him and over her and burned her soul to cinders.

Later, much later, as dawn crept pink and lavender over the hills of the Aventine, Xander woke alone.

TWENTY-SEVEN

Once upon a time, when she was a little girl no taller than the weathered brick lip of the Drowning Well, Morgan's mother had told her a story.

"I'm going to tell you a story," she announced with that faraway look in her eye that sometimes made Morgan slightly afraid for a reason she didn't understand. The song she'd been singing died on her lips as if the wood fairies had snatched it right out of her mouth.

They were walking hand in hand through hazy morning sunshine, knee-deep in the drifts of wild heather that grew like weeds on the brink of the New Forest, watching tiny white butterflies flit with bumpy grace around bluebells and buttercups, listening to the sweet symphony of birdsong and breezes whisper through pines.

"A thtory," Morgan whispered, enthralled, with the baby-girl lisp she hadn't shed until she was six, watching her mother's coffin being lowered into a rime of hard winter ground. She looked up at her mother—alive still on that verdant spring morning—and saw what she always saw: a fairy-tale princess with skin white as milk and a bittersweet smile and a galaxy of sorrow in her leaf-green eyes.

Even as a small child, Morgan recognized that her mother was beautiful, and very, very sad.

"There once lived a girl named Kalamazoo," her mother began, and here Morgan giggled, liking the sound of the name. Her mother's pale gaze slanted down to hers, and she began again, her lips tilted up at the corners. "Kalamazoo," she said, "was a headstrong girl, ahead of her time, very smart and strong and independent. She was pretty, too— some even said she was blessed by angels on the day she was born, so pretty she was—and curious, and kind."

Her mother's voice took on a darker tone. As if the sky itself knew what was coming, a cloud passed over the sun. "But Kalamazoo had one…fatal…flaw."

They slowed and then stopped beside the huge, rotting trunk of an ancient pine, overgrown with lichen and ivy, felled by some long-ago storm. Her mother lifted her up, set her teetering on its edge so they were almost at eye level with one another, held her hands around her waist to steady her until her little bare feet found their balance over the rough bark. Her mother's feet were bare too; none of them ever wore shoes in the woods.

"She *wanted*," her mother said with deep solemnity, gaz- ing into Morgan's eyes. "She had everything, but she wanted other things, anything she didn't have. Her hair was dark and she wanted it to be gold, the sky was clear and she wanted

it to rain, her home was in the woods and she wanted—
she so badly wanted—to live in the city. She wanted to be a
girl who spoke exotic languages and danced the Argentine
tango with a handsome stranger in a smoky bar and was able
to say blithe, self-possessed things like, 'Oh, thank you for
the lovely invitation, but I'm jetting off to Cannes this week-
end for the festival.' Kalamazoo dreamed of all the things
she didn't have and went around all the time with her soul
lusting so badly after all those unhad things that it hung out
from her body like an untucked shirt.

"And that," said her mother ominously, "is why the goblins were able to get her."

Morgan's eyes widened. "Goblinth?" she whispered.

Her mother nodded. "Goblins, you see, aren't like us.
They don't eat regular food. They have no use for meat and
milk and sweets. What they eat…"

Morgan's little heart pounded in her chest.

Her mother leaned closer. "…are souls."

Though it was warm, Morgan shivered, wishing she
could tuck her soul down somewhere safer inside her where
the goblins couldn't get it.

"But they can't just *take* our souls. Oh, no, that's not how
it works at all! They have to make us *give* our souls away,
freely. And do you know how they do that?"

Morgan stuck her thumb in her mouth and furiously
sucked on it.

In an empty, leaden voice, her mother said, "Hope.
They prey on our hope. Sweeter than honey and more
heady than wine, hope is the lure they use. They whisper in
our ears that all those things we so desperately want we can
someday have, and so we go around lusting and dreaming
and letting our souls drag us around with want until finally

we're so tormented we don't notice our soul has slid right out of our body like a snail slides out of its shell and we've been carved hollow.

"And that's what happened to the lovely Kalamazoo. Inch by inch, day by day, hope by hope, her soul slipped away and the goblins devoured every last morsel of it. Without her soul, the poor girl quickly wasted away and died, and when they buried her, nothing would grow around her grave, not even a milkweed, because anyone who dies without a soul is cursed forever."

Imagining the goblins and the grave and the barren ground, Morgan squeaked in terror.

Her mother lifted her up. Morgan nestled trembling against her chest, hid her face in her mother's soft hair. They began the long walk back to Sommerley.

"Hope is a drug, my love," her mother murmured gently in her ear. "Hope is a tragedy. It will haunt you with its bittersweet perfume and addle your senses and ultimately drive you mad. Creatures like us cannot afford the insanity of hope, because everything we are and ever will be can be found within fifty miles of where we stand now. There can be no more for us. So watch your soul carefully, sweet girl. Watch that you don't give the goblins what they hunger for. Watch for hope within yourself and don't be afraid to do what Kalamazoo didn't: crush it."

Morgan had been hardly more than a baby then, but she remembered the story of Kalamazoo as vivid as fireworks against the night sky, and now—sitting cross-legged on the dewy back lawn of the safe house, wretched with Fever and heartbreak, watching the sun rise in a fiery orange ball over the eastern horizon—she knew why her mother had told it.

Because, like her, Morgan *wanted*. Maybe it was a genetic thing, passed down in her DNA, maybe it was just bad luck. But Morgan had been haunted by that old bitch Want all her life, and though her mother had tried to warn her that her very soul was in danger, she hadn't listened.

Want had done its worst. It had driven her to make the greatest mistake of her life, one with the costliest toll. And now Want's evil cousin Hope had hatched inside her like a dragon's egg and she would be devoured from the *inside*, her soul driven out to the goblins' feast.

Xander was the warmth that had incubated this terrible egg of hope. With his hands, his lips, the poetry of his words, and the glowing dark burn of his eyes, he had grown hope inside her until she could barely breathe with possibility.

What. If.

The two words by themselves were harmless. But put them together—what if?—and harmless grew fangs and sucked out all your blood.

She couldn't afford another costly mistake. She knew now what she had to do.

She heard pounding footfalls in the house, echoing through empty rooms. Her name was frantically called, faint, then closer, louder. The sound of the back door flying open, hitting the outside wall with a sharp smack that sent a tangle of sparrows shrieking from the branches of an elm into the morning sky. Heavy breathing, a long pause, then halting footsteps brushing light as butterfly wings over the grass and he was behind her. He stood there for a moment silently, and she felt the weight of his gaze like warm pressure on her back.

"What are you doing out here?" Xander murmured, his voice full of concern. "It's cold. Come inside. Come back to bed."

Come back to bed—just that was enough to make her waver. She set her teeth against the need it stirred inside her, the pain his proximity caused. The hormones of the Fever were bad enough, but her heart, oh, her heart...

"It's beautiful, isn't it?" she mused, watching the orange sunrise, watching the sky lift from purple blue to amber to brilliant pink, translucent as a jellyfish. "When I was a little girl I always wondered if sunrises looked the same everywhere else. Like on a beach in Fiji, or someplace else I'd never see...would this look just the same?"

She sensed how he tensed, heard his breathing falter, just for a second. Then he came closer and knelt down behind her on the wet grass, the scent of spice and skin and *maleness* doing its best to tear her in two.

Without touching her, his voice very low, he said, "Tell me."

God, to have someone know you like this. Without a cross word from her, without even a look, he *knew*. It made her shiver with misery. A night of shared breaths and bodies and heartbeats, of wordless secrets passed between flesh, and hearts can knit and fuse together like two healing fragments of splintered bone.

Morgan wondered why her mother hadn't warned her of this, too. Eviscerating this newly healed organ seemed a thing even more terrible than having a goblin devour your soul.

"What happened last night...this...thing...between us..."

She faltered, breathless, struggling. Xander's hand pressed against her lower back, slid under her hair, spread warmth over the space between her shoulder blades. His thumb began a slow tracery of her spine, and she curled her bare toes into the wet grass. A ladybug landed on her instep and began a clumsy, zigzagging amble over her foot. It didn't tickle; she felt nothing at all.

"This can't end well. There are no happy endings for people like us, Xander," she whispered, staring at the sky. "We both know that."

It was a long, long while before he answered. His thumb kept a slow rhythm over her skin. When he finally spoke he sounded older, and very tired.

"Yes."

She was surprised how much that hurt, and what a relief it was he hadn't tried to lie. She bowed her head and closed her eyes. He slid his palm up her neck and cupped the base of her head with his hand.

"But we have a while yet," he said, softly pleading. "We have today, and tonight, and eight more days and nights after that. Some people live their whole lives and never get that much."

She inhaled a long, shuddering breath, and then his hands were in her hair and his lips were on her shoulder, her neck, her cheek. She braced against it, trying not to crack, trying to push him away, but then he took her in his arms and clasped her against his chest and she broke, ashamed and enraged that there was nothing to be done about it all but cry.

"Let me go—I can't—we can't—"

She couldn't get it out, but he knew. He knew what she meant.

"One more day, then," he urged, cupping her face in his hands. His eyes burned hot and desperate, brilliant as dying suns. "Give me one more day, just until the Fever breaks—"

"No! I'm already too—"

He kissed her, hard, cut her off before she could say *too far gone. I'm already too far gone.* He kissed her as if it were the last time he'd kiss anyone ever again, and it muddled her brain and ignited the Fever until all her *nos* were crisped to ash in the inferno of her desire for him.

"*One,*" she panted, breaking away. "When the Fever breaks—"

"It will be over," he promised, gathering her in his arms. "It will be over and we'll never talk about it again."

She was nodding, she was crying, she was trying to crush the horrible, rushing onslaught of adrenaline that made her heart pound and her blood boil dry.

Hope, she thought, delirious. *You evil bastard. One more day, and then I'll drive a stake through your fucking heart.*

Xander put an arm around her back and another hooked behind her knees, and he lifted her off the grass in one swift move as if she weighed nothing, nothing at all. He brushed his lips against her forehead, tucked her against him, and ran back to the house with her cradled gently in his arms like a treasure, like something fragile and precious and fleeting, a broken-winged sparrow almost healed enough to fly.

Mateo was jolted awake by the loud, echoing clang of a metal door slamming shut.

Pain throbbed through his shoulder and back, the cold floor beneath him leached the warmth from his body, the sharp, acrid tang of alcohol and urine burned his nostrils. He opened his eyes and stared in blank incomprehension at his unfamiliar surroundings.

Cement block walls on three sides, a barred metal sliding door on the fourth, a cracked cement floor with a round center drain. Rows of glaring fluorescent lights shone down from the ceiling overhead.

His mouth went dry as bone.

He was in a cell. More correctly—a *cage*.

He leapt in one swift motion to all four paws and stood tense and bristling in the center of the square cage, testing the sour air with his nose, gauging the danger with all of his senses. Threads of faraway conversation flitted to his ears, disjointed words that were muffled by the low drone of an ancient air conditioner and the whir of a helicopter hovering unseen somewhere far above the roof. He picked out several words—*astonishing, investigation, specimen, tests*—noting the fact that they were in English but concentrating more keenly on the tone of excitement in the speakers' voices.

The cage was bad enough, but that excitement boded even worse.

His gaze swept the sterile corridor beyond the narrowly spaced bars of the sliding door. He saw a stone floor, a few empty cages just beyond that were replicas of his own, and not much else. The full horror of his situation descended on him with breathtaking clarity, and he stood fixed, his mind a screaming tangle of memories, calculations, plans.

He remembered the three enemy *Ikati* males, he remembered the fight at the club, the chaos, the screams, the girl with the cellular phone, the police…his heart froze.

The police. Gunshots.

Julian.

Julian had been shot. He'd gone down on the dance floor in a spray of crimson blood while Mateo and Tomás snarled in rage and leapt at the shooter and the other *Ikati* males fled. They'd mauled the police officer beyond recognition, but there were others there, more shouting, uniformed humans with guns and batons and the Tasers that had ultimately brought him and Tomás down with jarring shocks from behind. He didn't remember anything after that, and now there were only questions left to taunt him.

Was Julian still alive? Where was Tomás? What were the owners of those voices going to do to them?

Pain flared in his shoulder as he limped to the front of the cage. His arm felt nearly torn from the socket—one of those feral males had sunk his fangs into it and given a great, whipping shake of his head—but it would heal faster when he was in his natural form. Not that he'd be able to Shift back to human, even if he wanted to. The change wouldn't come when there was any injury; even the smallest cut would prevent it. And he definitely wasn't going to call the Shift while in captivity, even if he stayed here long enough to fully heal. His captors couldn't see what he really was. His own life—and that of Julian and Tomás—depended upon it. One of his kind had never—*never*—been taken alive by humans. He knew without question that should it come down to it, should he be unable to find a way to escape, he would have to kill himself.

If necessary, he would rip out an important artery with his own teeth.

He eased silently to the front of the cell, ears flat against his head, scanning the walls and ceiling for any sign of surveillance cameras. There were none, and nothing else modern either. This facility looked and smelled half a century old. It wasn't a zoo, that much was clear, though a musty whiff of long-vanished primates emanated from moist cracks in the floor. Apes, he thought. Gorillas and orangutans. Other animals, too, living unseen nearby. A confusion of rodent and mammalian scents crowded his nose, but beneath it all there lingered a curious scent of decay. No, not decay, exactly, it was colder and more acrid, more like...death.

A jolt of fear rocked him with the realization that this was probably an animal shelter.

Judging by the smell of it, a *kill* shelter.

An angry, low growl rumbled through his chest. It echoed through the empty cage with an eerie, hitching twang and was immediately answered by another just like it, somewhere close.

Mateo's heart went into overdrive. He called a greeting with a low, huffing chirrup and limped over the cold cement to the front of the cage. His gaze darted over the opposite cages until suddenly he saw at the far end of the long corridor a sight that eased his heart rate, if not the churning chaos of his mind.

The hulking black figure of Tomás stared back at him with fierce, storm-lit eyes from behind the narrow bars of his own cage.

Mateo made a soft, disgruntled whine low in his throat— *can you believe this shit?*—and Tomás answered back with a clipped chirrup of frustration. Claw marks scored a ragged, red path down the side of his tapering nose, but otherwise he appeared unhurt. He reared up silently on his hind legs and, long tail snaking back and forth behind him, tested the strength of the barred door with his large, padded paws. It rattled and flexed under his weight but didn't give, and Tomás dropped back to the cement, growling his discontent. He began to pace back and forth in tight circles within the confines of the metal cage.

He was still pacing when the heavy door at the end of the long hallway opened and six white-coated humans walked into the room.

TWENTY-EIGHT

The female reporter on the evening news was blonde and busty and sported one of those toothy, salacious smiles perfectly suited for television. In one hand she gripped a mike, in the other, a sheaf of scribbled notes her gaze kept darting to as she reported on the headlining story. She stood in the glare of halogen lights in front of a squat, redbrick building that was windowless and ringed with a tall metal fence topped with razor wire that lent it the menacing air of a secret government facility or a sanatorium. A crowd the *polizia* was trying to herd away from the television cameras had surrounded the fence, chanting something about animal rights, while two helicopters flew overhead, raking the scene with jittering floodlights that cut through the night like white lasers and sent leaves and dust and hairdos swirling in the wake of their whirring blades.

"The injured suffered everything from broken bones to concussions in the fray," the reporter enthused, blue eyes sparkling, "and the police are not saying how these animals came to be inside one of the most popular and upscale dance clubs in the heart of Rome. Our sources are telling us there were *three more* panthers that escaped the scene and remain at large, but this hasn't been confirmed by authorities. For now all we know for sure is that the three that were captured are being held under quarantine while the decision is being made whether to transfer them to one of the euro zone's zoos or—because of the violent attack on the police officer—euthanize them."

Her smile became positively blinding. "Back to you, Reuben!"

Dominus clicked off the television with a push of a button on the remote on his desk, and the library drifted into silence. Smiling, he sat back into his chair, steepled his fingers beneath his chin, and let his gaze slowly rove over the sparsely lit chamber. The corners were all in shadow, and so was the high arch of the ceiling above, just as he preferred. Though candlelight flickered dimly from the iron braziers along the wall, most of the room was a mask of twilight, sullen and gloomy, in exact opposition to his mood.

Euthanization. How perfect. How utterly sublime.

It was an inviolable law of nature that even the most glorious creatures had their Achilles' heels. The wily fox had its eye-catching red coat, the swift hare had its tufted white tail, the grizzly bear was slow, the dolphin was trusting, the shark had to keep moving forward or perish.

For the *Ikati*, the weakness was even more profound. They could not Shift when injured. Evanescence became permanence. Mutable became fixed. Camouflage became cage.

Unless, that is, they had been inoculated against that particular ailment, as had the warrior class of the catacombs thanks to Dominus and a lifelong obsession with eradicating weakness in all its forms. Even nature itself had a weakness: science.

From behind him came the amused tenor of Silas. "It seems these interlopers won't be a problem after all, my lord. Providence is once again on our side."

Dominus didn't turn or invite him forward out of the shadows where he'd been standing for the last hour and would remain indefinitely until directed to do otherwise. He merely pushed aside the empty bowl of lamb stew he'd eaten for dinner at his desk while watching the international news and spoke to the hulking alabaster statue of Horus—god of vengeance, god of war—set directly across from him, against the wall.

"Fortune favors the bold, Silas."

And he had been bold, every day of his life. How thrilling that the culmination of all those years of boldness was so close to fruition. So, so close…

Dominus pressed a napkin to one corner of his mouth. "Has it arrived yet?"

"Not as of this afternoon, sire," Silas murmured with real regret. "However, there is the possibility of a late delivery. The courier was told to wait as long as necessary."

Dissatisfaction thrummed through him. He wanted the lab results before the *Purgare*. He wanted to be able to make an announcement that would lift all their spirits. He wanted to be able to tell everyone definitively *when* all their lives would change.

"Go and see if there is any word," Dominus instructed, pulling a thick notebook from a locked drawer in his desk. He set it carefully on the blotter and ran his fingers over the fine linen cover, darkened with use and frayed at the edges. Leather would have been more durable, but he found the idea of his life's work bound in the skin of a bovine corpse disgusting.

Silas murmured an acknowledgment and drifted silently to the door. Once there, he executed a low bow and straightened, allowing Dominus a clear view of the long, aquiline nose, the impenetrable black eyes, the small, secret smile.

Silas had good reason to smile. He alone knew the full measure of his King's plans.

"And bring that new female you acquired yesterday to the *fovea*," Dominus added, a flash of heat tightening his groin at the memory of the blonde tourist who had been snatched by one of the *Legiones* from a bar near the Pantheon. She looked a lot like the newscaster. Blonde. Busty. Stupid.

He wondered how loudly he could make her scream.

Silas bowed again and retreated silently into the opaque darkness of the winding corridor beyond the library. When he was alone, Dominus opened his notebook and began to write, his script fluid and precise:

In keeping with the results of Dodd's experiments with reproductive isolation, my calculations suggest a period of eight generations will be necessary to engender a permanent alteration in the gene pool to achieve speciation once the correct antiserum formula has been isolated and applied to the existing population. Further, through artificial insemination of stud-quality females and embryonic transfer to surrogate females we may concurrently increase the number of pure-Blood offspring, thereby exponentially expanding both breeding stock and pure-Blood subjects. In a matter of only a few generations, the enemy gene pool will be irreparably damaged and ultimately destroyed.

Along with their terrible legacy of war, ignorance, and unrelenting greed, Homo sapiens will vanish from the face of the earth forever.

Dominus set the fountain pen on the blotter, closed the notebook, and slowly exhaled.

And so their world will end, he thought with deep satisfaction, staring at Horus, *just as T. S. Eliot predicted. Not with a bang, but a whimper. And I will be the architect of it all.*

He locked the notebook away and rose, heading for the *fovea,* hoping Silas remembered to bring his favorite steel qilinbian whip along with the blonde.

The knock that came through the closed bedroom door was tentative, and so was the voice that followed it.

"Alexander," Bartleby murmured through the wood.

Xander tightened his arms around Morgan's body and pulled her closer. They'd spent the entire day in bed, making love, dozing in the semidark, not speaking of anything or anyone outside the walls of this room. He felt twilight descending outside, but he wasn't ready to get up yet. He was going to savor every last moment.

"Not a good time, Doc," said Xander quietly, looking down at Morgan's sleeping face. She still radiated the heat of the Fever, but it burned lower now. Soon it would be done...and so would they.

"I'm sorry to disturb you, but there's something you need to see." Bartleby cleared his throat, a worried sound. "It's important."

Morgan made a little noise in her sleep and burrowed closer to Xander's chest. He put his nose into the dark mass of her hair and inhaled deeply, wondering if this would be the last time he'd ever be able to do it. The thought sent a spike of pain through his chest.

"*Amada,*" he murmured. Beloved. He stroked a hand up her arm. "I need to leave for a minute."

She made another sleepy noise, protesting, and he pressed a kiss to her temple.

"I don't want to either, but I'll bring you something to eat," he whispered, nuzzling against her throat. She arched into him, responsive even when asleep, her fingers twined into his hair. He hardened instantly, eager for her—again—but there came another tentative knock on the door and he sighed.

Just a few minutes. He'd take only a few minutes, and then he'd be back, back with her scent and her skin and that slow, mischievous smile that melted his heart and inflamed his body...

He couldn't get enough of her. He couldn't imagine not being able to touch her, kiss her. Not now, not after they'd stared silently, rapt and amazed, into one another's eyes while their bodies and souls merged, over and over again. And he suspected, in a very dark, abandoned corner of his heart, he wasn't going to honor his promise to end things between them.

She would make him a liar, consequences be damned.

He pressed a quick kiss against the pulse in her throat and rose, pulling the sheet up to cover her naked body. She murmured something not quite audible—*goblins?*—then drifted back down into slumber.

He dressed quickly, strapped on the knives he was never without, and went to the door.

"I'm sorry," Bartleby said again when Xander stepped into the corridor. He shut the door softly behind him.

"What is it?"

The doctor shook his head, motioned to the stairs. "You'll want to see this." He turned and quickly made his way down the hallway with Xander close on his heels.

They climbed the stairs and entered the big media room with its somber, masculine decor of charcoal walls, black leather sofas, glass-and-stainless-steel coffee and side tables. Recessed lights in the ceiling glowed softly off the flat screen that hung above a sleek black credenza.

A large red banner across the top of the television screen read, "Rare melanistic panthers captured in vicious attack."

Xander's blood turned to ice.

And then came the grainy video captured by an eyewitness. Motion and chaos, wobbly images of a panicked crowd shoving and screaming, the impossible sight of six huge, snarling black panthers attacking one another on a dance floor. A shot rang out, then another, then one of the animals collapsed, three of them bolted, and the other two turned on the officer who'd fired and began to rip him to shreds. A solemn male voice spoke over the video.

"As you can see from this disturbing video, these animals are highly aggressive and dangerous. Wildlife experts tell us these particular animals have been living in open areas and feeding on large prey and may have even been somehow genetically enhanced, evidenced by their enormous size in comparison with the norm for the species. Like the other panthers that have been captured and killed over the past several years in this area, these nocturnal predators are so large it is unlikely a novice wildlife enthusiast was able to raise these big cats unnoticed in the middle of an urban area.

"Several members of the European Union's Wildlife Preservation Fund, including the preeminent evolutionary biologist Dr. Hermann Parnassus, are expected to arrive in Rome tomorrow to provide expert opinion and conduct testing on the animals. The authorities are urging citizens who live nearby to stay indoors until the other three panthers are captured, but even once they are the question will remain: From where did these extraordinary creatures come?"

Downstairs in the bedroom where he'd left Morgan, Xander's cell phone began to ring.

"Shit," he breathed, frozen with disbelief. Bartleby lowered the volume on the television while the screen switched to scenes of the hospital where the police officer was being treated, the facility where the animals were being held. He noted the address.

"It's them, isn't it?" Bartleby asked, glum. "Mateo and Tomás and Julian?"

Xander nodded, listening to his phone ring and ring. To his ears, the innocent sound was as ominous as a volley of gunfire. It had to be Leander. If the Assembly had seen this, they would use it as evidence of guilt. Such flagrant violations— Shifting in public, allowing it to be filmed, being captured by humans—would undoubtedly trigger three executions. *If*, that is, Mateo, Tomás, and Julian made it out of captivity.

Which they would. He would ensure that much. But he wasn't going to save them so they could then be executed, that was for sure. So he was going to save them and then... help them disappear.

It wasn't even a choice. It had to be done. And quickly.

"If they're being held it means they're hurt, which means they can't Shift," Xander said, his voice shaking. Adrenaline coursed through his veins; he wasn't sure if he could Shift either, wasn't sure if his stomach wound had entirely healed. He'd be going in blind. "Which means it's going to be tricky getting them out. We'll have to find a way in, use subterfuge, find a way to distract—"

"We don't need subterfuge," Bartleby said, blinking at him from behind his spectacles. "We'll be able to just walk right in."

Xander raised his eyebrows.

"My dear boy, I'm a *doctor*, remember? And a specialist with these particular...beasts." He patted the tufted clouds of his white hair, adjusted his bow tie, and sent him a wry smile. "Also I'm extremely handsome. And charming. I can talk the birds right out of the trees. Whoever is holding our boys simply won't be able to resist me." His smile grew wider. "Especially when presented with official documentation."

Though Xander's body was still frozen with disbelief, his mind broke through the thaw and snatched at Bartleby's genius plan. "Dr. Hermann Parnassus."

Bartleby executed a bow, managing to make it look both elegant and mocking. "At your service, sir."

Downstairs, his cell phone began to ring again. "How long do you need?"

Bartleby shrugged. "About twenty minutes. After all these years with you boys, I've become something of an expert on faking identities."

The ringing stopped. He heard a chime, indicating a new voicemail. "Make it ten," said Xander, and sprinted away, heading for the stairs.

The fog obscured almost everything and muffled all the sounds of the forest in its cool, clinging gray swirls. Eddies of it pooled around Morgan's feet as she walked over perfumed beds of leaves and bracken, searching for him, calling out his name, her voice nearly soundless in the endless mist.

She heard laughter nearby and stumbled toward it, catching her foot on the twisted root of an ancient, towering pine. She fell into a soft bed of dry needles and struggled to get up, but the needles had turned to quicksand, sucking her down, clinging to her skin, pulling, relentlessly pulling.

"Xander!" Morgan cried out helplessly, digging her fingers into the soft sand. She sank chest-deep and craned her neck, desperately searching the dark forest for him. The clawed boughs of trees loomed close and black overhead. "Xander, help me!"

And then there he was, walking slowly through the forest toward her in a ray of light, smiling, heart-stoppingly beautiful, a black-clad angel with swords sheathed on his back.

"Help me!" she gasped, the cold, wet sand sliding thick over her shoulders, her neck, her chin. It slid between her lips and she spat it out, choking. "Xander!"

He stopped beside the pool of sand and gazed down at her, beatific, his brilliant golden eyes dazzling in the gloom. "You're in too deep," he murmured, calm as morning. "A thousand kisses deep. Nothing can save you now."

The sand was in her ears, her mouth, her eyes. The silence of the forest echoed all around them. "Please!" she begged, crying, suffocating, drowning in darkness. "Please!"

"Farewell, my love," Xander crooned, smiling. "Give the devil my fond regards."

He turned and disappeared back into the forest. The darkness swallowed her whole.

"Morgan!"

She jerked up in bed, gasping, her hand at her throat. Something touched her shoulder and she reeled, swinging blindly at it.

"It's only me! Morgan! Wake up! It's me!"

Xander had her by the shoulders, shaking her awake. It took a moment before her mind registered it, recognized his voice and his scent, then she threw herself into his arms, trembling.

"It's all right," he murmured, holding her tightly against his chest. He sat on the edge of the mattress with his arms around her as she shook and blinked, trying to dispel the horrible feeling of doom. "You were having a nightmare. It was just a dream."

She squeezed her eyes shut. Just a dream. *A thousand kisses deep.*

He pressed a kiss to the top of her head. "I have to go out for a while."

She raised her head and looked into his eyes. They were worried, tense, and suddenly she was, too. "Why? What is it?"

He drew a long breath, and she edged out of his arms and sat staring at him with the sheet rucked up between them. "Mateo and Tomás and..." His voice wobbled. He swallowed and then said, "Julian. There was a fight. Those other males—they've been caught."

Morgan gasped. She drew the sheet up to her chin, the nightmare forgotten but a newer, darker dread taking hold. "Caught!"

He nodded, brushed a lock of hair from her forehead where it had fallen into her eye. "They're being held at some kind of animal shelter close by. I have to go help them.

You understand? Bartleby's coming with me. You'll be here alone for…a while." He swallowed again, looking pained.

"You don't think…" she faltered, drew her knees against her chest and hugged her arms around them, "…you don't think I'm going to run away, do you?"

He blinked, startled. "No. I know you won't—I know I can trust you. I just can't stand the thought of leaving you alone." He licked his lips and his voice dropped. "I don't want to be away from you."

Her toes curled in pleasure. She allowed herself to wallow in it for a moment while they stared at one another. She hoped to remember someday what this felt like, wishing with all her heart some tiny echo of this feeling would last. Even the faintest memory of it could sustain her for all the dark years to come.

If she survived the next week, that is. Though they'd shared something here—something precious—he was still what he was. If she didn't find the Expurgari…

That thought quashed the warm blossom of pleasure, and she looked away, heart pounding. "I'll be fine," she whispered.

He rose from the bed—he didn't seem to notice her sudden paleness—and pressed a soft, fleeting kiss to her cheek. The cell phone on the dresser began to ring.

"I know you will." He put a knuckle beneath her chin and tilted up her head so she had to look up into his face. "My fierce little warrior. But I'm not so sure I will be." His eyes darkened, and for a moment he looked haunted. Pensive, somewhere far away, he trailed his thumb slowly over her lower lip. "God, Morgan," he whispered, holding her chin, gazing down at her, "what you do to me."

The cell phone kept ringing. He never looked away from her face.

"Go," she urged, pushing his hand away. "Go get them. I'll be here when you get back."

He nodded, slowly backed away, then crossed the room and picked up the phone. He glanced at the number on the readout, then pocketed it with a dark sigh. He crossed to the door.

She said weakly, "Be careful."

He paused with his hand on the doorknob and just looked back at her. His intense gaze trailed over her face, her hair, her bare shoulders and arms above the sheet. One corner of his mouth quirked, then he pulled the door open and walked out of the room.

Midnight is historically viewed as the witching hour, when supernatural creatures appear and black magic is at its most powerful, but Xander knew from many years of experience that 3:00 a.m.—the devil's hour, deepest of the night, when all the world's abed—is best for hunting prey. Or in this case, staging a dicey, hastily conceived search and rescue operation. So it was just before 3:00 a.m. when he and Bartleby rolled to a stop in the black shadows of a grove of Roma pines that ringed a small urban park, and killed the engine of the huge black SUV he'd "appropriated" from one of his neighbors in the Aventine, a burly Russian he suspected was an arms dealer, judging by the automatic weapons—modified to high capacity—he'd found stashed in the spare tire well.

If all went well, they'd be back at the safe house in less than an hour and his neighbor would be none the wiser. If it didn't go well and he had to abandon the vehicle...his neighbor might be in a lot of trouble with the authorities.

The animal shelter was located adjacent to the ancient ruins of Largo di Torre Argentina, a large square of dirt and broken travertine pavers that hosted four crumbling Roman temples and the remains of Pompey's Theater where Julius Caesar was killed in 44 BC. Located just minutes away from landmarks such as the Piazza Navona, the Pantheon, the Colosseum, and the Campo de'Fiori, it was smack in the middle of ancient Rome.

Which posed some rather obvious problems.

"There's a lot of apartments around here," Bartleby muttered disapprovingly, peering up through the windshield at the rows of brick buildings surrounding the park. Hundreds of windows gleamed in the light from the streetlamps, windows that might be hiding watchful eyes.

"Hotels, too." Xander watched a pair of doormen at a boutique hotel across the street load luggage into an airport transfer van that idled at the curb. Two groggy tourists stumbled their way into the van, and it lurched away from the curb, coughing smoke, even before the door was shut. "But that's why it's called a clandestine op."

Bartleby lifted a pair of field glasses to his eyes and said, "Not a covert op?"

"Covert ops are about deniability," Xander explained, checking his weapons pack one last time. Inside were his daggers, a pair of wire cutters, a length of rope, a grenade, a canister smoke bomb, a lock pick, and six cyanide capsules encased in a blister pack in case the entire op went to shit. He never carried guns: too loud, too heavy, too unreliable. "Clandestine ops, on the other hand, are about secrecy."

The doctor lowered the field glasses and looked over at him. "What's the difference?"

Xander gave him a grim smile. "Politics."

Bartleby returned his smile. "Ah. Well, at least the tourist traps don't open for another six hours. Hopefully we'll be long gone by then, with no one the wiser." He pointed to something beyond the windshield, several blocks down. "They might be a problem, though."

Camped out on one side of the wire-topped fence outside the facility where his boys were being held were three mobile television trucks with their camera-topped jib arms extended high over their roofs. The press. Vultures.

"I saw them when we pulled up," Xander said. Only a few reporters were ambling around, smoking and talking on cell phones. The rest of the area was deserted. "At least the animal rights demonstrators are gone."

"They were probably too weak to stand up all night. A diet of tofu and lawn clippings will do that to a person." Bartleby leaned over, picked up a small stainless steel suitcase near his feet, and set it on his lap. He flicked two latches and popped it open, then pulled out a laminated photo ID on a lanyard, an official-looking document, and a business card—all fake, of course—and shut the case. He wound the lanyard around his neck, folded the document in fourths, put it in the front pocket of his white lab coat along with the business card, and turned to Xander.

"Ready to go balls to the walls?"

In spite of himself, Xander laughed. "You've been hanging around the Syndicate far too long, my friend."

Bartleby opened the door and stepped into the street. "I'll take that as a yes," he said, adjusting his spectacles.

He checked his wristwatch. "The taxi should be here any minute."

As if on cue, another airport transport turned the corner behind them. It crawled slowly down the street, searching for the address they'd called in to the dispatcher just moments before from one of the disposable cell phones Xander always kept handy.

"Are you sure about this, Doc?" Xander asked quietly, noting the slight tremor in the old man's hands as he watched the cab approach.

Bartleby inclined his head and gave Xander a penetrating look. "You boys are the only family I've got. You're like sons to me, and there's nothing I wouldn't do for any one of you," he said softly. Then he pursed his lips. "But don't let it go to your head. That's big enough already."

Xander saluted, suppressing a smile.

Without another word, Bartleby closed the door. He walked briskly toward the cab, whistling through his fingers. The cab jerked to a stop, and Bartleby got in. Xander watched from the shadows as the taxi slid by, made its way slowly down the street, then turned into the gated entrance in front of the shelter. The driver spoke into a wireless call box mounted on the wall in front of the gate. Nothing happened for several moments, then two armed guards appeared in the main doors of the facility and approached the taxi. One of them, tall and burly, exchanged words with Bartleby through the window, then took the documents he presented. The guard studied them briefly, then nodded.

A barked shout, then the press spilled from their mobile vans like a swarm of locusts. But too late: the taxi had already deposited the impostor Dr. Hermann Parnassus, who, striding quickly through with the steel briefcase clutched in hand, breached the inner sanctum of the facility's fenced parking lot before they could reach him. The gate swung shut with a solid *clang* behind him, and the guards, stone-faced and silent, followed Bartleby inside as the reporters shouted questions at their backs.

Xander started the car and took side streets and a back alley to skirt the facility. He parked the car behind it, close enough that he could carry his boys out if necessary, but far enough that he was out of sight of the reporters and any security cameras. He'd come in from the back or the roof, whichever was more expedient, while Bartleby provided a distraction to whomever might be inside.

It seemed simple enough. God knew he'd executed a thousand ops more dangerous and complicated than this. But a faint buzz of discontent, the feeling he was missing something, nagged at him.

As he slung the weapons pack over his shoulders and set off at a trot down the street, the soles of his shoes silent over the asphalt, the night air cool on his face, it hit him.

Armed guards. Barbed wire.

Why was an animal shelter surrounded by barbed wire?

TWENTY-NINE

Julian knew he was drugged by the way his limbs refused to answer his brain's instructions to move. He was thick-tongued and groggy, and his head weighed a thousand pounds. Maybe more.

"And the neocortex is considerably larger and more grooved than expected," a male voice was excitedly saying somewhere nearby, "surpassing that of even a human brain, indicating both advanced evolutionary status and extraordinary intelligence. But the most remarkable aspect of this mammal—and one that also suggests we are not dealing with a species we have seen before, in spite of its outward physical similarity to members of the *panthera* family—is a small organ located directly adjacent to the sinoatrial node."

There was a click, some rustlings, more clicks, then murmurs of surprise as the voice continued on.

"As you recall, the SA node serves as the natural pacemaker for the heart by sending out the electrical impulse that triggers each heartbeat. In these MRI scans you can see how deeply entangled the nerve network is between the ventricles of the heart, the SA node, and this new, unknown organ. What it suggests to me—and mind you, this is merely untested hypothesis at this point—is that this organ might be some kind of backup in case of heart failure, in the way a generator is used in the event of electrical failure. Or…" the speaker paused for dramatic effect, "…it might possibly be a separate electrical supply in and of itself."

"To power what?" chimed a voice, this one female.

Julian tried to move his head but couldn't, nor could he open his eyes. Jumbled memories surfaced. Strobing lights, pulsing music, screams.

"I don't know. It's a mystery. But since this subject"—Julian felt a touch on his spine—"who has, as you can see, been ear-tagged with the identifier TS-4187, is so badly injured, he's been selected for vivisection, which will tell us more. As you saw, the other two animals are doing much better, so other testing on them will begin as soon as Dr. Parnassus arrives."

Vivisection. Julian searched his foggy brain while the group—six people? Ten?—stood around murmuring words like *remarkable* and *breakthrough* and *discovery*. Vivisection meant…

Dissection. Dismemberment. Cutting.

While he was *alive*.

Fury gave him the strength he needed. Silently he lifted his head, opened his eyes, and looked around.

He was in a large, sterile room with white walls and white floors and shining metal surgical instruments laid out down the length of a polished steel shelf bolted to the wall like silverware on display in a wedding registry. In his animal form, he was laid out on his side on a long metal table with a tube attached with tape to a vein in his arm, a patch of fur shaved around it. The group of white-coated humans stood clustered in front of an X-ray light box on the wall, staring at the illuminated black-and-white film hanging from clips along the top.

When he let out a ear-piercing roar that shivered the rows of metal instruments and echoed through the room like cannon fire, however, they all jumped and stared at him, gasping and bug-eyed, mouths hanging open.

"Jesus Christ!" one of them shouted, lunging for a recessed panel on the wall by the door. "The anesthesia's already wearing off!" He slammed his hand against the panel, and it popped open, revealing a row of buttons. He stabbed a finger onto one of the buttons, and Julian felt a new heat surge up the vein in his arm.

He glanced down and froze, shocked and horrified by what he was seeing. Or more correctly, what he *wasn't* seeing.

His legs—both his legs—were gone.

Morgan stood silent and pensive in front of the steam-misted mirror in the bathroom at the safe house, staring down at the necklace and heavy medallion glittering gold in the palm of her hand. She knew the symbol depicted on the medallion, and seeing the large, stylized Egyptian eye made her blood run cold.

It was the same symbol the feral males at the hotel had tattooed on their massive shoulders.

She'd found it when she'd gone searching for something to wear in the dresser after her shower. Most of her luggage had been abandoned at the hotel in the rush to get Xander to the safe house, but Mateo had allowed her to bring two bags. The contents of both had been placed carefully into dresser drawers and hung in the closet by someone—it had to have been Xander—when she was sleeping.

The thought of his big hands carefully arranging her things brought a prick of tears to her eyes, and she swiped at them angrily with the back of her free hand.

Stupid. Falling for an assassin. For *her* assassin. Incredibly stupid.

She shook her head, took a deep breath, and focused again on the necklace.

It had been coiled in a corner of one of the drawers, hidden beneath the glossy silk of a red chemise. It had to be what Xander had taken from the man in white that day on the street near the Spanish Steps. She remembered Xander's kneeling down to search the clothing that feral Alpha had left behind when he'd Shifted to Vapor and disappeared over the rooftops, remembered the subtle flash of gold in his hand as he pocketed it. She'd seen that symbol somewhere else, too, she was *sure* of it, but where? Her mind, still heavy with the remnants of the Fever, refused to disclose it.

When she'd awoken, the Fever had been gone. Just... poof!...disappeared. Three days of the worst kind of hell and the sweetest taste of heaven, then done as if it had never happened at all. Except for a dullness in her brain that somehow vivid memories of Xander's beautiful, muscled body—beside hers, over hers, *inside* hers—managed easily to penetrate.

She was exhausted. Mentally, physically, emotionally depleted. Though they'd shared something she'd never thought possible, she and Xander had made a bargain, fair and square. Their—tryst? Dalliance? Mutual insanity?—was over when the Fever was over, which now it was. He was a man of his word and so would honor their agreement, but would she?

Gripped by a sudden, horrible vision of herself wailing and weeping at his feet like some pathetic castoff, hoping for some crumb of his affections, she felt a chill run down her spine.

You're in too deep. A thousand kisses deep.

She rubbed a clear circle in the middle of the steamy mirror and stared at her reflection.

Hope. Sweeter than honey and more heady than wine… her mother had been right. Hope was a drug that lured your soul right out of your body. How much of her soul had the goblins already eaten? How much did she even have left?

She felt a sharp pain in her hand and looked down to find her fingers gripped so tight around the necklace her knuckles were white. She eased her shaking fist open and gazed at the necklace, at the little red dents in her palm. In a flash of something like defiance, she wrapped the chain around her neck and fastened the clasp.

The medallion slithered down between her breasts and settled there with an ominous, foreboding *chink*. Something in the sound snapped through her haze and brought her upright.

Creaking chains and ancient metals, echoing corridors and whispering voices, darkness and incense and moldering stone. What? What was it?

She stood fixed, on the verge of it, unable to breathe. Seconds went by, minutes, but...nothing. Just that pale shadow of a memory, a skin-crawling brush of déjà vu. Suddenly she was cold, shivering. She rubbed her palms against her cheeks to get the blood back into them and reached for the towel to finish drying off from her shower.

As Morgan dried her body, as she dressed, as she moved around the darkened bedroom, tidying, stripping the bed, preparing to move all her things into one of the other unoccupied rooms, the medallion nestled heavy and cold between her breasts, and she was acutely aware of its alien weight, of how it never warmed against her skin.

The first bullet whistled by Xander's left ear, missing his face by inches. A second followed quickly after the first and embedded itself into the wall a few feet behind him with a *thunk* that dislodged a fine spray of dust from the drywall inside; a third found its target and hit him directly in the chest. He'd been prepared, so it Passed harmlessly through his body, but it still knocked the breath out of him.

Things were not going as well as planned.

Everything had been fine at the start. He'd Passed through the back wall of the facility after finding a spot where his senses told him it was safe—meaning deserted— on the other side. He'd held steady in the dark supply room he'd found himself in for just long enough to confirm the wires he'd cut in the fuse box out back were, in fact, the ones for the burglar alarm and motion detectors. He'd isolated Bartleby's voice from a babble of others somewhere near the front of the building, which meant the doctor had been successful in gaining access and now had the attention of what Xander hoped was the majority of the other humans in the building. He'd wound his way through the maze of dark hallways and rooms toward where his nose told him Tomás and Mateo were being held, sensing nothing out of the ordinary. He'd found the two of them, unattended, locked in large cages in a well-lit room and had quickly freed them and led them back the way he'd come, Mateo badly limping and silent, Tomás bristling and growling low in his throat, dripping blood from a wound on his face. They'd slunk out of the facility and into the SUV without the slightest hitch.

Simple. Everything was so simple.

Until, on his way back inside to find Julian, Xander had gone past one locked steel door and stopped short, arrested by the scent of blood.

So much of it the air was stained by its thick, rust-and-salt pungency.

A muscle in his jaw twitched as he stared at the door. He knew that like many animal shelters in Europe, shelters in Italy had a no-kill policy. Unwanted animals weren't euthanized; they were kept until adopted or sent to one of the many animal sanctuaries around the country. And in the case of animals that were mortally wounded or terminally ill, a cocktail of drugs was administered by injection for a quick, "humane" death.

So why all the blood?

He didn't bother walking through the door. He just Passed his head and shoulders through and looked around. Though the lights were out and the room was plunged in darkness broken only by the eerie blue glow of computer screens and digital readouts, he saw and smelled everything with perfect clarity and was instantly overcome by a horror so overwhelming he could not move another inch to save his life.

It was a long white room crowded with thousands of cages of every size, stacked in orderly rows one atop another, to the ceiling. Some were empty, but the ones that were occupied contained misery the likes of which he had never seen.

Hundreds of snowy white rabbits were immobilized in a long row of black plastic shoebox-size cages along the north wall, their bodies pressed by the cage on every side, their heads stuck through holes in front, their pink eyes covered in weeping sores and bloody discharge. Beside them were the cats, cramped by the dozen in breadbox-size chicken-wire cages, electrodes implanted into their skulls and wired to overhead panels, pacing listlessly or lying dead-eyed and drooling in their own waste. Along the opposite wall were the emaciated dogs huddled in the corners of their larger metal cages with every type of disfigurement: raw and bloody coats, missing limbs and eyes, open sores, no teeth, bleeding gums.

The monkeys were in the largest cages, reinforced with steel bars, like all the others barren of any food or water or even a soft place to rest their heads. With their old-man faces and keen, eloquent eyes, they were worst of all. As soon as he looked in their direction they all sent up a piercing, cage-rattling shriek loud enough to scour demons from their nests. They began to jump up and down, flail long arms, batter the bars of their cages.

All the ones that were still alive, that is. Macaque and chimpanzee and owl monkey corpses—skeletal and oddly human—littered the bottoms of cages, as worthless and forgotten as yesterday's newspaper.

The scream that tore from him came from someplace deep down in his soul that he hadn't known existed.

Death was a thing he was well accustomed to, a steadfast companion of his life for so many years it was as much a part of him as his own flesh. But *torture*...torture of thousands of innocent creatures so helpless they had no chance of escape, no ability to voice their misery and pain...this was something he'd never come face-to-face with, and his mind almost could not comprehend the evil of such a thing.

This was no animal shelter. This was an *animal testing facility.*

So humans could have their cosmetics, their perfumed soaps, their dryer sheets and sudsier shampoo, all of it paid for by the blood of millions of animals just as alive and aware and able to suffer as the keepers who mutilated and tortured them.

He ripped the solid metal door off its hinges and flung it aside. It collided with a loud, echoing crash against the corridor wall. The overhead motion-sensor lights in the testing lab blinked on, illuminating the horror in Technicolor while he ran like a madman through the room, roaring, smashing things, blind with rage. Banks of desks and computers and filing cabinets were destroyed, screw-top glass canisters in a tall, open cabinet exploded into sprays of caustic chemicals as a chair went flying into them, an island of square metal worktables in the center of the room sporting sinks and chain restraints crumpled like aluminum foil under his fists.

The monkeys shrieked bloody murder all the while, the dogs howled, the rabbits began to scream and wriggle, desperate to flee, unable even to turn their heads to look in his direction. The cats, crouched and bristling, just stared at him, ears flat against their Frankenstein heads.

Heavy footfalls and shouting voices from down the corridor told him someone was on the way. Multiple someones, most likely guards, most likely the armed ones who'd escorted Bartleby inside. Through his rage, Xander gathered his wits and removed another of his disposable cell phones from a pocket in his pants. He took photo after photo, then switched the video function to record and panned the room.

"You'll be out of here soon," he promised the screaming animals, his voice raw in his throat. "Just hang on a little while longer." He repocketed the camera and spun around just in time to see three armed guards appear in the doorway. They froze when they saw him standing amid the chaos. Like marionettes, their jaws unhinged in shock.

"*Fermo!*" one of them shouted after a moment of stunned silence. He hoisted the Glock .44 he'd drawn from the holster at his waist. The others followed suit. "*Fermo, o spariamo!*"

Stop or we'll shoot.

"Be my guest, assholes!" Xander shouted, furious. Then he lunged at them.

They got off three shots before they toppled like bowling pins under the full force of his weight. They crashed to the floor in a tangle of arms and legs. Cursing in Italian, one of the guards tried to wrench free of the stranglehold Xander had on his neck, but Xander bore down and felt bones snap with the brittleness of dry twigs. Slack-jawed, the guard fell still. The other two scrambled to their feet and started firing rounds into him, but when he leapt up, unharmed and snarling, they backed slowly away and started jabbering like frightened birds.

More running footfalls from somewhere far beyond the destroyed door. More faint shouts from unseen men. The monkeys' banshee shrieks drilled into his brain.

Xander smashed his fist into the face of the second guard, and blood spurted from his shattered nose. He slid to the floor and toppled to his side, where he lay unconscious, still as a corpse. The last guard lunged at him, but Xander was too fast, his instincts too honed. Xander had him by the throat with one hand squeezed around his larynx before the man had taken a full step, then lifted him high, entirely off the floor.

The guard clawed at his hand, but his grip didn't loosen. He tried to cry out but managed only a wheeze, eyes rolling, face beet red. His boots kicked out and met resistance: Xander's shins.

"Where are they keeping the third animal?" Xander shouted. This bastard knew everything, knew what went on in this torture chamber, and turned his eyes away for the sake of a paycheck. "The panther that was separated from the other two! Where are they keeping him?"

The guard tried frantically to escape. His eyes bulged from their sockets, veins popped out along his neck. He gasped, trying to speak. Xander heard a choked *please*, and it enraged him so much he saw red as the final shreds of his restraint began to snap.

"Oh, I'm sorry, are you in *pain?*" Xander hissed. He jerked his head toward the cages of animals. "Should we pour some toxic goo in your eyes and see if that makes it better? Or maybe slap some corrosive chemicals on your skin that will melt it away? How about a little impromptu surgery where I implant something into your skull so I can study how your brain waves spike when you're injected with a heart-stopping load of carcinogens?"

The guard took a swing, but Xander only leaned back, easily avoiding his fist.

"I've got everything I need right here to turn you into something from a horror movie, my friend, so you better start talking, and quick," he snarled.

His lips peeled back over his teeth, his canines elongated as the Shift began to pound through his blood, heating cells, electrifying. With a sound like a faint exhalation, a fine nap of black fur sprang from the pores all over his body. Amost there, *so close*, only a slight twinge in his injured side held him back from fully completing the turn and tearing the man's throat out with his fangs.

Yes, the beast in him roared, clawing just under his skin, writhing to be set free. *Yes!*

When he spoke again, his voice took on a deep, animalistic quality, coarse and barbarous, entirely inhuman. It rumbled through the room, echoing, and all the animals screamed anew.

"Where is the third panther?"

The guard stiffened, mouth gaping in a silent scream. His face darkened to purple. He released the contents of his bowels into his pants with a loud, malodorous *plfflolff!*

Xander dropped him, and the man crumpled to a heap at his feet, coughing, clutching at his throat. Boots pounded down the hallway, closer.

"Where!"

"Second floor," the terrified guard rasped. Shaking and coughing, he spat blood onto the white tile. "Surgery suite on the second floor." His eyes rolled back in their sockets, and he passed out cold.

Xander turned, ran the length of the room past the shrieking and howling and screaming and baying, and Passed through the back wall just as half a dozen more armed guards burst through the ruined doorway into the deafening chaos.

Nausea rolled through Julian in wave after hot, sickening wave. Lights strobed red and orange beneath his closed lids; he felt movement and big, gentle hands beneath his body. Sounds, warped slow, penetrated the blackness he floated in as if from somewhere very far away or underwater. There was pain, but it mostly kept far away, too, only occasionally swooping in low to nudge him with sharp talons.

He was aware of being lifted, of being spoken to, of moving swiftly through space, though how that was possible he didn't know since he was paralyzed. He didn't much care, truth be told—despite the nausea, the blackness was warm and comforting and he wasn't inclined to leave it anytime soon. After a while cool, fresh air brushed his face and he sucked it deep into his lungs.

That helped the nausea. He sank a little deeper into the comforting blackness.

"Julian!" said a male voice he vaguely recognized. Whoever it was sounded really worried. Panicked, really. The voice said, "If you die on me, I'll fucking kill you!"

Ha. Ha ha. He liked the owner of that voice, whoever it was. He drew in another breath, feeling his heartbeat slow. Liking how peaceful he suddenly felt. His body began slowly to melt.

"Julian!"

Fainter sounds reached his ears, animal sounds, low grumbling, yowling, hissing sounds, and with the sound of an engine turning over the movement changed from jerky to smooth. Something wet and rough passed over the side of his face, something wet and cold nudged his nose. For a moment he wanted to try and open his eyes, but then the darkness called once again and he turned back to it, melting, sinking, falling, surrendering happily to the endless void.

That almost-familiar beseeching voice called out his name over and over again, until, finally, it fell silent as Julian dissolved into darkness.

THIRTY

With his dead father's elaborate Victorian silver letter opener held carefully between two fingers, Dominus slit open the sealed manila envelope in his hands. The sheaf of papers from the lab in Milan that emerged from within was an inch thick, bound by a black jumbo clip at the top corner. He dismissed the bowing servant who'd brought it and without returning to his desk began quickly to skim the summary page on top.

...nucleotide represented as sample A in report successfully replaced by sample G...

As he read, the manila envelope dropped unnoticed from his fingers and silently floated in a sideways drift to the floor at his feet.

...mutation replicated in successive testing...

His heart began to pound. His gaze skipped down farther, to the bottom of the page.

...positive test results achieved.

His arms, strangely numb, lowered to his sides. He raised his head and stared at the stone statue of Horus against the wall, glowering blank-eyed into the gloom. Outside a new day was dawning, but here in the dank belly of the catacombs, darkness held fast. Twenty-five years it had taken him, but now he would rise from the darkness, take back everything that had been stolen from his kind, and rain death on that spreading stain that was humanity. All he needed now to complete his happiness was that unmated full-Blood beauty he'd seen at the Spanish Steps.

And by this time tomorrow he would have her. Demetrius's dreams had attested to that.

"My lord?" murmured Silas, emerging from his ever-present silence in the shadows of the library. He approached in a rustle of robes and the smoky tang of incense they always burned to diffuse the scent of mold that saturated everything.

"It's time, Silas," Dominus whispered, gripped suddenly by the fear that to say it aloud would jinx it. But he was a man of science, a man of action—he didn't believe in superstition. He straightened and spoke louder. His voice echoed through the room. "I've finally done it. It's time."

He turned to find Silas staring at him with a look of stunned disbelief. He sank to one knee on the stone floor, pulled the gold medallion he wore around his neck out from beneath the collar of his robe, and kissed it.

Seeing him on his knees got Dominus's mind to working. "I feel like celebrating," he announced, walking to his massive oak desk. He opened a locked drawer and carefully set the report inside. He laid his hand flat on it for a moment before locking the drawer again. "Go get that new blonde I had last night."

Still on his knees, Silas shakily replied, "She was not able to withstand your...attentions, sire. She died in the infirmary just an hour ago."

Dominus's brows rose. He gazed at his servant, silent.

"I shall find you a replacement," said Silas, rising. He bowed. "Immediately."

Dominus smiled into the gloom, victory singing through his blood.

"Make it two." He thought of the full-Blood female again—her lush body, her exotic scent, her mind a surprising, sweet tangle of brilliance and loneliness and guilt—and a surge of heat washed through the room. "And make them brunettes," he said, smiling.

Xander crouched on the balls of his feet with his back against the rough bark of a twisted umbrella pine at the top of the grassy, ruin-dotted Palatine Hill, looking out over the breathtaking view of the morning sun climbing over the Forum and Circus Maximus below. From this elevation all of Rome was laid out before him like a banquet: the six other famous hills, Vatican City, the Colosseum, the endless miles of twisting streets and red-tiled roofs, the ancient Aurelian Walls that enclosed the city, the snaking green Tiber, the surrounding countryside and far-flung, smoke-purple mountains.

It was a view fit for a king. Which was exactly why he'd chosen it.

A cool morning breeze ruffled his hair, and he closed his eyes a moment, savoring the relief it brought his overheated skin. He was drenched in sweat; the skin on the palms of his hands had blistered and rubbed raw; all his muscles ached.

Grave digging was hard work. Harder than he remembered.

From beside him Bartleby quietly said, "Are you all right?"

A quick glance left revealed the equally sweaty and disheveled doctor leaning on his shovel, gazing down at Xander with real concern in his eyes. Xander swallowed and looked away. "No," he murmured honestly. He wasn't sure if he'd ever be all right again.

The doctor's slow exhalation was almost drowned out by the harsh squawking of two ravens chasing a peregrine falcon away from their nest in one of the trees nearby. The old man slowly sank to a crouch, using the handle of his shovel for support, then sat back abruptly on the grass with a great sigh as if relieved to no longer be standing. They sat in silence for a few minutes, looking at the view, the brilliance of the rising sun, the flattened, choppy patch of disturbed grass and dirt directly in front of them that housed the shrouded remains of Julian, six feet under.

"He'd approve, I think," said Bartleby, gazing slowly around. He set the shovel down next to Xander's on the grass between them and brushed a few clinging clumps of dirt from his hands.

Xander's heart clenched in his chest as a memory seared an agonizing path through every nerve in his body. The doctor had said those exact words—with the exception of changing the *he* to *she*—the last time they'd done something like this together, nearly twenty years ago. He'd never forgotten a single detail of the day Esperanza died nor, he suspected, would he ever forget a single detail of today.

So much death. So much loss. Idly he wondered if he'd be alive in another twenty years to look back on this. He decided he hoped not.

"This is my fault," he said morosely, drowning in self-loathing.

"He was a big boy, Alexander," Bartleby answered sternly. "He made his own decisions. There was absolutely nothing you could have done to prevent him from fighting—"

"He should never have been at that bar in the first place," Xander interrupted, running a hand through the sweaty mess of his hair. "I'd never have allowed it."

"Now you're his mother?" The doctor's voice was gently chiding.

"They left the safe house because of me!" Xander exploded. He leapt to his feet in a fluid motion, adrenaline singing through his veins, his anger finally breaking free after being held in check all night. He stared down at Bartleby with flexed fists and the overwhelming need to punch something bloody. "We fought! I drove them out! *Me* and my stupid, asinine—"

"Stop it!" Bartleby snapped, rising to his feet with surprising agility. He stood in front of Xander, staring up at him with livid, blazing blue eyes. "Stop blaming yourself for everything bad that happens and twisting it around to make it your own fault! You can't control everything, Alexander, and Julian was no exception! And may I remind you because you seem to have forgotten—they *had* to leave. And not because of any fight with you."

At that, Xander shuddered. Yes, he was right. Julian, Mateo, and Tomás had to leave because there was a female in heat in the house...and he should have gone with them. He'd refused to leave Morgan alone because of what he wanted from her, because of how she made him feel and the man he thought he almost could be, a happier man, a *better* one, just by being near her, awash in her smile and her scent and the dark, tantalizing depths of her eyes.

He'd chosen Morgan, and now Julian was dead.

Bartleby narrowed his eyes at him, scrutinizing. "Whatever you're thinking, I guarantee you it's wrong."

"I'm thinking what a wonderful guy you are," Xander said between clenched teeth.

Impossibly, it brought a smile to Bartleby's face. "At least you haven't lost that charming sense of humor."

Xander growled and looked away. The morning sun was bright in his eyes—too bright—and for a moment he closed his eyes against it. Immediately, too many images flared beneath his closed lids, ghosts rising to taunt him in his misery.

Finding Julian near dead in the surgery suite at the testing facility, the chemical stink of drugs all over him, speeding away in the stolen SUV to the safe house, frantically trying to revive him even after all signs of life had disappeared. Bartleby pulling a sheet over his big friend's body, going to care for Mateo and Tomás in the impromptu infirmary he'd set up for them in the gym. Stumbling in shock out of the room in search of Morgan, only to find her gone from the room they'd shared, all her things moved out, the room sterile and clean as if she'd never been there at all. Standing outside the room she'd moved into, smelling her scent beyond the locked door.

Locked. She'd locked the door against him.

He could have easily broken it down, but he knew what she meant by it. The Fever was over. *They* were over. And in his state of anguish and utter self-loathing, it had torn a hole in him wide enough to drive a truck through. Everything good in his life inevitably ended. And the better the good thing, the more catastrophic the ending.

For every gift, an equally terrible price.

He'd decided while he and Bartleby had driven to this place in the predawn dark with Julian's shrouded body in the back of the car that he was cursed. Because of who and what he was, because of the life he'd lived, because from the very beginning he'd been unwanted, an outsider in a world he could see but never touch, his very being was tainted. Like the gentle rain that turns to ruinous floods or the morning sun that rises to scorch all the earth dry at noon or the soft breeze that becomes a hurricane, anything he touched started out fine but always turned to shit later.

Cursed.

So it was better Morgan stayed away from him. Better she wanted to stick to their agreement, better she thought he did, too, though it would kill him to even think of not being near her again, not touching her again.

Because he knew without doubt he was in love with her. He was totally gone. She infuriated him, she drove him to distraction, she baited him and challenged him and defied him, but for all that, she calmed him in a way no one ever had. And after years of his being dead, she made him feel alive.

With her, he felt...whole.

"We should get back. I need to check on Mateo and Tomás," Bartleby said, rousing Xander from his thoughts. He opened his eyes to find the doctor gazing solemnly at him, a furrow between his brows.

Xander nodded, a chill like ice spreading through his gut. He leaned down to retrieve the two shovels and handed them to Bartleby. "Give me a moment," he said.

Bartleby laid a gentle hand on his shoulder. "Take your time," he murmured with understanding, then turned and slowly walked down the sloping hill toward the car, a grave-digging shovel clasped in each hand like a pair of morbid walking sticks.

Xander stared down at the freshly disturbed patch of grass at his feet. He felt, for the first time in his adult life, fear. Mingled with regret and the kind of acid, devouring sorrow that doesn't have a name, it was almost completely debilitating. For a moment he didn't know if his lungs would remember how to expand and contract. He almost hoped they wouldn't.

How much pain can a heart take before it just stops beating? he wondered, swallowing around the flame of agony in his throat. Surely it couldn't endure much more?

"Good-bye, old friend," he said, head bowed. "I'm sorry. Wherever you are, I hope you can forgive me for all the ways I've failed you." He took a long, slow breath, then lifted his head and stared out over the sun-kissed rooftops of Rome, red and gold and glimmering in the morning light.

"Maybe I'll see you soon," he whispered.

When he and Bartleby arrived back at the safe house, he found Morgan curled up on the black leather sofa in the media room with her feet tucked beneath her body, chewing on a thumbnail as she watched television. She was so absorbed in the program, she didn't hear when he came in and stood staring silently at her from the doorway. She was dressed entirely in black, leggings and a long black cowl-neck sweater belted at the waist to make a knee-skimming dress. Her feet were bare, her hair was pulled back in a loose bun, her face was devoid of makeup.

She was, as always, breathtaking. His heart broke all over again.

"We're back," he said tonelessly, and she jumped.

"Oh!" She leapt from the couch and faced him, pale as snow, the hand at her throat shaking, pulse pounding furiously in the hollow of her neck. "I didn't—I wasn't—" she stammered, blinking, and adjusted the neckline of her sweater, closing it tightly around her throat. "I was watching TV. They said—the news said someone gave an undercover video to the press showing animal abuse at that facility…and the authorities have gone in to shut it down…" She trailed off, waiting for him to reply.

He said nothing. He'd already forgotten about the phone with the photos and video he'd dropped off early this morning at the local news offices. At this moment he could hardly remember anything at all; it took every ounce of his concentration not to cross the room and yank her into his arms. He wanted to bury his nose in her hair, bury himself in her warmth and scent and softness, cry like a baby while she held him and wiped his tears away.

"I was so worried," she murmured, staring at him, her eyes soft.

Cursed! he screamed at himself, and stayed put. He forced his face to stay in the expressionless mask it had grown accustomed to over so many years and said, "The Fever's gone, isn't it?"

She shifted her weight from one foot to another. A flush spread across her pale cheeks under the weight of his stare. She nodded, looking absolutely as miserable as he felt, and bit her lip.

Inwardly, he groaned in torture. He wanted to bite that lip himself. His hands clenched to fists at his sides, and he stood staring at her, willing himself to remain where he was until his body vibrated under the agony of push/pull, stay/go, hold/ break. But the Fever was gone, she'd locked him out of her bedroom, they had a deal, and anyway he was no good for her.

He had to let go.

Only he had no idea how he would do that when being with her suddenly seemed more important than air.

Obviously uncomfortable with his rigid silence, she tentatively said, "I didn't hear you come in last night. How... how did it go?"

"Mateo and Tomás are upstairs in the gym," he answered, his voice absolutely flat.

"Oh, Xander," Morgan breathed, visibly relaxing. "Thank God. And—and Julian?"

He looked away, ran a hand over his head. It took a few tries before he was able to mutter, "He's dead. We buried him this morning."

Her shocked gasp brought his head around. Morgan sank to the couch, a hand over her mouth, wide-eyed. "Oh my God," she said in a small voice from behind her hand. Her eyes were huge and dark. "I'm so sorry, Xander. I'm so sorry. What...what happened?"

He glanced away, unable to take the emotion on her face, let alone deal with the crushing weight of his own. It felt like someone had parked a truck on his chest. "I didn't get there in time, that's what. Bartleby says it was an overdose of Telazol, an animal tranquilizer."

She made a little noise of horror, rose quickly from the couch, and took a few steps toward him, her hands held out as if she wanted to embrace him.

He took a swift step back. "Don't," he said, hard. "Don't touch me."

She came to an abrupt halt and blinked at him, her eyes filling with tears. "It's not your fault, Xander," she whispered.

The eighteen-wheeler on his chest began to do wheelies. He closed his eyes and took deep, steady breaths, trying to block out her scent and his need for her and the awful, paralyzing reality that she didn't really want him. If she had, she'd never have locked that door. This—this was nothing but pity. How had he not seen this before?

She felt *sorry* for him.

"I know what you're thinking," she went on, moving another step closer, "and it's *not* your fault. I know how much he meant to you; I know you must have done everything you could to help him—"

"*You don't know anything!*" he shouted, all his misery and longing and rage finally boiling over. Shaking and panting, he went on, the words tumbling from his mouth before he could stop them. "Don't waste your precious time worrying about it because it's *over*! It's *all* over! There's nothing I can do to change it now, and talking about it isn't going to help! So why don't you just do what you do best and think about *yourself*! Why don't you just concentrate on your own goddamned problems and figure out how you're going to accomplish what you came here for so it's not a total waste of everyone's time and my best friend's *life*! Because if it wasn't for *you*, none of us would have been here in the first place! If it wasn't for *you* and your fucking 'different sort of life,' Julian might still be alive!"

She stood there in stunned silence, mouth agape, livid spots of red on her cheeks as if she'd just been slapped very hard across the face.

Immediately he was ashamed. Cursed and shamed and in love with a female he could never have and—oh, yes, let's not forget—was supposed to kill sometime very soon. Though obviously he wouldn't, because he *couldn't*, which was just another catastrophe waiting to happen, courtesy of Fate's unrelentingly cruel sense of humor.

"Oh, fuck it all," he spat. He turned on his heel and stalked out of the room.

In a daze, Morgan watched Xander go and felt something inside her leave with him.

If it wasn't for you, Julian might still be alive.

If she thought she had been acquainted with pain before this moment, she was wrong.

She moved in a daze to the door, unseeing, unsure of what she would do, aware only that she had to get away from this room, get away from this house, get outside into the air where she could clear her head and think and maybe release the scream that was burning a hole in her chest.

If it wasn't for you...

She found her heels where she'd left them near the dresser and slipped them on. She walked unsteadily down the corridor, then took the stairs one at a time, slowly, her legs leaden, the soles of her shoes clicking unheard against the wood. She crossed the third floor and took another set of stairs to the staged model house above, then went outside to the backyard and stood on the porch, blinking at the sun, cold with shock in spite of the warmth of the morning.

If it wasn't for you, Julian might still be alive.

He was right, of course. She realized that as she stared at the grass and the trees and the white fence and the bottom-less azure sky above, bile rising in her throat. She was the hub this entire shit storm revolved around, and she had no one to blame but herself. Wanting and wanting and wanting her whole life through, she'd dug a hole so deep there was no climbing out of it now. And everyone around her was beginning to fall in, too.

The only way out was to make it right. To do what she'd come here to do—find the Expurgari.

And then—what then? Forget she ever knew Xander?

Yes, came the sneering answer from her subconscious. *Forget him, because he thinks you killed his best friend. And sweetheart, he's probably right.*

Her eyes filled with tears, and she stifled a sob behind her hand. How much easier it would be for him now, when the time came. How much easier to slide that knife between the vertebrae in her neck.

I still have time! she thought desperately, spinning around unsteadily to stare at the house. It seemed menacing in the morning sun, full of hidden danger and a palpable charge, as if it were a giant, ticking time bomb.

As it had innumerable times since she put it on, the medallion around her neck drew her hand like a magnet. It lay stone-cold and ominous against her chest and gave her the same disquieting sense she'd had since she'd first glimpsed it that there was something here she was missing, a clue this necklace held, a puzzle piece she didn't know how to make fit. It scraped at her mind, over and over, as irritating as a fingernail scratching down a chalkboard.

The Alpha. The Expurgari.

Somehow they were related. But how? And how would she ever find him?

She stood there staring at the house as if it held some kind of answer for a long, long time, how long she didn't know. Cars passed by on the streets beyond the yard, birds sang in the trees, the mechanical thrum of a lawn mower broke the stillness of the morning. Then finally a thought occurred to her and she stood breathless with the horror of it.

She wouldn't ever find the Alpha, or the Expurgari. She was fooling herself.

And the man she was in love with…was happily going to kill her.

A shudder wracked her body. With a low moan, she dropped her head into her hands.

A clock began to chime inside the house, counting the hour in low, mournful tones. Five, six, seven…off in the distance a church bell began to ring, mirroring the chiming clock, then another, then another, faint, melancholy tolling that reached her ears from far-off churches all around the city, announcing the time.

Morgan stiffened. Her mind turned over, then her stomach. Slowly, slowly, she moved her head and gazed off into the distance, where she saw through the morning haze the enormous golden dome of St. Peter's Basilica glittering like a Fabergé egg atop the Vatican. She turned back and gazed at the safe house, at the empty façade that hid all its secrets below.

Below.

The puzzle pieces came together with a cold, solid *click.*

Though they had felt his energy diffused all around them at the Vatican, the feral Alpha had evaded detection because he wasn't in the basilica. He was *beneath* it, safely out of sight, just as hidden and sheltered as they were in the underground rooms of the safe house.

Holding her breath, she backed one step away from the house, then another. Without bothering to think, Morgan turned and ran for the back fence.

THIRTY-ONE

Over two thousand years ago, or so the story went, the first *Purgare*—Purging—was held in a secret spot on the banks of the winding Tiber river where the giant sycamore trees bend low and weep their silver-green leaves into the burbling waters near the tiny Tiberina island in what is now the very heart of Rome. The spot had been abandoned for more and more rural locations as Rome grew up and spread sprawling over the flood plain of the Campus Martius around the river, and was now located well north of the city in a quiet place still unclaimed by man.

The location had changed, but the ceremony—solemn and ancient—had not.

Every month on the full moon's apex the ashes of all the half-Blood *Ikati* who had not survived their Transitions the month prior were taken from the small clay urns they were placed in after cremation and transferred to containers fashioned from squares of white raw silk tied with cords of hand-spun gold. Green apples were placed atop the ashes to pay the hungry ferryman's tithe to the netherworld; a small bundle of sparrow grass brought the unlucky soul peace. One by one, as the names of the dead were called by the Alpha of the tribe, the bundles were placed on slender balsa-wood planks with lit beeswax candles at either end and set into the river, where they bobbed and dipped and finally caught flame. Mothers and fathers and sisters and brothers and cousins and friends would watch in silence as the flaming bundles drifted away on the restless river until they slipped with a hiss and coils of rising gray smoke beneath the surface of the dark water, on their way to their final resting place at the bottom of the vast, enchanted Mediterranean.

Eliana sometimes wondered if there was a huge pile of *Ikati* ashes mounded like drifts of silt at the mouth of the Tiber where it drained into the sea.

Because she was full-Blooded, the King's daughter, and referred to as *spem futuri* by the eldest of the tribal elders—hope for the future, whatever *that* meant—Eliana was considered too precious to attend the monthly *Purgare*. She stayed under guard inside the catacombs where she'd been born and had spent every waking moment of her life.

But tonight, oh, tonight—she would finally break free.

The past few days she'd been a frazzle of nerves and twitchery and pent-up emotion held in check only by the sobering realization that to fail in this—to be caught—would mean disaster. She wasn't thinking too closely about that, though, because her full attention and indeed imagination had been captured by the thought of being alone—*outside!*—with Demetrius.

With heat and powerful need in his eyes he had agreed to her request and simultaneously exposed his own desire. He wanted her as much as she wanted him, and now she had her proof, evidenced undeniably by his willingness to risk death just to be alone with her for a few hours. How exactly he was going to manage it she still wasn't sure, because he hadn't spoken a word to her in the past few days, had just looked at her with that silent, burning intensity whenever their paths had crossed. But she knew he would figure out a way. Though Celian was the leader of the *Bellatorum*, D was the most clever, the most willing to take risks and defy authority, and she loved that about him. She had only to shake her guard long enough to get to the sunken church, then D would handle the rest.

She was sighing in anticipation when her father walked into the flickering light of her large, white-on-white, candlelit bedroom.

"Eliana," he said, and she jumped, guilty.

"Father!" She leapt from the overstuffed chair near her four-poster bed and snapped shut the book she'd been devouring: Lonely Planet's *Guide to Rome*. "I didn't expect to see you this early. Good morning!"

Though there were no clocks in the catacombs, she knew it was morning. Dawn and dusk were felt keen as hunger pangs even far belowground. Regardless, clocks were entirely unnecessary: the *Ikati* of the catacombs had nowhere else to be.

"Good morning to you." A small, secret smile flitted across her father's lips, and he crossed to her quickly over the stone floor strewn with plush rugs and embraced her.

"I'm going to be occupied all day, but I wanted to see you before the last *Purgare* tonight," he said, low, into her hair.

Eliana pulled back and frowned at him, studying his handsome face, his burning, coal-black eyes, so like her own. "I don't understand. What do you mean, the last *Purgare*? We'll have another one next month. And the month after that."

He took her chin in hand and gazed down at her, those dark eyes alight with a wild, feverish victory that took her breath away with its strange edge. She'd never seen him so wired. In truth, he looked a little…unhinged.

"I have an announcement to make, something that concerns all of us," he murmured, holding her face in a way that made her nervous. It was possessive, more like a jealous lover than a father, and she stepped back, out of his embrace. He noticed her discomfort and his eyes flared. "Something that concerns you, too, daughter of mine," he drawled, a new hardness in his tone.

Eliana had been in the middle of another step back, but she froze instantly and so did the blood circulating in her veins. "Me?" she whispered, thinking only of D. Her heart became a stampede of wild stallions in her chest.

How could he know of their plans?

His small smile grew wider, revealing his perfect, ultra-white teeth. Dressed elegantly and with care in his usual impeccable white that set off his burnished skin and tousled black hair to model-like perfection yet exuding the kind of raw menace usually found only in violent criminals, he looked like the love child of Cary Grant and Blackbeard the pirate. He stepped nearer, closing the distance between them, that undercurrent of menace chilling the air in her already cool bedchamber.

"You are my life, you know that," he said, taking her shoulders in his hands. His voice was very low, controlled, giving nothing away. His eyes burned. "And your happiness is my only concern, beautiful Eliana. It's what I've worked so hard for, all these long years."

His fingers curled into her skin, and once again she fought the urge to step back. She'd never been afraid of him before, but there was something in his eyes...something so very dark.

"Father," she managed, swallowing the panic that was clawing at her throat, "what are you talking about?"

He lifted his hand and leisurely brushed back a strand of hair from her suddenly perspiring forehead.

"I'm talking about destiny," he whispered. "Yours and mine. Ours." He made a sweeping gesture with one hand, indicating, she thought, all her kin who lived together in darkness beyond the rounded walls and burnished light of her room. "We were gods once, Ana, so long ago, before our destiny was stolen from us. But now we can take our destiny back and be gods once again. *I've finally done it.*"

Relief flooded her, and she almost sagged into his arms, her heartbeat thrumming like a hummingbird's. "Your project," she breathed, trying to gather her wits. He couldn't read her mind, but he was exceptionally good at reading her face. "Oh, Father, that's wonderful..."

She trailed off because she really hadn't the slightest idea if it was wonderful or not. No one could be secretive the way her father could, and for all the years she'd been alive she was aware of his work in the lab, aware of some grand scheme involving the fates of all her underworld kin, but he revealed almost nothing except to a very few of his closest confidants, and she wasn't among them.

Her father took her face in both his hands and vehemently whispered, "My beautiful daughter. Your young will rule the earth."

Eliana's heartbeat grew faint. First because her father seemed entirely beyond reason and second because she did not want *young*, and never had. But…did she have a choice? She was about to open her mouth to ask, but her mercurial father released her and smiled in a way that made all the tiny hairs on the back of her neck stand on end.

"You will be at the convergence room at dawn tomorrow," he commanded, "to stand by my side when I make the announcement. In the meantime, get some sleep." His voice grew softer. "You look a bit…frazzled, my dear."

Oh, he really had no idea. She sank back down into the overstuffed chair, trying to control her breathing, when a burst of inspiration hit. She cleared her throat and gazed up at him through her lashes. "I am frazzled. I haven't been sleeping well, lately, Father."

His brows shot up. "Oh?"

She nodded, then cast her gaze to the floor at his feet. "The new guard you assigned as my escort…"

"Yes?" he said sharply, instantly tense.

"Well, he…makes me uncomfortable." This was absolutely true. The new guard watched her every move like a hawk. She didn't know what had happened to the old—friendlier—one and didn't dare ask; her father's decisions were never questioned.

"Uncomfortable," Dominus repeated, deadly soft.

Eliana glanced up at him. "It's just…it's just the way he looks at me."

Dominus drew in a sharp breath. His head whipped around to the entrance of her bedchamber, where the guard stood vigilant outside, just his elbow and booted right foot visible beyond the heavy swagged drape that partially covered the rounded doorway.

"He hasn't done anything inappropriate, Father," she rushed to assure him, knowing it might save the guard's life, "but still I would feel better if you could assign me someone else. Perhaps tomorrow, after the announcement? I'd be fine for just one day without a guard, I'm sure."

He turned to look at her with narrowed eyes, and her heartbeat skyrocketed again. Terrified he sensed her little deception, she pleaded, "I'll sleep better tonight without someone new watching me. I'll be fine, just for one day. One night. I really don't think I can sleep knowing he's there."

"Why didn't you tell me this before?" he hissed, stepping closer to loom over her. "I would have dealt with him—"

"I don't want you to *deal* with him, Father, please! Just— just let me have another guard. Tomorrow."

He considered her in silence for several long, tense moments. Then his face softened and he said, "As you wish."

Really? She couldn't believe that had worked. She put a shaking hand to her face, adrenaline wreaking havoc on her nerves. "Thank you," she whispered.

He bent and planted a kiss on the top of her head, then abruptly turned on his heel and walked toward the door. He paused just before passing over the threshold and said over his shoulder, "By the way, a very special guest will be arriving this morning. Someone who'll be staying with us from now on, who I hope you'll...like...as much as I do."

His voice, low and husky, throbbed with emotion. Her ears pricked. "A guest?"

He turned slightly and met her curious gaze. That menacing smile of his made another appearance. "Yes. I'll introduce you tomorrow morning, after the announcement."

"Why not today?"

His face grew flushed, his eyes hot. "Because today we'll be spending some time together, getting to know one another better."

Eliana stared at him, confused. Was this why he was in such a state?

"Who is this guest?"

A gleam came into his eyes, one that made her scalp prickle with dread.

"Your new mother," he answered. Then he turned and disappeared beyond the door, leaving Eliana gaping after him in shock.

By the time Morgan arrived at the Vatican, the morning sun had risen over the rooftop of St. Peter's and bathed the vast cobblestone square in warm, golden light. It was too early for the tourists, but the Swiss Guard was ever present, and she made her way across the sun-washed square to a lone guard posted at the top of the stairs on the left side of the entrance to the basilica, hoping to draft him into her plan.

He was a large man, physically imposing even in that silly, striped Renaissance uniform with boot covers, white gloves, and white ruff around his throat. The rapier at his hip, however, looked more ominous than silly, as did the sidearm strapped to his other hip, and she approached with caution. When she finally stood directly in front of him, he made no indication he was aware of her presence except for a slight inhalation of breath. Looking up into his pale blue eyes—affixed on some point above her head—she saw his irises dilate.

Just as Xander's had when he'd stared down at her as he pushed himself inside—

Stop! Morgan screamed at herself and bit her tongue hard to banish the thought. With her hands now trembling and her heart thrumming, she turned her attention back to the guard.

"Excuse me," she said. He completely ignored her.

Hmmm.

She lifted both hands to pull her hair back from her face as if she were going to make a ponytail. It forced her rib cage to lift, and her breasts—unfettered by a bra—pressed against the clinging fabric of her dress. "Excuse me, *signore?* I think I'm a little lost. I'm looking for the tour that goes below the Vatican? The necropolis tour, I think?"

She'd heard of this from the cab driver on the way over. There was some guided tour of the rarely seen areas beneath the Vatican, ancient grottoes and catacombs with tombs of long-dead saints, including the tomb of St. Peter around which the entire church had been built. It sounded like the perfect place to start her search.

A muscle in the guard's jaw twitched, but he still didn't respond. Obviously he was well trained to ignore all manner of foolishness from the tourists. Or just stubborn as hell.

Either way he was dust, because now this was personal.

Morgan dropped her arms and shook her hair back, then slid both hands slowly down the front of her dress, over her waist and hips, smoothing imaginary wrinkles. She shifted her weight to one foot and thrust out her hip, then jauntily rested her hand on it, gazing at him with an intensity she knew he felt, because the faintest hint of color flushed his cheeks.

Thank God for peripheral vision.

"I'm sorry," she breathed in a conspiratorial tone, stepping closer, making sure to exaggerate the roll of her hips, "I know you're probably not supposed to talk and I don't want to disturb you, but if you could just give me an idea? Maybe"—she coyly twirled a lock of her hair between her fingers—"point me in the general direction?"

He swallowed but said nothing.

Mulish bastard. She pursed her lips. Leisurely, she lifted the lock of hair to her mouth and dragged it back and forth across her parted lips. "*Per favore?*" she said, very throaty.

His gaze flickered down to her mouth, and his nostrils flared. "*Ufficio Scavi,*" he blurted, brusque. She didn't understand and her brows lifted.

His gaze darted right to a small black door recessed in the stone wall perhaps a hundred yards away, beneath a huge statue of a robed woman in traditional habit. Another damn nun.

"*Ufficio Scavi,*" the guard said again, more forcefully, now staring at her mouth.

"Oh," she said, understanding. *Ufficio*—office. Office of the...*Scavi?* She jumped when the guard answered her in heavily accented English, his voice low.

"I'll take you."

Was it her imagination or was there a double entendre there? "Why, I'd just love that," she purred, gazing up at him through her lashes. She was gratified to see his flush deepen.

He took her by the arm and quickly led her down the wide marble steps and over the worn cobblestones to the Plaza of

Protomartyrs around the side of the basilica. They passed beneath an arched corner and went through the squeaking black door of the *Ufficio Scavi,* which swung shut with an echoing *thud* behind them. They were in a small stone antechamber, totally unadorned, cool and quiet as a tomb. An arched doorway directly in front of them had steps leading down into a tunnel swallowed in gloom. They were alone.

"Wait," the guard said, releasing her arm, and pointed to the floor. "Here. First tour at nine."

"You've been so helpful! Thank you so much. *Grazie,*" Morgan breathed, doing her best impression of a damsel in distress. A damsel whose heart hadn't recently been ripped—beating and bloody—from her chest. Sweetly smiling, she trailed a finger down the soft folds of the collar of her sweater dress, exposing as if by accident the top swell of her breasts, the cleft between. "May I show you something, since you've been so nice?"

The guard blanched. His gaze flickered to the closed door; then he stepped forward and licked his lips as if she were a trussed and roasted Thanksgiving turkey and he hadn't eaten in years. He lifted his hand to her face, but before he could touch her she had him by the wrist.

Quietly, she said, "Stop."

Obediently, he froze midstep. His face wiped blank.

"You're going to answer a few questions, then you will leave this room and forget you ever saw me. Understood?"

The guard stared at her, his blue, blue eyes utterly blank.

"*Capisce?*" she insisted.

Slowly, he nodded.

"Good," Morgan said, keeping her grip on his wrist. With her other hand she pulled the medallion from beneath the draped collar of her dress. "Do you know this symbol?"

The guard nodded again.

"What is it?"

"Horus," he said in a monotone, "*Dio della vendetta.*"

Dio—God. OK. *Vendetta*…revenge? "God of revenge?"

The guard frowned a little, concentrating. He said softly, "*Sì.* Er…vengeance."

The god of vengeance. It sent a chill down Morgan's spine. She swallowed around a sudden lump of fear that lodged like a stone in her throat. "Where can I find this symbol in the necropolis?"

"The tomb of the Egyptians," he intoned, staring at her chest. "Tomb lettered *Z*; symbol of Horus is painted on the north wall."

Painted on the wall? "Anywhere else?"

He blinked, slowly lifted his gaze to hers, and with a vague motion of his hand said, "*Ovunque.*"

Morgan stifled a frustrated sigh. "English, please."

The guard gazed blankly into her eyes. "Everywhere," he said, very soft.

"What do you mean, *everywhere?*" Morgan said sharply, so that her voice echoed off the stone walls.

"Paintings," he calmly responded, "statues, frescoes, the obelisk in St. Peter's Square, the pope's hat—"

"The pope's hat!" she exclaimed, astonished.

"—wood carvings, tile work, tapestries, stonework—"

"Enough! Stop."

He fell silent, waiting for her next command, while Morgan tried not to hyperventilate.

Everywhere. The feral Alpha's symbol was all over the Vatican. Even on—good Lord—the pope's hat. How? Why?

"I don't understand. Why would the symbol of an Egyptian god be all over the seat of the Christian church?"

A faint smile curved his lips. "Their gods were here long before ours. We just…" he floundered, searching for a word in English, "…*appropriato*. Stole them. Reconfigured."

Morgan's mouth dropped open, then snapped shut. She didn't have time for this. "Are there any other entrances to the catacombs?"

He shook his head. "Only in the pope's private chambers, but there you cannot go."

Oh, but she could. But at the moment she was at the entrance to the necropolis, so she might as well start here. She gave the guard's wrist a final warning squeeze and said, "You will return to your post and forget me."

The guard blinked down at her and wistfully murmured, "Forget you."

"*Sì*. Go now. Go."

He nodded slowly, then turned on his heel, went through the door, and let it swing shut behind him.

The moment he was gone, Morgan turned and made her way down the narrow flight of stairs, her heart pounding, light diminishing behind her with every step. At the bottom of the steps was a series of narrow passageways constructed of red bricks that led off in every direction, lit with dim spotlights at long intervals. The air was humid and stagnant, the ground uneven dirt. Several richly engraved stone sarcophagi were assembled near the entrance, beyond which was a larger main corridor with a map in English and Italian on the wall that showed the various tombs of the necropolis. Feeling excitement mixed with crushing dread, Morgan located the Egyptian tomb on the map and set off in search of it.

She passed tomb after tomb, both large and small, cold, shadowed rooms of brick and earth with stone sarcophagi resting in niches in the walls. Motifs of stags and vases and flowering vines, perfectly preserved, decorated walls and ceilings; remnants of colorful mosaic tiles survived in patches over the floors. The corridor narrowed at length, the brick walls showed more signs of deterioration, the air became clammy and thick. Around another corner, and she began to feel claustrophobic. The ancient walls, now flaked and uneven, pressed close; the light dimmed to a faint greenish hue.

Just as she was beginning to panic that she was lost, the weak light of the entrance to the tomb of the Egyptians appeared around another corner, illuminating the gloom like a phantom in a graveyard.

Her heart in her throat, Morgan stepped hesitantly into the tomb. Six elaborate stone sarcophagi and four empty niches lined the walls of the square mausoleum; several alabaster urns and shards of broken pottery lay in one corner. On the north wall, just as the guard had said, was the painting of Horus, god of vengeance.

It was massive and strangely vivid in the half-light, rich with color and an eerie dimensionality that made it seem to bulge from the wall. A bare-chested warrior with the sun-haloed head of a falcon and huge, flaming wings fanning out from the middle of his back floated over a mob of prostrate worshippers gathered at a riverbank. He held a sword in one hand and a staff in the other, bands of gold surrounded his muscled biceps, a linen garment hung from his hips. But the eyes were by far the most striking of all. Black and piercing above a sharp, elongated beak, they seemed uncannily *alive*.

Morgan took an involuntary step back, dropped her gaze, and saw, in the right corner of the painting, a cutout in the stone roughly the same size and shape as the medallion that hung around her neck.

Her heart pole-vaulted over her breastbone.

Feeling like a character out of *Indiana Jones*, she unclasped the medallion from her neck and shakily approached the small niche in the wall. Without breathing, she set the medallion flush against the ancient brick and jumped back with a yelp when the lid of the sarcophagus directly behind her popped open with a puff of dust and the low groan of stone on stone.

"Oh, hell, no," she said into the ancient, sinister hush. "You've *got* to be kidding me."

The answering silence was deafening.

She stood in the center of the mausoleum for several minutes, arguing the pros and cons with herself. She'd found what she'd come looking for—possibly—and now she could go back and tell Xander...ask for his help...

If it wasn't for you, Julian might still be alive.

Right. Xander was the last one who would want to help.

Fighting back the sudden, bitter onslaught of tears, Morgan snapped the necklace back around her neck, strode over to the sarcophagus, and pushed the lid wide open. Peering down, she saw a set of impossibly narrow steps descending into impenetrable blackness. She sat on the edge of the hulking stone coffin and swung her legs over, then, moving as silently as her feet would allow, stepped down into darkness.

THIRTY-TWO

D stared down at the folded note in his hand. *Change of plans*, it read, in the lilting, elegant script he recognized as Eliana's. *Meet before* Purgare? *Sunken church. One half hour.*

He dismissed the blushing young handmaiden who'd brought it with a curt nod that made her blush deepen. As she backed quickly out of the room and fled into the safety of the dark corridor beyond, D slowly unwound the tape around his knuckles.

His bare chest was bathed in sweat, the muscles in his arms and shoulders ached, his breathing was heavy, but he was satisfied that the punching bag he'd been beating the life out of for the past hour had served its purpose. He'd be calmer now, his head clearer.

And he was definitely going to need that.

He left the gym with his duffel bag in hand and went to the adjoining multiroomed thermae, where warm spring waters bubbled up naturally from the bedrock far below. He was alone in the baths at this hour, but he didn't bother with his usual postworkout soak. He got himself clean as quickly as possible, dried off, and dressed, then, after a quick side trip to stash the duffel in his footlocker in the private quarters of the *Bellatorum*, set out for the sunken church.

On the way, he burned Eliana's note with a lighter and let the ashes drift to the ground.

No one would miss him at this hour. The *Bellatorum* were allowed personal time prior to the *Purgare*, and in any case, Celian, Lix, and Constantine—all now healed—had decided to play with a quartet of nubile young *Electi* the King had grown bored with and gifted them for their pleasure.

Our pleasure, he thought grimly. *But I'm not interested in anything other than what I'm going to meet now.*

Twenty minutes later he'd wound through the maze of catacombs and stood silent in the shadows of the sunken church, waiting for her beside a crumbling stone column next to the corridor that led deep into the bowels of the catacombs he'd just emerged from. He stood there breathing, feeling his heart pump in his chest, feeling anticipation clench the muscles deep in his belly.

He felt ravenous. Exultant. Alive.

He sensed rather than heard her approach. She was silent as midnight but carried with her a tangible current of power, refined yet electric. As she passed the threshold into the sunken church and glanced nervously around, he moved swiftly from his position hidden against the column, grabbed her by the arms, and spun her around, her wrists held tightly behind her in both his hands. She gasped as he pushed his body against hers and held her, pinned, to the wall.

"Demetrius!"

"Tell me again," he said, very low, his face mere inches from hers, "why I'm risking my hide to be here?"

Panting a little, she stared up into his eyes. Her skin was lucid in the moonlight that spilled over the floor from the small windows high above in the rounded room.

"Because you want to," she said, breathless.

He stared down at her parted lips, feeling the clench in his belly grow into a burn. "Not good enough," he said, slowly shaking his head.

"Because...I want you to?"

He cocked his head and considered her, enjoying the heat and softness of her body pressed against his, prolonging the moment. Jesus, she looked good enough to eat. Dressed in tight black leggings, black boots, and a black sweater that hugged every curve, she was probably the most beautiful thing he'd ever seen.

He lowered his face slowly, watching her eyes widen, watching the pulse in her neck grow jagged. Slowly, softly, he ran the tip of his nose down the column of her throat and inhaled, deeply, against her skin. He felt himself harden, knew she felt it too because her breathing hitched and, subtly, she arched into him.

"I need something more definitive than that, *Principessa...*" he murmured, letting his lips skim her exposed collarbone as he spoke.

"Oh. In that case, how about this?" she breathed, then leaned forward and took his earlobe between her lips.

D froze as heat detonated in his body. Eliana sucked gently on his earlobe, running her tongue over and around that tiny piece of flesh he had never known had so many nerve endings, then lightly pressed it between her teeth. He pulled away, took her face in his hand, and darkly said, "Oh, little girl, you *really* shouldn't have done that."

Then he lifted her up and tossed her over his shoulder so she hung upside down behind his back. He turned and ambled across the moonlit floor, heading to the door that led outside, into the night.

"Demetrius!" Eliana squealed, pummeling his back with her fists. "Put me down! Put me down this instant!"

He slapped her hard on the bottom and enjoyed her mortified howl.

"Sorry, Your Highness," he drawled, "but I'm not taking orders tonight."

She gasped in horror or astonishment, he couldn't tell which, and D broke into a smile. His arm easily spanning both her thighs, he maneuvered his way through the hidden doorway that led outside and around a thicket of wild raspberries that grew along the rounded wall. Eliana grasped his belt to steady herself as he walked, alternating between pleading and demanding that he let her down.

"Stop squirming or I'll put you down and take you over my knee," he threatened, and gave her bottom a soft pinch. She quieted instantly with a sharp intake of breath, and his smile grew wider.

God, this was going to be fun.

On a damp patch of clover around the east wall of the sunken church, he abruptly set her back on her feet. Before she could protest, he put one hand over her eyes—it covered most of her face—and spun her around so her back was against his chest. He pulled her close. "Are you ready?" he murmured suggestively into her ear.

She trembled against him and clutched the arm he'd wrapped around her chest. "Ready for what?" she whispered.

Oh, yes, she was ready. Her voice gave her away. The heat and longing in it flooded him with carnal urges, but he was able to control himself, just barely. Because right now he wanted to give her something she—and everyone with a soul—deserved.

Slowly, he removed his hand from her face. "For Rome."

She exhaled sharply. Her body fell utterly still.

Before them lay the glorious, decadent labyrinth of humanity's most magnificent city, the crown jewel of man's achievement and imagination, the pulsing, vibrant heart of the planet that had beaten for over two and a half thousand years. Renaissance palaces and baroque basilicas, medieval bell towers and Etruscan tombs, a sprawl of tiled rooftops as far as the eye could see washed fairy-dust gold by the huge, orange moon that lazed like a fat pumpkin over the distant black hills. A huge cloud of starlings rose in a tangle into the star-dusted dome of the sky, flashing quicksilver until they vanished into the horizon, and off in the distance the enormous stone bulk of the Colosseum crouched in the center of it all, striped gold and black like a sleeping tiger.

A little spasm wracked her body, and he looked down into her face. Her eyes were huge, unblinking, filled with tears. He gently turned her to face him.

"Eliana," he whispered, contrite. Had he done something wrong?

She turned her head and gazed into his eyes. "Thank you," she said, her voice choked.

His heart melted. A single tear tracked down her cheek, and he brushed it away with his thumb. "Silly girl," he said gently, "you're not supposed to cry at the start of a date. Cry at the end, like I do."

"You, cry?" she scoffed, sniffling and wiping away the moisture around her eyes. She took a breath and straightened her shoulders. "I find that very hard to believe, Mr. Kick Ass."

D stared down at her in mock indignation. "Mr. Kick Ass? I'll have you know I'm very tenderhearted, Ms. High and Mighty."

It was her turn to feign affront. "High and Mighty? I'll have *you* know I'm very humble and meek."

He stepped closer, smiling. "Really? *Meek*, are you?"

She tilted her head and gazed up at him through her lashes, playful. "Well. Meek for a princess, anyway."

"Hmmm. That's what I thought."

He trailed his fingers over the side of her face and jaw, because he wanted to, because he could, because he loved seeing the effect his touch had on her. Even in the dark he saw her flush.

"And I'm sure you don't *date*, in any traditional sense of the word," she said, less steady than before.

His hand slipped around the back of her neck, and he drew her against him. Her hands lifted to rest lightly against his chest.

"Now why would you think that?" he murmured, lowering his head to hers.

Her fingers curled into the front of his shirt as his lips brushed her temple, slid barely touching down to her jaw. He paused at the corner of her mouth.

"Because there are too many women throwing themselves at your feet to bother with dating," she breathed, her lips barely brushing his. "You can just take them to bed and dispense with all the formalities."

He fisted his hand in the hair at the nape of her neck and gently pulled her head back so she was forced to look up, into his eyes. "There is only one woman I want to take to bed," he said, his voice husky, all teasing gone, "and I'm ready and willing to provide any kind of formality she requires, for however long she requires, in order to do so."

She stared at him with dark intensity, all bedroom eyes and Mona Lisa lips, moonlight weaving blue magic in her hair.

"No snappy answer for that, *Principessa?*"

"Well," she murmured, bemused, "I can't quite figure out if that's incredibly offensive or incredibly hot."

A low chuckle rumbled through his chest. "Don't over-think it. Just go with your gut."

Her gaze dropped to his lips. Her cheeks heated. "Incredibly hot, then," she whispered, and rose up on her toes to softly press her mouth against his.

It slew him. She was so sweet, so beautiful, so good—and she wanted him.

Him.

He moaned into her mouth, hardening instantly when her tongue slid against his. She wrapped her arms around his neck and pressed herself against him and kissed him with an ardor that took his breath away. He'd wanted to kiss her like this for years, but now that he had her in his arms, her mouth on his, he felt light-headed and woozy and was suddenly afraid he might do something to hurt her, afraid he might be too rough and scare her away.

He broke the kiss, panting, and set her away from him with both hands.

She blinked at him, her expression that of a scolded puppy. In a small voice she said, "What is it? Did I do something wrong?"

"Jesus, *no*," he groaned, wincing, "you did everything right."

Her puppy-dog frown deepened. "I don't understand."

His voice came out whiskey-rough, aching. "Eliana. Do you have *any clue* what I want to do to you? How much I want you? How much self-control it takes not to peel those pants off your perfect, delectable body and fuck you right here? Now?"

"Oh," she said, paling. Her eyes grew huge. "Oh, my. We're back to incredibly offensive or incredibly hot territory."

"It's just the truth! I've wanted you every second of every day for *years*, and now that you're here, alone with me, I'm finding it very hard not to—"

"Fuck me?" she interrupted, staring him dead in the eye.

The barest hint of a rakish smile lifted her cheek, and his mouth dropped open.

"Are you *smirking* at me, Ms. High and Mighty?" he growled. He tightened his hands around her arms and pulled her closer.

"I wouldn't dare, Mr. Kick Ass," she said innocently. "Knowing what a twitchy hand you have. I'm afraid I'd get such a spanking I couldn't sit for a week."

"Oh, you really have no idea," he breathed, closing the final distance between them. He pinned her arms around her back again, pressed himself against her, and took her chin in his hand. He stared down into her eyes and said, "I'd love to turn that beautiful ass of yours the perfect shade of pink, and be inside you and make you moan my name and promise to belong to me forever. Make no mistake, Eliana, I want to make you mine. *All* mine. I want to do very bad things to you, things no one has ever done to you before or ever will again. And what's more, I want you to learn what pleases me and do it because you want to, because it makes you happy. Because *I* make you happy."

She stared at him with her mouth hanging open, her eyes popped wide.

"But we're not going to do any of that until I've shown you this city you've lived beneath your entire life and we've had a very honest talk about what exactly it is you're after here, because I'll tell you right now I'm not interested in just one night and I'm not going to share you with anyone else. Including your father. Do we understand one another?"

She swallowed and nodded her head.

"Good." He leaned in and kissed her very softly, first taking her lower lip between his teeth, then sliding his tongue into her mouth, careful to hold back when she arched into him and made a sound in her throat that sounded perilously close to surrender.

"First things first, sweet girl," he whispered, then pressed a chaste kiss to her forehead and released her. "Let's go see Rome, shall we?" He held out his hand.

A little unsteady on her feet, she reached for his hand and closed her cool fingers around his own. She swallowed again and sent him an amused, slightly disoriented look. "Are you always this bossy?"

He grinned. "Someone's got to stand up to you. Your ego is completely out of control."

"*My* ego!" She laughed, following as he led her away down the sloping grassy hill.

"And yes, I'm always this bossy," he said over his shoulder. "In fact, I'm just getting started."

"Yeah, well, good luck with that, Mr. Kick Ass," she scoffed. "You're not the only one who's used to giving orders. If you can dish it out, you better be able to take it."

D heard her sweet, low laugh from behind him and was glad she couldn't see the huge grin that split his face.

Yes, he was going to take it. He was going to take it *all*.

"What the hell do you mean," breathed Xander, cold with shock, "you *don't know* where she is?"

He'd just returned from a full day wandering the streets of Rome, trying to distract himself from thoughts of Morgan, only to see her face on every brunette in the city. After he'd left her in the morning he'd been so strung out it had taken him all day just to calm down enough to return to the safe house, and when he had, she'd been nowhere to be found. In mounting panic, he'd combed every foot of the house and had finally found Bartleby and Tomás—back in human form, healed from the shallow cuts on his face—sitting at the kitchen table.

"We—we thought Morgan was with *you!*" Bartleby stammered, blinking. "I didn't see either of you since we came back from…Julian…this morning…I assumed you were together! I was with Mateo and Tomás all day in the gym!"

In a quietly hostile voice, Tomás said, "Mateo will be fine in a day or two. If you care."

Xander sucked in a breath and stared at Tomás. He deserved that, he supposed, but still it felt like someone had just twisted a hot dagger deep inside his gut. "Of *course* I care!"

"Funny way of showing it, her over us and all," Tomás said, still with that blade-edged tone.

Xander couldn't deny it. Everyone in the room knew it was true. He sank down into the nearest chair, rested his elbows on the table, bowed his head, and wrapped his hands around it. He closed his eyes and took a deep breath, fighting panic and the urge to jump up and flee into the gathering dusk outside, screaming her name.

Into the tense silence he said, "I'm sorry. You're right. But..." he swallowed and closed his eyes, "...but I love her. I love her, Tomás, with every fucked-up atom of my being. She resurrected me, understood me, gave me a reason to live. I never thought...I never thought I could feel anything like this again, and this time it's even...*more*. It's everything. I just couldn't leave her here alone."

He heard Tomás's hissed exhalation of breath, but he *felt* Bartleby's smile.

"God*dammit*, Alexander," snarled Tomás through clenched teeth; then he fell silent.

"Well," said Bartleby, chipper all of a sudden, "I for one think you make a lovely couple."

"Couple of what?" Tomás muttered under his breath, but the doctor ignored that.

"Where do you think she went, Xander? Where are you going to look for her?"

Xander lifted his head and stared at Bartleby in desolation. "I don't know," he whispered. "I don't know how I'm going to find her." *And after the way I treated her this morning, she most likely never wants to see me again.*

Tomás snorted loudly. Xander looked at him, and he crossed his muscled arms over his chest and glared back at him. After a moment he huffed out a breath as if he'd come to some kind of unspoken decision. "For a smart guy, you can be colossally stupid, you know that?" he snapped.

"I'm sorry, Tomás. I'll do anything to make it right between us—"

"Oh, shut up, for fuck's sake. I'm not talking about us anymore!"

Xander blinked at him, confused, and Tomás rolled his eyes to the ceiling.

"Give me patience, God," he said between stiff lips.

Bartleby sat looking back and forth between the two of them, chewing on the inside of his lip.

Tomás uncrossed his arms, laid his hands flat on the table, and leaned forward. "You have her Blood inside you," he said very slowly, as if speaking to someone exceptionally dense. "You. Can. Find. Her. *Anywhere.*"

Fire erupted on Xander's skin and ran scorching over every muscle, nerve, and bone in his body. "Blood follows Blood," he whispered, breathless.

It was a saying as old as their race, with a dozen different meanings. For parents who passed Gifts to their offspring, for tribe members who swore fealty to their Alpha, for positions such as Matchmaker and Keeper of the Bloodlines that were held in perpetuity by a single family, handed down from father to son through every successive generation.

For the binding tie created when one *Ikati* shared the fluid in their veins with another.

Xander leapt to his feet, and his chair crashed to the tile floor behind him. "Tomás, I have to go—I'm sorry—tell Mateo—"

"Yeah, yeah," Tomás muttered drily, waving his hand. "I know all about it, lover boy. And don't worry, we'll be fine.

Go find your pain-in-the-ass princess and bring her back in one piece, will you?"

And with that, Xander knew he was forgiven. He launched himself at Tomás, dragged him from his chair, and crushed his arms around his brother's back. Tomás hugged him back briefly, then disentangled himself from Xander's arms with a disgusted look.

"Go on, fuckface," he growled, fighting a smile, and pushed Xander toward the door.

He went willingly, shouting over his shoulder, "When I get back we're going to talk about hiding you and Mateo from the Assembly!"

"Hiding, shmiding," he heard Tomás mutter from behind him as he barged like a freight train through the back door. "I was planning on retiring anyway."

Xander knelt on the grass in the backyard, staring up into the purple-blue twilight. The strength in his legs had deserted him, and he didn't know how exactly this was going to work anyway, so he figured he might as well get close to the ground in case he was inclined to fall flat on his face.

He spread his hands over his flexed thighs, closed his eyes, and breathed.

"Morgan," he murmured. "Love. Where are you?"

Distant traffic murmured. Leaves rustled in the trees. Cool, soft air brushed his skin.

Nothing else happened.

He shifted his weight and tried again, focusing on her name, repeating it silently like a mantra, clearing his mind of all else. After several minutes of this his left foot began to tingle; it was falling asleep.

He ground his teeth in frustration. How the hell was this supposed to work? He had a random thought to go back inside and ask Tomás, but instantly thought better of it. He had to be the one to do this, and he had to do it alone.

A wet snuffling at the back fence caught his attention. There lurked the beagle, staring at him wide-eyed through the knot in the painted white wood. It froze when he let a low, rumbling growl build in his chest, then took off yelping when he sat forward on his haunches and snarled like an animal, like the animal he was.

Stupid dog. He remembered the first time he'd seen it, when he and Bartleby had sat here together and the doctor had so pointedly asked Xander if he was in love with Morgan. He chuckled, remembering it, how in denial he'd been just moments before he'd gone downstairs and surrendered himself to the first emotion he'd felt in two decades.

And God, what emotion it was. Sweet and fierce and beautiful, just like her. Passionate. Consuming. Demonic.

Memories rose to assault his senses: her eyes, skin, hair, lips, scent. Words spoken, hushed and reverent, hoarse and pleading. Pleasures shared. Skin on heated skin. Love. He swallowed to try and ease the ache in his chest, breathed deep to counteract a sudden light-headedness. "Morgan," he softly groaned.

And then a rushing cold wind engulfed him, roaring in his ears.

Underground—clammy air—dusty stone—bones and shadows and—

Danger. She was in danger, and terrified.

Xander leapt to his feet. He gazed out over the rooftops of Rome, feeling a pull like gravity, his blood scorching fire through his veins. Her name like a drumbeat inside his head, loudest when he looked west, deafening when he spied the golden, rounded rooftop of St. Peter's Basilica.

All the breath left his body as if he'd been punched.

"I'm coming, baby," he snarled, and took off in a flat-out run.

THIRTY-THREE

Morgan awoke to a jackhammer pounding pure agony through her skull.

With a moan, she lifted her head, wincing in pain. A quick glance around revealed a vast, shadowed stone chamber decorated by an eccentric hoarder with a fondness for Edwardian Gothic decor and the color red. Every inch of floor space was crammed with antiques that looked valuable and very old, and everything was saturated in shades of fresh-spilled blood, from the patterned rugs to the elaborate velvet-upholstered furniture to the woven tapestries on the walls. Even the heavy iron braziers that lined the walls had candles of red that cast a demonic, dancing glow over everything.

The chamber was retrofitted with an enormous, intricate limestone skeleton that hugged the soaring walls and created the illusion of the interior of a medieval cathedral with clustered columns, pointed ribbed vaults, and flamboyant tracery in stained-glass windows that looked out onto nothing. There were statues and oils and carved figures of saints, gargoyles leering down from peaked columns, suits of armor and displays of antique weaponry, rows of crested flags hanging far above.

It was astonishing, morbidly beautiful, and very cold. No fireplace or other visible source of heat warmed the chamber, and the damp, clinging air sank down to chill her bones.

And there was the matter of her *head*.

She gingerly explored the back of her skull with her fingers and found an enormous, tender knot lurking just behind her left ear. When she pulled her hand away it was slick with blood.

"Damn," she muttered. What had happened? The last thing she remembered was the tomb of the Egyptians, the sarcophagus, the steps—

"My apologies," said a low, silky voice to her right, "but my guards tend to be a bit overzealous in their treatment of intruders. How are you feeling?"

She snapped her head around—the room went spinning—and there he was, the feral Alpha in white. He was as slickly handsome as she remembered, reclining on an elaborately carved velvet divan a few feet away. He watched her with hooded black eyes and a lazy, sinister smile.

Her body went cold, colder even than the room. "*You*," she whispered.

He looked faintly amused. His brows lifted. "My name is Dominus, Morgan. And yes, me. You were expecting Santa Claus?"

Fight-or-flight adrenaline coursed through her body, electrifying, primal. She kept herself in the chair through sheer force of will, but her hands began, slightly, to shake.

"How do you know my name?"

"I know everything about you, elegant guest. Your strengths and weaknesses, your greatest joys, your deepest fears. You might even say I know you better than you know yourself. The inside of your mind is a very...interesting place to be." His sinister smile grew wider. "By the way, you're in terrible denial about that problem of yours."

She stared at him, the shaking in her hands growing worse by the second.

"In love with an assassin?" he mused. "Hired to kill *you?* Tsk. That's more than just your garden-variety self-loathing, my dear. That's truly pathological. "

Morgan tried to leap to her feet—and couldn't. Horrified, she looked down at her legs, but there were no restraints, no visible injuries, just the chair beneath her, another chunky dark velvet affair that looked transported from an eighteenth-century bordello.

I don't need restraints to keep you where I want you, deliciae, a voice whispered in her mind.

Even without spoken words she heard his amusement, his smug tone of victory, and the anger that flooded her body finally provided some much-needed warmth.

"Stay the hell out of my head!"

His face darkened. Suddenly she couldn't move her arms either. They fell limp to her sides, and though she tried frantically to get them to respond, nothing happened. It was as if her spinal cord had been severed at her neck.

"Demands are not something I tolerate from my females," Dominus said, deadly soft, gazing at her from the shadows with menaced focus like a predator contemplating its next meal.

"Since you know everything about me, you should know I'm not *yours*," she snapped.

Pain exploded in a white-hot firework behind her right eye. She stiffened and gasped.

Languidly Dominus unfolded himself from the divan. He came to stand beside her and slowly stroked a cold, cold finger down her cheek, watching its progress with glittering, hungry eyes.

"Aren't you?" he murmured. His smile struck a note of pure terror in her heart.

Stand, came the unspoken command.

Without a breath of hesitation, her limbs leapt to comply, and she was on her feet, speechless and furious and terrified, her body a puppet to his invisible strings. The pain behind her eye radiated through her head, searing, blisteringly hot, and she had to bite her lip hard to keep from screaming.

Dominus began a slow circle around her, inspecting, smiling his malevolent smile. She was frozen, mummified, unable even to move her eyes to follow his progress. She felt a soft touch on her shoulder, a slight tug as his fingers combed through her hair, a gentle hand caressed her back. As his hand slid down to linger possessively at her waist, her skin crawled as if a thousand spiders were scuttling over her body.

"All of this is mine," he murmured. "Your every thought, your every feeling, every muscle and bone and sinew in this perfect, beautiful body is mine. And from now on, it always will be."

"*No.*" Half whisper, half moan, it brought him to a standstill.

"No?" came his softly spoken challenge. The pain in her head gathered into a shrieking, howling monster with sharp, gnashing teeth that ripped and tore and shredded her flesh, a dragon devouring villagers and spewing fire inside her skull.

Dominus said, "You sound unconvinced. Perhaps a demonstration is in order."

He grasped her by the wrist and lifted her arm away from her body, turned it in various positions until he found one he liked. Then with a murmured, "Stay," he released it, took up her other arm, and repeated the same procedure, then angled her head. In a moment she was posed like a Renaissance statue in the posture he'd chosen, and she stood helpless in suffocating, blistering agony, buried alive.

"Venus in chains," Dominus murmured, transfixed.

His gaze raked over her figure, ravenous, and he looked for a moment as if he would pounce on her and devour her whole. But he took several slow, deep breaths, and the rabid excitement in his eyes eventually dimmed. "Pain is a very powerful motivator, Morgan. Most creatures will do anything to avoid it. Anything at all." He licked his lips, slow and deliberate. "Can you guess what I require from you in order for the pain to go away?"

Unable to answer, she made a high-pitched sound of terror that sounded like a mouse when it spots the cat in midleap.

"*O-be-di-ence.*" He drew it out, lovingly emphasizing each syllable. "You will obey me in all things. You will do whatever I ask without hesitation or I will leave you standing here like this, in agony, until you rot on your feet. Which, I happen to know from experience, takes about three weeks." With an elegant gesture of his manicured hand, he indicated a pile of bleached bones jumbled in a huge, hideous white mess in one dark corner beside a basalt statue of the devil.

Her heart heaved. Sputtered. Started up again with a painful throb.

Dominus moved closer. "But I don't want to do that." His voice was tender now, stroking, and his eyes had grown soft. He touched a finger to her lower lip. "I have other things in mind for you. For *us*. Give me your word you will behave and I will release you, and we can begin again."

"And in return?" she whispered, stalling. Sweat beaded along her hairline, trickled in a cold rivulet down the back of her neck. "If I agree to…obey…what will you give me?"

First he looked angry: his eyes flared; his handsome mouth drew to a hard, flat line. He dropped his hand from her face and made a fist at his side, and she braced herself for a punch. But then another emotion softened his face, and for a moment he looked younger, almost wistful.

"Are you *negotiating* with me?"

He sounded amused, amazed, but most of all intrigued.

"I would like to *not* rot on my feet," she said, faint. "But I will if it means I have to sacrifice free will. I'd rather die on my feet than live on my knees, which if you *really* knew me would be obvious." She moistened her lips. "And because you don't—that makes me think you might be full of shit."

He inhaled a sharp, astonished breath. His mouth dropped open. His eyes, coal black and burning, popped wide. He stared at her in silence while the candles sputtered in a sudden cold breeze and the blood roared wild through her veins.

"No one has ever spoken to me like that," he hissed, unblinking. A flush of crimson rose up his neck, and for a horrible, breathless moment, he did nothing at all.

Then—impossibly—he began to laugh.

It echoed through the vast chamber like a thing alive. It bounced off the walls and split into a hundred different laughs, each one darker and more sinister than the last. He sat back down on the velvet divan and gave himself over to it, head thrown back, eyes closed, white teeth shining in the gloom. In a moment his laughter tapered off and he composed himself and sat gazing at her with a finger rubbing his full, smiling lips.

"You amuse me," he said, surprised. "I had no idea when I chose you that you'd be so…interesting." And with a little flick of his hand, he released her from his control and the pain simultaneously vanished.

Morgan collapsed into the overstuffed chair, gulping air, fighting down nausea, hot and sour. Her mind wasn't working, her body wasn't working. She had to *think*!

"Ch-chose me?" she managed.

"To help me infiltrate the other colonies," he replied, matter-of-fact. "My people had been watching them all— well, the three I knew of—for years, looking for a weak link, for someone who didn't fit, someone rebellious, someone, perhaps, who might want a little," he waved his fingers, coyly searching for a word, "*vindictam?*"

Vengeance.

"But we could never find a chink in their armor. Until… you. And you were so ripe for the taking." He smiled. "So much loneliness. So much *anger*. Turning you was hardly any work at all."

An iceberg slid silently over her and crushed her with its cold, massive weight. Suddenly, horribly, she understood everything with a blinding, brilliant clarity, like sunlight reflected off snow. "Oh my God," she whispered.

"Yes," he smiled wider, "I *am* your god, Morgan. God of vengeance, god of war, god of salvation, who will release our entire race from the oppression of man. It's taken a lifetime of planning, but now all the players are positioned perfectly on the board and the *Ikati* will, finally, have checkmate. No little thanks to you."

Her stomach heaved. The sudden, wretched knowledge of what he had done, of the part she had so willingly played, burned like poison in her throat.

"You—you planned this," she sputtered. "You planned all of this! *You set me up!*"

His smile grew dangerous. "You were an easy target."

"You killed your own kind!" she shouted as blood flooded her face. "You had them tortured! You worked with *humans*—"

"Destruction is one of nature's mandates, as the Marquis de Sade so eloquently said," he answered calmly, "and a king must be willing to sacrifice a few rooks in order to win a war. And as you know, lovely Morgan, we have been engaged in war since the beginning of time."

She hated him, hated him with a ferocity that made her heart pound and her fingers itch to claw his eyes out. "You *bastard*! We've been hunted for centuries—forced to run—forced to *hide*—"

"*Silence!*" he shouted, and leapt from the divan.

He began to pace in front of her, lithe and menacing, bristling like a caged animal. He ran an agitated hand through the mane of his silver-black hair.

"*They* started this. *They* declared war on us. Are you familiar with the old adage 'Keep your friends close and your enemies closer'? That is what the Alphas of my lineage have done since the Inquisition began in twelve thirty-one. My ancestors quickly realized that a church-sanctioned mass-murder spree was a golden opportunity to infiltrate the bastion of human leadership and wreak a little havoc of their own, *vengeance*, if you will. What a wonderful excuse to kill humans! And in such imaginative ways!" He stopped pacing and turned to look at her. His voice dropped an octave, and his expression sent a chill of fear over her skin.

"And that is when the organization was first formed."

"The Expurgari," she whispered.

"The Purifiers," he agreed, nodding. "At first the goal was only to kill as many humans as possible. Thousands were slaughtered, branded heretics, and the church never suspected a thing. They gave us gold, mountains of gold, for the wonderful job we did. We pretended to be their most devout disciples, when all we really wanted was to see their blood run in the streets. And it worked out perfectly...until, in our travels rounding up all their falsely accused, we discovered another colony of *Ikati*, living hidden in France."

He resumed his pacing. "Up until that point, we thought we were the only ones. Our records only go as far back as the Roman soldier who brought back four strange, orphaned children from Egypt after Cleopatra was defeated by Caesar Augustus at the battle of Actium. But once the colony in France was discovered, the goal of the Expurgari changed."

Morgan breathed, "There is no colony in France."

Dominus stopped pacing. He smiled. "Not anymore."

"Why?" Her voice broke. "Why would you want to wipe out an entire colony of your own kind?"

"I don't," he said, offended, then shrugged. "My ancestors were a little less big picture than I am, however. They didn't like rivals any more than humans do."

"But *you're* killing the Keepers of the Bloodlines! You're torturing women—the Queen of our colony—"

"Yes, that," he said, sour, and returned to his position on the divan. He spread his arms over its scrolled back and fixed her with an intense, penetrating look. "That was a mistake, brought about by the idiotic leader of one of our less organized cells. Humans are so unreliable, but there's so many of them and so few of us...they've been useful minions, for the most part, but what happened at your colony was not planned. He was supposed to take the Keeper, as you know, but unfortunately bungled the job and wound up with a female instead." A wry smile crept over his face. "I understand your Alpha took care of him, however."

Morgan moaned, squeezed her eyes shut, and dropped her head into her hands. It was worse than she'd ever thought possible, the worst thing she could imagine, a nightmare from which there would be no awakening.

She'd found the feral Alpha. And she'd found the head of the Expurgari.

They were one and the same.

"I don't understand," she whispered through her fingers. "I don't understand."

"My plan was never to destroy the other colonies, Morgan," he said softly, as if to a child. "The Alphas, yes—there can be only one King, and that is me. I wanted the Keepers because they would tell me everything I needed to know about each colony, about the Alphas, the most Gifted Bloodlines, about their defenses and weaknesses and their more disgruntled members who might be convinced it was time for a change. And then I had to kill them, obviously, so they didn't expose me."

"But...why?"

She wasn't looking at him, but she heard the smile in his voice. "Because we are going to come together as one, as it was always meant to be. We will combine our resources and infiltrate their gene pool and take back everything that was stolen from us so long ago. And then...we will rule the world." His voice dropped to a zealous whisper. " 'Vengeance is mine, saith the Lord.' Such a lovely sentiment, don't you think? The human Bible is full of little gems like that; their god is a petty, bad-tempered sort with some substantial insecurity issues, but on this he got it right. Vengeance *is* best left to the gods. Best left to *me*."

Morgan shuddered. Beautiful and genius and completely insane, he had lured her into his trap and she had fallen willingly, like a honeybee drunk with the heady smell of nectar.

He came and stood beside her, touched a gentle hand to her hair. "Think of it," he said, reasonably, as she shrank away. "No more running. No more hiding. No more living like mice, shaking in the baseboards. We'll be free, Morgan. *Free*." His voice hardened. "And you—more like me than you're willing to admit—will stand beside me. As my Queen."

She stiffened, all her muscles tensed for flight, but before she could move he sensed her intention and yanked her head back with his hand fisted painfully in her hair.

"Or," he said, gazing down at her, perfectly controlled, "you will end up there."

He pointed, moving his hand and her head so she was forced to twist around in the chair, craning her neck.

Beyond the horned statue of the devil, beyond the gruesome pile of bones, even farther into the long, sliding shadows of the room stood a modern glass case against the wall, lighted from within to illuminate the contents, row after row of large, screw-top jars with bobbing dark somethings inside.

Heads.

Row upon row of heads preserved in pale yellow liquid with staring wide eyes and clouds of dark hair, desiccated flesh peeling from skulls, lips shrunken and curled back over grinning teeth, the very same heads Jenna had shown her what felt like a lifetime ago.

A roar rose in her ears, pain throbbed in her skull, she felt faint and nauseous and cold. The shaking began somewhere deep in her stomach and spread to her arms and legs, leaving her weak, wobbly as a foal.

"As I said before, I do not tolerate demands, and I do not tolerate disobedience of any kind," Dominus said, holding her fast. "One act of defiance," he lifted the index finger of his other hand, "*one*, and I will not hesitate to put you in my trophy case along with all the others who didn't see things my way."

He smiled down at her, excitement burning hot in his eyes. "Obey me, submit to me, rule with me," he whispered. "Or die. Choose. Now."

Without thinking, without breaking eye contact, Morgan opened her mouth and very quietly said, "Fuck. *You.*"

Faint surprise registered in his coal-black eyes. He blinked. Then, with his hand still fisted painfully in her hair, he rose to his full height and dragged her, limp, along with him.

"Interesting choice of words."

He opened his fist and released her. She staggered back, panting in sudden terror, until she was brought up short by the icy, invading claw of pain that punched through her chest and flared out in a cold, crackling frost all over her body. The cold spread, hardening her muscles, immobilizing her. Once again she was trapped, breathless, held hostage inside her own body.

With his arms folded across his broad chest, Dominus said, "Yes, very interesting choice of words, considering what I'm about to do to you."

His tone was light, but the fury on his face was not, and if she thought she had been afraid before, she knew this was to be an education in fear.

Suddenly, with the numb, jerky movements of a marionette, her hands lifted and began to pull at the material of her dress, grabbing at it, sliding it up over her hips. She stared down at her alien hands in horror, and all she could think was, *Xander! Xander! Xander!*

"Oh, yes, thank you for reminding me," Dominus said. "Your boyfriend is coming to save you, but I kill him before he can. Just thought you'd like to know. Now," he said, his tone a little lower than before, "let's get you out of that dress."

And before she could open her mouth to scream, her own puppet hands had pulled the dress over her head and let it fall in a silent puddle to the bare stone floor.

THIRTY-FOUR

D had shown Eliana as much as he could in the few short hours they had between twilight and the *Purgare*, cramming it all into a whirlwind, epic trip.

The Forum, the Colosseum, the Pantheon, his favorite ancient ruins and curio shops and the artifacts and arcades of Trajan's market, the decadent Baths of Caracalla, the Piazza Navona with its lavish baroque fountains and busy cafés. He kept a motorcycle—Italian, of course, a sleek, muscular black Ducati—covered in a garage near the Domitilla, and they'd flown around the city with her thighs pressed against his, her arms wrapped tight around his waist, her heat and softness molded into the hard muscles of his back.

He'd never been happier in his life.

But now it was nearing midnight. Time was short.

"We have to get back," he murmured, watching her devour a triple *stracciatella* gelato at the small sidewalk café they'd stopped at to eat.

"What *is* this?" she exclaimed around a mouthful, tapping the little wooden spoon against the plastic cup. "It's like heaven in my mouth!"

Seeing her like this—awed, excited, full of wonder—was the best gift he'd had in a long, long time. Maybe ever. He inhaled, smelling citrus blossom from a pair of nearby lemon trees, tasting a bittersweet flavor on his tongue he imagined was the fleeting taste of joy.

"Chocolate chips with cream. Next time I'll buy you the cinnamon pear."

She swallowed the mouthful of gelato and batted her lashes. "Next time?" She put the wooden spoon in her mouth and slowly sucked on it, holding his gaze.

He leaned over the table and gently grasped her wrist, forcing the spoon out of her mouth. "Yes, next time. And stop sucking so suggestively on that spoon, or I'll think you're teasing me on purpose."

"And then you'll have to spank me," she whispered, eyes alight with mirth.

He growled and pulled her out of her chair and onto his lap. She squealed and dropped the cup of gelato while an elderly couple at a table nearby tutted their disapproval.

"Don't make me do it right here," he growled, nuzzling her neck.

She giggled and wrapped her arms around his shoulders. "Promises, promises," she said, a little breathless, and then gazed at him with those dark, beautiful eyes that lit his soul aflame.

"*Principessa*," he murmured, enthralled, "I would die a thousand deaths to wake a single morning to that smile."

"Well," she teased, leaning down to press her lips against his, "let's hope it doesn't have to come to that."

And then they were kissing, passionately, oblivious to time or place or dark or light, wrapped so completely in one another, nothing else existed in that moment, nothing at all.

She broke away first, and he let out a soft moan at the loss of her warm, sweet mouth, at the bitter ache of withdrawal.

"I don't want to go back," she whispered, grasping the leather collar of his coat. "Not yet."

He opened his eyes. "We have to. You know we have to."

She traced the bow of his upper lip with the tip of a finger, trailing fire across his skin. "Are you going to keep pretending you can't stand me?" she asked in a small voice.

D shook his head, bewildered by her beauty, by the sweet, loving look on her face. "Not if you don't want me to," he answered. He was rewarded by that brilliant smile again.

"Well, maybe just until we figure out…how…how we're going to…"

She faltered, blinking, and he laid his head against her chest and closed his eyes. Her heartbeat thumped strong and even and calmed the burning fire in his chest.

"Don't," he whispered, inhaling the scent of her skin. "Please don't."

He knew there was only one way they could ever be together. Only one thing would cure what ailed them, and he couldn't bear to think of it right now. Because the therapy would most probably kill the patient.

She took pity on him, he thought, because she sighed and then fell silent. "All right," she said after a moment. She pulled away from him and stood, smoothing her sweater, pushing back a strand of choppy dark hair from her face. Without looking at him she said, "Back to Hades, then."

He stood. With a swift glance in his direction, she turned and made her way to where the bike was parked, and he followed her, silent. She waited for him to swing his leg over the seat and start the bike, then she grasped his arm, stepped astride, and settled in behind him.

On the long, cold ride back to the sunken church, Dominus couldn't help the feeling that though he was happier than he'd ever been, something, somehow, was about to go terribly wrong.

The first of the screams echoed faintly down the long corridor just as Constantine pulled himself out of the nubile young female and collapsed, naked and panting, beside her on the pillow-strewn bed.

He listened for the sound again, that far-away, poignant scream of anguish, but it didn't come, and he thought he must be imagining things. Living in the land of evernight had a way of doing that to you.

It's too damn pink in here, he thought, irrationally irritated, looking around at the ultrafeminine decor used throughout the harem. He'd been here for over four hours, and he was sore and chapped and badly dehydrated, itching to get away from the overload of pastel. Even the damn ceiling was hung with blush fabric, sheer, gossamer panels that drifted overhead like rosy clouds and fell down to shroud the oversize bed. He felt stifled, a little panicky, as if staying one second longer in this cotton-candy room would cause his own skin to become stained pink.

What was wrong with him? He'd just enjoyed the most energetic female he'd had in years, the cream of the King's crop, so to speak, still lying beside him in a sweaty stupor, but he felt no satisfaction. He felt, actually, like getting up and tearing something to shreds.

He'd been feeling like that a lot lately. Especially every time he laid eyes on Dominus.

"That was amazing," the female purred. He realized without regret that he didn't know her name. She rolled lazily to her side and rested her hand on his chest. "Fancy another go—"

But before she could finish, Constantine jerked upright in bed and spat, "Quiet!"

She huffed indignantly and pulled away. "Asshole," she muttered, rising from the bed in a snit. She pushed through the panels of fabric, bent, and snatched her gown from the floor, where he'd left it, torn hastily from her body, hours ago. "You *Bellatorum* think you're *so* special—"

"*Quiet*, I said!"

There it was again. The scream. He hadn't imagined it after all.

"What the fuck?" he whispered, eyes trained on the arched doorway on the far side of the chamber.

The bedroom, used only when the King made a visit, was one of several clustered together around the central hub of the harem where the *Electi* lived in boring, sumptuous leisure. Lix and Celian were in the two rooms beside his, and as he leapt from the bed and pulled on his pants, he heard Celian's voice from the doorway, dark as the corridor outside.

"Constantine."

"Yep. Coming."

He finished dressing and left the room without a backward glance. Lix and Celian, both radiating tension, were already dressed and waiting in the narrow corridor for him.

"Sounds like it's coming from the *fovea*," Celian said, low. He hadn't bothered with a shirt, and the huge muscles of his arms flexed as he shot a glance down the long, shadowed corridor winding toward the King's chambers.

"One of Dominus's playthings?" asked Lix. He ran a hand through his long, disheveled hair, following Celian's gaze. "He just picked up two new ones this week—"

"That sound like a human to either of you?"

No. It most certainly did not. Human screams could never reach that pitch. But Constantine couldn't tell if it was male or female…

The three of them looked at each other.

"Where's D?" Celian finally said.

"We, uh," Lix shot a nervous glance in Constantine's direction, "we didn't want to tell you. In case Dominus found out—you wouldn't get in trouble. Since you've just healed…from last time…"

Celian's face hardened. "In case Dominus found out what, exactly?"

"D is with the *principessa*," Constantine answered, and took a step back when the heat of Celian's anger pulsed over him like a furnace with its door blown off.

"Eliana?" he hissed, eyes flashing. "What the hell is he doing with *her*?"

"I'm not exactly sure," said Constantine, holding Celian's furious gaze, "but I've got a pretty good idea."

The scream came again, a high, sustained note of pain from somewhere far off in the darkness of the catacombs. All three of them froze, listening.

Celian said, "I have a very bad feeling about this. Be ready for anything."

And with Lix and Constantine hard on his heels, he set off at a dead run toward the *fovea* and the high, wavering screams.

Running as fast as his feet would take him, Xander sprinted across the worn cobblestones of St. Peter's Square, heading directly for the portico of the basilica and the bronze masterpiece Door of Death, carved with images of a crucified Christ and the Virgin Mary ascending to heaven.

He Passed straight through it just as a pair of Swiss Guards leapt to stop him from their posts at the soaring marble columns that flanked the door. He heard their shouts from outside, growing fainter as he ran into the center of the vast, shadowed cathedral. Past the nave, past the baptistery, past the transepts with their haloed, blank-eyed statues of the founding saints in stone niches, his boots striking loudly over the elaborate inlaid floor.

He came to a sliding halt near the chapel of St. Sebastian, brought up short by a twist in his heart.

Here, sang the ghostly, lilting tune of the Blood tie that had drawn him across the city.

Panting, heart pounding, he slowly approached the chapel. It was as before when he and Morgan had tried, unsuccessfully, to locate the Alpha when he'd been inside her head. Lighted casket with the body of a long-dead pope beneath the towering mosaic of the martyrdom of

St. Sebastian, baroque paintings in the cupola and corbels, faint stench of decay and death.

Dark, disembodied tremor of feral *Ikati* everywhere.

He combed over the entire chapel, searching frantically, but there was nothing, no one, no hidden entry or secret passage or door, just that magnetic pull of their connection.

"*Morgan!*"

He shouted it at the top of his lungs because he couldn't think of what else to do. It fractured into a thousand parroted cries of her name that seemed to take on a life of their own, taunting his ears, mocking him as they reverberated through almost six acres of yawning space, bouncing off marble and glass and stone. He was so close; she was somewhere nearby, terrified, and he couldn't find her, he didn't know where to look, he *had to do something—*

From somewhere far beneath his feet, the faintest, faintest echo of a scream reached his ears.

Xander leapt back as if the floor had burned him. He stood staring down, arrested, his heart frozen solid in his chest.

On the floor in the middle of the chapel was painted a colorful coat of arms, surrounded by a circle of Greek lettering. It featured a pair of crossed keys above a golden shield that depicted the image of an olive branch–bearing dove with a trio of fleurs-de-lis. Floating above the shield was a crown.

And just above that, painted in bold strokes of black and gold, was the all-seeing Eye of Horus.

Xander dropped to his knees and pressed his shaking hands flat against the cold marble.

Beneath. Below. *Underground.* But—how?

The scream came again, and the how no longer mattered. All that mattered was Morgan, and she was somewhere down there, beneath his feet.

Just as a group of armed Swiss Guards burst through a side door near the entrance to the basilica, Xander closed his eyes, concentrated, and was swallowed like a stone dropped into water by the ancient marble floor of the church.

THIRTY-FIVE

Someone far beyond the brimstone sea was controlling her muscles. Someone beyond the sea chanted a refrain of *burn, burn, burn,* and because of him she was smoking, she was blistering, her flesh had all melted away.

"Xander," Morgan moaned, voice raw from screaming.

"Oh, yes," said the demon controlling her body, stoking the fire that crisped her bones, "I imagine he'll be along anytime now. Perhaps I should revive you a bit for your reunion." He chuckled, a sound like red-hot pokers stabbing through her ears. "We wouldn't want you to miss the unhappy ending, now would we?"

Suddenly the fire dimmed and she was ripped panting and coughing from the scalding brimstone lake to find herself chained naked—unharmed, all in one piece—to a rounded stone wall.

"Welcome back, Morgan," Dominus said, smiling serenely. "And how are we feeling?"

The room spun. Dark and circular, it sported black walls so high the ceiling was lost in shadow. It felt very much like being at the bottom of a well. A blood-spattered well, because all along the walls from eye level down were smeared dark trails of crimson, some old and flaking, some bright and hideously fresh.

The room was devoid of ornament save for a huge rusted metal rack drilled into the stone from which dangled a sadist's collection of playthings. Steel and leather and wire whips, chains and pokers and saws, masks and knives and metal things she couldn't name but recognized as implements of unspeakable atrocities nonetheless.

Morgan stared at the tools and the splatters of gore on the walls. Her mind began to clear. The enormity of the situation edged in.

"That was really a rhetorical question," Dominus mused, stepping closer. "I won't make you answer it." He lifted his hand and very gently, as Morgan shrank back against the rough, frigid rock, caressed her bare breast.

Her wrists were shackled overhead with what felt like steel or iron; her ankles sported the same. But she was still able to move her body. And as he stroked her and watched her writhe, intently watched the disgust and fear and anger play over her face, Morgan realized he could have simply held her frozen in place with his mind. But the lust burning bright in his eyes told her that he found the physical display of her fear so much more arousing.

She stilled, closed her eyes, and swallowed back the vomit rising in her throat.

Fuck him. *Fuck. Him.* She wouldn't give him the satisfaction of watching her squirm.

"Oh, Morgan," he sighed, and she heard the exasperation in his voice. "Honestly, this is beginning to become tiresome."

And he slapped her across the face with so much force she tasted blood.

"Touch her again," shouted a furious voice from behind him, "and I'll eat out your fucking heart!"

Morgan sobbed, Dominus spun around, and Xander leapt, snarling, from the shadows of the opposite wall.

Then everything happened at once.

With the force of runaway trains colliding from opposite directions, they smashed into each other and fell in a bellowing tangle to the floor, trading vicious punches, howling like rabid wolves, an unholy noise that reverberated through the room. They rolled over and over until they hit the rack of whips and knives and chains. With a terrible squealing shriek of buckling metal, the whole thing wrenched from the wall and came crashing down on top of them.

Three huge males appeared in the doorway to her right. They skidded to a stop as they saw Dominus and Xander grappling beneath the pile of instruments and the ruins of the rack. A fourth male—bald, pierced, and tattooed—appeared in the arched doorway on the opposite side of the room. He took in the scene in one swift glance and froze. His hard face blanched; his expression turned incredulous, then, strangely, elated.

Dominus leapt clear of the debris and landed a dozen feet away, crouched and snarling, his attention still focused on Xander, who had thrown off the crumpled rack and struggled to his feet in the middle of the debris. When Dominus spied the bald male on the opposite side of the room, a look—savage, bloodthirsty—passed between them.

"You didn't tell me he was immune to mind control!" Dominus screamed, teeth bared.

The male stared back at him, hatred darkening his face. "I didn't tell you a lot of things."

Dominus stared at him for one fleeting, suspended moment. Then, horrified, he whispered, "Eliana."

With the suddenness of a switch being thrown, the temperature in the room dropped thirty degrees. Ice formed on the walls, rose in long, crackling white fingers up the black stone. Morgan's breath frosted out in pale clouds in front of her face. The air itself began to shiver and hum.

Then something happened.

It was like a detonation. All the air sucked into a tight core and then exploded, lightless and silent, in a blast that ripped through the room. It flung the tattooed male back against the wall with devastating force. He was suspended there for a moment, spread-eagle, gulping ragged breaths, his huge body twitching. Dominus pulled a small dagger from his belt and flung it across the room.

With a sickening *pop*, it sank deep into the male's chest. He slid down the wall and crumpled to the ground.

As one, the three males at the door let out a deafening roar of fury. The bare-chested one and the long-haired one launched themselves across the room and landed, sliding into a jolting stop, against the stone wall beside the wounded male. Their companion, a beautiful male with classically perfect features, stood rigid in the doorway, staring in horror at the scene. He looked toward Dominus and Xander—who was now well clear of the debris and crouched to pounce on Dominus—and reached into the waistband of his pants and pulled out a handgun.

"Xander!" Morgan screamed.

And just as Xander spun to heed her warning, Dominus snatched a wicked-looking blade from the mess of weapons on the floor and plunged it into his back.

Impossible! her heart screamed. Then her voice rose to echo it, ripping its way out of her like a thing with claws, gutting her as it went. She screamed and screamed and watched in helpless horror as Xander sank to his knees, lips parted in surprise, wide eyes focused on her face.

"I told you, Morgan," snarled Dominus, teeth bared as he glared at her. A fine spray of Xander's blood was misted across the pristine white linen of his shirt. "I told you I win!"

"That's what you think," said a hard voice from her right.

Then there was a thunderous *crack* of noise near her head, a flash of light, a wave of hot, pressurized air and the smell of gunpowder. Dominus staggered back several steps and a small, perfect hole appeared in the center of his forehead. For a moment he looked confused. From the hole trickled a tiny rivulet of blood. He touched a finger to it.

Looked at his hand in incomprehension.

Frowned.

Then slowly pitched backward and fell unmoving to the floor.

A few feet away, Xander wavered on his knees, fell forward onto his hands. Blood from the wound in his back had rained an inkblot pattern over the backs of his legs and the stone on which he knelt. His face was white, white as the frost on the walls.

"Xander!" Morgan screamed, straining against the wrist restraints. "*Xander, no!*"

The male in the doorway beside her tucked the gun into his waistband and came to stand in front of her. "*Paenitet,*" he said, gazing at her with those black, black eyes. "I'm sorry. We are not all like him."

He unchained her, snapping the restraints circling her wrists and ankles as if they were twigs instead of iron. As soon as she was free she ran, sobbing and nearly blinded by tears, to Xander and flung her arms around his neck. She heard his sharp inhalation, heard the faint, faint sound inside his chest.

"You were right, I'm afraid," he murmured, pressing his face to her hair. He slumped sideways and she caught him, eased him down to the cold stone. He gazed up at her, pale and solemn, as she cradled his head. "About happy endings. I should have known it would end like this." His lips, so full and soft, lips she'd kissed with dark, dark greed, curved to a wry smile. "I'm not the hero. I don't save the day." His eyelids fluttered, his voice grew faint. "I don't get the girl."

"No, no, no, no, no." She kept repeating it, sobbing hysterically as blood bright red and warm began to pool beneath her. "Xander, please, stay with me, stay with me!"

"I wasn't going to do it," he murmured, gazing up into her eyes. "You know that, don't you? I wasn't ever going to… hurt you." He drew a long, shuddering breath, and his voice dropped to the barest of whispers.

"I could never hurt you. I love you too damn much."

Then his eyes closed and his head dropped to the floor.

With three pairs of hands on his arms, back, and shoulders, D was lifted to his feet.

"Fuck, you're heavy," muttered Lix from behind him. "What've you got in your pockets, rocks?"

He didn't recognize the wheeze that came out of his throat as his own. It sounded like the death rattle of a very old, very sick man. The knife embedded in his chest sent out wave upon wave of excruciating pain, blood flowed hot and fast down his chest, the room had lost its shape. He was helpless to stand without support, as all the strength had left his legs.

"Some of us have actual muscle, Lix," he croaked, sliding very close to the wall of wavering gray fog that lurked in the corners of his vision. Breathing too deeply made the fog roll closer; that knife had punctured a lung. As evidenced by that sickening rattle in his chest.

At least it had missed his heart. That male on the floor didn't look so lucky.

"Shut up, both of you," Celian snapped. "If we don't get you to the infirmary fast, you're going to bleed out before we can sew you up, D."

D remembered the last time he'd been sewn up. A faint smile crossed his face.

"We've got to contain the situation," said Constantine. He eased his shoulder beneath D's raised arm, took hold of his hand, and hoisted it around his neck, wrapping his other arm around D's back. On his other side, Celian did the same. "We could have a mutiny on our hands if we don't handle this right."

"Trust me, no one's going to miss him," Celian muttered, glancing at Dominus's body. A pool of blood had seeped from the bullet wound and formed a perfect circle around his head like the gory halo of some biblical devil.

His daughter might, D thought, then sucked in a breath as pain shot down his spine. Celian and Constantine had taken several steps forward, managing his weight between them. They made their way slowly across the room.

"Even so, the *Legiones* might make a move on us," Constantine said. "We're going to have to present a united front, be in control, manage what happens next. In other words, take decisive action. Nature hates a vacuum, boys, so let's not give 'em one."

His voice very low, Lix said, "And her?"

No one had to look to see who he meant. On her knees beside the pale, still male they'd chased at the Vatican, the female rocked back and forth silently, shaking, both hands over her face. Her unbound hair shrouded her naked shoulders and back in gleaming mahogany.

Celian spoke. "As far as I'm concerned, the enemy of my enemy is my friend. And I think we've all seen enough bloodshed. Let them go."

D didn't think that male was going anywhere, but he was unable to speak. Pain had his tongue.

"Here." Constantine pulled his gun from his waistband and nudged it into the hand D had wrapped around his shoulder. "Just in case things get ugly on the way to the infirmary."

And as soon as he had his fingers curled around the metal grip of the Glock, D heard the advancing echo of boots from far down the corridor. Someone was running to the *fovea.*

Of course. The *Legiones.* They'd been drawn by the sound of gunfire.

He closed his eyes, trying to conserve strength. And when he opened them again, Eliana was standing in the doorway they were headed to, staring at them in white-faced, open-mouthed shock. Her gaze darted around the room. The chaos. The blood. Her father's body.

The gunshot wound in his forehead.

She glanced back at Dominus, and all the color drained from her face.

"You," she breathed, staring at the gun gripped in his right hand. Her gaze, horrified, uncomprehending, skipped back to his. "*You!*"

Constantine and Celian froze, and his own heartbeat ground to a standstill.

"No. No," he whispered vehemently, chilled as if ice had been injected into his veins. A storm erupted in his body, a howling white squall of dread and panic. She had it all wrong; she thought it was *him*—

"No. Eliana! It's not what you think!"

But she had backed from the doorway into the deeper shadows of the corridor and, before he could say another word, turned and disappeared.

THIRTY-SIX

Gentle rocking, warmth and softness, the cries of seagulls, and the tang of salt water ripening the air. The sound of water lapping lightly against wood. The scent of tropical rain, sweet and warm.

Hell, Xander mused, wasn't nearly as bad as he'd expected.

Pondering that, he allowed himself to drift on an aimless current of dreamy carelessness, rising and falling with that lovely rocking motion that lulled him so completely. He thought any minute the pitchforks and sulfurous rain would appear, so he didn't bother to open his eyes. And anyway, the light that glowed red behind his closed lids was a little alarming. Better to put it off for a minute and enjoy the calm before the storm. Or whatever this was.

A little sound caught his attention. It was nearby, very soft and dark and troubling.

A sigh.

An exhalation from some pitchfork-wielding fiend, no doubt, anxious to cart him off to the next circle of hell as soon as he opened his eyes. Well, screw that. He was staying right here. He hadn't felt this relaxed in years. He clamped his eyes shut so tightly his face crumpled into a scowl.

And then that little sigh turned into a gasp, fraught with concern.

The rustle of fabric, the sound of something creeping nearer, a cool touch upon his forehead. He flinched, swearing, and the fiend cried out his name.

"Xander!"

Even in hell he recognized that voice. It cut through his dreamy laxity like a knife through butter, and his eyes flew open. And his heart—oh, his heart—

"You're awake," breathed Morgan, leaning close over him with her hair draped all around her face like a veil of burnished, silken bronze.

If he wasn't already dead, he was pretty sure he would die of a heart attack.

"I...don't...think so," he murmured, staring up at this beautiful apparition. He reached out and touched a finger to her satin cheek. Her irises burned vivid emerald, that circle of yellow around the pupil blurred just slightly by the moisture welling in her eyes. "This is a wonderful dream, though. Very realistic."

She laughed and sobbed at the same time, then pressed the back of a shaking hand against her mouth. She hitched up her dress and sat beside him, and for the first time he realized he was on a bed. In a room. No—a cabin? The sky shone deepest azure through a round porthole edged in brass set high in the wood-paneled wall; the ceiling was painted aqua and populated with dolphins and seaweed and eels slinking through coral. The spoked ship's wheel clock on the dresser beside the bed read 4:17 p.m.

"It's not a dream," she said, "and here, I'll prove it to you."

Then his beautiful ghost leaned over and pressed her lips against his. When she drew back, they were both out of breath.

"Well," said Xander. "I did say it was realistic. Perhaps a little more proof is in order." He pulled her down to him, ignoring the sudden pain between his shoulder blades, and kissed her hard and deep with his hands pressed against her face, his fingers threading through her hair.

She broke away first—again—and quietly laughed. "You're feeling better."

"I thought you were a fiend."

She raised her eyebrows. "Did you now?"

"And this was hell. I thought I was dead. How am I not dead?"

Her eyes grew soft. She brushed back his hair from his forehead and smiled. "Well...I sort of saved your life. Again."

Xander took a breath. "Oh. Not very manly of me, needing to be rescued so much, is it?"

"It is an awful lot of work," she agreed, somberly nodding. Then she lifted a shoulder and dropped her gaze to the knitted azure blanket across his chest. She picked at the material, chewed on her lower lip. Her voice lowered. "Someone has to look after you, though. And since I'm so... fond of you, well, I suppose it might as well be me."

As his heart swelled inside his chest, Xander had to work very hard not to smile. He reached for her hand. "We can save each other," he whispered, and pressed his lips to her knuckles.

She bit her lip, and that moisture welling in her eyes finally overflowed. Tears tracked down her cheeks. She buried her face in his chest.

"You found me," she said, muffled, into the blanket. "You came for me, Xander, you *found* me—"

"I'll always come for you, *amada*," he murmured, stroking her hair. "Don't you know that? You're my heart. You're my soul. I'm not going to let a little thing like you being kidnapped by a madman and held in his secret underground dungeon keep me from my heart and soul. You're not getting away from me that easily."

She sobbed into the blanket.

"Hush now, sweet girl." He gathered her into his arms and held her against him until she quieted and all her tears were spent. "Tell me what happened."

She sighed, snuggled closer to him, and began to talk. She told him how the males of the catacombs had helped her, how they'd cared for him in their infirmary, how close he'd come to death. She told him how they'd quashed the rebellion that had stirred when the other members of the colony learned of the King's death, how they'd installed the one named Celian as the new leader, how the King's daughter had fled the colony with her brother and a handful of others and had not yet been found.

"But the best part is," she said quietly in conclusion, "now that I did what I was sent to Rome to do, I've been given a full pardon. And the Queen has honored her promise to me." She lifted her eyes and gazed at him. Light from the window caught in her hair, warmed the tips of her lashes. "I can go wherever I want. *Live* wherever I want. I'm free."

He stared at her blankly. "I don't understand."

"Dominus. He was the head of the Expurgari. We found him, so…"

"The head of the Expurgari," Xander repeated slowly.

She shook her head. "I'll explain it all later. Right now you should rest. You look a little pale."

He caught her wrist and held it, pulling her closer to him. He sat up in bed and ignored the searing pain along his spine. "You mean—we're *not* fugitives? This trip—this boat—"

"Oh!" she said, startled. "No! God, no, we're not fugitives. All five of us have been completely cleared."

He stared at her. "All *five* of us."

At that exact moment, heavy footsteps pounded over the roof above his head. A smile flitted over Morgan's lips as she watched him follow the sound with his eyes as it moved overhead, growing softer then louder, thumping down what sounded like a flight of stairs. A dark head popped in the high, round window, then disappeared; someone had jumped up to look in.

A heavy hand knocked on the door.

Then to Morgan's amused "Come in," Tomás and Mateo burst through the door.

"Hey, asshole," Mateo said, smiling. "You look like death warmed over."

Tomás nodded a greeting and leaned his huge frame against the wall. "Fuckface."

"Bartleby is on deck, making dinner," Morgan said gently, seeing Xander's open-mouthed astonishment. "Your friends here are quite the fishermen."

"So far I've caught blue marlin, yellowfin tuna, wahoo, even *sailfish*," Tomás bragged. "Kadavu is amazing!"

"Kadavu," Xander repeated, finding it hard to know where to look. His brain wasn't translating information properly. He had to be hearing this wrong.

"Fiji," said Mateo with an eye roll, as if it should have been obvious. "Seventy-five miles of pristine barrier reef with water so clear you can see the bottom of the ocean from the boat. Jungle-covered volcanic hills, mangrove bays, snow-white beaches...what?"

He trailed off because Xander had closed his eyes. He was sure he was deathly pale.

Morgan leaned close to his ear. "I told you I always wanted to see a sunrise in Fiji," she murmured, her hand on his arm. "So now I'll get to see one. Or..." she giggled, and it made his blood sing, "...maybe two or three."

He opened his eyes and saw her devilish grin and began to laugh, a hoarse, shaky sound that hitched in his chest and caught in his throat and made Morgan's grin falter. His laughter died, and he roughly pulled her against him and buried his face in her hair.

"Jesus, woman," he said, ragged, all restraint gone, "do you have any idea how much I love you?"

She pulled back and gazed down at him, eyes alight. "Probably not as much as I love you," she whispered, then bent to kiss his lips.

"Jeez, get a room," grumbled Tomás, but Xander hardly heard it. Against her protests, he hauled Morgan on top of him and wrapped his arms around her, ignoring the ache between his shoulder blades and in his chest, caution at last thrown to the wind. He heard the cabin door close softly and the sound of footsteps receding.

"Marry me," he said between breathless kisses, struggling to rid her of her dress.

"I doubt there's a priest on this island," she replied with a low laugh, then sat up and pulled the dress over her head. It was discarded to the floor, and she lay back against him, her skin warm against his. "There are just beaches and coves and coconut trees. And anyway, you're in no shape to stand at an altar, my love."

He took that as a challenge and pulled her close. "Allow me to demonstrate exactly the shape I'm in." He took her hand and maneuvered it beneath the covers, to the straining hardness between his legs.

She laughed again, and it was like honey to his ears, sweet and dark and delicious. "Oh, how I do admire an ambitious man. But you're still healing. A few more days and then—"

"And then you will be sore for a week," he growled, nipping at her neck.

She allowed him that much, relaxed back against him so he could trail his hands over her bare skin and inhale her scent and kiss her, and all the while she smiled at him like a cat with all the cream.

"What is that mysterious look of yours, love of mine?" he whispered, stroking her face.

"Do you notice anything different about me?" she said coyly.

He let his gaze drift over her naked body. "If I say no," he said, husky, "how much trouble will I be in?"

"A lot," she laughed, "considering you're the one who put the damn thing on!"

He frowned and she stretched back her head, gazed at him from beneath her lashes, and trailed her fingers down her throat with a flourish. "Your friend Mateo is quite good with a blowtorch. Didn't even leave a mark."

He inhaled sharply. The collar: it was gone. Feeling a tightness in his chest, he brushed his fingers over her neck, the fine sweep of her collarbones. The blowtorch hadn't left a mark, but a faint ring of circular bruises the size of his thumb marred the perfect skin just over her jugular on the left side of her neck. He clenched his jaw and closed his eyes, disgusted with himself.

I will never, he thought as a violent rush of love and possessiveness swept through him, *do anything to hurt her again.*

He opened his eyes and quietly said, "I was wrong to do that. I've been wrong about so much. You'll have to be patient with me, Morgan, because I'm stubborn and temperamental and I'm going to make stupid mistakes, probably a lot of them. But I swear I'll do my best to make you happy every single day of your life, if you let me. I will love you, and no other, until I take my last breath, and when I'm dead I'll keep on loving you. Forever."

She swallowed and turned away for a moment, took a few deep breaths. Her eyes closed and then blinked open, and she turned back to him and whispered, "I was wrong about something, too."

"What?"

She smiled and cupped her hand against his face. "There *are* happy endings for people like us. Welcome to our happily ever after, my love."

Then she leaned in and very softly pressed her lips against his.

EPILOGUE

Saturday, the twelfth of August, 20—

Another sweltering day, another endless night. Everything is so different here. It is difficult to adjust.

My brother and I and a small group of loyalists from the colony have settled near the basilica of the Sacré Coeur in Montmartre, on the top floor of a tall building at the crest of the city's highest hill. Sometimes we are lost in the clouds here. Sometimes it seems the horizon stretches on forever.

I find myself often wandering the shadowed crypts of the nearby catacombs, so much more familiar than my new house in the sky. On those wandering walks, my mind is a black tangle of schemes and memories and unanswered questions. Like a ghost I haunt *the twisting corridors in those silent, dark hours before dawn, my thoughts a sea of hungry rats, chewing holes in my mind, devouring the memory of the naive girl I was. Devouring any shadow of softness that still lingers.*

I wish the hungry rats would eat the memory of him.

But that is the one thing they leave untouched. Traitorous rats.

At least I'm not alone; that I don't think I could bear. I have others here to help me finish the work my father started—and this will be difficult, as his journals were left behind and he never shared his vision with me—others that believe as I do that what he had planned for his people must have been good, that his death must not go unavenged. We are few and they are many, so for now I must be content to stalk the bone-lined corridors of les carrières de Paris while plans are made and alliances are forged.

While the blueprint for vengeance is drawn.

"Eliana."

She spun from her desk at the sound of the voice, relaxing only when she saw the familiar face at the door, the piercing dark eyes and aquiline nose.

"You scared me," she said, irritated. She closed her journal, pushed back the chair, and went to stand at the tall, dormered window. The oppressive heat of the day had given way to an evening thunderstorm; rain peppered the glass, running down the panes in long, silvery tears.

"I'm sorry, my Queen."

He'd taken to calling her that of late. It got on her nerves.

She spoke to the window, not bothering to turn around. "What is it?"

"I've received word from your father's lab in Milan. The reports you requested."

Now she did turn, so quickly she lost her balance and had to set a hand against the sill to steady herself. "You have them? Where are they?"

A large manila envelope was produced from behind his back. He held it out, smiling. "Here. Shall we review them together?"

Eliana took several small, hesitant steps forward, her heart like a hummingbird trapped in her chest. Her father's reports. This would tell her what he had discovered, what he had spoken of so rapturously—and vaguely—the night he was killed.

Killed by the man she'd nearly convinced herself she was in love with. The man who had used her so badly, who'd plotted to take her father's kingdom for himself.

She knew that courtesy of the loyal servant who now stood in front of her. He'd discovered the plot himself, had been on his way to warn her father just before he was killed. At least, that's what he'd said when he'd found her that night, hysterical and incoherent. He'd served her family for so long—unfailingly, with no expectation of reward—she knew it was right to listen to him when he said they had to flee Rome and start fresh somewhere else.

She knew he was the only one she could trust.

Filled with a swell of gratitude for him, she said, "Yes. We'll review them together. And…thank you. Thank you, Silas. You've done so much for me. I couldn't have done any of this without you."

Silas smiled, a slow, spreading grin that overtook his entire face but didn't touch the frozen depths of his black, black eyes.

"Oh, no, my Queen," he murmured, moving closer. "It is *I* who could not have done it without *you*."

ACKNOWLEDGMENTS

First and foremost, I want to give special thanks to Eleni Caminis, my amazing editor at Montlake. Your enthusiasm, professionalism, sense of humor, and tireless cheerleading kept me sane whenever I was about to go off the rails. Working with you is a dream, and I couldn't be more grateful for your support. Plus, you have great hair. (How can one person be so cool?)

To the rest of the team at Montlake Romance: YOU GUYS ROCK! It's like *wunderkinder* wonderland over there. Jessica Poore and Nikki Sprinkle in particular deserve kudos for sheer awesomeness. Thank you for always patiently responding to the crazy writer people you assist. (Other crazy writer people, you know, not me.)

Also big hugs to the incredible Brooke Gilbert and a deep bow to the sheer fabulosity that is Ms. Daphne Durham. I'm so grateful to all the special people I've met at Montlake and Amazon, and I'd like to go on record as saying Jeff Bezos is a genius not only because he's built one of the best companies in the world, but also because he knows the importance of hiring the right people and giving them the tools to be *amazing*.

I owe a debt of gratitude to Marlene Stringer, agent extraordinaire. Without you I'd probably still be in query hell. Thank you for your dogged determination and business acumen; I've learned a lot from you.

To Melody Guy, who caught all my goofs and gaffes, I would like to bestow the Nobel Prize for developmental editing. (Unfortunately I'm not on the selection committee, but I'm totally going to send them a strongly worded letter.) And to Renee Johnson, thank you for dealing with the serial comma issue, among other things!

I also owe a special shout out to Lily Yao, aka Eagle Eye, who caught a glaring mistake before it was too late. Xander and I thank you.

And finally to Jay...you had me at "It'll never last." You saved me from disaster once, and you keep on saving me, every single day. I love you.

ABOUT THE AUTHOR

J. T. Geissinger is an author, entrepreneur, and avid wine collector. Her debut novel, *Shadow's Edge*, book one of the Night Prowler Novels, was published in June 2012, and she is at work on a third book in the series. A native of Los Angeles, she currently resides there with her husband and one too many cats.

3756701R00228

Printed in Great Britain
by Amazon.co.uk, Ltd.,
Marston Gate.